# THE CAT'S EYE CHRONICLES

## Books in this Series

THE CAT'S EYE CHRONICLES #4

# Ferran's MAP

## T. L. SHREFFLER

ISBN 978-0-9851663-8-0

# CONTENTS

# THE CITY OF CROWNS

THE CROWN'S RUSH

EAST BANK

WINDMILLS
(MORE TO THE EAST)

OUTER WALL

FLOWER
DISTRICT

KING'S PALACE

WEST BANK

THE REGENCY

BRIDGE

WEST GATE

THE ROYAL ROAD

REGENCY WALL

SMOKESHAFTS

WIND
TEMPLE

TOURMALINE ST.

SOUTH GATE

THE DOCKS

THE BATH

HEALER'S
SEMINARY

N
nw    ne
W        E
sw    se
S

# PROLOGUE

G randmaster Natrix stood at the top of a sandy ridge, the iron-gray ocean to her back. Heavy clouds covered the sky, sending down flurries of snow. Below her, dozens of Named assassins littered the training ground, practicing hand-to-hand combat. The assassins worked tirelessly despite the weather, bracing themselves against gusts of wind and using the ice to their advantage. At this distance, they looked like black crickets darting among the gray slush of the dunes.

As she watched, a second figure appeared on the ridge beside her, materializing through the storm.

Her lip curled, her eyes still focused on the training ground. "You've returned," she said, as though musing about the weather. "I wonder where you've been—he who once dedicated his life to this colony."

Grandmaster Cerastes raised a thin eyebrow. He looked weary, his pale skin sallow. Gaunt cheekbones protruded from an intelligent, angular face, matured by age. His deep-set eyes gleamed with a poisonous light.

"Are you reprimanding me?" he said, a touch amused, but mostly hostile.

Natrix gazed at him. She noted the ragged condition of his black robes, the depressing downturn of his lips. His hair was sleek and perfectly black, falling to his waist. A strange scent tainted his clothes—the gritty musk of a city, and the vague stench of humans and horses.

Then she nodded to the dunes below them, focusing on one assassin in particular.

"Your Viper has become quite good," she said, shifting her weight from one hip to another.

She wore a close-fitting black shirt, clasped with a vest. Born of Fire and Darkness, all of the Sixth Race were resistant to cold weather. Her tall black boots were made of toughened hide, with no soles, allowing her feet to move freely. A series of various-sized chakrams hung from her waist, steel rings with edges as sharp as blades. They could be hurled with deadly accuracy, slicing off heads and limbs with the force of her throw. Tightly braided rows of black hair covered her head. Her eyes were the bright green hue of aloe.

Cerastes followed her gaze without comment.

A smirk came across her pale lips. "In your absence, he has trained with Lachesis. Another few years and he just might become a Grandmaster himself."

Cerastes appeared impassive, but Natrix knew the statement rankled him. Grandmasters did not like sharing students, especially talented ones. "Has he unlocked the fifth gate?" Cerastes asked quietly.

"No," Natrix said, her eyes following the figure of the Viper. "But he is close."

Eight years had passed since the Naming of the Viper. In that time, Natrix had watched Cerastes' student progress rapidly and tirelessly. He was far better than her own savants—even the Named Adder, her best student, who wielded his saber with dexterous speed.

Assassins, especially Grandmasters, kept their emotions under tight control. Yet bitterness had crept in over the years, perhaps even jealousy. Natrix wished she could work with such a motivated student, one who took his training into his own hands, compelled by his own inner drive. Even without a Grandmaster, even if the Hive did not exist, even if Viper were the very first of the assassin race—she had little doubt he would be able to unlock the seven gates. He harbored a talent that founded tradition. He proved the Hive's ways were not just fabrication, but a true part of their nature.

And because of that realization, she eventually lost her envy of Cerastes. The Viper's skill was not one of superior instruction. Some assassins were simply born to the task, gifted by the Dark God with deft hands and a keen mind.

She studied him on the training field below. He moved like flowing water, using his opponent's energy to his advantage, pulling his assailant forward and off-balance, then striking with his entire body—foot, knee, hip, forearm, open palm. The Adder twisted, and the Viper turned with him, able to anticipate his opponent's next move. He knocked the Adder to his knees. As she watched, her own student was forced to the ground, prostrate in surrender.

Cerastes turned away and walked across the top of the ridge, moments away from vanishing again. Months had passed since he had last appeared in their colony. Natrix wouldn't let him leave so easily.

She cleared her throat. "The Hive wonders at your absence," she called out to him, a slight challenge to her tone. "They are running out of patience and will erase your name from the records of our colony. You will become a hermit master like Lachesis, a ghost in the woods, all but forgotten."

Cerastes paused, replying over his shoulder, "What I do with my time is not the Hive's concern. My attention has turned to greater matters."

"The other Grandmasters don't care about your hobbies," Natrix said. "They want to know where you've been. Personally, I wonder at this path you've chosen. Is it wise?" Did Cerastes understand the severity of his absence? Why would a Grandmaster abandon the Hive—his traditions, his reputation, all he had ever achieved? "We were *savants* together, Cerastes," she reminded him. "We trained side by side. You mastered the ways of our kind, and now, after a lifetime of dedication, you shun the Hive so easily?"

Cerastes faced her fully, the shadow of a sneer on his lips. "Perhaps if you knew more of our race's heritage, you would shun the Hive as well."

Natrix hardened. "We must serve our colony and all those who live within it. I don't know what you're searching for, Cerastes, but consider—if our ways are not enough for you, nothing else will be, either. Ambition is a hunger that can never be satisfied. It's a dangerous path, not the way of an assassin."

"Ambition is not what drives me," Cerastes replied staunchly. "A thirst for knowledge, perhaps, but only in search of higher truth."

"Does nothing else matter to you? What about the Viper? Have you no duty to your own student? The boy relied on your instruction." She shook her head. "Grandmasters are meant to teach. Instead, you hoard your skill like a human hoards gold. The Viper deserves better!"

"I owe him nothing," Cerastes said coldly. "He has made his way."

Natrix watched Cerastes, trying to read his face. She sensed discomfort in his rigid stance. She pressed on.

"You've forsaken your duties to the Viper and the Hive. The Grandmasters won't tolerate it. You must understand what you are throwing away."

Cerastes raised his eyebrow. "I didn't come here for a lecture, Natrix. My decisions are my own. I know the sacrifice I am making."

"Then why stand on this ridge? If you wish to leave the Hive, why come back at all?"

Again, he said nothing.

Natrix suspected his reasons. As ruthless and logical as a Grandmaster might be, the bond between mentor and student was strong. Once broken, such intimate trust between student and teacher could turn to powerful hate; Cerastes must know that.

She pointed to the training field. "Our best students shall one day become our greatest rivals." Her eyes found the Viper. "You are not as invincible as you think."

Cerastes remained silent. They watched the Viper sheath his dagger and turn away from his defeated opponent. The young assassin crossed the training ground toward a fringe of trees on its opposite side.

"You should keep good relations with him," Natrix said solemnly. "Some day he will be a Grandmaster, and you will be old, and then you'll be that fool bleeding out in the snow." She pointed at the training field again, where the Adder now sat holding his rib cage, his blood staining the ground.

Cerastes gave Natrix one last look, then strode away, vanishing into the ever-thickening gusts of snow.

Viper left the practice ground. He crossed the sandy, slushy dunes to the hard-packed snow of the woods and entered the barren forest, heading back to his village. The trees and shrubs were stripped of leaves, comfortingly silent, like gleaming skeletal hands. A series of animal tracks—from a gray squirrel living in a nearby knotted oak—crossed the path before him. He caught sight of a fox in its white winter coat crouching beneath a bush, its ears pointed forward with acute concentration. As he watched, a small field mouse erupted from the snow. The fox pounced but missed, then chased after it.

Viper removed his shirt as he walked, letting the snowflakes strike his hot skin, invigorated from his hours on the training ground. A steaming plume of vapor accompanied each breath, visible on the chill air. His muscles sang from long hours of practice, pulsing with each heartbeat. Now was the ideal time to meditate. *Winter is a time of reflection*, Lachesis taught. *A time of frozen streams, of suspension. When the outside world is dormant, we are better able to focus on that which lies within us.*

Lachesis spoke of the seven gates: physical locks born into each member of the Sixth Race to help contain the full power of their demon. A shard of the Dark God lived within each of the Unnamed, a monster of destructive power seething just beneath their skin. Every now and then, children were born with their gates unlocked; they usually died within a few weeks, if not days. The demon's power dissolved their flesh, heart and lungs, killing the vessel along with itself.

Assassins of the Hive were trained to unlock those gates, to eventually master their demon—or meld with it. Each gate brought Viper closer to his full evolution—his highest potential—and greater prestige within the Hive.

The first four gates were the easiest to unlock. Most assassins accomplished that before they were eighteen.

The first gate, that of the mind, allowed Viper to hear the demon's voice in his thoughts.

Opening the second gate allowed him to channel the demon's strength and endurance into his physical body.

The third gate, that of magic, had its limitations—yet he was able to summon his shadow from the ground, to use as a cloak, a means of defense, or for minor spells.

Finally, the fourth gate was that of form: becoming the demon, allowing it to overtake his body and physically manifest. Only after opening the fourth gate could one become a Named assassin. Since the age of fourteen, Viper had been able to manifest his demon, and over time, he had become acquainted with its ways.

The fifth gate, a doorway into the shadow realm, remained blocked. His demon could cross over into the world of Wind and Light—but how did a man enter his own shadow? The key to unlocking the fifth gate lay in deep meditation, finding the door within himself and opening it. Then he would be able to open shadow portals between different lands, traveling hundreds of miles instantaneously.

"Soon," Grandmaster Lachesis said only a few days ago, "soon, you will break through the fifth gate, and the secrets of the shadow realm shall be yours."

Then only the sixth gate would remain. Eventually, after exploring the hidden paths of the shadow realm, one unlocked a new demon—a second, stronger form of his darker self. Only then, as a Grandmaster, could he choose a name separate from the Hive, uniquely his own, to be included in the scrolls of the Hive's history.

And the seventh gate? No one spoke of the seventh gate.

Viper paused next to a large boulder. He brushed the snow from its peak and climbed easily onto it and sat in a cross-legged position, quieting his thoughts. It was easier to meditate after physical exertion; his mind was quieted and ready to sink into his body.

He placed his hands palm-down on his knees and took deep breaths, allowing the tension to leave his neck and shoulders. His mind pooled at the base of his skull, becoming still as a frozen lake, empty as a riverbed. Time slipped away, removing its chains. He heard only the slow thump of his heart.

Somewhere deep within him, a dark pit opened, an eager, gaping maw. *Come,* the demon whispered. *Come....*

The sudden sound of footsteps, intentionally loud, broke Viper's concentration. Assassins did not make noise in the snow. He recognized the pace of the steps, the subtle brush of robes against the ground.

His eyes opened.

Cerastes stood at the fringe of trees.

Viper stared at him.

His Grandmaster had been absent for years, occasionally appearing in their colony without warning, only to disappear again with little explanation. He visited rarely and said few words to Viper during his visits. Before his long absence, Cerastes had spent much of his time with books and scrolls, delving into the ancient lore of the Dark God and the history of their race. Viper suspected Cerastes' thirst for knowledge eventually led him away from their colony, but he couldn't know for sure.

Cerastes' doings had weighed heavily on him. Viper could barely contain his own self-doubt. In some ways, he felt like he had failed an unspecified test. Despite his unrivaled progress, his Grandmaster had lost interest in training him. Perhaps Cerastes simply found him lacking in some way.

When Cerastes had first disappeared, Viper had felt lost, cut adrift and listless without guidance. Other Grandmasters had turned him away; no one dared take over Cerastes' tutelage. Grandmasters often became possessive of their students, particularly talented ones, and in the Viper's case, few were willing to risk Cerastes' wrath.

But as time wore on, the possibility of Cerastes' return seemed less and less likely. Finally, a year ago, an eccentric hermit had come to their colony—Lachesis. He was of the Hive, but not a member of any specific village. Viper eventually received new instruction under the unusual Grandmaster, although he felt no true loyalty to Lachesis or his teachings. This strange man was not of their colony; he was a traveling vagabond who visited various factions of the Hive, then disappeared for months on end, much like Cerastes. Viper was still alone.

As he gazed at Cerastes, Viper felt that powerful bond again. This was his true master, the one who had melded him into a lethal weapon, who had made him as strong as tempered steel.

Viper felt a distinct tightness in his throat as he waited for Cerastes to speak. However, no words were forthcoming. Finally, he asked his master, "Why are you here?"

"To check on your training," Cerastes said.

*A lie,* Viper sensed, though it was difficult to read his old teacher. "My training is no longer your concern," he said, hiding his disappointment. "I study under Grandmaster Lachesis now."

Cerastes' eyes remained flat and expressionless. Viper's skin prickled. He had never seen such an eerie, unreadable look. A thin veil seemed to cover Cerastes' face, hiding something utterly grotesque. *This is wrong,* Viper thought.

"Come," his Grandmaster murmured, and raised his hand in a beckoning gesture. He moved slowly, almost mockingly. "Let us spar. Show me your new skill."

Viper couldn't resist the invitation. He slid off the rock and drew his dagger, then crouched slightly, prepared to fight. Cerastes drew a similar dagger from his belt. This would be an equal match—at least, as equal as master and student could be.

Cerastes lunged without warning. His hand became a blur of motion. He thrust his blade directly at Viper's heart.

Viper knocked the blade to one side, then dipped under Cerastes' arm and came up beside him. He landed a solid punch to the ribs, then a vicious kick to the sternum.

Cerastes grabbed Viper's leg and dragged him off-balance, twisting him until he fell into the snow. Viper allowed himself to fall, rolled quickly back onto his feet, then unleashed a series of blows that forced Cerastes back across the clearing.

Still, his Grandmaster evaded each strike with ease. Viper felt as though he was battling the wind.

Finally, Viper caught Cerastes' wrist and pulled him sideways, knocking him off-balance. As he rammed his shoulder into Cerastes' ribs, the Grandmaster stumbled backwards. Viper kept pushing at him, dragging his master to the ground until his knife pressed firmly into Cerastes' navel.

Then, just as the Viper tasted victory, his Grandmaster disappeared from beneath him. Viper collapsed in the snow, disoriented. His knife struck the frozen ground.

Cerastes reappeared beneath a nearby tree, materializing from thin air. *The fifth gate.* He had opened that portal instantly and had used it to outmaneuver his student.

Viper sat up, his eyes narrowed to slits. "You have an unfair advantage," he spat.

"Assassins use any and all advantages in combat," Cerastes returned.

"Perhaps." A hint of rebellion lit his gaze. "Lachesis teaches differently. Engaging a lesser opponent is pointless, if only to show off one's skill."

"Then you admit you are the lesser?"

Viper's glare hardened. "I never claimed to be anything else."

"And this Lachesis...." Cerastes clasped his hands behind his back. "Is he your new master now? Is he the one who taught you to harness your demon, who made you a Named assassin?"

Viper's lip curled, but his years of discipline kept him from jumping up. He bowed his head stiffly and stayed on the ground.

"No, Grandmaster," he murmured.

"You've grown sloppy, Viper," Cerastes said flatly. "Lachesis is too encouraging with his words. You are far from reaching the fifth gate."

"Then I will strive harder."

Cerastes smiled—an empty expression. "I see my absence has sorely impacted your progress. Lachesis is a wild hermit. His teachings are untried and unproven. Do you really think you will reach the fifth gate by meditating hours on end? Lachesis is fooling you. He's stalling your progress and wasting your time." His eyes sharpened. "He fears what you may become."

Viper didn't want to believe Cerastes' words, yet he knew his Grandmaster would never mislead him. The bond between mentor and student remained strong despite Cerastes' absence. Viper had trained and studied at his Grandmaster's side since childhood, almost since birth—and a child's loyalty was not easily shaken.

"What do you suggest I do?" Viper asked. Although he kept his eyes trained on the ground, he could feel Cerastes' approving gaze.

"Come with me," his mentor said, his voice low and heavy, as though burdened by some unnameable secret. "Join my side and I will teach you to harness the fifth gate. I will teach you all the forgotten secrets of our kind."

Viper looked up. For years now he had struggled on his own, always anticipating his master's return. He had yearned for this very moment....

Yet strangely, now that Cerastes had made his offer, Viper did not feel swayed. Over time, he had found ways to stand on his own in the Hive, to continue training without his Grandmaster's guidance. He had built a new life. The Hive, after all, was more than just a place. It was a community, a rigid one, but consistent all the same, and saturated with tradition. This was his home.

"You would ask me to leave the Hive?" Viper asked.

His Grandmaster gave only the slightest nod.

In that instant, Viper knew where he belonged. "I can't go with you."

"Are you afraid?"

"No," he replied. "I won't turn my back on our people."

"And this is how you perceive me?" Cerastes' voice became withering. "Someone who has betrayed his race?"

"No," Viper said quickly. "I didn't mean—"

"Then speak what you mean."

Viper stood up and sheathed his dagger. "You've chosen your path," he said clearly. "It is time I choose mine. I won't leave the Hive."

Cerastes' eyes became dangerous. For a moment, the thin veil slipped, and Viper saw something malicious, even monstrous, upon his face. Then the look passed.

"A pity," Cerastes said as he turned away. "You're certain? I won't ask again."

Viper didn't hesitate. "I'm certain," he said. "But you will always remain my first mentor. Wherever you go, Grandmaster, your shadow shall encompass me." He bowed to his mentor's retreating back.

Cerastes hardly seemed to hear him. A slight wind touched his long, black hair and rippled through his robes. Then he entered the shade of the trees and was gone.

Viper stood back. He felt suddenly bereft, as though the air had left his lungs. He made his hands into fists, wondering if he had made the right choice, yet knowing it didn't matter now, the moment had passed, it couldn't be changed. He had allowed his teacher's absence to affect him for too long. It was time to let go.

He stared at the place where Cerastes had vanished, and allowed himself to sink into the solitude of the forest. *Farewell*, he thought, and watched the falling snow bury his Grandmaster's last footprints.

# CHAPTER 1

The Dawn Seeker sailed upriver, impressive and sturdy, a three-masted schooner with billowing white sails and over a dozen cabins. The ship traveled up the Little Rain, a small tributary of the Crown's Rush, headed inland from the ocean. The rainy season had made the tributary deep and wide.

The Little Rain traveled through flat marshland and dense forest, lined by juniper thickets and bristling blackberry bushes. Early morning fog cast the world in gray, brooding light. Tall trees loomed over the riverbanks, fading in and out of the mist.

Sora dangled her legs over the crow's nest. She always took the dawn watch, as she liked the tension in the forest at daybreak, and the birds twittering in excited song at the first hint of silver light.

The crow's nest of the Dawn Seeker sat high upon the central mast, dozens of feet above the ground. From this height, Sora could see Captain Silas' crew stirring on deck. The night workers filed inside as a fresh crew took over their stations, adjusting the sails and manning the wheel, calling out to one another, laughing. She could smell fresh bread baking, as the aroma drifted up from the galley. Her stomach let out a sudden, loud complaint. While she wanted nothing more than to climb down and eat breakfast, she felt stiff and cold, her woolen cloak damp with moisture from her three-hour watch.

*But I can't leave yet*, she thought. When Captain Silas first assigned her to the crow's nest, he gave her a long lecture about sailing upriver: the danger of opposing currents, lightning, driftwood, debris, tree limbs and rocks in the shallows. The ship's safety relied on a good lookout...and so breakfast would have to wait.

Her eyes drifted to a figure on the deck below. At first glance, he appeared to be lying prostrate on the wooden boards, but a closer look revealed a series of short, quick press-ups. His hot breath misted the air. His hands were placed opposite his shoulders, his palms flat on the deck, his back rigidly straight. She didn't know how many press-ups a man could do in one sitting, but she had counted at least two hundred.

He trained every morning around this time—the same as her watch—and ran through a strenuous routine of exercises: twenty laps around the deck, a series of kicks and jumps, then a long chain of attacks using daggers or swords. His broad, powerful shoulders immediately caught her eye. A myriad of scars, visible even at this distance, covered his back. She wondered if he had removed his shirt on purpose, if he knew how much it distracted her. *No,* she thought, *he doesn't want anything to do with me.*

She hardly spoke to Crash these days. Not after what had happened on the Lost Isles.

"Hey!" a familiar voice drifted up to her. She glanced toward the base of the mast. Burn, the giant Wulven mercenary, swung himself easily onto the rigging and climbed upward. His movements were startlingly graceful, despite his size. Within a half-minute, he stood on the ropes just beneath her feet. "What are you doing up here, looking so gloomy?"

She tried to smile, but it didn't stay. "Just tired," she mumbled. That was half-true. Honestly, she had been out of sorts since leaving the Lost Isles, and for more reasons than just Crash. Her eyes drifted to her left hand, which lay curled in her lap.

Burn smiled, a fearsome expression on his square face. His teeth were as sharp as lion-fangs, a trait of the Wulven race, and his long incisors jutted past his lower lip.

"Is the moisture bothering your wound?" he asked. "Perhaps Lori can give you a soothing balm."

Sora shook her head. "No, it's healed." The scar in the center of her palm was from her battle with Volcrian: a circular crater, still pink, with new skin. But her wound seemed to go deeper than mere flesh. Since battling the mage, she hadn't heard a whisper from her Cat's-Eye necklace.

She resisted the urge to touch the small, green-tinted stone at her neck. The Cat's Eye was more than just a simple rock, but a magical artifact with its own form of consciousness, sharing a psychic bond with her mind. It protected her from magic, absorbing supernatural energy like a parasite; if she removed the necklace, that psychic bond would break. She would fall into a coma, or even die. *Most likely die,* she amended. She had worn it for almost two years now, and there was no going back.

Usually the stone murmured softly to her, nudging her thoughts, responding to the world around them. Yet now, when she stretched out her mind and sought its presence, she felt a muddy, dull quagmire at her fingertips. *Wake up,* she thought, touching upon the internal bond. *Where are you?*

There was only silence, like the billowing morning fog.

Her troubled frown deepened. She looked at Crash. He had finished his routine and sat on the deck to stretch out his muscles, cooling down.

"Hmmm," Burn grunted deep in his throat. "Is *that* what's occupying your mind? Quite a good view from up here." He winked at her.

Sora grimaced. Then she redirected her gaze to the forest.

"You should go speak to him," Burn suggested.

"Speak to Crash? Why?"

Burn gave her a humorous look. "First, so I can eat dinner with both of you again. And second," he paused, "so you can put your heart at ease. I know what happened. I saw you on the deck of the ship when we left the Isles," he admitted.

A tremor of horror ran down Sora's spine. "You...you what?"

"I saw you two speaking, and a bit more than that."

*The kiss.* Oh that terrible, stupid kiss! "It's not what it looked like," she cut him off, her cheeks red. "There isn't anything between us. I mean, there *wasn't* anything between us. I...uh..." she stuttered. "He's a hard person to understand. I think he just needs...." *What? Needs what?*

"A hearty breakfast? Perhaps a knock upside the head?" Burn guffawed.

Sora scowled. "I don't know and I don't care," she huffed. *I don't care about him at all,* she repeated to herself.

Despite all they had faced together, the assassin remained enigmatic and withdrawn, and she had taken to avoiding him. They seemed to have fallen back into their old ways, repeating their roles from two years ago, when he had first kidnapped her and dragged her into his world. Back when he had been so easy to hate, so easy to blame for all her troubles.

Over time they had fought side-by-side, shared nights by the fire, learned to trust and rely on each other. They had grown steadily closer, until the kiss.

Now everything was the same—yet so horribly different. *I can't,* he said that night on the ship as they sailed away from the Lost Isles. *I can't be that person for you.* He was of the Sixth Race, after all. Ruthless and deadly, with a past she was just beginning to understand.

Now he kept a steady distance from her, as though she were an infatuated young girl. The thought made her at once furious and dismayed. She felt she deserved more of an explanation, or at least an attempt at normalcy. She glared at his dark figure on the deck. *Cold bastard,* she thought.

"Have you considered he's just as bad at this as you are?" Burn asked. He leaned back on the rigging, settling his weight on the ropes.

"Bad at what, exactly?" she hedged.

"Talking."

"Talking? Explaining himself, you mean? I told you, there's nothing between us."

"And I'm a Harpy with no wings! You've been circling around each other like two cats in a closet. It's hard not to notice. Even the Dracians are talking."

"The Dracians talk about everything."

"Right," Burn agreed, then gave her a searching glance. "But have you heard what they're saying?"

"What do you mean?"

Burn hesitated. "Tristan thinks Crash hurt you...physically," he said. "Some sort of wife-abuse, without the wife part."

Sora's face drained of color. "He said that?"

"Yes, about twenty times over the past week."

Her jaw clenched.

Burn reached out and patted her foot. "The sailors are restless. Not much for them to do but spread stories. Just thought I would warn you, before you hear it from someone else."

Sora sighed. "It's my own fault, I suppose," she muttered. Burn looked at her questioningly, but she shook her head. "It's not true, of course. But I might have confided a bit too much in Tristan...." Her voice trailed off. After Crash's rejection, she had sunk into a depressed state. Tristan saw her distress and swooped in, all too willing to take the assassin's place. His attention had been difficult to turn down. Tristan was handsome, charming, and her same age. He brought her seashells and tried to make her laugh. If she had been any other girl, she might have fallen head-over-heels for him.

Then she had complained about Crash's coldness. A petty thing to do, but there it was. Tristan had been furious that the assassin would scorn her. *You don't need him,* the pirate had said. *Not when you have a hot-blooded Dracian at your side.*

Then he had tried to kiss her. Twice.

Sora winced at the memory. The very touch of Tristan's lips against her cheek had brought a startling revelation—she didn't love him, and she never could.

"He's probably jealous," Sora said, realizing she had been quiet for some time.

Burn raised an eyebrow. "Of course," he agreed. "And perhaps a bit angry at you. Dracians are passionate creatures. The rest of the crew half-believe his story...."

Sora glared. "It's just gossip and drunken speculation! Tristan should lay off his cups. The Dracians can think what they like—I don't care."

Burn nodded. "Fair, but your mother hasn't known Crash very long, and the Sixth Race carries a reputation. Don't be surprised if she asks you about what happened. Word will reach her eventually. It's a big ship—but not that big."

Sora bit her lip and looked down at the assassin. Crash seemed to be taking longer than usual this morning, drawing out his stretches. She had the sudden suspicion that he could hear them talking. He wasn't human, after all. Not entirely. Only a few weeks ago, she had learned the truth about his race, that Crash was one of the Unnamed, a child of the Dark God. He contained a demonic power she couldn't begin to understand. Did he know about the rumors? She felt a twinge of embarrassment. *What a mess....*

"How do we stop this from getting out of hand?" she asked Burn, suddenly concerned. A few more weeks of travel still separated them from the City of Crowns. What if the Dracians became so worked up, they tried to throw the assassin overboard? *Goddess help them,* she thought.

"Go to the source, I suppose," Burn said, rubbing his chin thoughtfully. "I tried to speak to Tristan...but he took offense, said I'd insulted his honor by calling him a liar." He let out a short bark of a laugh. "Dracians! Full of pride and passion, and not a lick of sense! I think you'll have to speak to him."

Sora didn't relish the thought. Confronting Tristan about the assassin, perhaps in front of the entire crew, sounded excruciating.

Burn swung easily up next to her, landing on the crow's nest. The wooden boards shuddered beneath his weight. "Go down and get some breakfast. My turn to play lookout," he said, and tousled her hair fondly.

Sora nodded, suddenly reluctant to go. Up here she felt above the Dracians' gossip; it was nothing more than petty speculation. Down there, she would have to walk around on deck, knowing what they all thought. How long had these rumors been flying around? She remembered a few conspicuous moments over the past week: a flurry of murmurs every time she passed Tristan's table in the mess room, strange looks from crewmen, a few nosy questions from her friend Joan.

Her cheeks flushed suddenly. Joan had asked pointedly about her experience with men. The honest truth? She didn't have any. Only that one night with Crash on the Lost Isles, learning the fire of a kiss, the addictive nature of a touch. She had no experience with love—and the mere thought of *making love* still left her blushing.

She bit her lip in distress. Perhaps the rumors weren't as well-hidden as she thought.

She sighed and climbed down the rigging, wincing as her stiff muscles flexed. The wind shifted abruptly, blowing in her face, and she wrinkled her nose.

"Do you smell something?" she asked. A pungent stench, like rotten vegetation, floated on the wind.

Burn nodded. Wolfy senses were far more heightened than humans. "Been smelling it for days. Seems to be from the forest."

Her eyes traveled to the line of trees. The fog was slowly burning off as the sun rose in the sky. It would be a cold, clear day, heralding the winter months to come. Large pine trees and cypress crowded the bank, thick with untamed foliage, arching countless meters above the river and branching into tall canopies overhead. Bright green willows leaned over the Little Rain, trailing their branches in the murky water. Birdsong filled her ears: the shrieks of meadowlarks and the sharp tat-tat-tat of woodpeckers, even the coo of an owl perched somewhere in the dark branches.

She couldn't divine the source of the smell and wrinkled her nose again, sniffing the air, reminded of her venture two years ago through Fennbog swamp, where the ground had reeked of sulfur. *We're not far from Fennbog now, are we?* she wondered.

No, actually she didn't think they were anywhere near Fennbog, but that didn't explain that rancid smell of rotting plants.

Burn waved to her as she continued climbing down the rigging.

The mess hall of the Dawn Seeker doubled as a game room and meeting room, depending on the time of day. In one corner, a series of steep wooden steps led down to the galley, the ship's kitchen.

Sora sat down at one of the long wooden tables and ate without disturbance. Breakfast was a humble affair of red beans, rye bread and two strips of fatty bacon. The breakfast hour had already passed and most of the crew were either resting from the night shift or manning the ship. Only two other Dracians inhabited the hall—Joan, a red-haired woman who sat with her legs boldly splayed out on a bench, and another man who Sora didn't know by name. The two spoke in quiet tones over cups of hot tea.

Just as Sora raised the last bite of food to her mouth, a hand grabbed her wrist. She gasped and spilled the last of her beans.

"Mom!" she exclaimed.

Lorianne stood above her daughter with a steady, searching gaze. "You un-wrapped your bandage," she said, taking note of Sora's scarred left hand.

Sora yanked her wrist free. "Well I feel fine."

"The skin needs to toughen up. What if you tear it again? That rigging is rough on your hands."

Sora started to protest, but Lori whipped out a strip of gauze and grabbed her hand, swiftly wrapping it. Sora waited impatiently. She didn't like being fussed over. She could take care of herself.

"What kind of Healer would I be if I let my own daughter neglect her wounds?" Lori muttered as she worked.

Sora gritted her teeth. "You're overly concerned," she insisted.

"And you're pouting," her mother returned.

Sora sighed. She wished she knew her mother just a little better; then she would feel more free to speak her mind.

She had known Lori for less than two years. When Sora was a baby, her mother had left her in the care of a rich nobleman, hoping she would be raised with all the wealth and privileges that her own blood couldn't afford. *His own seed was useless,* her mother explained once. *But he lived in denial. A man's pride, you see. So it was easy for me to convince him that you were his daughter.*

According to her mother, Lord Fallcrest married Lorianne within a few weeks of meeting. Eventually he discovered Lori's common bloodline and gave her an ultimatum—either disappear, or face the King's law. She was forced to leave her baby behind, however, as Lord Fallcrest still believed the child to be his own.

*He always doubted me,* Sora thought, caught up in memories. She would never know for sure if he saw her as his true daughter. He had always remained distant, especially in those final years, traveling often to the City of Crowns.

She thought back to her Blooming ceremony and the end of her stepfather's life. The Blooming marked her transition into adulthood, and should have attracted herds of hopeful suitors. Instead, her stepfather was murdered and she was kidnapped and taken on an unanticipated adventure—which eventually led her to Lorianne's doorstep.

It all left a strange taste in her mouth. She didn't always understand her mother's decision to leave her with a nobleman. For seventeen years she believed she was a Fallcrest, born into Second Tier nobility. It was hard for her to see herself any other way.

"Come," Lorianne said, interrupting her daughter's thoughts and releasing Sora's freshly bandaged hand. "Let's go for a walk."

"A walk?" Sora asked, nonplussed. There weren't many places to go for a walk aboard the Dawn Seeker. She had been circling the deck for weeks now.

Lori waited for Sora to stand up from the wooden bench. Then they walked together out the door, arm in arm.

"I'm composing a letter to Cameron," her mother explained. "I thought you might like to add something to it."

Sora shrugged. She doubted her mother would go to all this trouble to compose a letter. No, something else was occupying Lori's mind, and thanks to Burn, she thought she knew what it might be.

Once outside, they circled the deck, their arms linked. The two women shared the same blond hair, Lori's straw-straight and worn neatly above her shoulders, while Sora's fell in long, heavy waves down her back. Sora had her mother's blue eyes, if a little darker, less like the sky and more like the iron blue of a deep, cold lake. She had a wider mouth, a slightly more pronounced chin, and a few inches more in height. Still, anyone who looked at them could see they were related.

As they walked, several Dracians hailed Lori with various greetings.

"Fair morning, Healer!" one called.

"And the day just got fairer!" another added.

"Your hair is like the dawn!"

Sora resisted the urge to sigh. Healers commanded a lot of respect from the different races. Sometimes it was useful—but the Dracians' blatant flattery grated on her nerves.

"Ahoy, mistress!" another sailor hailed Lori as they rounded the aft of the ship. "Do you have time for an appointment this afternoon? Got a terrible fungus on my toe."

Lori nodded graciously. "Of course," she said. "Come by the sickroom after lunch."

The Dracian dropped the rope in his hands and gave an exaggerated salute. Their race came from a union of Wind and Fire, and they were theatrical to the bone.

Sora grinned at his antics, but the sailor didn't return her smile, and instead turned back to his job.

Her mother noticed. She spoke casually as they continued to walk. "I've heard some strange rumors around the ship," she began.

Sora considered a number of responses, but remained silent.

Her mother gave her a sideways glance. "The Dracians like to embellish, but it *does* make me wonder...."

"Rumors?" Sora fumbled. "I'm not sure." Then, just as they rounded another corner of the deck, she came face-to-face with the last person she wanted to see.

Crash stood with his shirt in his hands, his hair damp. A series of wet footprints led to a large water basin on the deck. By the look of him, he had just rinsed off. Sora recalled his fierce regimen of exercises in the early morning fog. He looked fit and bristling, his shoulders straight and wide, his arms powerful, his chest hard and defined. His hair, perfectly black, fell in front of his eyes. His face always reminded her of a wolf or a jackal, sharp and cunning, with a straight nose, a defined jaw, and a firm mouth that rarely cracked a smile.

Sora's heart thudded awkwardly in her chest, missing a half-beat. Her mother paused beside her. She became aware of a lull in the activity of the ship; a few nearby Dracians cast curious looks in her direction. *Don't feed the rumors,* she told herself firmly. She raised her head a notch and gave the assassin a warm smile.

"Training?" she asked, trying not to stare at the water droplets trickling down his chest.

He raised a dark eyebrow.

"Walking?" he asked in return.

Sora flushed.

He pulled his black shirt over his damp body and turned to walk away. Sora dared to glance at her mother, who watched both of them closely.

In an attempt to appear normal, Sora tried to speak again. "Uh...nice day out, isn't it?" she asked, stepping after him. She winced. *Much too forced!*

He kept walking. "No different from yesterday." His voice held a rough edge. Only a month ago, he was taken captive and tortured by Harpy soldiers. They had placed a sunstone collar around his neck. The light of the stone had burned into his flesh. The scar still marked his collarbone, and his voice had never fully healed.

Sora didn't feel like giving up quite yet, so continued, right on his heels. "The fog burned off," she offered. "Nothing like a clear winter sky!"

Crash looked upward. "Funny thing about fog," he said.

"Oh?"

"It plays tricks on your ears. Sounds tend to carry."

"Oh?" she repeated softly.

"Aye," Crash murmured. "Though I suppose Burn knew that."

Sora opened her mouth, then shut it promptly. Her footsteps came to a halt.

Crash continued walking down the side of the ship, heading toward the galley. She watched him. Her hands slowly curled into fists. *He knows,* she thought. *He knows about the rumors, and so does the whole damn ship.* Humiliating. She had the sudden urge to throw herself into the river.

Her mother's hand suddenly landed on her shoulder. "Here," Lori said, steering her toward the railing. Sora leaned up against it, swallowing the frustration in her throat.

Lorianne cast a sharp look at several gawking Dracians, who hurriedly ducked their heads. Her hand moved restlessly around Sora's upper back, massaging the stiff muscles.

"What happened between you two?" Lori asked. "You barely speak to one another. You've been out of sorts since the Lost Isles."

"Nothing. Nothing happened."

"You can tell me about it, you know, if there was a disagreement, a fight of some kind," Lori hesitated, "or if he hurt you."

"Mother!" Sora snapped, turning to glare at her. At times, the word still felt strange on her tongue. "How could you think that of Crash? Just because he's an assassin doesn't make him violent." Goddess, it sounded desperate even to her own ears—of course assassins were violent, especially the Sixth Race. They were creatures of Darkness and Fire. They fed on chaos. She tried again. "You don't actually believe the Dracians, do you?"

Lori gave her a searching look. "No," her mother finally said. "But I worry about you. Crash is...not very approachable. The Sixth Race is difficult to read." She paused again and continued carefully. "We have a lot to consider about him, now that the Shade is trying to summon the Dark God."

Sora shook her head. "You can't blame Crash for that," she said.

"I don't," her mother replied swiftly. "But we don't know much about him. We don't know his previous alliances...."

"Then you believe the rumors?" Sora balked. "You believe Crash would hurt me?"

"No, I just want you to be cautious!" her mother exclaimed.

Sora frowned stubbornly. Her mother's lack of trust bothered her more than anything else. Did the entire ship see her this way? As a young girl in the thrall of a ruthless assassin? Who knew what the Dracians were really saying? Burn said "abuse," but perhaps he had tried to soften the blow. *Used*, she heard in her mind. *Taken by force.* Any of these concepts could be part of the rumor mill.

Her mother touched her arm, and Sora couldn't abide the sympathy, the distraught look that crept into Lorianne's gaze.

"I'm not a defenseless victim!" she almost shouted. "Crash saved my life countless times! I can't believe you would doubt him. Just keep out of my business, would you? I know who my friends are." Then she turned quickly on her heel and stalked across the deck, thumping her feet as hard as she could, wishing she could snap each wooden plank in half. She was relieved that her mother didn't follow.

Deep underground, Krait knelt on one knee and bowed her head. Above her, the ongoing churn of gears grated through the heavy granite stone.

Shadows filled the domed, circular chamber. Summoned by Grandmaster Cerastes, she was transported under the earth by a shadow portal, an instant doorway. She didn't know where this chamber resided, perhaps deep beneath the City of Crowns, or perhaps buried under a mountain range hundreds of miles away. It made no difference. Cerastes had called, and she had come.

To her left knelt another assassin, clothed similarly in plain black garb: a member of The Shade. She had yet to meet him. Cerastes kept their order hidden from the world, even from each other. Higher-up members rarely gathered together except for training, or to study the Dark God's lore. She wasn't sure why Cerastes had summoned them here, but as she raised her head, she thought she might know the answer.

At the center of the chamber hovered an eerie, nightmarish apparition. The creature made her skin crawl and adrenaline rush through her blood. It seemed molded out of mist and shadow. A tattered black cloak encased its evanescent form, creating the illusion of a body. Beneath its hood, only empty space stared out. It shifted back and forth, flickering in the air, as though it might vanish completely.

A circle of fine chalk on the ground kept the creature contained. Krait didn't know much about magic, but she knew this was an ancient spell taken from *The Book of the Named.* Her master had imprisoned this *thing* for his own dark purposes.

"Cobra tells me the Viper is indeed alive and has returned to the mainland," Cerastes remarked from behind them. The chamber seemed filled by his presence. One long, calloused hand rested on each of their shoulders, connecting the two assassins.

Krait forced herself not to shudder beneath his touch.

"For the past month, Cobra and his savants have kept watch over the minor tributaries that feed the Crown's Rush. He tells me that Viper has returned from the ocean."

Her heart quickened at Cerastes' words. She had first encountered the Viper almost six months ago in the port city of Delbar. Before that, Cerastes' infamous protegé had been thought dead. Their battle was fast and violent, and she had barely escaped with her life.

Krait felt a twinge of uncertainty—almost jealousy. The Viper was *her* discovery. So she dared to speak.

"Master," she murmured, "you assigned me to watch for him at the gates of The City of Crowns—"

"And Cobra found him first," Cerastes cut her off. "We can't afford to wait and let him slip past our ranks unnoticed. Winter solstice will soon be upon us. I must ensure that the Viper arrives with the weapons on time. And if we can persuade him to do so willingly...even better."

Krait ground her teeth. Her thoughts made it imperative that she speak. "He has more than one weapon?"

"Yes," Cerastes said. "He carries the sacred spearhead and the sword hilt. He has already killed the bloodmage who initiated the plague. A pity, but not detrimental to our plans." His voice turned deceptively soft. "Does that ease your mind?"

Krait bowed lower and pressed her lips shut. Clearly, she had overstepped her bounds.

"You and Cobra have been of great service these past weeks," Cerastes continued. "With *The Book of the Named*, I've been able to harness the last of the wraiths, the keeper of the third sacred weapon."

Krait's eyes slid over to the phantom, which gave off a cold, deathly energy—unnerving, even to one of the Shade's elite.

"The Viper travels with a group of others," Cerastes explained. "We have yet to discern if they are a threat. I want to see what they're capable of. To that end, you and Cobra shall be my trusted eyes and ears."

Krait's gaze went to Cobra kneeling nearby. He was a slight man, narrow-shouldered and unassuming. A long scar mutilated half his visible face. A black cowl obscured his nose, mouth and lower features. His green eyes remained focused intently—almost fervently—on the stone floor.

This time, Cerastes' silence seemed to encourage questions.

"Exactly what do you wish from us, Grandmaster?" she asked.

"Observe them from a distance. I want to know what Viper's allies are capable of."

"Capable of killing a bloodmage," Cobra offered. His voice sounded nasally and thin, as though he spoke through a broken nose.

"Yes, but what else?" Cerastes intoned. "Knowledge is a weapon. We cannot be taken off-guard." The Grandmaster released their shoulders and began pacing around the outer circle of the chamber. Perfectly black hair trailed to his waist, blending with his dark robes. A heavy gold chain with the emblem of a boar's head upon it, the human king's royal seal, hung around his neck. Only recently had he begun wearing it, though Krait didn't know why. Cerastes kept much of his doings secret, sharing only what was needed to know for a mission.

Her Grandmaster paused at the side of the circle. "Look at this creature from the Dark God's realm," he said, his voice echoing. "Is it not beautiful?"

Krait raised her eyes slowly, gazing at the phantom. "Your power is unrivaled," she murmured.

Cerastes sneered. "This creature is not my work," he corrected. "It was summoned from the Dark God's realm...but that is unimportant now. Do you see its weapon?" Cerastes stepped very close to the barrier of powdered bone. His face came into full view: gaunt, angular cheeks, a narrow jaw, deep-set eyes and a stern nose. Subtle lines marred his brow and lips. His form was lean and powerful beneath his robes, his muscles taut and defined over decades of vicious training. He looked capable of cruelty.

The wraith lunged in his direction, coming up against an invisible barrier. It paused, unable to pass over the white line. The two stared at one another, hood-to-hood. Then the creature let out a horrible shriek—a piercing, unnatural sound—and raised its arms.

Yes, she saw it then: a longbow, seemingly molded from onyx. A black arrow manifested between the wraith's hands. The phantom drew the bowstring taut and aimed the arrow directly at the Grandmaster's chest but did not release it. Rather, the creature held the arrow drawn, trained on Cerastes' heart, quivering.

"A creature of wrath, bred of vengeance," Cerastes murmured. "Immortal...unstoppable. And here, the black arrow, the Dark God's third artifact. Somehow, we must separate the weapon from its keeper...." He trailed off, deep in thought.

Krait watched silently. The wraith didn't look like an easy opponent; it wasn't a physical being, but an apparition of mist and shadow. She wondered if she could actually strike it, or if her hand would pass right through. She watched her master's pensive face as he stared at the wraith. She knew he planned to contact the Dark God in some way by using *The Book of the Named* and the sacred weapons. He would need to retrieve the bow from this creature and collect the last two weapons from Viper. But she knew nothing more.

*Why is he showing us this?* Cerastes didn't flaunt his trophies without some purpose. She shifted. "What are your plans for the Viper?" she asked softly. "Does he also seek this arrow?"

Cerastes released a slow hiss, then spoke without looking at her. "He will come for the last weapon. He travels with the same Dracian who once kept *The Book of the Named*. Perhaps we have found ourselves an adversary...." He paused as though amused. "He knows of us and he will seek us out. Perhaps that's to our benefit. The sooner we retrieve the weapons, the better." He looked at Cobra. "I must know the Viper's plan. And I want to know how he killed the first two wraiths."

Cobra twitched, his body tight with anticipation. "It shall be done, Grandmaster," he murmured.

Krait frowned. "And after we have the weapons?"

Cerastes replied coldly, "We shall see."

Krait lowered her head. Cobra's rigid stance seemed to mock her disobedience—a reminder of just how unworthy she felt as Cerastes' student. She wanted to impress her Grandmaster and earn his favor. But her eagerness to serve made her talk out of turn, anxious to exceed his expectations. She yearned for his blessing, like a wayward child seeking a parent's approval.

Six years ago, Cerastes had found her, emaciated, lying on the beach. A half-dead shell, her memory had been full of gaping holes and horrific nightmares. Through his majestic powers, Cerastes had restored her burned-out eyes and built her spirit anew—consequently, she served his will without question.

That bond of loyalty gave her a sense of purpose—the seed of a new identity. Given how low she had once fallen, and how high he had raised her, she would do anything to repay him.

"Go now," Cerastes said, and raised one long-boned hand. The shadows coiled in the corner of the room, circling until they formed a misty portal. "Return to me as soon as you have learned their plans."

Krait and Cobra stood as one. Then Cerastes spoke again, "Cobra, stay for a moment. I have one more task for you."

Krait wore the composed mask of an assassin, but she couldn't dismiss her jealous thoughts. Why would Cerastes choose Cobra? He might be superior to her in skill, but he was still a new member of the Shade. Did Cerastes not trust her with his plan? *He has no reason to doubt me*, she thought. A willing tool, she would do anything he asked without question. Cerastes must know that.

*We all have our place*, she told herself. *As hands of the Dark God, we must do as we are asked, and nothing more.*

Krait bowed slightly to Cerastes, then turned her back to Cobra and swiftly traversed the room. With a running leap, she jumped through the portal into inky darkness.

# CHAPTER 2

The Dawn Seeker contained a surprising amount of cabins below deck, each about the size of a closet, with just room enough for a narrow cot and a porthole window. Sora's room contained her bags, a change of clothes and a lantern. She hid the two sacred weapons—the sword hilt and spearhead—in a bag under her cot.

Her staff rested behind the door. The gray-blue pole stood about two hands taller than Sora's head. The initials K.W., perhaps the insignia of some past owner, had been lovingly carved into the wood.

She had purchased the weapon in Mayville two years ago, when she first left Fallcrest lands, before journeying through Fennbog swamp. The staff was made of a rare kind of wood only found in the Bracken, an ancient forest in the far East, where travelers said the trees were so old, their roots and branches had grown together into a single living organism. The wood of those trees could not be cut by humans, but could only be carved by magic. Any artifact made of "witchwood" had to predate the War of the Races, when magic had been an everyday occurrence.

Sora lifted her staff and her arms tightened in anticipation. She intended to lose herself in a long, hard workout. It had been several weeks since her last bout of strenuous exercise. She left her cabin and headed to the bow of the ship.

As Sora walked, she thought of her mother's warning. Now more than ever, she needed to trust Crash. The next leg of their journey would be the most dangerous.

On the horizon lay the City of Crowns, home to the King and the most powerful nobility in the land. And within that City, the Shade awaited: a secret cult of the Sixth Race, trained since childhood in the art of killing; they worshiped the Dark God and wanted to resurrect His power.

Sora's small band now followed the Shade on a desperate hunt for *The Book of the Named*, an ancient text that contained secret knowledge of the Dark God. Lori and her friend Ferran, a once-renowned treasure hunter, claimed the book would help them stop a deadly plague from consuming the land. The disease had already spread over a hundred miles, from the lowlands to the coast. Sora didn't know how helpful the book might be, but without it, they didn't have much to go on. No one knew much about the plague, and the only way to cure it was to use a Cat's-Eye stone.

Crash denied any knowledge of *The Book of the Named* or the Shade. He said the cult was only a rumor among the Sixth Race, and she believed him. *I can't let myself doubt,* she thought, turning her staff over in her hands. In the past month, Crash had more than proved his friendship, his alliance, his intentions. Why couldn't Lori see that?

Sora reached the bow of the ship just as they rounded the next bend in the river. Shouts arose from the crow's nest; countless Dracians leapt to the jib and yardarm, adjusting the sails and rudder to guide the long schooner around a sharp turn. The ship slowly tilted to one side, making its lumbering way upstream. She could hear Captain Silas yelling obscenities at a hapless young sailor who had tangled up the ropes.

As the ship passed through a thick copse of poplar trees, the Little Rain straightened out into a wide, flat stretch of water, heading further inland. The current slowed considerably, the banks half-buried in cattails and watercress. Any number of obstacles lay hidden beneath the murky, sluggish water.

She heard Captain Silas roaring orders behind her, directing his men to steer the ship toward the center of the river.

"Straighten her out, boys! I'll have your heads if we hit bottom!"

Sora stood at the pointed nose of the Dawn Seeker, where the figurehead of a charging horse protruded from the woodwork. The wind shifted, and she smelled that strange, pungent odor again, like a pile of rotting fruit. She leaned against the railing and gazed out at the riverbank, wondering what the source of the smell might be.

Suddenly a strange vibration moved through her, causing chills across her body. She looked up, surprised, and raised a hand against the sun's glare. *No, wait, that's not the sun....*

"Sora!" a familiar voice called. Caprion! He sounded unexpectedly distraught.

The winged Harpy plummeted from the sky and Sora stumbled backward, narrowly avoiding a collision. Caprion landed on the deck next to her, a frantic expression on his otherwise handsome face. His hair looked mussed, his clothes unkempt. She blinked up at him. His keen violet eyes were wide open. Fear?

As creatures of Wind and Light, all Harpies had pale hair and bright, luminescent eyes. Their voices were entrancing and hypnotic. Their wings looked solid, but were really manifestations of pure energy, starlight solidified into feather and flesh. Sora had learned recently that Harpies earned their wings through a complicated test called The Singing. A young Harpy would pitch his pristine voice far above the heavens. If his Song was strong enough, a star would sing back, and the light of that star would channel into his body, manifesting as wings. The larger a Harpy's wings, the greater the strength of his star, and the more magical power he controlled.

Caprion was not a normal Harpy, but something called a seraphim. He carried six wings on his back instead of just two, and had the rare ability to hide and display his wings at will. He told her it was for his own self-preservation—if he displayed all of his wings at once, the constant energy would wear out his body, shortening his life. He had joined their party on the Lost Isles, where he helped them escape the Harpy Matriarch in exchange for passage overseas.

"What?" Sora asked. "What's wrong?" She glanced around. Three days ago, Caprion and two Dracians flew off to investigate the surrounding forest. She thought that might have something to do with the growing stench, but Silas had claimed they were scouting the river for large debris and other obstacles.

"A town," Caprion said, out of breath. "We found an abandoned village in the woods. I need to speak to your mother."

Sora nodded, taken aback. "A village? Out here?" They were countless miles away from any roads or civilization.

Caprion headed down the side of the ship. His feet lifted easily from the wooden deck after a few steps, and he glided forward, half-flying.

Sora jogged to keep up. "Where are the other two Dracians?" she asked.

"No time to explain. Where is your mother?"

"In the sickroom, I suppose, probably tending a patient...."

"Tell Silas to drop anchor. We need to stop the ship immediately!" Caprion went below deck.

Sora stared after him. Then she ran back to the bow of the ship, where she last remembered seeing Captain Silas. But when she got there, the good captain had disappeared, replaced by a half-dozen sailors.

"Where is Silas?" she called, grabbing the arm of the nearest Dracian. The sailor gave her a startled look, then shrugged.

Sora gritted her teeth in frustration. For a mid-sized boat, it was certainly easy to lose track of people.

As she turned around, she glanced over the side of the ship at the riverbank. She saw a pile of rotted wood and mulch, but then something unexpected caught her attention. She paused, her gaze traveling back. She blinked. Then squinted. *Is that a body?* She stared harder, moving along the railing as the ship continued upriver.

A thin, crumpled body lay among the reeds. It was female, covered in muck from the river. Water lapped around the woman's legs.

"There's a woman!" she yelled, pointing over the side of the railing. "Hey! There's a woman on the riverbank!"

The Dracians were too busy straightening out the boat, furling and unfurling various sails, and swinging the jib back into place, to pay Sora any heed. She looked up at the crow's nest where Burn sat high above the ship, his head looking in the opposite direction. She needed to get his attention.

*Nothing else for it.* Sora cupped her hands to her mouth and screamed, "Woman overboard!"

Two or three heads turned to look at her. She saw Burn's ears twitch and he looked down, leaning over the edge of the crow's nest. She signaled to him, then pointed over the side of the boat.

Burn put his fingers to his lips and whistled loudly. "Aye!" the Wolfy picked up her cry, roaring in his deep, brassy baritone, "Woman overboard!"

The sailors looked around in confusion. Sora waved her arms animatedly. "We need to drop anchor! Where is Silas?" she called.

Then, seemingly from nowhere, Crash appeared on deck. He strode to her side, swift as a shadow. "What is it?" he asked. He gave her a quick once-over, then his voice turned wry. "You don't even look wet."

Sora glared. "Not me, of course! There's a woman over on the banks. She looks injured." She pointed to the thick patch of weeds and half-rotted logs. "See her?"

Crash followed her pointing finger and stared for a moment.

"Caprion returned," Sora continued impatiently. "He said there's a village in trouble nearby and we need to stop the ship."

"Not our problem."

Sora growled, "What if she's still alive? She'll die of exposure before long! By the four winds, *where is Silas?*"

Crash let out a short breath, then stepped onto the railing without a word. He cast her a glance as if to say, *This had better be worth it*, then leapt from the boat into the water.

Sora gasped as he fell smoothly through the air and entered the river with hardly a splash. Within seconds he broke the surface of the water and swam powerfully toward shore. The boat continued forward and she momentarily panicked. "Man overboard!" she screamed. "Drop anchor! Stop!" She waved her arms wildly at the Dracians on deck.

Captain Silas finally strode onto the bow. He was a short man, as all Dracians were—only an inch or so taller than herself. He was dressed tastefully in a starched white shirt and long blue greatcoat with tall black boots. A leather thong tied back his silky red hair, the color of shined copper. Dracians were usually lighthearted and mischievous, but today he wore an irritated scowl.

"What is this about?" he demanded as he stalked toward her.

Sora raised her chin a notch. "Caprion said there is an abandoned village in the forest and we need to drop anchor. Also, two of your men didn't return with him. And...!" She pointed to Crash's figure in the water. "There's a woman on the banks. Crash jumped the railing to help her."

The assassin reached the shallows and began trudging through the thick mud and cattails, his black hair slick with water. Silas saw him, paused, then looked skyward with great exasperation.

"What a waste of a day," he muttered. "I should toss you all overboard!" Then he turned back to his crew, who were waiting expectantly up on the rigging. "You heard her, lads! Drop anchor!"

The crew scurried to obey.

He cast her an angry look. "Let's hope the anchor catches on something. Otherwise your assassin will have to find his own way to the City of Crowns. And if any of my men are missing, I'll cut off that damned Harpy's wings!" He turned and stalked off.

Burn whistled twice more from the crow's nest as the rear anchor dropped into the water. Sora could feel its sudden weight drag at the back of the boat. They continued to surge forward a short ways; then the anchor caught against the bottom of the river and the boat came to a sudden halt.

"Lock her in!" Silas roared from the wheel. "Secure the front anchor! Raise the sails! Get off your arses and work!"

Sora waited impatiently as the sailors prepared a small skiff to travel ashore. Eventually, her mother and Caprion appeared on deck, deep in conversation. When Lori saw her, she asked immediately, "What's this about a woman?"

Sora pointed over the side of the boat to the nearby bank, where Crash knelt among the tall reeds next to the woman's form. It was hard to tell if she was injured or dead.

"Can you take us down there?" Sora asked, turning to Caprion.

The Harpy nodded, then made a few swift gestures with one hand, a wordless sign language that Sora had seen him use before, though she didn't know its significance. A white light began to engulf her, starting at her feet and slowly working its way up her legs. She felt a vibration pass over her skin, like music with no sound. A similar light crept over Lori's body. Next, with a wave of his hand, Caprion lifted Lori and Sora swiftly into the air and transported them over the side of the boat. As gently as a leaf on the wind, they crossed the Little Rain tributary.

Their brief flight over the river felt terribly unnatural to Sora. She retained her sense of gravity, as though she stood on solid ground, even as the water flowed underneath her. Her Cat's Eye remained silent—a disturbing sensation, since it usually responded to any sort of magic, warning her with the sound of bells in her ear. She subconsciously touched her left hand to the stone, gripping the necklace in her bandaged palm. *Where are you?* she thought worriedly. She felt a slight stirring in the back of her mind, but that was all.

Finally, they reached the tall cattails where the woman's body lay. A few yards downstream, Ferran leapt over the narrow bow of his boat. He sloshed through the shallows toward them. He was a tall man of athletic build, a few years older than her mother, with brown hair and quick gray eyes. Lori waved to him as he neared.

Sora went directly to Crash on shore. He took a step back as she approached.

"The plague," he said quietly.

Lori overheard him, and pushed them both out of the way to make room for herself.

"The plague?" she echoed, not truly a question. She pulled a handkerchief from her pocket and tied it around her mouth, then knelt next to the woman, turning her over on her back.

The woman appeared pale and motionless, as good as a corpse, though when Sora looked closer, she noted the fragile rise and fall of her chest. Lori motioned for Ferran to grab the woman's shoulders and they dragged her out of the water, onto the bank. She checked the woman's pulse and breathing, her eyes swiftly taking stock of her symptoms.

"It's the plague," she confirmed. "Her pulse is weak. Another hour and she'll be dead."

"What is she doing out here all alone?" Sora asked. "Was she looking for help?" No one answered, of course, because no one knew.

Her mother checked for other injuries, touching the woman as little as possible. Lori finally sat back on her heels. "I can't treat her here," she said. "We'll have to move her back to the ship."

"Isn't this plague contagious?" Caprion asked logically. "Not to sound inhumane, but is that such a good idea? You would put Silas' crew at risk."

The four looked at him. The Harpy stared back expectantly.

Then Crash said dryly, "On that note, where are the missing members of Silas' crew? I suppose something *inhumane* happened to them?"

Caprion shot him an angry glare. "We passed over a village in the forest. It appeared abandoned, but the Dracians wanted to investigate."

"And they...disappeared?" Crash asked.

"We became separated," Caprion replied. He became troubled and looked at Sora. "When I found them, they were not themselves. They became violent. Something affected their minds. I had to leave them behind. Is this a symptom of the disease?"

Everyone in the circle seemed alarmed.

"I don't know," Sora admitted. She felt very cold. "Someone has to tell Silas."

No one seemed eager to do that.

"This woman must be from the village," Lorianne suggested. Her eyes returned to the prone figure on the ground. "If we can cure her, we can find out what happened. From what I've seen, deranged behavior can be a symptom of the plague, but only in its very late stages, just before death, when the sickness reaches the brain." Lori chewed her lip in thought. "If we remove the Dark God's magic from this woman's body, then we can safely move her to the ship. Sora?" She turned to her daughter. "We need your Cat's Eye."

Sora was deep in thought, pondering why the woman appeared abandoned on the riverbanks, all alone. It seemed strangely foreboding. She touched her necklace subconsciously. "I...uh, what?"

"Use your Cat's Eye to draw out the Dark God's magic," her mother repeated.

Sora looked back to the prone body, uncertain. "Right," she murmured. Her four companions watched her, waiting. She tried to prompt the necklace into action with a surge of thought, but nothing happened. A bit of sweat broke out on her brow.

Ferran joined their circle around the woman. He frowned as his eyes searched Sora's face. He, more than anyone else there, seemed to notice her hesitation. He wore a Cat's Eye as well, the only other bearer she knew. Most of the stones were destroyed after the War of the Races, tossed back into the ocean from whence they came, deemed too dangerous to continue using after the war. Knowledge of the stones had been forgotten over time, just as humans had forgotten about the races, their magic and lore.

Sora hadn't told anyone about her trouble activating the necklace. She was hoping the issue would fade away with time and that the necklace would return to its former self, but it seemed like the longer she waited, the worse the problem got.

"I'll try," she said quietly. She knelt down at the woman's side and placed a hand on her arm. At this point, she expected the necklace to release a fierce jingle of bells and glow with a bright green light. That light should flow from Sora's hand into the poisoned body and seek out the Dark God's taint, then draw the black energy into itself, absorbing and nullifying its power, thus releasing the victim from the plague.

She expected that—but nothing happened.

"Just a minute," she mumbled, aware of her mother's expectant gaze.

Suddenly, the injured woman shuddered. Her eyes opened, showing pure white orbs rolled back into her head. Then her pale hand whipped through the air and grabbed Sora's arm. Her face twisted into a terrible grimace, somewhere between a scowl and a smile—a frenzied leer. Then she launched herself off the ground.

Sora cried out and stumbled backward, taken by surprise. She twisted her arm and broke the woman's grip, then shoved her away.

The leering woman crawled after her, but Ferran stepped between them. He caught the woman by her neck, gripping her under the jaw, and lifted her clear off the ground.

Sora gasped, falling back onto the wet dirt of the riverbank.

A bright red Cat's Eye, embedded in a leather cuff on Ferran's wrist, glowed. The stone flared crimson, and the light spread over the woman's body, up her neck and over her face like a scarlet cowl. As it entered her mouth, her jaw stretched wide. A banshee's cry ripped from her throat. Tendrils of black smoke spewed from her lips as the dark curse was expelled from her body. The Cat's Eye drank in the toxic residue like water spinning down a funnel.

Then, unexpectedly, the woman began to cough and hack. Her body stiffened and convulsed. A black, tar-like substance spilled from her lips, gushing down the front of her muddy shirt. A hideous smell drifted from her body, like rotten meat, heavy and pungent in the air. Ferran didn't loosen his grip, but held the woman aloft as she vomited. Finally the spasms passed, and the woman went limp in his hands, her shirt stained dark with phlegm.

With rigid self-control, he set the body gently back on the ground. Then he turned to the river, a disgusted grimace on his face. He staggered the first few steps.

Sora knew what that felt like. Usually the Cat's Eye became energized and jubilant after absorbing magic, but the Dark God's power was different. It tasted like moldy sewage water.

Ferran barely reached the river before he vomited, emptying the contents of his stomach into the flowing current. Lori rushed to his side, a worried frown on her face.

Sora watched the two interact—the way her mother hovered near Ferran's side, her hand resting on his shoulder. How she rubbed his back. Sora noted the closeness between the two of them. It made her feel awkward.

Finally, Ferran sat down on the banks, his arms resting on his lanky legs, his head bowed. He took deep, long breaths. Lori rummaged through a pouch on her belt, perhaps for an herb to settle his stomach.

Sora rubbed her arms, disturbed by Ferran's violent reaction. She remembered curing a farmer from the plague almost a year ago, but the nausea hadn't been nearly that intense. Was the plague growing stronger? More difficult to dispel? Or did Ferran simply have a weak stomach? She doubted it—the man drank like a fish.

Realizing Crash was standing only a few inches from her side, Sora looked up and met his gaze. He watched her, and she felt that bond they had created on the Isles, when touching and talking had felt so natural.

"Your Cat's Eye should have responded to that," he said quietly.

She wanted to turn away, but his eyes wouldn't allow her. His gaze was bright green in the sunlight, too vibrant against his dark hair.

"My necklace has been acting strangely," she admitted. "Since the Isles, I can't control it as I once did."

"Why haven't you said anything?"

She glared at him, suddenly irritated. "Because you won't talk to me for more than a half-minute."

He stared at her.

Sora felt her bubble of anger grow. "I thought we agreed to be more open with each other!" She jabbed a finger into his firm chest. "I thought you said you would be there for me. That we were *a team!*" She jabbed him twice more, for emphasis.

Crash caught her wrist and glanced around. Caprion stood only a few meters away, staring at a pile of moldy leaves, very obviously eavesdropping.

"This isn't a good time to talk..." Crash said.

"Then when?" she demanded, trying to wrench her hand back. But he wouldn't let go. "*When* are we going to address this? You can't avoid me forever. Half the crew are talking about us!"

Crash's face darkened momentarily, a look that made her want to step back.

"Well, it can't go on," she pushed. "You need to do something. Avoiding the rumors makes you look like a coward." She nodded firmly, proud of herself for stating her thoughts so directly. Yes, a coward. It felt good to say that, like untying a hard knot. *A frightened, stupid coward.*

She could tell her words affected him, but only because she knew him so well. She saw the marginal hardening of his lips, the tightness around his eyes. *Good*.

She continued in a fierce whisper, "You told me not to doubt you. Well, now I doubt you more than ever."

Crash's grip tightened a notch on her wrist. He held her eyes with his, their faces so close she could feel the heat of his skin. His firm glare intimidated her, just as it always had, but she didn't back down. If anything, it only made her more determined.

"Hey," Lori called suddenly. "What's going on?"

Sora glanced up at her mother, who stood a few yards away with Ferran, both observing Crash with suspicion and concern. She knew what they must look like—the assassin's hand on her wrist, their faces close together, scowling at one another.

"Absolutely nothing," Sora said, and yanked her hand back.

Crash let go this time, though he seemed unsettled, first crossing his arms and then checking his scabbard, like he didn't know where to place his hands.

"Feeling better?" Sora asked Ferran. His face looked drawn and tired, but not terribly so. He nodded to her, though he didn't reply.

Then the sick woman stirred on the ground.

The travelers paused and glanced down at her prostrate form. When she coughed, her pale, cracked lips parted and a wheezing breath escaped.

"Help..." she murmured.

Sora moved quickly to her side, relieved for the distraction.

"We're here," she said softly, kneeling next to the woman's head. "We're here to help you."

"No," the woman croaked. Her eyes fluttered and she tried to lift her head, but the effort was too great. Sora wondered if the woman was fully conscious, or perhaps consumed by a fever-dream, a delirium. "My village...my children...help...."

Sora looked at her mother's pale face.

"What about your children?" the Healer demanded. "Where are they?"

"My village...help them...." The woman groaned and flung out her hand, attempting to point in a direction. Her eyes opened and rolled upward, searching the forest. She pointed to the thick, tangled woods. Her arm swayed and then landed in the dead leaves above her head, stretched to the North. "My children...

please...help...." The woman shuddered and her eyes closed again, her body returning to a limp, flaccid state.

Sora turned uncertainly to Lorianne.

"We need to go to this village and see what happened," her mother said.

"It's a long trek through the forest," Caprion pointed out. "We could fly there much faster."

"What of the plague?" Sora thought to ask. "Ferran and I have the Cat's Eye to protect us, but the rest of you...."

"I'll be fine," Crash said.

Caprion cast him a narrow look. "If the assassin goes, then I go as well," he said. The two glared at each other.

Ferran shifted on his feet, shoving his hands into his pockets. He chewed on a long yellow reed from the river, spinning it between his straight teeth. "Troublesome," he murmured, and raised an eyebrow at Lori. "Sora raises a good point. You don't have protection against the plague. It could be dangerous for you...."

"It's a risk I'm willing to take," Lori said. "If the plague has spread this far, and grown this strong, then the entire Kingdom could be at terrible risk. Much has changed since we traveled to and from the Lost Isles."

"A small village in the woods is hardly indicative of the entire Kingdom," Crash said.

Lori shot him a fiery look. "What did you say, Viper?" she asked. "If you have an opinion, speak up."

Crash remained solemn. "There's nothing we can do. Her children are already dead. If not, they'll die very soon."

"And what of the missing Dracians?" Lori demanded.

Crash shrugged. "I don't see the point of risking our entire crew over the fate of two men."

"Of course he would say that," Caprion said to no one in particular. "His kind value death over life. Cut down the weak and leave them to rot. Isn't that the way of the Hive?"

*The Hive.* Sora remembered that term—the name of a colony where Crash spent his childhood. Or perhaps it wasn't just a simple colony. Perhaps the term meant something more.

Crash stared at the Harpy dangerously. Tension settled over their group, and for a moment his hand twitched toward his dagger. But the assassin contained himself.

"No," he said levelly. "Quite the opposite—I won't put *Lori's* life at risk."

Sora saw a look of surprise pass over Caprion's face.

Crash turned to Lori. "You're a Healer and a valued asset to our team. I won't allow you to risk your life."

Lori gazed at him for a long time. Then, finally, she nodded.

"But we can't leave the Dracians behind," Sora said. She looked at Caprion. "There's a chance they're still alive?"

Caprion looked uncomfortable. "I honestly don't know if they're still alive, and I'm not immune to the plague. I took a risk returning to the ship. I feel fine, but perhaps the sickness is slower to work on me. I could be infected."

"He's not," Ferran interjected. "My Cat's Eye would sense it. But he brings up a good point. Perhaps he should stay behind."

A brief silence fell as the five companions regarded each other.

At that moment, the skiff from the Dawn Seeker arrived. Silas stood at the bow and jumped ashore before his crewman could secure the boat. "Well?" he barked. "Where are my missing men?"

Sora felt the situation coming to a head. She could see the temper flare on Silas' face.

"They were infected by the plague," she started.

"I had to leave them behind," Caprion said at almost the same time.

Silas hesitated mid-step. He didn't seem sure where to unleash his fury—upon Caprion, Sora, or the whole lot. He looked like he wanted to strike someone in the jaw.

Then he pointed at Ferran. "Go get them," he growled.

Ferran raised an eyebrow. "Your men are probably dead," he repeated. "The risk involved—"

"You have a Cat's Eye, don't you?" Silas snapped. "You can take the risk. I don't abandon my crew. Fix this, or find your own way to the City of Crowns."

The treasure hunter chewed his reed stubbornly and said nothing.

Lori finally indicated the woman on the ground. "She needs my care," she said. "And she might have information about what happened in the village. Permission to bring her on board, captain?"

Silas studied the prone figure. "Does she have the plague?" he asked.

"Cured it," said Ferran.

Silas beckoned impatiently. "Then bring her aboard. The rest of you," he scowled, "find my men and bring them back. You have until nightfall. You hear me? No wandering about! If you don't return by tonight, consider yourselves stranded." Then he whirled back to his boat and flounced away.

"A fat lot of help he is," Sora muttered.

"Hypocrite," Ferran agreed.

Crash looked skyward, and Sora followed his gaze. It was close to noon. The sun set early this time of year and they only had a few hours at best.

"How soon can we get to this village?" he asked no one in particular.

Caprion answered, "It's about two miles away. I can't transport all of you. I'll have to make several trips."

"I think we can make our way on foot," Ferran said.

Sora gave him a questioning look. "Is it truly necessary to walk? It would be much faster to fly."

"Better to search the forest," Ferran explained. "See what we can find on the ground."

Crash nodded agreement. "Caprion can fly, since he's susceptible to the plague." The assassin stared at the Harpy as though intentionally pointing out his weakness.

Caprion looked uncomfortable. Sora didn't think he was used to being at a disadvantage.

Then Ferran chimed in, "I'm curious to see what we might uncover in the woods. The state of the forest could tell us a lot more about the plague than an abandoned village. And let's not forget the stench." He wrinkled his nose to emphasize his words.

Caprion shrugged. "As you wish." It seemed they had reached an agreement. Ferran helped Lori carry the sick woman to Silas' skiff. The Healer looked reluctant to go, and cast Sora a concerned look, mouthing the words *"Be careful."*

Sora felt a sudden stab of uncertainty as she watched her mother sail back to the ship. Lori was just as much a warrior as the rest of them. She obviously wanted to join the hunt, but she didn't have a Cat's Eye to protect her. Sora considered returning with her to the boat, but she couldn't stand the thought of waiting for

Crash and Ferran on the ship, surrounded by clowning Dracians and the irascible Captain Silas.

For a moment, she and Crash were alone. The assassin paused by her side.

"Will your Cat's Eye protect you?" he asked.

Sora's mouth felt dry. "It should," she finally said, though she wasn't all that certain. The bond with her necklace wasn't broken, just clogged, somehow dormant. But she knew the Cat's Eye would protect her in a real emergency, if anything, for its own self-preservation. That was simply the nature of the stone.

Crash nodded, then turned away. Without another word, he started into the forest, following the woman's trail through the underbrush toward the village.

Sora started after him, fingering her necklace in thought, her brow furrowed. She felt a strange chill on the back of her neck. Who knew what they would encounter in the village?

But it was too late to argue. Caprion summoned his white magic and lifted smoothly into the air, soaring above the trees. She, Ferran and Crash continued through the woods toward the plague-ridden village.

# CHAPTER 3

They followed the woman's trail through the woods. It was easy to pick out. Even Sora could see the half-footprints in the damp soil, torn leaves, broken branches and strands of snagged clothing. She knew how to walk softly in the wilderness, but Crash's steps were completely silent, as though she followed a ghost and not a man.

Ferran brought up the rear. The tall, lanky treasure hunter chewed idly on his reed from the riverbank, making little attempt at stealth.

As they walked through the forest, the smell of decomposing vegetation grew stronger, and Sora began to see evidence of its source. Small berry bushes close to the ground were bare of leaves, their fruit rotting from emaciated branches. Blighted tree trunks sprinkled the forest, covered in black splotches, a sign of slow decay. The deeper into the forest they traveled, the worse the trees became.

They entered a grove of toppled oaks with deteriorated roots twisting into the sky. None of her companions spoke, but continued through the devastated grove, climbing over the ancient trees. At this point, the ground was soft and spongy and the stench was almost intolerable. The forest was being choked of life, dying from the ground up.

Finally they reached the village. Crash motioned for them to crouch behind a row of thick bushes. They peered between the shrubs. Sora waited for a sign of life—the shout of voices, the laughter of children, a barking dog, anything—but only silence greeted them. Even the birds were quiet.

To her eyes, the village looked like it had once belonged to nomads and gypsies. Unpaved roads cut through a cluster of shacks and shanties with little rhyme or reason. She had heard of wandering river-folk inhabiting the Crown's Rush; wayfarers who lived on giant rafts of misshapen boards, who steered with slender oars and lived in lean-to cabins with canvas roofs. She had never met such people, but looking at the haphazard arrangement of wooden buildings, their roofs little more than thick oilcloth, she could only imagine a large group had settled here in an attempt at civilization. That would explain the village's isolated location—hidden deep in the forest, yet close enough to a river to travel easily. The people had probably traded downstream at other established towns. This way, they avoided the king's taxes.

The woman on the riverbanks must have been desperate for help. Anyone who found this little town could report it to the King's guard and initiate a raid. Most of the river-folk would be imprisoned or perhaps even executed, depending on the extent of their crimes.

A rustle of branches and flurry of leaves announced Caprion's landing. He appeared through the foliage. Sora saw his nostrils flare as he inhaled the rank stench of the woods.

"Where did you last see the Dracians?" Sora asked him. The village looked completely abandoned.

"On the opposite side of town," Caprion said, indicating the deserted streets. "I didn't spot them on my last pass-over. They might have left the area." He rubbed his hands over his arms. He seemed uncomfortable on the ground, shifting from foot to foot.

*It must be the forest,* Sora thought. Perhaps the power of the plague was already affecting him.

"The Dracians are most likely dead," Crash offered.

Sora wrinkled her nose at him. To her knowledge, the plague didn't work that fast—unless it had grown stronger than before. She thought of the rabid aggression of the woman by the river. If the Dracians weren't dead, they might be in a similar state. *Dangerous,* she thought.

"Shall we look for them?" she suggested.

"Seems safe enough to walk around," Ferran muttered around his reed.

"For you, perhaps," Caprion replied. "I'm not immune to the plague. This place is tainted by the Dark God's essence. I can't stay on the ground."

"Then you can keep watch from above," Sora said. "If you see anything suspicious, just call down to us."

Caprion disagreed. "I think I'll sweep over the forest once more, see if the Dracians haven't traveled into the woods. They might be walking back to the river on foot."

"I thought you said they were deranged?" Crash asked darkly.

"Exactly," Caprion agreed. "They're a danger to the ship. I'll scan the area and make sure they haven't wandered off." Then he launched back into the air, flying up through the trees. He seemed relieved to be leaving the ground. Sora watched him go.

"Useless," Crash muttered under his breath. Then he turned to a large pine tree overgrown with ivy. He started climbing easily up the trunk. Chunks of dry rot came away under his hands but hardly slowed his pace. He reached the first branch a good dozen feet above the ground, then continued to a higher perch.

Sora shared a questioning glance with Ferran. Finally, Crash stood perhaps three dozen feet above the ground. At this height, he had a good vigil of the entire town.

Finally, he called down, "There is a large building on the opposite end with something blocking the door—perhaps a collapsed villager. That would be a place to start looking."

Ferran yelled back, "Are you coming with us?"

"You have two Cat's-Eye stones," he replied. "I'll keep watch for now."

Sora felt somewhat relieved. She had been on the verge of asking Caprion to stay, but Crash was an even better lookout. Caprion was still adjusting to the mainland, and this was his first encounter with the plague. She trusted Crash's experience much more.

"Let's go," she said determinedly, and drew her staff from the sling across her back. The witchwood felt heavy and reliable in her hands.

Sora and Ferran strode side-by-side into the town. She felt tense and anxious, but Ferran walked in a casual way, as though taking a nice afternoon stroll. No matter where he went, he gave off an air of confidence, never rushed or hurried. Sora slowly relaxed as they walked further into the village. They didn't speak; the hollow town didn't seem to permit it.

She vigilantly searched the houses, pausing to gaze through a few smudged windows, looking for any sign of inhabitants. Several clotheslines swayed gently in the breeze, strung up between buildings. Most doors were closed, but a few had been blown open by the wind; piles of leaves were accumulating inside the darkened rooms.

Sora and Ferran walked through the ghost town without incident. As they neared the far side of the village, Sora could see the building Crash had indicated. It was by far the most complex structure, a full-sized townhouse that must have served many purposes: meeting hall, schoolhouse, hospice. The brick walls looked sturdy and fairly new. Mismatched tin sheets covered the roof. A wooden emblem of the Wind Goddess hung above the large oak double doors, and several wind chimes adorned the roof's overhang, clanging hollowly in the breeze. The emblem and bells looked much newer than the rest of the building. Sora wondered if the townsfolk had gathered here after the plague broke out, and had prayed to the Goddess for mercy and healing.

She wasn't as superstitious as most country folk. She knew a body must be healed through medicine; prayer was a spiritual reprieve, but miracles were not always granted. At least not the kind the townsfolk needed.

As they approached, she saw the figure of a man collapsed outside the front door. From a distance, he appeared more like a sack of flour or grain, so covered in dirt that his entire face was brown. *Caprion must have missed him from above*, she thought. As they neared, she could make out a wild bush of red hair and a fierce, tangled beard. Sora wavered in shock as she recognized the first of the two missing Dracians. His body was slumped to one side, half-fallen on the ground as though he were asleep. His skin had the pale-white hue of a fresh corpse.

Her stomach churned as she neared him. She had seen corpses before, far too many, especially during her battle with Volcrian. She didn't need to check the Dracian's body to know he was dead. As she paused next to him, a great pit of sadness opened within her. She recognized him from the ship, though she didn't know him by name. One of Tristan's friends. *He died within hours of contracting the plague,* she thought. How was that possible? When she first came across the disease, it took a week or more before a man's life ended.

And where was the second Dracian?

She and Ferran turned to look at the front door of the building, which swung slightly on its hinges. The wind chimes clinked above them, a lonely, muffled sound. Sora's skin prickled. She had the sudden desire to leave the village as quickly as possible and never return. Somewhere deep in her mind, she felt her Cat's Eye stir, but it quickly returned to silence.

She didn't want to open those doors.

But, Ferran did.

With a sigh that said *Well, nothing else for it,* he reached up, took the heavy brass handle and dragged the door open. It screeched terribly.

Sora was struck by a sickening smell, far worse than the decaying forest. This stench of rotting bodies—damp, sullen and bitter—immediately brought bile to her throat. A burst of flies escaped through the door, swarming up around the rooftops. Several flies immediately dropped to the ground, as though struck dead by the light of the sun.

Ferran met her gaze. "You don't have to go in."

Sora considered for a moment. She really didn't want to see any more corpses. Yet a morbid curiosity grew within her, a question she couldn't deny. *What happened here?*

She shook her head and wordlessly followed him.

They entered the building gingerly and stood just inside the front doorway. Bleak midday light filtered through a series of tall, slanted windows. Once inside the dusty room, she could see long rows of benches pushed near the walls. The floor was filled with cots and cushions, blankets and pillows. Wind chimes hung from the rafters and burned incense stained the floor.

Everywhere, there were corpses. Men, women, and children; infants, adolescents, elderly. Pets—over a dozen cats and dogs, a few goats and pigs. All killed by the plague.

Sora took a step back. Families of the sick must have gathered here, trying to care for their loved ones, unknowingly exposing themselves to the Dark God's taint. Before long, the entire town must have been affected. The woman lying near death on the banks of the Little Rain had probably gone for help; who knew how long she had waited? Sora looked around. Some bodies were stiff with rigor mortis, their cold hands desperately clutching: husbands embracing wives and wives gripping children. They probably died just a few days ago. Their flesh appeared mostly intact, except for the blackened nails and flaky, patchy skin: telltale signs of the Dark God's taint.

"We're too late," she said softly, gagging on her own words. She put her arm up to her mouth.

Ferran strolled further into the room and prodded one of the bodies with his boot. "Your mother isn't going to like this," he murmured. His face twisted against the stench. He glanced around one last time before turning back to the door. "We've seen enough. Time to go."

As though summoned by his voice, something stirred at the back of the room. She heard a few soft thumps, then the low scrape of a bench moving.

Ice slid down Sora's spine. *Impossible*—by no means could anything be alive here. She clutched her staff firmly in hand, her ears straining as she caught the sound of rustling fabric. The wind?

"What's that?" she asked. Her heart began to pound.

Ferran turned toward the noise. He paused, eyes narrowed.

"Get out," he said abruptly.

Sora frowned and hesitantly took a step back. "What is it?"

"Sora, get out now!" he commanded, raising his left hand in front of him. The Cat's Eye gleamed at his wrist and a shield of red light fell in front of them. At that moment, several shapes prowled forward from the shadows.

It took a long moment for Sora to recognize the creatures as wild dogs. Pus oozed from their eyes and ears; their fur was wet and matted from some unknown fluid. Her Cat's Eye jingled maddeningly and she knew the dogs were completely contaminated by the plague.

With several guttural roars, the pack of diseased hounds lunged toward Ferran with rabid energy. He could never take on so many animals at one time. She couldn't leave him.

"Ferran!" she shouted, then swung her staff at a nearby hound. The blow should have snapped the creature's back, but the beast took the hit without flinching, then turned on her and snarled.

"Use your Cat's Eye!" Ferran yelled.

Several frenzied dogs converged on him. Ferran passed his left hand through the air as though gathering a handful of invisible ropes. Then he made a powerful pulling gesture. The first three hounds stumbled forward, their jaws stretched open, piercing shrieks coming from their throats. Strands of darkness shot from their gaping mouths as though they had been yanked out by Ferran's fist. His Cat's Eye absorbed the dark magic, sucking the cords into itself with an ear-splitting *snap!*

Sora stared in mingled shock and awe. She had used her Cat's Eye many times—but never with such masterful control.

Following his example, she turned to three more encroaching hounds. She held them at bay with her staff while she reached into her mind, begging her necklace to respond, desperate for its reply. Finally, she heard a dull jingling in her ears and the necklace glowed at her neck. Green light surrounded her body like a shield. She tried to reach for the hounds as she had seen Ferran do, but it seemed impossible—she didn't have his power of command over her stone.

*My staff,* she thought. Witchwood held magical properties, and she had used it once before to channel the Cat's Eye. Sora focused. When her staff glowed green in her hands, she swung it at the hounds and struck the nearest one across the muzzle, then beat down the next two dogs, one in the ribs and the other in the chest. At each impact of her weapon, dark smoke poured from the mouth of the beast. Her staff smashed through their skin like breaking open a beehive, releasing gusts of black smoke. The necklace absorbed the dark energy.

As soon as the magic entered her necklace, nausea spiraled through her. She stumbled to one side, sick and dizzy, close to losing her balance. She couldn't keep up. The Dark God's taint was like poison. She already felt the need to vomit.

Then she heard an unexpected moan from behind her, and whirled to face the door of the building. To her shock, she saw several corpse-like villagers rising from the last row of benches. They looked wasted and skeletal, and a ravenous gleam lit their eyes.

One moved to block the doorway. She recognized a shock of red hair—his skin was as pale and corpse-like as the woman by the river. He snarled at her with ferocious intensity, spittle flying from his lips.

Sora raised her staff and rammed it into the Dracian's face, toppling him behind a bench.

Her Cat's Eye murmured weakly at her neck. It flickered, and then the glow slowly faded from her staff. She backed away from the villagers toward the center of the room, clutching her weapon before her. Her necklace couldn't handle another dose of the plague. She needed time to recover.

Then a new figure blocked the doorway. Crash entered the room, sword in one hand and dagger in the other. A grim and terrifying expression marked his face. As soon as he set foot in the building, the shadows seemed to grow along the walls until the whole room darkened.

Sora watched, stunned. She had never seen him like this.

The assassin turned to the plague-ridden villagers. At the sight of him, the corpses recoiled and hissed, cringing, raising their hands meekly like slaves beneath a whip.

Crash struck down a man to his left with his sword, slicing off his arm with a mighty heave. The shadows twisted around Crash's body like living snakes, then shot toward another corpse and dragged the man to the floor. The corpse wailed in frustration, then the shadows plunged into his mouth, cutting off his voice.

Sora watched, horrified and entranced. Her Cat's Eye let out a fierce rattle of alarm. She had never witnessed this kind of magic. Crash manipulated the darkness. A lethal aura emanated from his presence, striking her cold with fear. She wondered, then, if she was witnessing the demon's power.

She turned around just as another ragged hound flew at her, growling. She smacked the dog over the head. Dark mist smoked from its ears, but no blood. Sora staggered again, almost falling to her knees as the plague entered her necklace. *No more,* she thought, as though the Cat's Eye had spoken aloud.

Ferran seemed to have reached his limit as well. He came to her side while Crash took on the remaining villagers. "Come," he panted. "Let's go."

As they began to run, she heard a much deeper rumble. Then she saw a black cloud accumulate toward the back of the room. It slowly formed into a shape. Strands of smoke curled into arms and legs resembling a giant spider. She clutched her necklace in one hand as fear gripped her heart. The smoky beast attached itself to a corpse. Sora watched in horror as it drained the corpse to a dry husk, becoming more solid and real as it did, then released the body back to the ground.

The creature turned to look at her, and she found herself staring into ten gleaming red eyes. As it took a crawling step toward her, Sora screamed.

The beast released a high-pitched, keening wail. Darkness spilled from its body like tar, then gushed across the floorboards toward them. Her Cat's Eye jingled loudly in warning. Sora stared, paralyzed.

Ferran saw the monster, grabbed her arm and dragged her toward the exit. "Run!" he yelled.

Sora felt a scream welling in her throat. No way out. *No way out!* She didn't know which way to turn.

The shadow-creature wailed again and rushed toward them, its many legs reaching out in every direction.

Then, unexpectedly, the sound of bells crashed over her ears, as strong as an ocean's wave. She stumbled to her knees, crying out. A fierce and smoldering rage spread through her body, setting her blood on fire. Then she felt a horrible, building pressure....

*Flash!*

Blinding light—and a rising howl, somewhere between a wolf and a mountain lion—filled the room. Blue energy poured from her necklace in a cascading river. A shape formed in front of the wave: a mane of bristling quills, four massive paws and spiraling horns as thick as branches. She knew this ferocious beast—knew it, but couldn't believe it.

The *garrolithe* burst from the Cat's Eye like a rampaging lion, filling the room with blinding light. The corpses and hounds screeched as it tore through them, ripping apart bodies, scorching the wood beneath its paws. Trails of blue fire followed in its wake.

The plague-monster's black, tar-like body scattered before it, splitting into a thousand crawling slugs that wriggled and wormed across the floor. Some lifted the roof tiles to escape, others bled through cracks in the windows or forced their way under the door.

The light from the *garrolithe* grew until Sora clamped her eyes shut. She heard the windows shatter. She didn't feel the arms that lifted up her body, or hear the footsteps as she was carried outside; she didn't feel the wind against her face or the sunlight on her skin. She heaved dryly, choking on her own breath.

Then darkness crept in, stealing her strength and senses.

# CHAPTER 4

C rash followed Ferran through the decimated village, holding Sora tightly in his arms. They moved at a slow jog, Ferran limping from his mangled boot. The howls of the garrolithe continued for another minute, then abruptly stopped. Crash didn't know what that meant. He saw Sora's glowing Cat's Eye begin to fade, returning to its normal dull sheen. Her face looked pale, but she didn't appear to be wounded.

Worry knotted his brow. He tried to reason through their battle, to understand what had happened, but in all honesty, he could hardly focus. The demon writhed inside of him, excited by its use of magic, pounding against his ribcage, as fierce as his beating heart.

*They're here,* it whispered maniacally, dancing beneath his skin. *They're here!*

Crash sucked in a deep breath, reining in his thoughts and firmly shoving down the beast, which churned in his gut. Its presence seemed stronger now after he had come into contact with the Dark God's essence. He was barely in control.

*Enough,* he thought, focusing on moving forward, on Sora in his arms: his anchor.

They neared the edge of the village. The wind rushed through the trees in a shimmering green wave, carrying the scent of decay.

For a moment, he glimpsed a vague silhouette perched high above the ground.

Crash paused in mid-step and studied the ancient oak. The wind calmed. The branches stilled and the leaves became a knotted curtain, hiding the trunk from view, but he knew what he had seen. *Not Caprion,* he thought. The Harpy would have hailed them. *Not anyone familiar.*

He felt more curious than concerned. The tree and its mysterious passenger stood a dozen meters away—not an immediate threat.

The demon's words suddenly took on new meaning. *They're here.*

He had to investigate.

"What is it?" Ferran asked, tension in his voice.

"Take her," Crash replied, and gently placed Sora into his arms. "I'll meet you in a few minutes."

Ferran took the girl, lifting her easily. His gaze wandered to the trees, then to the silent village. "Where are you going?"

"I won't be long. Take her a safe distance away," Crash said. "I'll catch up to you."

Ferran finally relented. He continued through the woods, back toward the Little Rain, eager to leave the village behind.

Crash waited for Ferran to disappear through the underbrush before he approached the tree. Then he caught a glimpse of Caprion's gleaming form far in the distance, a hundred meters or so in the sky. The Harpy circled slowly on the wind, his wings flickering in and out of view. Crash clenched his teeth. *Coward,* he thought. Did the seraphim know about their battle in the courthouse? Did he know the fate of the Dracians, or the danger he had put them in? *No matter,* he thought. Caprion wouldn't have been much use. The Dark God's plague would have overcome him; those wings could only defend against so much. But why didn't he fly down to greet him now?

*He's trailing me,* Crash thought. *Suspicious bastard.* But perhaps it was a good thing. At least he had someone watching his back.

He neared the base of the large tree. No sense hiding his intentions. The person in the branches wanted to be noticed. As he walked, he felt that darkness stir again. The demon knocked against his ribcage. A thin, wheedling voice penetrated his thoughts.

*Will you listen now?* it grinned.

Crash pushed it away. *No.*

He reached the base of the tree and looked up through the branches. He didn't see the mysterious figure. Then a rustle in the underbrush caught his attention.

*They're baiting me,* he thought. Someone wanted him alone in the woods.

Crash's hand roved to his dagger, feeling the firm steel blade through its sheath at his belt. He thought of Sora's pale face—of the garrolithe that exploded out of her Cat's Eye only a few minutes ago, robbing the girl of her senses. He was sorely tempted to return to her side. But he knew this visitor had come just for him.

Crash took off running into the woods. He caught a glimpse through the canopy of the Harpy following him from above. Crash ignored Caprion and focused on the chase. He heard the rustle of branches up ahead, the light rhythm of footsteps. His visitor knew how to run in the forest without crashing clumsily through the underbrush. *Trained in the Hive,* he thought. Despite a few scuffs in the dirt, the stranger's footsteps left no mark. The crushed leaves seemed intentional. Crash followed swiftly. *The Shade. They're here. They have to be.* And then he thought, *It's about time.*

Finally he reached a small clearing in the woods. The trail of crushed leaves and snapped twigs vanished before him. He stopped and turned in a slow circle, scanning the vegetation. The stale smell of rotting wood met his nose.

Then he saw it. A dark shadow in broad daylight where none could exist, like a stain on the fabric of the world. As he watched, a figure stepped from behind one of the trees. He was shorter than Crash, below-average height for one of the Sixth Race, and slight of build. His identity remained hidden by a hood and a black cowl tied around the lower half of his face, but Crash recognized the venomous green eyes of his own race, the reptilian coldness of the man's gaze. One eye drooped slightly from a long scar that trailed down his forehead, continuing across his cheek before vanishing beneath his half-mask.

Crash looked for weapons but saw none, only a pair of strange gauntlets covering the man's fists. The metal gloves were serrated along the sides, creating jagged blades along his wrist and forearm. Crash had never seen such a weapon before, but doubtless this man was one of the Named. He could tell by the unwavering certainty of the assassin's gaze.

"Viper," the man said. "*He who hides in the grass.*" His voice sounded thin and stifled, as though his nose were twice-broken. "Bit of a lone wolf, aren't you? I didn't expect you to come to me."

Viper raised an eyebrow. He glanced at the surrounding trees, searching for more of the Shade. Despite the aloof nature of his people, they usually didn't travel alone. Assassins were typically assigned to task forces, teams of three savants with a Named assassin at their lead, or on more deadly missions, several Named assassins acting in concert. He doubted the Shade would send only one man to confront him. *What are they playing at?*

"I take it you're responsible for the decimation of the village?" he asked directly.

"Were you impressed?"

*Disgusted, perhaps.* "It was messy work."

The man bowed ironically.

"How did you find me?" Crash asked.

"We've been following you for some time now."

He paused, remembering a separate incident in Delbar before his voyage to the Lost Isles. He should have known they would follow him.

"Our master has taken an interest in you. He wants to meet you, Viper. He wants to share his vision."

"Who is your master?" Crash asked, though he already knew the answer. In the seaside city of Delbar, he had killed two of his own race who sought the Dark God's weapons. In that musty, darkened bell tower, he had pressed a dagger to a woman's throat and demanded the name of her leader. *Who do you serve?*

She had spoken a name he never expected, a name he once revered—Cerastes, *he who kills in the sand.*

The stranger let out a wheezing laugh. "He knows about you, Viper. How you were executed. How you slunk away in the night and abandoned your colony. There are many who will come for you now. Many who will kill for your Name."

"Is that what you're here for?" Crash asked. "My Name?" He drew his dagger, allowing the sunlight to play off his sharpened blade. "If you want it, then take it."

The man shook his head. "I have a Name," he said. "I've come to offer you restitution, Viper. My master will welcome you by his side. Your transgressions will be erased. You will be reborn as one of the Dark God's servants, blessed by His shadow. You've been given an honored invitation. Become one of us, and revel in His rising glory. What say you?"

Crash felt his skin crawl.

"I follow no one," Crash said softly. "And certainly not the will of the Dark God."

The unknown assassin gave him a piercing look. "Not even to further your practice?" he said, his voice dropping a notch. "My master makes a generous offer. He will continue your training. Wouldn't you like to unlock the fifth gate?"

Crash's eyes narrowed. The fifth gate: entrance into the shadow realm, that place between places, where darkness reigned and demons slept. Only by unlocking the fifth gate could he learn the full extent of his race's magic—the use of shadow portals, among other things. It was not an easy skill to attain. When last he tried, he had been too young, overzealous, not yet prepared to harness his demon.

"I won't be swayed," Crash said.

The unknown assassin seemed to be laughing, though he made no sound. "You say that now, Viper," he murmured. "But what our master wants, he takes. He will weaken you. We know about the false life you've created. The people you think you care for. The ones closest to you. We shall pick them off...." The man's eyes glinted dangerously. "We will chip away at them until you have nothing left but your true calling."

Crash gripped the hilt of his blade.

"Take your time, Viper. Consider it," the man said. Then, fast as a whip, he turned and leapt through the black portal.

Crash lunged and tried to grab him before he could escape, but the portal shut with a whistling snap. He landed on the crushed leaves between the tree trunks. Staggered. Then stood.

The assassin and the portal were both gone.

Crash scanned the forest, prepared for an unseen attack, but after a long minute his tension eased. He glanced at the sky. Caprion had disappeared. How much had the Harpy witnessed?

He turned back toward the village and started running, hoping to catch up with Sora and Ferran. The assassin's threat lay heavy on his mind. *The people you think you care for.* Crash cursed himself over and over. How long had the Shade been trailing them? How much did they know about his journey? About his companions?

*Don't jump to conclusions,* he told himself. His kind were skilled at manipulation. Chances were, they knew nothing of his life. They were planting seeds of fear, hoping to set him off, testing to see what he would respond to. He recounted his actions since leaving the Lost Isles. He had stayed far away from Sora. He had spoken briefly and casually with Burn. He kept to himself whenever possible and reluctantly worked alongside the Dracian crew. For all the Shade knew, he was the same man who had left the Hive, lost, with no connections to the world.

And at that thought, he suddenly felt furious, like a wild horse put to the reins. *They will not control me with fear. After all this time, do they really think I will return to the fold?*

The demon smirked within him. *Soon*, it murmured, *they come.*

The forest stretched out below Caprion. He saw endless green pines jutting into the air, disrupted by stark gray bracken and the occasional patch of golden leaves. A sharp wind heralded a different kind of winter than he had experienced on the tropical islands of his homeland. He had never seen snow, though he could see it now on the distant mountains.

The Little Rain river resembled a long, silver scar across the green earth. He glided slowly toward it, unhurried. His companions wouldn't reach their ship for another hour or so, and he didn't see the point of returning before that. In the meantime, he wondered what had transpired in the village, and about the Viper's strange meeting in the woods.

His thoughts were disrupted by a humming, pulsing vibration at his hip.

Intrigued, he paused to hover briefly on the wind and reached for a pouch at his belt. After some rummaging, he withdrew a small ovular sunstone that trembled and glowed in his hand. At his touch, a quiet song began to play—a melody he hadn't heard in years. Still, he remembered the notes as clearly as the day he first sang them, when he sealed them into this stone.

It was *her* song. *Her* stone. Impossible that it would play now, because she was dead.

He banked his wings and turned in an easy loop, considering the small white stone in his hand. It was meant to play in her presence. He had written it as a lullaby of sorts, to keep her company in his absence. He had never spent enough time with her.

But it shouldn't play now. It couldn't. She had been gone for years.

*Its magic is weakening*, he decided. And as the magic left the stone, it released a whisper of years long past, nothing more.

He briefly considered throwing it away—allowing the stone and its whispered melody to vanish into the wide expanse of the forest. He hesitated, trying to make himself let go. Below him, a gust of wind rippled through the trees, like riffling the pages of a book. Watching the branches shimmer and sway, for a moment he remembered other trees on the Lost Isles, the scent of citrus on the wind, and warm evenings shared with a young, dark-haired girl.

He stole her life. He had broken every promise he ever made. Yet now, hearing her song, he could see her face again. He could almost meet her eyes....

Then the stone fell silent.

He fingered its smooth surface. He had kept it all these years out of pure sentiment, but it no longer served a purpose. He should have destroyed it long ago.

With a deep breath, he released the stone from his hand and allowed it to fall into the forest. His heart quickened, and he fought the urge to dive after it. He watched the small, shining rock plummet away—and then it was gone.

*It's better this way,* he thought.

He continued toward the Dawn Seeker, which drifted like an acorn on the long shining expanse of the Little Rain river.

Sora awoke to a sharp twig jabbing her in the back. She opened her eyes, blinking in the harsh sunlight. Her head pounded. Her chest felt heavy, difficult to breathe.

She climbed into a sitting position and her vision swam momentarily. She tried to blink her eyes clear, holding her hand to her head, then pulled it away, her palm sticky with blood. Head wound? No...it took her a minute to realize the blood seeped from the scar torn open on her left hand.

"Oh, good, you're awake," Ferran's voice reached her. She turned and found him standing a few yards away, leaning up against a tree, whittling away at a piece of wood in his hands. He sucked on a stem of grass between his teeth.

Ferran always seemed to have something in his mouth: a cinnamon stick, sweet-grass, hard-candy, ginger roots. She wondered if he once smoked tobacco leaves. It was a rich man's habit and he hardly looked like a rich man, with his hair mussed from their fight in the village, a few cuts and bruises along his arms, and his stained tunic torn down the front. He had once been the most renowned treasure hunter in the Kingdom of Err, or so her mother said. In Sora's opinion, he seemed little more than a drifter, someone with no roots and no destination.

Sora could understand her mother's attraction to him, though Lori never spoke of it. Ferran carried a daring sort of charm, a certain disregard for rules that made him, well, *exciting*. He seemed younger than his age and full of boundless energy. Lorianne acted as though the two were just old friends, and treated him as a nuisance at times—and yet Sora noticed how her mother laughed around him, and how wide she smiled. They were always together....

Her thoughts made her uncomfortable, and she looked away, avoiding Ferran's quick gray eyes. She picked a few leaves from her shirt.

"Where's Crash?" she asked. "What happened?"

"You don't remember?"

"Well, yes, I remember...." The image of the *garrolithe* remained vibrant in her mind. She had felt the beast crouching nearby in her sleep, looming over her body, but obviously, it was long gone by now.

Ferran dropped his whittling to the ground and kicked it away. Then he crossed to her side and settled himself among the moldy leaves.

"I take it your Cat's Eye hasn't been acting right for a while?" he asked, shifting the reed in his mouth.

"No, it hasn't. It's been very hard to control." She felt relieved to talk about it. Ferran wore a Cat's Eye himself, but his friendship with Lori made her unexpectedly awkward around him. She wasn't used to her mother spending time with a man.

"I'm used to always hearing it in the back of my thoughts, but lately it's been silent. Today is the first time it's reacted to...well...*anything*, since the Lost Isles."

"And the more you worry about it, the worse it becomes." Ferran squinted at the trees in thought.

"Yes, actually. I hadn't thought of it that way."

He flashed her an easy, reassuring smile. "It's not permanent. But in order to use the stone, you need to have strong mental discipline. If you're overly stressed and worried, that clogs up the bond. Makes it hard to focus. You were raised a noble, weren't you? I assume you were privately tutored and took written exams?"

Sora nodded, remembering her years of tutelage at the manor. Yes, she had learned arithmetic, history and literature. She had studied economics for a time, though eventually her father put a stop to it, saying such topics were for her husband-to-be.

"Well," Ferran continued, "no matter how well you prepare for an exam, if you're too nervous, you can't organize your thoughts and you won't remember anything. It's the same idea with a Cat's Eye." He tapped the red stone on his wrist cuff. In this light, it looked like nothing more than a large, ovular ruby. "If you have too much on your mind—too much worry and stress—you won't be able to control the stone. The more you doubt yourself, the harder it becomes. Your bond with the Cat's Eye should be a natural connection, taken for granted, like breathing."

"It used to be...."

"Then my guess is, when you first wore the necklace, you weren't afraid of its magic. You were *open* to the stone's power. But something happened to change that. I don't know what you endured on the Lost Isles, but I think it's weighing pretty heavily on your mind."

Sora considered his words. The previous leg of her journey had been fraught with peril. First, their ship sank near the Lost Isles. Then she fought the *garrolithe* in the Crystal Caves. Crash was imprisoned and tortured by Harpies, and finally, they battled Volcrian. She was forced to create a bond with two different Cat's-Eye stones in order to kill the mage. Luckily, she hadn't died in the process.

She glanced at her blood-caked, bandaged palm.

Beyond all of that—though it seemed pathetic—she had to consider the kiss. That unforgettable kiss on the bow of the Dawn Seeker when she and Crash had left the Isles. She hadn't been the same since.

"I fought the *garrolithe* in the Crystal Caves," she said quietly. "That's where all of this started."

"I was getting to that," Ferran replied. "Your Cat's-Eye stone has been imprinted by powerful, ancient magic. The *garrolithe* is no simple work of sorcery. It is a war-spell called a *mecha-animist*."

"A mecha-animist?"

Ferran nodded. "Before the War of the Races, skilled sorcerers would make magical little pets called *animists* and keep them as companions, or sell them to wealthy families. But when the war started, sorcerers from different races would come together and unite their magic, creating terrible beasts of power.

The mecha-animists were true monsters meant for battle. I've only seen one such creature before; they are very rare. And *very* dangerous."

"But how...?"

He didn't wait for her question: "The beasts were created by magical energy, and therefore immortal, unless destroyed. The *garrolithe*, as you call it, is now contained inside your stone. Imagine wearing a lion around your neck—it won't come when you call, and it won't respond to your begging or pleading. It's a wild creature—it wants to be free."

"Then what should I do?" Sora asked.

"You need to tame it."

Sora bit her lip, uncertain.

"It all comes down to your strength of will." Ferran gave her a pointed look. "To use the Cat's Eye, you need a greater level of mental discipline than you've had up to this point. More power requires more control."

Sora sighed and leaned back on her hands, wincing as a rock bit into her injured palm.

"Great," she muttered. "More complications."

"Don't look at it like that," Ferran said reproachfully. "You're very lucky, you know. We all are. Without the *garrolithe*, we'd most likely be dead."

She nodded—true, but she was too distraught to appreciate his words.

"So what now?" she asked. "How do I fix the stone?"

"There's nothing wrong with the stone." Ferran reached up and prodded her forehead. "You need to fix your *mind,* my girl."

"And how do I do that?" She gave him a disgruntled look.

"I'm going to teach you. It will take time and commitment, but seeing as we won't reach the City of Crowns for a little while, I think you can manage that."

Sora recalled how Ferran had wielded his Cat's Eye against the undead corpses. His control was effortless, like watching Crash with his swords, or her mother tend a wound. She knew she had a lot to learn from him, and the more she considered it, the more eager she became. She desperately wanted to reclaim her connection to her Cat's Eye. It wasn't just a tool or a weapon—she felt, somehow, as if she had lost a very dear friend.

"I need to be productive. I need to get better at this. All of it." She smiled at him, surprised that she felt like smiling at all. "When do we start?"

Ferran suddenly yawned; his reed started to fall out of his mouth, but he caught it in time.

"Well, I promised your mother I would fish with her tomorrow. We're heading into catfish territory, and I've heard that some grow seven feet in length and weigh over 200 pounds...." He stopped, perhaps realizing his digression. "The day after. Evening is the best time."

Sora nodded eagerly.

"Feeling better?" Ferran asked, sticking his toothpick back in his mouth.

"Much better," she sighed. "I'm ready to go back to the ship." She couldn't wait to get out of this forest, with its blighted trees and blackened berries.

Ferran stood up. "We're ready!" he called.

Crash appeared between the trees. Sora stared at him, tall and dark against the late afternoon light. Had he heard their entire conversation? *Of course*, she thought.

She expected him to ignore her as he had been doing, but his eyes skimmed over her before he motioned to Ferran to take the lead. The treasure hunter strolled into the forest at a leisurely pace, backtracking through the woods.

Meanwhile, Crash fell into step beside Sora. She glanced sideways at him, staring at the sharp line of his jaw, his tousled black hair. He seemed distracted, his thoughts as distant as his gaze. She was suddenly reminded of his short battle with the villagers, how the shadows had surrounded him in a dense cloak, how he had manipulated the darkness like it was an extension of his body. She hadn't thought he could wield magic. *But of course he can. He's one of the Sixth Race.* What kind of magic did the Sixth Race use? The question was on the tip of her tongue, begging to be asked. But that also scared her. He had a demon inside him—did she truly want to know more?

"Have you seen Caprion?" she asked instead. "He didn't follow us back from the village."

Crash shrugged, not meeting her eyes. "He flew off over the woods. Maybe he found something of interest."

Sora could tell he was lying. *He's hiding something,* she thought. Her brow darkened. "Maybe he's in trouble," she said. "It's not like him to vanish on his own."

"Then maybe he went back to the ship." He changed the subject. "Your hand is bleeding. You should have Lori look at it when we return."

If he meant to distract her, it worked. Weeks of silence, and now a sudden show of concern?

"I've had worse injuries," she glared.

"Wounds can fester."

"So can feelings."

Crash raised a dark eyebrow. "Are you festering?"

"That's not what I meant," she grumbled. In fact, Sora wasn't quite sure what she meant. For weeks, Crash had kept his distance. It seemed unfair for him to suddenly swoop in and care about her again. Or pretend to care. She just wanted him to explain himself.

"I miss you, I guess," she finally admitted. "I thought we had something different between us. I don't know." *Well done. I sound pathetic.*

Crash let out a thoughtful breath. Then he said, "This is my fault."

Sora waited for further explanation, but none came. She found herself growing annoyed again.

"Don't act like I didn't have a choice in the matter. I kissed back."

He hesitated. "I recall that."

"I didn't mind it at all."

"I see."

"In fact, I enjoyed it." *There.* "Not that you asked. Or cared to ask." She tried not to sound bitter, but it was impossible to hide.

Crash caught her wounded hand abruptly, holding it up between them. Sora almost tripped. They came to a halt. She could handle his rebuffs, his cold shoulder and even a mean word or two. But staring him in the face...*this* was hard.

"I know you enjoyed it, Sora," he said, holding her by the wrist. "But you understand that nothing can come of it."

"Yes, I do understand that," she said. *Another lie.* "But I don't understand why you have to avoid me."

"I'm not avoiding you."

"Yes, you are! The whole ship notices. And the rumors—"

"I'll handle the rumors," he cut her off. Then he added more gently, "I'm still here, Sora."

She met his gaze. He sounded stern, but a softness entered his eyes, a slight glimmer that she recognized. Some of the tension drained from her shoulders.

"I haven't left your side," he repeated.

Then he undid the bandage from her hand. He inspected her palm, pressing lightly on the reddened skin around the wound.

"Does this hurt?" he asked.

"I...uh...." she muttered, struck dumb by his simple touch.

He grinned, a wry quirk of his mouth. "No infection, then."

The wound looked like a popped blister. Her blood had burst through the fragile new tissue. Sora recalled the excruciating heat that had consumed her body when the *garrolithe* appeared. She chewed her lip in thought. *Will it be this way every time I use my Cat's Eye?* More questions for Ferran once they began training.

Crash reached into the pouch at his belt and withdrew a strip of clean linen, then began freshly wrapping her hand. She wondered if he had brought the linen just for her, anticipating that she might open the wound. She took a deep, steadying breath. Yes, this was what she missed—his closeness, knowing she could lean on him, and that he wanted her to.

When he finished wrapping her hand, he continued to hold it, looking down at it thoughtfully. He seemed to be wrestling with himself.

"Are you fond of him?" he finally asked.

His question took her off-guard. "Who?"

"Tristan."

"Really?" She couldn't suppress her slow, wide smile. "Not at all. In fact, I rather detest him at the moment."

"Good."

Sora blinked. *Is he jealous?* Could a man like Crash even feel jealousy, and over a clowning Dracian, at that? She felt supremely satisfied, but then a sense of foreboding crept over her. Crash's expression remained dark, his thoughts turned inward.

"Why do you ask?" she prompted.

He didn't reply immediately.

"What are you planning?" she asked again.

"Why does it matter?" he hedged. "I thought you weren't fond of him."

*He's teasing me,* she thought. *He has to be.*

"I'm *not* fond of him," she said, flustered. "I want the rumors to end, but...non-violently."

"And you assume I would resort to violence?"

"Well...."

"I'm wounded."

She rolled her eyes. "Oh, come now! Don't play innocent. I know how you are, Crash!"

"Do you?"

"Yes."

He suddenly raised her hand and blew softly against her palm. The brush of air sent chills all the way down her arm. Sora's mouth dropped open.

"Then don't worry about it," he finished. He released her hand and continued along the path through the forest.

Sora stared after him, at a complete loss. She watched his retreating back, trying to regain her voice.

"If you don't know what to say, at least keep walking!" Crash called before disappearing into the trees.

Sora's mouth snapped shut and she scowled.

"Arrogant bastard," she muttered, and followed him into the woods.

# CHAPTER 5

Caprion met them on the banks of the river. Sora noticed that he and Crash avoided speaking to one another, or even making eye contact, which seemed unusually cold, even for them.

The Harpy transported them back to the Dawn Seeker, where the crew had assembled. Captain Silas listened grimly to the news of his two missing crewmen, then stalked off, grumbling about a wasted day of travel. The rest of the crew eagerly flocked around Ferran, offering him a tankard of cold ale in return for the full story.

"I would tell you," Ferran replied, holding up his hands. "But I need to get back to my boat. Can't just leave her behind."

"Ach! I'll watch over her," a short Dracian offered eagerly. "Just tell us what happened!"

Ferran allowed himself to be convinced, perhaps a little too easily. Sora watched as, with an ironic grin, he followed the crew back to the mess hall as the Dracian left to watch his houseboat. She shook her head. By tomorrow morning, his story would be embellished beyond recognition. *Not that it needs much exaggeration,* she thought. Ferran played to the crowd and the Dracians enjoyed a tall tale.

Lori approached Sora's side once the Dracian crew had dispersed. After her eyes silently assessed Sora for injuries, she gave her a tight hug. Sora noticed that her mother looked tired.

"Our patient didn't make it," she explained. "There was no chance of saving her."

Sora gave her mother a reassuring squeeze. "You did everything you could."

Her mother smiled sadly, then returned below deck to clean up her workroom.

Sora sank back against the railing with a weary sigh, and enjoyed a moment of silence. She still hadn't fully recovered from her encounter with the *garrolithe*. Retiring early to bed sounded very appealing.

Then an unexpected light entered her vision. Caprion flew down from the crow's nest and landed nearby. She still wasn't used to him falling from the sky, and she jumped slightly, taken aback.

He turned to fix her with an intense, worried look. "I need to speak to you about something," he said in a hushed voice.

*What now?* she thought. "Can't it wait for tomorrow?" she asked, exhausted.

"It's about Crash."

Sora frowned. "What is it?"

"After you left the village, he went into the woods. I was circling overhead, keeping watch, and I followed him—"

"Sora!" a voice suddenly interrupted. She glanced across the deck and saw Tristan striding toward her. She stared at him, nonplussed. The Dracian was a handsome young man, a year older than herself, with pronounced dimples and a strong cleft chin, straight white teeth and a mop of sleek red hair.

He observed her annoyed expression and his grin faltered, if only for a second.

"Join us in the mess hall," he invited. "Ferran is telling quite a story!"

"I was there, remember?" she said dryly. "And he's not the only one telling stories aboard this ship. I've heard a lot of strange rumors going around."

Tristan gave her an odd look. "Oh, come now! What rumors are these?"

Sora crossed her arms and waited.

"You mean about the assassin?" he relented. He searched her eyes. "You deserve much better than him."

"Then you admit it!" she declared. "You've been talking about me to the other Dracians! And about my own personal, *private* business!" She silently berated herself for ever confiding in him.

"He's a demon, Sora," Tristan said, as though telling her the sky was blue. He reached out and caught her hand. She tried to wrench it away, but his grip tightened. "I was doing you a favor. Maybe if you saw how the rest of the ship reacted, you'd understand. The Sixth Race are toxic. They feed on death. They're not meant to have friendships or...or lovers." He let the word hang for a moment.

Sora felt her cheeks flush. She became acutely aware of Caprion standing behind her, listening to the whole exchange.

Then a charming smile came over Tristan's face. "Dracians, on the other hand, know how to treat a lady."

Sora's embarrassment shifted to rage. "By spreading nasty rumors? Yes, you're quite the charmer."

"Is that sarcasm?"

"No!" she snapped, pulling her hand away from him. She stalked off across the deck, heading for her cabin. She passed Caprion on the way and shot him another hot glare. "I've heard enough bad news about Crash for one day," she snarled. "Keep your nasty opinions to yourself!" She hoped neither of them followed her.

Sora went below deck, experiencing an immediate sense of relief, and entered her cabin, hoping to find some peace and quiet.

Crash stood at the stern of the Dawn Seeker, gazing over the river as league after league of water slowly vanished behind him. His eyes scanned the tall trees, the muddy banks. The Shade could be watching him at this very moment. *Why don't they attack?* he wondered. *What are they waiting for?*

He could take it as a good sign. Perhaps the Shade didn't have the manpower to attack Silas' ship and the Dracian crew. He thought of their small band of warriors: a Healer, protected by the grace of the Goddess; two Cats-Eye bearers, a Harpy seraphim, a Wolfy mercenary and himself. Perhaps the odds were in their favor.

Somehow, though, he doubted that. Not with Cerastes at the head of the Shade.

He thought of the unknown assassin he had encountered in the woods. He didn't dare take the man's bribe seriously. Still, the thought of continuing his practice—not just maintaining his skills, but actually improving them—was more attractive than he wanted to admit. Opening the fifth gate would give him the ability to open shadow portals, to effortlessly travel across hundreds of miles in the blink of an eye. It would bring him that much closer to the power of a Grandmaster, which had been his ultimate goal before he left the Hive.

Of course, such skills could not be attained without a price. Pursuing the darkness changed a man. With each gate he unlocked, he would lose another piece of himself. He had seen it happen to Cerastes over time. The extent of his Grandmaster's coldness had become unnerving toward the end. His ability to manipulate others without conscience, to end innocent lives, to gaze upon both good and evil with detached indifference, showed the strength of his demon. Crash had felt that same emptiness within himself.

A soft glow teased the corner of his eye. Crash turned, already knowing who stood behind him.

Caprion hovered several inches above the deck, his feet not quite touching the wooden boards. He carried himself with a certain gravity, his arms crossed before him, his face stern. The Harpy's pale hair moved slightly in the cold wind.

Crash crossed his arms as well. "What?"

"I saw you in the forest," Caprion said. "I saw you meet with another of your own."

"I don't know what you're talking about."

To most others, the Harpy's voice sounded soothing and melodious, but to Crash, it was like a fork scraping a plate. He clenched his jaw in irritation.

"You do," Caprion murmured, and hovered closer. *Punching distance,* Crash thought. "I want to know who you met with."

"You mistook what you saw."

"Perhaps," Caprion said in cold amusement, "but I'm sure the others on this ship would be curious to hear about it. Particularly Sora. She's having a hard time trusting you these days."

"Is that a threat?"

"No," Caprion said. "Just stating facts. You met with a member of the Shade. I'm certain of that. I've learned as much about you as I could from Burn and the others, and exiles of the Hive don't stay in touch with old friends."

"And what do you know of the Hive? Or the Shade, for that matter?"

Caprion raised an eyebrow. "I don't know much about the Shade," he mused, "but the Hive? Your kind are not a mystery to me. You intimidate your companions easily enough, but I have killed demons before, and I won't hesitate to do so again."

Crash looked the Harpy up and down and sneered. "If you're so eager to kill me, then why haven't you?"

"Because Sora, for whatever reason, is fond of you. But that fondness won't save your life if you become a threat. I have met innocents of your race—those worthy of redemption. But your darkness has matured past that point. I watch you struggle with your demon. I watch it waver in your shadow. I saw it slip out of you in the village. You are a danger to your companions."

A self-deprecating smile touched Crash's lips. "You don't know me at all."

"Then tell me, if you're so innocent—what does the Shade want with you? Who did you meet in the woods?"

Crash leaned back against the railing, no longer concerned. "I don't know. I didn't anticipate they would make contact. It's *quite* the mystery."

The Harpy stared at him long and hard.

"I'm not a member of the Shade," Crash emphasized.

"Hm. Surely they offered you something? Some sort of bribe?"

Crash's guard went up. He wasn't a fool—this man was not his friend, and he didn't know what to expect if he revealed the truth.

"I'm not who you think I am, Harpy," he snapped. "Your suspicions are off-base. Go find someone else to spy on."

Then he turned and walked away, heading to the cabins below deck.

Close to midnight, Crash sat in his cramped cabin fully awake, slowly polishing his Named dagger, deep in thought. The lethal blade ended in a trailing point, perfectly balanced, made for piercing and tearing flesh with optimum efficiency. A bronze snake, tarnished with age, adorned the handle.

Reflecting on his interaction with the Shade, he could only draw one conclusion: they wanted him to join their ranks. Which meant they must not have many trained assassins in their midst. Why else seek out a disgraced member of the Hive—someone so willfully insubordinate?

Or perhaps that was Cerastes' game. Perhaps the Shade only recruited those who were already separated from their colonies, who were desperate to find a place to belong. The Hive was not so much a single place, but a cluster of separate communities kept hidden from the larger world—even from each other. To leave the Hive was not just to leave one's home, but to abandon a densely interwoven web of rituals, codes and hidden hierarchies.

His kind seemed solitary on the surface, but no assassin of the Sixth Race was truly meant to live on his own. They needed the Hive to survive—to make sense of their lives. Five years had passed since Crash abandoned that world, and he still felt its loss, a certain lack of roots and boundaries, as though a great tree had been torn up from the ground.

Perhaps the Grandmaster still felt a bond with his old student. Why else would he risk exposing the Shade just to make contact? It seemed a bold move, even for a man who feared nothing and no one.

Crash pondered that. Was Cerastes' confidence misplaced? He still felt a deeply ingrained need to shelter the Hive, to keep the secrets of his people hidden, despite the Shade's plot. He hadn't told anyone of his encounter, and didn't intend to. But that didn't mean he was loyal to Cerastes' cause.

*They threatened you,* a soft voice murmured inside him. *They will hurt the ones you've adopted as your own.* He thought of Sora's questioning glance in the woods as they walked back to the Dawn Seeker, and felt another surge of anger toward the Shade. *I can protect her,* he thought. He didn't know exactly *how* to protect her, but introducing her to his past would only put her at further risk.

*I shouldn't have touched her,* he thought, remembering their interaction in the woods. He gripped his knife in frustration. He had acted foolishly, holding her hand in the open forest, so close to where the Shade had confronted him. But her nearness made him act impulsively, made him feel fierce and invincible, able to throw caution to the wind.

He tried to sweep her from his thoughts, but kept returning to the wide curve of her lower lip, her short, curvaceous body strengthened with well-toned muscles, her delicate wrists, her long fingers clasped inside his own. She still poised her hands like a lady, the natural inclination of a highborn woman. It didn't matter that her blood was common; she carried herself like a noble, whether she realized it or not.

He shook his head, trying to forget the touch of her skin against his. He knew nothing could ever come of this, not with the Shade watching. A touch, a look—where would it end? Back on the Lost Isles, he allowed himself to pull close the sweet heat of her body and trace her lips with his own. He remembered her clumsy, timid kiss—how she had bloomed under his guidance until her mouth grew soft and responsive.

*Innocent*, he thought, and grimaced ironically. *Too innocent for me to ruin.*

She was young. She would find another man, like Tristan, to fill that place in her life. She deserved a man with simple intentions and an open past, who wouldn't drag her into danger, who wasn't raised by a people ruled by death. The simple truth? She was safer with Tristan, and perhaps the Dracian had a greater capacity to love.

But, he had to admit, the thought of sharing her, of allowing another man to take that innocence, to draw those sighs from her lips—it summoned an anger equal to what he felt for the Shade.

And suddenly his Grandmaster's voice surfaced, weaving through his thoughts, proof that the Hive still lived in his mind—and always would.

*Illogical*, he heard clearly. *We are not like the other races—we are not creatures of the Wind. Love, like fear, is a choice. It weakens our control, clouds our thoughts, lowers our inhibitions. Never forget—all that we touch is destined to end.*

Crash remembered that lesson well. Over and over, he had witnessed it. Savants occasionally fell in love, forbidden trysts occurred, and harsh punishments were meted out to those who disobeyed the will of the Hive. A man in love was not himself. He was vulnerable, easily led and manipulated, and that was unacceptable for an assassin. The Shade knew it—and he knew it, too.

*Don't forget what you are*, he thought, and slid his finger intentionally over the blade of the knife, allowing it to pierce the pad of his thumb. He watched a vibrant drop of blood form between his split skin.

A dark presence swam up inside of him, responding to his mood.

*You sound like a simpering child*, the voice murmured.

*No one asked you*, Crash thought.

The demon laughed. *You can't hide from me, little snake. Take her, if that's what you want. Spend yourself. I know what you crave—why fight it?*

Crash grimaced. *Silence, fiend.*

The demon showed its fangs. *So noble*, it mocked. *So sincere.*

Crash turned away, ignoring it.

The demon snarled, demanding his attention. *Do it*, the beast pressed, climbing up his throat to perch behind his eyes, furrowing his brow. *Take her. She told you herself—she wants you.*

Crash grabbed his dagger suddenly and flung it into the wall—*thunk!* It quivered, embedded deeply in the wood. He seethed for a moment, rage flickering behind his eyes. *Press me once more, and I will slit both our throats.* If anything could hurt Sora—if anything could ruin her, could break her in two—it was the malevolent and sick-minded beast that cursed his body. He would not let that happen.

The creature shuddered, then slunk to the back of his mind. It faded from his thoughts, though he still sensed it just beneath the surface of his skin, taunting him, biding its time. Since the Dark God's weapons had entered the world, his demon had become increasingly difficult to control, and such bouts of inner struggle were now commonplace. He trained each morning for more reasons than to keep his skills sharp—he had to remain strong to contain the beast within him.

Crash struggled for a moment to rein in his emotions. Eventually, his blank, cold mask fell back in place. Then he pulled his knife from the wall and headed out the door.

He slipped down the hallway past several cabins. For such a narrow ship, the Dawn Seeker contained a lot of rooms. Most cabins held no more than a small bunk and a porthole window, barely bigger than a closet. Noise traveled an exceptional distance through the walls, though at this late hour, most of the crew were asleep, except for the handful manning the sails.

He counted the doors as he went by and soon found the one he sought. Soft gold light shone through a crack under the door. He paused, glancing around to make sure the halls were empty.

A thick wall of shadow stood to his back. He glared at it.

*No one will see you,* the demon whispered in his thoughts.

*My threat still stands,* he warned.

The demon shied away, but couldn't resist a response. *Are we playing tonight?* it murmured, eagerly prancing against the bars of its cage. *Shall we eat him? Shall we twist his bones and peel his flesh?*

*No,* Crash replied, forcefully turning away from the darkness. He faced the cabin door, leaving the shadow to his back.

Another surge of anger rose in Crash's throat. *He dirtied her name,* the demon said in a toxic whisper. *A name is a precious thing. He deserves my fire.*

*He deserves a lot of things,* Crash agreed.

*Let me out,* the demon whined.

*Silence,* he ordered. His body shuddered. The dark presence gave up and crawled away, fading again.

Crash waited until he was certain the beast wouldn't interfere. Then he turned the doorknob. The door opened halfway and bumped into the side of a cot. Lantern light spilled into the hall.

Immediately, a man's voice cursed. "By the six gods, Joan! I told you, not tonight!"

Crash stepped into the room.

Tristan froze when he saw the assassin. His face drained of color. The Dracian stood half-clothed in his undershorts, literally caught with his pants down, his shirt half-unbuttoned and trousers tossed thoughtlessly on the floor. He was a hand shorter than the assassin and a few years younger. His coppery hair looked tangled and greasy, his cheeks flushed from drinking, eyes hooded and bloodshot.

In two steps, Crash grabbed the man by his collar and heaved him effortlessly into the air.

"Aye!" Tristan yelled. "Aye, put me down! Help! Help!"

Crash slammed him against the wall. "Shut your mouth," he hissed.

Tristan's eyes widened and his mouth snapped shut. The assassin hauled him around by his shirt and forced him out of the room, half-dragging him down the hallway. The Dracian stumbled. Pathetic whimpers issued from his throat, embarrassing for a full-grown man, but Dracians weren't known for their courage.

"Wh-where are you taking me?" Tristan gasped as Crash shoved him into the night. The assassin spun him in a half-circle and rammed his back against the railing. He pushed the Dracian until he was halfway over the side of the ship. Tristan almost screamed, but Crash's knife-like glare shut him up. The Dracian glanced over his shoulder at the black water of the Little Rain tributary. Goosebumps rose on his skin. Crash knew the scent of fear like a predator on the hunt; Tristan reeked of prey, of undisciplined, weak-minded cowardice.

Crash didn't draw his dagger; he didn't need the man pissing on his boots. He spoke directly into his face.

"If you say anything more to hurt Sora, I will slit you navel-to-jaw and tie your intestines in a wreath."

"I-I-I'm sorry, sir, I won't, I swear it, I won't say a word."

"Oh, you're going to speak," Crash said, cutting him off. He leaned Tristan farther over the railing until he was completely off-balance, his arms flailing pathetically in the air, one foot off the ground. "You're going to tell everyone you're a liar. That you've wanted Sora since you first laid eyes on her, but she doesn't want you back. That she rejected you, and you lashed out like a coward." Crash loosened his hold slightly, letting Tristan fall a few inches over the rail. The man let out a short squeal of terror. "And if I hear you spinning tales again, I will cut out your tongue and sew your lips shut. Are we clear?"

"Y-yes, sir."

"I didn't hear you."

"YES!"

Then Crash pushed him overboard.

Tristan screamed like a wounded sow all the way down to the water, ending in a loud *splash!* The sound drew another sailor's attention. He swung down from the rigging, landing on the deck nearby.

"What happened?" the sailor demanded.

Crash gestured over his shoulder. "I hope your friend can swim," he said. Then he turned back to the cabins below.

The sailor ran to the railing and leaned over the side, let out a colorful string of curses, then grabbed a long line of rope and dashed to the rear of the ship.

Crash allowed himself a small, self-satisfied smile. Then he headed below deck.

# CHAPTER 6

Sora awoke a few hours before dawn. She lay in bed, staring at the wooden ceiling. The ship swayed peacefully. Today Captain Silas would most likely bring out the sweeps, long oars used to manually row the ship upriver. He was counting on the winter rains to begin. The storms usually blew inland and would propel their ship up the Little Rain to the Crown's Rush.

Her mind traveled to her brief conversation with Crash the day before. She flexed her injured hand to test the wound beneath her bandages. Suddenly, she knew what she had to do.

Sora stood up and dressed herself in a thick woolen shirt, belted at the waist, and snug cotton pants. She pulled her boots on one by one, stretching out her cramped legs as she did so. She was used to spending nights under the stars, which made sleeping in a small, cramped cabin difficult. She often felt suffocated, as though shut in a tight box.

She strapped on daggers and slung her staff over one shoulder, then climbed on deck. She exited the row of cabins and walked down the side of the ship, where she paused next to a large barrel.

Crash was stretched out horizontally along the aft of the boat. She knew he would be there, as he always was at this time. As she watched, he finished a quick set of press-ups, then ran through a series of sprints across the deck. His breath appeared in small bursts of vapor and he had yet to break a sweat.

He finished his sprints and removed his shirt. The sky held only a slight tinge of gray, but in the dim pre-dawn light, she could see the scars that traced his powerful back. They crisscrossed every which way, some long and thin where blades had cut, or perhaps whiplashes. Others formed white, rough craters—perhaps puncture wounds from arrows or daggers. They were small but numerous and formed a fine web across his shoulders, like constellations drawn on tan parchment.

She knew his longest scar began at his jaw and cut down his chest in a jagged white line. The bloodmage Volcrian had dealt him that wound many years ago. It should have killed him, but Crash was not a normal man.

A new scar sat red and angry at the base of his throat, partially healed from the Isles. It looked as though someone had jammed a red-hot poker straight between his collarbones. His voice still hadn't fully recovered from the sunstone's burn. His tone sounded rougher, deeper than she remembered. As an assassin, it only made him seem more lethal when he spoke, like small rocks grinding behind his words.

He paused after another set of crunches, then stood to face her, watching her quietly.

Sora left the protection of the barrel and stepped into the open.

"A long time ago, you called me your student," she said.

He considered her for a moment, then nodded.

"I'd like to be that again...if I may."

A slight smile crossed his face, a wry tug of his lips. Wordlessly, he sank into a fighting stance, his knees bent agilely and his hands held naturally before him, slightly below eye level. He beckoned her with a quick flick of his wrist.

Sora felt mildly surprised. *Well, that was easy.* Then she mimicked his position, but her stance was not as smooth or comfortable. Her legs strained from her slight crouch and she hesitated before putting her left foot first. It had been a while since she last practiced hand-to-hand combat and her muscles were cold.

She first came to know Crash in the depths of Fennbog swamp, where he taught her to leap nimbly over roots and through tree branches, to duck and weave, block and punch, and kick with enough force to break ribs. Now—after uncovering the truth of his race, the hidden darkness of his past—she would come to know him again.

She approached him warily and decided to attack head-on. She gave a swift jab at his face. He easily swept her hand to one side with his open palm. One attack led into the next, and she attempted to knock him off-balance, but he intercepted all of her blows.

Moving faster as her muscles loosened, she caught him behind the knee with a deft kick. He fell gracefully and rolled back to his feet, coming up behind her. A quick volley of strikes and jabs ensued. Now she found herself on the defensive, relying purely on muscle memory and instinct. She tried to anticipate each blow, but he moved too fast for her to watch his hands.

Finally she saw an opening. She lunged, intending to upper-cut him in the jaw, but he caught her hand at the last minute and spun her around, pulling her against his chest. He locked her arms in front of her, tightly holding her wrists. She gasped, surprised by their abrupt change of position.

"Softly," he murmured against her ear, his breath unexpectedly hot on her cold cheek. "You're too rigid."

"You're too fast," she countered.

"You'll be faster if you relax." He held her like that for a moment too long, it seemed, or maybe she became overly focused on the warmth of his skin, the tight coil of his arms. Then he released her.

"You're worse than I remember."

She flushed. "I...I know," she relented. "It's the Cat's Eye. Usually it helps me."

Crash raised an eyebrow. "So you've been cheating?"

She wrinkled her nose, resisting the urge to grin. While training with her mother, she had learned the Cat's Eye could aid her in hand-to-hand combat. The souls of past bearers still resided somewhere deep in the stone, centuries of warriors, their skills at her fingertips if only she had the control. During battle, she could feel the old warriors stir; not as specific people, but as a source of strength, a sixth sense to guide her hand and improve her reflexes.

But now the necklace seemed stifled. It offered no hidden power, no secret help. She was just a normal girl with a few years of practice under her belt, sparring with a skilled assassin.

"Again," Crash said, and returned to a crouch. They repeated their brief battle, except this time he critiqued. He never spoke harshly, but he called out her missteps, her inconsistent footing and lack of balance. His words offered no encouragement. Everything he said was coldly logical, without flattery or pretense, but she knew this side of him. She understood his method of instruction.

"You're wasting energy," he pointed out when she overextended her reach. "Get closer before you attack."

"But you'll grab me!"

"Then wait for the right moment," he said. "Everyone lets down their guard, even a Grandmaster."

She frowned, uncertain. *What's a Grandmaster?* Obviously someone far more skilled than she. *No time to ask.* She came at him again, targeting under his ribs; a swift punch to the abdomen could deal a lot of damage.

He trapped her arms again and pushed her back against the railing of the ship, easily overcoming her. She let out a breath of frustration.

"Will you at least let me try?" she hissed, aggravated. How could she practice when he didn't come down to her level?

She tried to escape his grasp, but he pinned her in place. He trapped her in a living cage. She could feel his entire body against her. As her heart slowed and her head cleared, she found herself completely preoccupied by his closeness, his height and strength. The memory of their first kiss came to mind, and she tried not to weaken against him. She glanced up and met his impenetrable gaze.

"What are you thinking?" she asked, hoping he didn't notice her distraction.

"That if I were the enemy, you'd be dead right now."

His words broke the spell. Her lips twisted in defiance. She slipped to one side and ducked halfway under his arm before he grabbed her again. He spun her around effortlessly and locked her against the rail.

"Wrong," he murmured. "Try again."

She twisted her arm inward to break his grip, then threw a punch at his exposed neck. He trapped one hand and she attacked with the other, aiming for his solar plexus. He blocked her again, easily deflecting each blow until her arms felt tied in a sailor's knot.

Finally they stood face-to-face, locked together, noses inches apart. "Better," he said briefly.

"You're enjoying this," she said, her voice huskier than intended.

His lips twitched. He watched her.

She cleared her throat self-consciously. She waited for him to release her, but he didn't.

Finally, she asked, "Why are you doing this?"

"To gauge your skill."

She blinked. "I thought you were just trying to humiliate me."

His sudden smile stole her breath. "And why would I need to taunt my own student?"

"Then...you'll teach me?"

"Of course," he said, as though she were a fool to doubt it. "Soon you will need to defend yourself against the Shade, with or without your Cat's Eye."

Sora hesitated. She hadn't encountered the Shade before, but if they were anything like Crash....

"Are the Shade as skilled as you?"

"Some of them."

Her face turned stubborn. "Then I will have to try harder."

She used that moment to slip from his hold, drop to the ground and roll between his legs. She leapt to her feet and dashed across the deck before he could catch her.

"Ha!" she exclaimed. "I win!"

She stopped at the row of cabins and danced lightly from foot to foot, her heart hammering with exhilaration. She laughed at his bemused expression, her breath rising in small puffs in the cold air.

"Be on guard, Crash!" she called. "I'll have your back against the railing next!"

He shook his head slowly.

"Weapons?" he offered.

Sora took a deep, refreshing breath of crisp morning air. Then she unslung her staff from her shoulder and held the weapon crosswise in front of her, all too ready to continue. Dawn light brightened the sky, summoning a chorus of birdsong from the forest. A variety of hoots and trills rose from the dense pine trees.

Crash drew his thin-bladed sword and assumed another fighting stance, clasping his weapon lightly in one hand, his wrist strong and flexible. They began to circle each other slowly, responding to each other's movements.

Sora felt much more at ease with her staff. When they finally clashed, she was able to hold her own for several minutes. Crash paused every now and then to adjust her hands and show her subtle techniques, ways of blocking and striking in one smooth motion. Sora lost track of the number of rounds they practiced; over time, she could feel her muscles strain, her hands ache with each strike of his sword. The exertion felt good—addictive.

Before she knew it, the sun was high in the sky and the ship was bustling with activity. A few sailors watched them from the rigging, munching on sweet rolls for breakfast.

Then a furious voice roared across the deck. "Sora!"

She stopped mid-swing, almost dropping her staff. Crash halted as well, his sword inches away from her left ear. She looked up in bewilderment, and then a terrible thought struck her. *Oh, no!* She had completely forgotten about her shift in the crow's nest!

Crash seemed to read her mind and allowed the point of his sword to touch the deck. He didn't seem terribly surprised by the interruption.

Sora scowled, suspecting he had kept her late on purpose.

"Why didn't you remind me?" she asked.

"Why didn't you remember?"

She was unable to think of a response.

Captain Silas rounded the corner of the ship, descending on them like a storm cloud.

"*Sora!* I told you not to abandon your post! By the four winds, do I have to chain you up there myself?" His eyes looked bloodshot in fury, or perhaps from a late-night bottle of wine. He paused when he saw her, red-faced from exertion, next to Crash. He sized up the situation in two seconds and rolled his eyes heavenward, releasing a loud, exaggerated groan.

"I take it you've found a better use of your time?"

Sora stuttered at first. "I-I didn't intend...."

"Well?" Silas snapped.

She straightened her spine. "Yes," she replied. "I have."

Silas' mouth opened, then clicked shut. Sora expected the Dracian to release one of his infamous tantrums, but he remained quiet. As his eyes shifted behind her to the assassin, his lips pulled into a distracted frown.

"A certain son of mine told me a strange tale this morning," he said gruffly.

Sora had no idea what he meant. She looked at Crash for an explanation, but the assassin simply shrugged.

"Your son enjoys spinning tales," he replied. "Someday it will get him into trouble."

Silas hesitated once more, as though considering any number of responses; then he pointed his finger directly at Crash. "That may be true," he said viciously.

"But if I hear of one more incident aboard my ship, *you'll* be the one left floating downstream."

The assassin didn't reply, but swung his sword in a lazy circle.

Silas pointed for another moment, then flicked his hand dismissively. "Fine. Sora, you've been switched to lunch duty. You weren't much of a lookout, anyway." He whirled around and headed back toward his cabin. He stalked off, yelling more orders at his crew, reassigning her hours in the crow's nest.

Sora turned back to Crash. "I guess I should head down to the galley," she said self-consciously. She felt a little embarrassed about forgetting her duties that morning, but the time spent with Crash had been worth it.

"Tomorrow, then? In the morning?" she asked.

The assassin nodded. His eyes held her gaze too long, and perhaps she saw his expression soften...but she didn't want to read too much into it.

She gave him a little wave and turned to leave, her heart pounding strangely in her chest. She remembered the brush of his strong calloused hands, his long and nimble fingers, his arms trapping her against the railing. She thought of his full attention upon her, observing each small movement, every flaw and breath.

Tomorrow they would train again. Her stomach tightened at the thought. She hoped he didn't notice her response to his touch—but she knew he saw everything.

In the evening of the next day, Sora left her staff and daggers in her cabin and climbed on deck. Caprion met her near the figurehead of a charging horse on the bow. He lifted her to Ferran's houseboat that trailed along after the Dawn Seeker, towed by a long piece of rope.

Ferran sat on the railing at the fore of his boat, his long legs dangling over the river. A half-chewed cinnamon stick was tucked behind one ear, obscured by his unkempt brown hair. He wore a tattered leather greatcoat with a stained tunic underneath, worn black pants and no boots. She knew her mother had taken Ferran's shoes for mending the day before. He didn't seem in a great rush to replace them.

*Better for balance,* he told Lorianne knowingly. *Less smell, too.*

She paused next to him and looked out over the water. In the distance, past the sails of the Dawn Seeker, she could see a growing ridge of snow-capped mountains. The tallest was called The Scepter. It was said to be cursed—that long ago, in the time of the Races, Kaelyn the Wanderer had killed a great demon and buried it among the massive cliffs. All who traveled there were destined to perish.

At the foot of The Scepter resided the City of Crowns. Sora had never been there before. As she gazed at the gray mountains, a cold, moist wind swept up behind her, blowing strands of hair across her face. Full winter would come soon. Captain Silas predicted it would rain tomorrow, and perhaps for the next week. If she turned to look over her shoulder, she could see glowering storm clouds heading inland from the ocean, hiding the vivid sunset. Rain would soon overtake their little ship.

Beyond the mountains, the sky was a deep, swelling indigo, and she could see the first stars of the night.

"We'll reach the City of Crowns just in time for the winter festival," Ferran said. He studied her from the corner of his eye. "Have you been?"

Sora shook her head. "No, but I've heard of it." Who hadn't? Young noble-women planned year-round for winter solstice: a two-week festival of elaborate feasts, fine wines, unforgettable scandal and legendary debauchery. It marked the end of the year when accounts were closed and profits made. A marriage proposal at winter solstice was immensely good luck, heralding a lifetime of good fortune and health.

It didn't seem so long ago that she lived as a noblewoman herself. The ladies of the high plains had chatted ceaselessly about the prestigious parties thrown by the First Tier. Through stories and gossip, she had come to know the richest families in the Kingdom as if they were her own neighbors. They all seemed like outrageously dramatized characters in a book: the Ebonaires, powerful and darkly elegant; the Seabournes, staunchly loyal to tradition; the fiery, ambitious LeCroys and the educated, silver-tongued Daniellians.

And with all of the masquerades, young ladies never knew who they might dance with. The prince could steal a kiss on winter solstice eve, and a girl might never know.

*So long ago,* she thought, and yet the memories arose easily, as though she had sat in Lady Sinclair's parlor just yesterday. A tangled mix of anxiety and displeasure settled in her gut. *I never want to go back to that life.*

Second Tier nobility were not as well off as the First Tier, especially those Sora grew up around, who lived on small estates in the country. If anything, they glamorized the winter festival even more. The girls studied fashion, plays, topics of note, First Tier etiquette and courting, courting, courting—all in hopes of visiting the city and landing a rich husband.

But winter solstice wasn't just for the wealthy elite. Its tradition spanned the entire Kingdom. Last year for the first time, Sora had celebrated among the lower class with her mother. It marked the beginning of winter, when the sun reached its lowest point on the horizon, signaling the dark, snowy months to come. Ale and wine, fermented from summer's harvest, flowed aplenty. Farmers slaughtered old and sickly animals, and prepared feasts of beef, pork, goat and lamb, to avoid feeding extra livestock through the winter.

In her mother's small town, they strung bells along the streets, and villagers wore painted wooden masks on winter's eve. The masks were meant to remind people of their true nature: as children of the Wind, they were ever-changing, and their inner spirits bore no face. Beneath the masks, the troubles of the old year dissolved, and a new year was embraced when they were shed at dawn.

And Sora learned another piece of the tradition: farmers believed that the boundary between the Dark God's realm and the world of Wind and Light weakened on winter solstice. Young children didn't stray far, as dead spirits might come to take them away to the underworld.

Sora wondered if there was any truth to that.

"Enough pensive staring into the distance." Ferran stepped down from the railing on his bare feet. "Let's find a quiet place where we can concentrate. Too many distractions here."

Ferran lit an oil lamp and led her into his humble cabin. A potbellied stove stood opposite to a long cot, with a narrow strip of floor space in between. Shelves above the stove carried boxes of dried meat, rice and jarred vegetables. They sat on the floor between the stove and cot. Sora could hear the rush of water outside and the occasional thump of driftwood striking the hull.

"You've meditated before, I take it?" Ferran asked.

"Yes. A lot." Sora winced at her last words. Actually, she hadn't meditated since boarding the Dawn Seeker.

"Good, then I'll skip to the point. Have you ever tried guided meditation?"

Sora frowned. "No."

"Even better. I want you to sit down comfortably and take a few deep breaths. Close your eyes. Relax and empty your mind."

Sora did so without complaint. It took her longer to clear her mind than it ever had before. A year ago at her mother's cabin, there had been few distractions from her training. She had learned from books in her mother's library that meditation was a strong method of connecting and controlling the Cat's Eye. She had spent hours under the thick pine trees allowing her thoughts to slip away. Eventually, she had been able to forget the ground, the birds, the sky—there was just the silent, open pit of her body, and of course, the stone.

Now thoughts of the winter solstice hung over her head, stressful and troubling. She sank deeper into herself, the worry smoothing from her brow. Her muscles began to relax. Silence brushed against her ears. Her thoughts soared in and out of her consciousness like errant birds, until they faded away.

Then, in the new stillness, uncontrollable images began to arise: her great fall in the Crystal Caves, when she finally learned the truth about the Sixth Race; Crash's torn and bloodied body in the Harpy prison; the long and strenuous battle with Volcrian and the second Cat's Eye's broken bond. Pain. Blood. Light. Each sudden burst of memory struck her like a physical blow. Her heart twisted. *I can't face this again,* she thought.

She clenched her teeth against the urge to scream.

"Breathe," Ferran's voice reached her softly, piercing the cloud of her mind. "Breathe, Sora."

She drew one deep breath after the next, as though bearing the pain of a broken leg. *Breathe.* She had to calm herself. If she didn't, she would crumble.

It seemed like an eternity passed, but she slowly sank back into her body, using the energy of the earth to ground herself. The images still flickered, though dimmer now. She remained there, breathing methodically, waiting.

And then, she felt it. Weak at first, it pooled inside her belly and spread outward—peace. The knowledge that she was safe, unharmed and still breathing. Whole.

Ferran seemed to know when she had reached that point. Only then did he speak.

"Sora," he said quietly. "I want you to find your bond with the Cat's Eye."

It seemed that her reply came from another part of her mind, a place separate from logic and reason.

"It's here," she said through heavy lips.

"I want you to take that bond and hold it in your hands. Do you see it?"

Outwardly, she didn't move. But in her mind, she glanced down. The images came to her like a dream. A thin cord of green light flowed through her hands. She gripped it.

"I have it," she murmured.

"Good. Now what do you see in front of you?"

Deep in the trance, she looked up. She stood in a garden behind her manor. Large rose bushes bloomed on a white trellis that spanned a stone wall. She could smell them suddenly—sharp and sweet, heavy with perfume.

"I'm in a garden," she said.

"Lovely," Ferran replied. "Do you see the path?"

"Yes."

A series of gray flagstones led around the horse stable to a wide field of long grass and wildflowers.

"I want you to follow it."

She did so.

In her mind, she walked over the gray flagstones, past the stables and out toward the field. The colors around her seemed impossibly saturated, every detail pronounced. The stone path led her to a corral at the far side of the field. She didn't remember it. As she walked, she could see the wooden stakes wedged solidly into the ground, with metal poles fashioned between them. A large iron gate barred its entrance.

"Where are you now?" Ferran asked softly.

"A horse corral. It's locked."

"Climb the gate," he instructed. "Don't bother with the lock."

She followed his directions and gripped the metal pole, pulling herself over the side of the fence. She dropped to the ground on the opposite side, then stopped. The vision changed. Her manor disappeared, the field, and the forest beyond. Now it was just the corral. The gated walls seemed like bars to a prison.

"Something's here with me," she said.

A chill crossed over her skin. She looked around the corral. A large, hulking shape stood at its center with its back turned to her. She waited for the shape to fully take form, then recognized four paws, gleaming white fur, a thick mane of bristling quills and two long, spiraling horns. Her heart quickened and she almost lost focus. *The garrolithe.*

"Breathe," Ferran murmured.

She waited until the fear passed. The garrolithe remained motionless, as though oblivious to her presence.

Finally, Ferran continued, "Look down at your hands. Do you see your rope?"

She looked down. The green strand still flowed between her fingers. She gripped it reassuringly, aware that she wasn't alone in this vision. No, the Cat's Eye was here with her.

"I have it."

"Look again," Ferran said. "What do you see?"

She blinked and the rope coiled around itself, forming a noose. That did not surprise her.

"A lasso," she said.

"Approach the garrolithe. When you reach its side, take the end of the rope and slip it over its neck."

Sora clasped the rope. She stepped softly across the corral. The beast did not move. As she neared its side, she saw its eyes were closed. It appeared to be asleep. Its head was massive, its jaw thick, like a white lion; her hands looked minuscule against it. She was just tall enough to slip the noose around its neck, if she could get close enough.

She began to loop the noose over its great mouth. But the moment she touched its fur, its eyes snapped open, shining with vivid blue light, far brighter and sharper than a summer sky.

A loud, coughing roar burst from the beast's throat, ending in the high shriek of a wildcat. Then the beast turned on her violently, thrashing its head. Sora stumbled, and the noose fell to the ground. The beast turned its long fangs on her, snapping and snarling. She shouted in fear and scrambled back across the dirt. The garrolithe leapt after her, eager to rip out her throat.

*Snap!*

Sora pitched forward, gasping for breath, her eyes wide open. A scream caught in her throat. She looked around wildly, prepared to fight for her life. But all she saw were the timbers of the boat, the potbellied stove and Ferran's cinnamon stick rolling thoughtfully in his mouth.

"I didn't say it would be easy," he grinned.

She inhaled, trying to calm her racing heart.

"What happened? What was that?"

Ferran laughed at her bewilderment. She glared at him in annoyance.

"I don't understand," she began again. "I saw the garrolithe. It was sleeping, but I woke it up, and now...." Now she could feel its energy writhing in her stomach like a nasty bout of food poisoning.

"You didn't get the noose around it," Ferran said, as though that explained everything in the world.

"But the Cat's Eye...."

"You have to harness the power of the garrolithe," Ferran repeated, as though she might be hard of hearing. "Get it? Harness the power? That's the beauty of this exercise. It's quite straightforward, really."

Sora resisted the urge to roll her eyes. "Have you done this before, or are you making it up as we go?"

Ferran shrugged. "Nothing wrong with a bit of improvisation. My techniques have all worked for me, but I've never had to teach anyone else." He adopted a more thoughtful look. "Your Cat's Eye used to belong to Dane. Your father, you know."

Sora glanced away. Ferran and Dane had been old friends, or so her mother once told her, but Sora didn't know Ferran well enough to start hashing out family history. She had met the man only three weeks ago.

Ferran raised an eyebrow, noticing her withdrawal.

"What I meant to say," he explained, "is that you're the only other person I've met with a Cat's Eye, since Dane died. These artifacts are very rare, and much has been forgotten." He took the cinnamon stick from his mouth and turned it thoughtfully in his hands. "I've worn this stone for twenty years. Most of what I've learned has been through trial and error, and at times, bitter experience. Hopefully I can teach you to avoid some of my mistakes."

She gave him a searching look, but he didn't explain. She shifted her position on the hardwood planks. Her legs had fallen asleep.

"How long have we been sitting here?" she asked, realizing how cold it was.

"Two hours, I'd say. Perhaps a little more."

Their lantern flickered, almost out of oil. She glanced at it.

"I should probably get back," she said.

"I'll signal Caprion."

Ferran stood, picked up the lantern, and walked outside. Sora followed him a bit more slowly. Her thoughts lingered on her vision of the corral and the monster within. She sensed the garrolithe still pacing, its fiery eyes watching her from beyond the barred gates.

# CHAPTER 7

Cerastes stood at the cliff's edge. The desert wind raked its hard, dry fingers through his hair. Miles of red sand stretched before him into a wavering, mirror-like distance. A trailing cloud scarred the burning blue sky.

His eyes slid to the base of the rocky plateau where he stood. A large encampment sprawled at his feet. Tents and fires dotted the ground. At this distance, the noise of the camp did not reach him, though he could see rows upon rows of nameless savants standing on the cracked, dry earth. They practiced chains of combat moves, all in coordination, like skilled dancers crossing a ballroom.

A trickle of satisfaction entered his thoughts. They came here to serve the Dark God. They came here to learn the secrets of their race, to obey, and to restore an ancient order.

Cerastes turned to the cliff face behind him. The massive plateau towered over the barren landscape. The book in his hand had led him to this place. Still, the plateau presented a puzzle. He found no markings, no signs, no indication of the Dark God's resting place...and yet he could feel it nearby in his bones.

He knelt with his ear to the rock. Through the cavernous walls of his body, through the echoing space between heart and lung, between pounding blood and seeping breath—he listened.

The red stone murmured.

His ears did not know the language. And yet his heart—which some would call a shrouded, crippled deformity—leapt at the sound. Because Cerastes' heart was not dead, nor blackened, nor damaged, as some might believe. It was as clearly crimson as the blood of a martyr, as the fires that burned in the Dark God's realm.

*For nothing,* he thought. *For nothing, I have sought You out. And for nothing, I shall fulfill this task.*

Because to live for nothing...to worship it, as one might the core of oneself, and dismantle all trappings of worldly identity...to live only in the moment, with few wants or desires, free from attachment and reward.... That was the final calling of an assassin. To know the true emptiness of all creation: life, a momentary flash of light, conceived from nothing and destined to return to its original state....

In this way, Cerastes knew the truth of the world. Life was not sacred, nor was death. All was a cycle. And beyond life and death, in those realms of emptiness—where the Elements vanished after creating the world—only there could one find peace.

The Dark God yearned to return the world to emptiness.

One could not live so long as an assassin and ignore that call.

The Sixth Race were not meant to rule. His kind did not have emperors or kings. They served their practice, their Grandmasters and the Hive. He knew this instinctively. He had lived it. For decades he had strictly obeyed his people's traditions, asking more from his body and mind than even his fellow Grandmasters could tolerate. But it was not enough. Eventually, after decades of study, he had reached the pinnacle of his practice. He could gain no more from the Hive.

And then, with nowhere else to turn, he had delved into the ancient secrets of his race. He had traveled to distant lands where the ruins of their once-civilization could be found in wasted tombs. He salvaged books and half-burned scrolls, and traced the ancient runes left on tombstones and crypts.

Only then did he see the Hive's traditions for what they truly were—diluted. Miswritten. *Weak.*

From those ancient relics of his race, he gained knowledge of the Shade. He learned a doctrine far more valid than taught by the Hive.

And he faced the truth: the races were slowly dying. One day, their knowledge, their sacred practices, their magic and their gods would be lost forever, becoming footnotes, then mythology, then dust on the wind.

Why should humans live while the races died?

What greater right did they have to exist?

If his kind were destined to fade from the world, then the world should fade with them.

He listened to the earth murmur. He pressed his hands against the hot, crimson rock. In that enclosed silence, he heard the Dark God speak—not words he could repeat aloud, nor even truly a language, but a sensation, an instinct greater than his own. The message swelled through his body.

And then the silence was broken.

A quick series of footsteps approached on the cliff behind him.

"Master," a soft voice said. "The two have returned. They await your presence."

He rose from the rocky ledge and brushed the dust from his robes. Then he turned to the long series of wooden steps that led back down to the desert. He dismissed the nameless savant with a wave of his hand. Then, with another wave, he summoned a black portal and stepped through it. The darkness clasped him in a familiar shroud.

Within seconds, the desert landscape dissolved around him, replaced by a gust of wintry air. The sound of passing carriages and human voices reached his ears. Above him, he no longer saw the burning sky, but 200 feet of scaffold—a tower worthy of a king.

He descended the wooden staircase into the gray afternoon light. King Royce's workers swarmed over the tower like busy birds constructing a nest. *Such shallow creatures,* he thought, watching them dispassionately. The humans he had met were a step above livestock, imbued with material intelligence yet ultimately devoid of depth. They barely questioned their own existence. They lived mindlessly, mumbling prayers to their Goddess, until they dropped dead on the ground.

He left the rickety staircase and entered the half-constructed stone base of the tower. The sounds of construction echoed through the hollow center of the building. Above him, hundreds of feet of brass gears and steel ropes filled its height. A new trophy for the human king—and the perfect guise for The Shade's purpose.

Darkness pooled unnaturally at his feet. He waited until the human workers dispersed. Then, with an assertion of will, he melted through the stone floor and went below ground.

The stone chamber dampened Krait's words. After making her report, she allowed her voice to die on the musty air. The crunch of heavy gears carried on above her, an ongoing grind through the earth. Cobra knelt nearby on one knee, his eyes feverishly trained on the ground.

Her Grandmaster remained silent, but the wraith at his back seemed to mirror his thoughts. The phantom flickered back and forth agitatedly, flying in restless circles, occasionally ramming up against the barrier of its invisible prison. It let out a piercing wail without warning. Heavy stone swallowed up the sound.

She waited. Cerastes thought. The gears churned. The wraith spun.

"And the Viper seemed distracted by this girl?" he finally asked.

"Yes," Krait intoned. She thought her master looked disappointed by the news, though she couldn't fathom why.

"It seems our Viper has fallen in love," Cerastes murmured. "How *regressive*." He paused, his eyes trailing along the wall, as though rewriting some passage in a book. "Still, I suppose this can be used to our advantage."

"He seemed strong enough when I faced him," Cobra offered.

"It won't last. He's distracted by this girl. Yes, this changes things." The Grandmaster gazed at the wraith. "How close are they to the city?"

"Well in time for winter solstice," Krait said.

"Bring the girl to me when they arrive."

Krait did not expect this.

"We can bring her sooner," Cobra hissed. "We can bring her now...."

He fell silent under Cerastes's stare.

"No need to rush," their master intoned. "We will trust in the Dark God's timing and wait for their arrival. Once we have the girl, then Viper will come to heel, and the weapons will be ours." His gaze fastened on Cobra. "You know what you must do."

Cobra bowed his head. "Yes, Grandmaster."

Krait glanced at her fellow assassin. She sensed a hidden agenda. What other mission did Cerastes refer to? She wondered, then, if she should voice her misgivings about Cobra. Even now, he spoke out of turn and did not follow the subservient doctrine of the Shade.

She imagined how that conversation would go.

"The Shade grows stronger in the Dark God's shadow, but there is still much work to be done," Cerastes said. "Do not disturb me until you have the girl."

Krait and Cobra bowed in succession, then turned as one to the shadow portal. With a few swift steps, Krait dashed through the misty portal and found herself transported instantly back to the slums of the city. She arrived on the bank of an abandoned water canal, long since overrun by waste and sewage. Reeking, sticky mud sucked at her boots. Rain fell heavily from the sky. Dim lantern light illuminated a row of thatched houses across the channel.

A moment later, the air wavered and Cobra appeared by her side. He stood there, twitching and shifting, and took a moment to adjust his gauntlets. Krait watched him out of the corner of her eye. For an assassin, he could never stand still.

She faced Cobra, meeting his toxic green eyes. She still hadn't seen the entirety of his face, and she didn't want to. Whatever his disfigurement, she could tell it was gruesome.

Most of the Shade were like Cobra: maimed and discarded assassins, rejected from the Hive and left for dead. Cerastes became their saving grace. Despite their solitary nature, her kind wasn't meant to exist on their own. The Sixth Race thrived on structure. Cut off from the Hive, assassins became manic and deranged. With time, they slowly lost their minds to their demons.

Cobra struck her as someone who had once come very close to that point.

"I'll handle Viper," he said in his oily voice.

She glared. "Cerastes ordered us to bring him *the girl*," she said. "We must obey."

Cobra's eyes crinkled. "You must obey, perhaps," he said. "Cerastes gave me a different mission."

"I doubt that. You're too unpredictable. He wouldn't trust you."

Cobra shifted from foot to foot, full of unreleased energy. "Unpredictable, am I? Only fools mindlessly obey orders. Cerastes sent you after a weak human because he didn't think you could handle Viper."

Krait's anger burned cold and clear. "You think I'm weak?"

"In Cerastes' eyes."

Krait drew a short crop from her waist and struck Cobra across the cheek. *Crack!* Given their close proximity, the blow was brutally strong.

Cobra stumbled back, taken off-guard. The strike tore off part of his mask. He threw up his arm to shield the exposed half of his face.

Krait shifted her weight to one hip and crossed her arms.

"Next time I'll remove your skin—whatever's left of it."

Cobra wiped a trail of blood from his cheek. Then he raised his cowl and covered his face again. The corners of his eyes creased.

"What else can you do with that whip?"

"Strike off your manhood, if you like," she snarled.

Cobra laughed—a wheezing sound. "Perhaps you could, but make no mistake—you *are* weak."

He stalked forward, closing the space between them. Krait stepped back, but he kept coming.

"That's why you follow every word he says," he hissed. "You live in fear. You can't survive without the Shade. You think the Dark God really has a place for you in His shadow—some great destiny. You *need* it, don't you? Of course you do, because you have no demon. Without the Shade, you're a useless shell. That's why you lap up your master's words like a dog."

Krait reached behind her and loosened the long bullwhip from her back.

"Then you admit you're not loyal to Cerastes?" she asked.

He scoffed. "Put your weapon down, little snake. Only a fool would make Cerastes his enemy. I, too, have reasons for joining the Shade. But not for the Dark God's might. Not to become a servant. Where my desires lead, I follow."

"An assassin should have few desires."

"So say the brainwashed slaves of a dying tradition."

Her hand tightened on her whip. "I can't let you walk free, knowing your true intentions. If you don't serve Cerastes...."

Cobra folded his arms. "Go on, then," he sneered. "*Waylay me.*"

Krait's whip struck his chest like lightning. Cobra staggered back from the blow, his breath stolen by the impact. Following the whip's circular momentum, Krait spun and cracked down again, aiming for his eye, but he twisted away. She left a long, bleeding cut up the side of his neck.

Cobra danced backward, but Krait attacked like a stinging wasp, her whip all but invisible. Her next blow struck his arm, then his tender outer thigh. With each vicious crack, she closed the distance between them. Soon the tip of her braided rope ran with blood.

Finally, she lashed out the whip and caught Cobra's heel, then wrenched him to the ground. The small man didn't weigh much, and she dragged him forward with a practiced hand. She would tie him up and return him to Cerastes....

Then, suddenly, he vanished before her eyes.

She blinked.

He reappeared directly behind her. She turned too late. Cobra slammed his steel fist into her face, connecting squarely with her jaw. Krait fell hard onto the mud, her vision blurred.

*The fifth gate*, she thought. But how? It took years to master....

Cobra's fist clamped down on her neck. He held her pinned.

"We're not so different, you and I. Cerastes made us both promises. To you, he gave a purpose, a new life. And I...I have my own interest in the Viper. Cerastes promised me that." She sensed his cold grin. "I love an angry vixen, but I won't hesitate to kill you, should you get in my way."

He shook her slightly for emphasis, then released her neck. For a long moment, she could only cough and wheeze through her bruised windpipe. The realization of his power felt even more crushing than his fist.

Krait reached for a knife at her belt, but Cobra's shadow twisted from his feet to her arms and held her to the ground. She was outmatched. He must be older than she first thought. He stood at the brink of Grandmastery. No wonder Cerastes had recruited him.

Shame grew within her. Despite training with Cerastes and the other students of the Shade, her skills had improved slowly. She wielded no magic of her own. The Harpies had destroyed her demon during her years on the Lost Isles. Using sunstones, they had ripped the magical core from her body. She could still feel the emptiness at the base of her skull where the demon's voice once resonated. She would never open the fifth gate; in fact, she couldn't even open the first.

Cobra stood over her, his eyes lit with poisonous fervor.

"You're a worthless little snake," he sneered. "One day, Cerastes will throw you away. Assassins like you are meant to be sacrificed." Then he walked away, back to the city, through the mud.

Krait lay still, her heart pounding. *Cerastes will throw you away.* Cobra's words rang with unnerving truth. Her master had a new favorite, and she couldn't compete.

She closed her eyes and put her hands to her head. Her temples throbbed with the memory of her stolen demon. Harpy voices echoed, sharp and metallic, in her ears. Searing light flashed. Burning heat. The images built and built, unlocked by Cobra's words, until she groaned under their pressure. A fierce, primal shriek welled in her throat, but she bit it back, unwilling to scream her weakness to the world.

And then, the images slowed.

A memory surfaced—only a glimmer. Cool hands.

Gone.

Krait stared up at the stormy sky, allowing the rain to strike her open eyes. She imagined they were tears—she hadn't cried since Cerastes repaired her vision. Tears were not meant for assassins. She would rather her heart be made of stone.

*Cobra lies,* she thought. Her Grandmaster would not betray her. She had a place in the Dark God's shadow—a purpose in her master's plan. And if that purpose meant sacrificing her life, she would not hesitate.

With renewed will, Krait rose silently to her feet. She was a broken puppet, a mimicry of an assassin, and no matter how long she lived, she would never reclaim what the Harpies took. She would offer her master something better, perhaps: unquestionable fealty.

Cobra played a dangerous game. Eventually, Cerastes would grow tired of him. Her Grandmaster did not suffer arrogance. The true strength of an assassin lay in discipline, which Cobra obviously lacked.

She thought of her brief battle with Viper in the city of Delbar, months and months ago.

Cobra wanted to confront him, but she didn't think he'd win.

# CHAPTER 8

S ora stood on the bow of the ship. She watched Silas' crew guide the Dawn
Seeker into the Crown's Rush. Over the course of the last mile, the riverbanks had crept inward and upward, narrowing until the current raged aggres-
sively. Silas' crew banked the sails and wrestled hard with the rudder. It took three
men to steer the wheel against the fierce current. The Dracians worked tirelessly,
yelling to one another above the storm, swinging the yardarm against the wind
and battling the hemorrhaging river.

Sora held her breath, gripping the rail, wondering if they would crash against
the trees or the rocky bank.

Then, finally, a fierce wind blew up from behind them.

"Unfurl the mainstay!" Silas yelled at the rigging. Then to the men at the tiller:
"Swing us hard to port! Hard to port!"

Some of the sailors turned to look at the mouth of the river, gauging the risk.

"*Now*, you lazy dogs!" Silas bellowed. He strode the length of the schooner,
tying down ropes where he could.

The ship groaned as the wind caught the sails and slowly moved forward.

"To port!" Silas yelled again, although the men at the tiller were already hard
to port.

Sora gasped as the ship groaned. She stared anxiously at the rocky banks,
imagining their ship twisting and slamming into the steep, jagged stone. Then,

within seconds, they slid past the threshold and into the Crown's Rush, leaving the Little Rain behind.

"Hard to starboard!" Silas continued to yell, his voice ragged from shouting. "Bring her out into the channel! We've made it, thank the winds!"

From that point, their schooner shot downstream like a well-crafted arrow. The crew cheered in victory. Sora let out a whoop of excitement, leaning over the bow into the fierce wind.

After several weeks of constant storms, the Crown's Rush appeared as wide and endless as the ocean. Iron-gray water flowed into the vague horizon, dissolving into vaporous curtains of mist and rain.

*From here, we will make good time,* Sora thought. Silas claimed they would be the last large vessel to enter the city from this direction. The snows would set in soon, and much of the river and its tributaries would be locked in thick ice, especially this far north.

As she watched the river, Ferran's boat shot ahead of them, much faster than the large schooner. A strong wind filled his small sail. He waved at them from the back of the boat where he manned the tiller.

Sora returned his wave, then left the bow, her face numb from the cold wind.

Days passed, each one blending into the next. As they neared the City of Crowns, more and more villages cropped up on the river banks. Small docks, fishing boats and ferries became a common sight. Silas rang a loud, heavy bell to warn smaller boats and rafts out of the way. Townspeople and farmers waved as they passed.

Twice they dropped anchor at small villages to trade for fresh vegetables and live chickens. Silas unloaded several barrels of limes, edible roots, dried seaweed and seashells.

"Best to stock up on supplies now before we reach the bigger towns," he said. "We'll have less bargaining power as we near the city." He started to explain to her the concept of supply and demand, and the value of limes in the country compared to populated areas further south, but Sora found the subject tedious.

They passed miles of barren fruit orchards. Harvest had long since passed, and the winter season had stripped the fields of fruit or leaves.

"These farmlands sustain the city," Ferran explained to Sora after one of their meditation sessions. They stood on the bow of his houseboat. "The Ebonaires own almost all of the orchards from here to the city itself. Their taxes pay for a third of the military's wages."

"Are they truly the richest family, next to King Royce?" Sora asked.

Ferran looked uneasy. "Richer, in fact," he admitted. "The king doesn't control every aspect of the realm. Politics are much more complicated than that. Many First Tier families fund his interests. Their wealth is the lifeblood of the kingdom."

Sora considered that, wondering how the Fallcrest family compared. They were country nobility, the Second Tier, who had won their title through military service many generations ago. Although her stepfather had owned several thousand acres of land, they hadn't harvested enough to live in the City of Crowns. They weren't like the First Tier, who could trace their lineage back centuries ago to the founding tribes of the Kingdom.

"How did your visualization go?" Ferran asked, changing the subject.

Sora grimaced. "Not well."

This time, she had climbed a tree near the corral, intending to drop the noose around the garrolithe's neck from above. Sensing her intentions, the beast had pulled her down and dragged her around in circles before trying to bite her head off.

Ferran had assured her it couldn't actually harm her...but Sora didn't know if she believed him. The garrolithe seemed very determined.

In truth, she dreaded the hours she spent delving to the roots of herself. Slowly, she had been able to reconnect with the necklace, but the long period of separation left her timid and doubtful. The bond didn't feel as natural as before.

"Keep with it," Ferran encouraged.

"How much longer will this take?"

"Everyone is different. There's no perfect method. Just keep trying."

Sora sighed in frustration. "It doesn't want to be controlled."

"Perhaps you shouldn't try to control it, then," Ferran suggested. He threw a chewed-up cinnamon stick over the railing, into the water. "Perhaps you're trying too hard. The garrolithe can sense your frustration. To the beast, it's another sign of weakness. Try to stay calm and assertive."

Sora nodded, but she didn't truly agree. No one could stay calm and assertive in the face of that beast. Each time she challenged it, the garrolithe came one snap closer to eating her.

"Worrying about it is the worst thing you can do," Ferran insisted, reading her furrowed brow. "You'll regain your control with time."

Sora sighed, feeling even less inspired. *I really am terrible at this.* She returned to the Dawn Seeker that day with even more frustration.

To take her mind off the Cat's Eye, she focused even harder on her training with Crash.

He took his role seriously, and often assigned hours of menial exercises to strengthen her muscles. He took her small size into consideration and taught her hand-to-hand combat in a style she hadn't learned before.

"You are a river, not a mountain," he told her during one particularly challenging lesson. His words seemed repeated from a distant past, perhaps something he had learned in his youth. "A river flows downhill over rocks, using the path of least resistance. This is how you fight. Have you ever held water in your hand?"

"Of course." Just that morning, she had cupped her hands and splashed her face with cold rainwater.

"And what happened?"

"Well...the water trickled through my fingers."

"Can you break it with a hard punch?"

She grinned at that. "No."

"Why not?"

Her eyes glinted. "It gives way beneath your hand."

"Exactly."

He demonstrated this idea in combat. If he threw a punch, instead of blocking with her arms, Sora was to grab his fist and pull him forward, putting him off-balance. Then she could deal a swift kick to the ribs, the groin, the knees, or even a jab to the neck. It was a smoother, softer way of fighting, one that didn't involve rigid blocks or tightened, heavy muscles.

"Most men, especially soldiers, learn to fight by the King's traditions," he explained as they practiced. "They use force against force, like stags butting heads. You want to be loose and pliable. Flow, and they will never touch you. Redirect their energy like a stream of water."

It went against her baser instincts. She wanted to brace herself for each blow, but over time, it became far more natural. Eventually she could spar with the assassin across the deck like two well-trained dancers. Each strike had a way of running into the next; each blow could be pushed aside, pulled up or down, or evaded completely. And she learned, over time, that his movement contained a rhythm. He favored certain combinations of attacks, certain patterns of the body.

"When you fight like this," he taught her, "it doesn't matter how strong or big you are. A child could defeat a giant."

*Yes,* she thought privately. *But I could never defeat you.*

At times, she caught him eyeing her with a thoughtful look. He didn't turn away when she met his eyes, but would hold her gaze with a hidden promise. *I am still here.*

# CHAPTER 9

Sora stood on deck in the pale light of dawn. Gauzy mist rose from the water of the Crown's Rush. She eagerly looked into the distance as they rounded a bend in the river. The storm clouds had dispersed several hours ago, revealing crisp, clear skies of pastel hues, from rose pink to robin-egg blue. The sun climbed over the hills to the east as they traveled downstream.

Now, in the light of dawn, the waterways were far more populated. Small riverboats skimmed the water. Fishermen chugged upstream, searching for trout or catfish. Sora's ears strained against the still air, and she thought she heard the distant tolling of a bell. Her fingers dug into the wooden railing of the ship. She held her breath in anticipation. The Dawn Seeker rounded the bend, and the City of Crowns came into view.

The city spanned both sides of the Crown's Rush. A tall sandstone wall rose up on the eastern bank, but the western bank had no such wall. Spiraling towers, chimneys and belfries stood as thick as a forest. Tiled rooftops all seemed to overlap each other, staggered like a tightly packed bookshelf. She saw taverns, street vendors, fishmongers, warehouses. Countless people walked alongside the river. The buildings were all strung together in a long row, like beads on a necklace. The western half of the city stretched on and on, disappearing into the misty horizon.

Her eyes returned to the eastern bank with its tall sandstone wall. She thought she caught a glimpse of the King's palace, but the giant towers were like pitchforks on the horizon, half-hidden by the wall. Far in the distance, she could see foothills rising up behind the city in a steep slant. Countless windmills dotted the hills. Sora had never seen so many windmills before, perhaps hundreds of them, all shapes and sizes. She stared for a long time, watching the distant wooden arms spin lazily in the wind.

"Leaves an impression, doesn't it?" Burn asked, joining her on the bow of the ship.

"Can't see much yet," she said. Her gaze returned to the crush of people on the western shore. "Why is there no wall on this side?"

Burn considered the tangled mess of buildings on the western bank.

"The city was originally built around the royal palace to the east. Eventually, the city grew until it crossed over the river. The west side is home to less attractive types, the lowest of the tiers all fighting for a place to belong. Lots of crime."

"It looks a bit run-down," she agreed. A forest of black chimneys spewed smoke into the sky.

Burn snorted. "The riverside is the nicer district," he said. "The deeper you travel, the more lawless it becomes."

"You certainly seem familiar with it."

"I'm no stranger to the lower quadrants of the city."

She glanced at him, curious. "Did you used to live here?"

He grinned disarmingly. "Anyone who lives long enough will pass through the City of Crowns."

They sailed onward. The river narrowed and widened at intervals. Silas guided their ship toward the south gate at the lower end of the city. It was the cheapest place to dock.

Eventually, Burn pointed downriver.

"See that line across the horizon?"

Sora nodded.

"That's a bridge connecting the two banks, newly constructed. It's more than a half-mile long. King Royce designed it himself. You probably already know, but he's a brilliant inventor. He also built the windmills and much of the plumbing beneath the city." Burn whistled through his long, sharp teeth. "It will be a sad day when his reign comes to an end."

Sora stared at the dark line on the horizon. The bridge crossed a narrow point of the Crown's Rush, tall enough for a five-masted vessel to pass under. She vaguely recalled hearing about it from her days as a noblewoman.

They passed under the bridge and continued to the southern docks, where the Crown's Rush expanded into a large lake. The Bath, Burn called it. Sora didn't expect the river to suddenly expand outward, becoming placid and smooth.

"At the far end of The Bath, there's a waterfall. Then the river continues to the south, branching out until it turns into Fennbog Swamp," Burn explained, and nudged her shoulder. "Sorry place that is."

Sora grinned, then her eyes returned to the eastern side of the city and the mysterious wall. Merchants had accumulated outside the southern gate on the boardwalk, their stores built of wooden posts and oilskin tarps.

"Best prepare to make land," Burn said.

Sora left the bow quickly and headed to her cabin, an excited spring to her step.

Docking the ship took twice as long as anticipated. As Silas found a vacant spot on the southern wharf to drop anchor, Sora readied herself in her room. The majority of her belongings would stay on the ship, but she made sure her blades were clean and secured to her belt. She braided her thick blond hair and washed her face. Then she tucked her humble coin purse inside her cloak.

Finally, she removed the Dark God's sacred weapons from under her bed: a rapier hilt and a spearhead. Her Cat's Eye stirred uneasily as she held them. The artifacts gave off a cold, uncomfortable energy.

Now that they were docked, Sora, Crash, Burn and Caprion would take the sacred weapons to the Temple of the North Wind. If they could speak to the High Priestess, they might be able to secure her help. Surely, the Wind Temple would believe them about the Dark God.

Meanwhile, Ferran would accompany Lori to the Healer's seminary, which was located on the other side of The Bath. She wanted to see the extent of the plague and how the Healers were treating it. Between their two parties, they were certain to uncover evidence of the Shade's presence, and perhaps track down *The Book of the Named.*

Sora wrapped the sacred weapons in a linen cloth and placed them carefully back under her cot. For now, they were safer on the boat. Then she headed out the door.

It was already past noon. Her three companions met her on the docks next to the boat. Crash and Burn took in the lead, with Sora and Caprion trailing behind. As they walked, Sora gazed about the boardwalk in wide-eyed curiosity. Countless ships of all different shapes and sizes were anchored outside the city. Caprion seemed just as curious, and kept drifting a half-inch off the ground in distraction, like a particularly buoyant leaf. She would touch his arm now and then, reminding him to walk like a human, and he would sink back down.

The river smelled much worse than Delbar's seaside port. In this area, where the Crown's Rush became slow and stagnant as it widened into The Bath, the water released a rank, noxious smell. She saw floating clumps of rotten vegetation, drowned rats and fish carcasses, old clothes, soggy wood and other debris.

"Do they throw everything in the river?" Caprion asked, appraising the water.

"Mostly," Burn said. "Don't drink it, would be my advice."

"And people do that?"

"If they're drunk or drowning."

"*Suffocating* would be more appropriate," Crash said dryly.

Sora caught Caprion's alarmed look and laughed.

"He's not serious," she reassured him. *At least, I don't think so.* She certainly wouldn't want to fall into that water.

The foot traffic became all but impenetrable when they reached the southern gates to the city. Sora noticed a dozen or so soldiers standing outside. They wore heavy suits of armor with the royal emblem of a boar's head engraved on their chest plates. As Sora watched, she saw the soldiers call out to people seemingly at random, stopping them, perhaps questioning them about their business. Some pedestrians flashed a piece of paper to the guards and then quickly walked free.

"Residency cards," Burn explained, noticing her look. "You can apply for one if you live on the east bank. They allow you to pass freely through the city gates. Otherwise, if the soldiers take notice of you, prepare for a long delay."

Luckily, all the soldiers were busy when they reached the gates. The crowds were so thick, their small group passed through unnoticed. A paved street, filled with wagons and horse-drawn carriages, stretched before them. Sora saw house servants, midwives, heavy-set merchants and baker's boys; she saw footmen and stewards in expensive uniforms, their house insignias pinned to their high collars, but no lords or ladies. *They must keep to a different district,* she thought.

In this part of the city, tall brick apartments lined the road, staggered on top of squat storefronts. The buildings looked square and utilitarian. Small waterways interrupted the streets, crossed over by footbridges. Sora found the canals charming, and she imagined them quite beautiful in the summer. Now, with murky clouds overhead, the tiny streams looked dull and gray, carrying dead branches and winter leaves.

Finally, they turned down a cobbled road called Tourmaline Street. They followed it toward the eastern side of the city, away from the Crown's Rush. Occasionally on street corners, she saw figures dressed in elaborate, billowing costumes, some in burgundy red with gold stripes, others in midnight blue with silver brocade. They wore delicately crafted porcelain masks beneath wide jesters' hats.

As Sora passed, one jester swept into a low bow.

She cast Burn a questioning look.

"A tradition in The City of Crowns," he explained. "The winter solstice festival is upon us. You'll see a lot more masked characters in the days to come. It's quite an ordeal, you know. Parades, fairs, markets, parties...."

Sora hadn't realized the festivities had already begun. Now that Burn mentioned it, she saw many storefronts decorated for the season. Some hung large wooden masks outside their doors; others dangled glass ornaments from windows. Streamers and banners adorned the sides of buildings: black for the evening sky, white for the dawn's renewal, and silver for that gray space in between, where time slowed and ghosts lingered.

A shiver of excitement ran down Sora's spine. She had always wanted to visit the City of Crowns for the winter solstice festival. Now she would finally have her chance.

As they traveled up Tourmaline Street, the buildings grew smaller and shorter, until finally Sora caught a glimpse of a domed temple arching above the city. She sucked in a short breath.

The Temple of the North Wind was built completely out of sparkling white granite. Even in the dull winter light, its surface gleamed from the countless flecks of quartz and mica crystals embedded in its surface. It was crowned by a domed roof made of shining gold. At the top of the roof spun the emblem of the Goddess, turning this way and that as a weathervane.

Perhaps even more surprising were the myriad of small, delicately shaped windmills that adorned the temple's roof. Their various twisting blades spun and twirled in the wind. Some were made of bronze, silver or copper, others gilded in gold leaf or studded with gemstones. All glinted with rainbow-hued light.

"Windmills?" Sora asked, breathless.

"Prayer wheels," Burn corrected. "The spinning blades represent the ever-changing will of the Goddess. When all of the prayer wheels spin at once, they say the Goddess has showered the city in blessings."

Sora imagined that would take a mighty blast of wind, indeed.

They walked ten more blocks before reaching the wide pavilion before the temple. As they entered the circular pavilion, Sora became aware of a growing crowd. The courtyard outside the Temple of the North Wind had been transformed into a campground. A granite wall and iron gates separated the masses from the temple itself. The city guards stood about, trying futilely to control traffic. None of the peasants seemed about to leave. Sora recognized sunburned farm types, burly trappers and fishermen. Many appeared sick. *Yes,* Sora confirmed. The plague had struck the city.

Burn came to a stop. The street traffic swirled around him like water around a boulder.

"Well," he said, his deep baritone carrying easily over the hubbub, "this isn't encouraging."

"It's just like the temple in Barcella," Sora agreed.

She remembered their visit to the Temple of the West Wind. There, she had used her necklace's ability to gain an audience with the High Priestess. She wasn't so sure that would work here. These people had a hardened look about them, and no acolytes stood at the temple gates, only glaring soldiers in heavy helms. If she and her companions caused trouble, they might be arrested.

"There must be some way...." she mused.

"I could lift us over the wall," Caprion offered.

Sora was tempted, but she ultimately dismissed the idea.

"Too many people. We'd start a riot."

They surveyed the pavilion in thought. The Temple of the North Wind had been built against the city's exterior wall, beyond which Sora could see a series of foothills. Atop those hills, a row of windmills spun idly in the wind.

She pointed to them.

"Perhaps it's less crowded behind the temple, outside the walls," she suggested. "At the very least, we can get a good look at the grounds from atop those hills."

No one offered an objection.

"I *am* curious about the windmills," Burn admitted.

After a moment, they started down an alley to the right of the temple, toward the city wall.

# CHAPTER 10

C rash led Sora, Burn and Caprion through a network of alleys to the eastern wall of the city, which separated The City of Crowns from miles of
foothills. Eventually, when they reached the wall, they found it to be fifty feet
high and impassable on foot. Sora didn't see any soldiers in this particular area.
They were probably standing guard closer to the Wind Temple.

Luckily, they had Caprion's aid. The Harpy lifted them easily over the wall
using his magic, and settled them gently on the other side—except for Crash,
whom he dropped indecorously to the ground. The assassin managed to land on
his feet, then shot the Harpy a glare.

They followed the wall until they caught a glimpse of the east gate, which led
directly to the courtyards of the Wind Temple. Sora was once again dismayed. A
battalion of peasants had besieged the east gate of the temple. She saw ox-drawn
wagons, tents, campfires and latrines. She could smell the taint of the plague on
the wind.

Countless peasants had taken up vigil on the eastern hills outside the temple
gates. Sora wondered why they were waiting. Perhaps they came to find solace
in prayer, hoping they could be healed by the grace of the Goddess alone. She
wondered how Lori and Ferran fared at the seminary, and imagined her mother
running into a similar crowd.

"Too many soldiers, too many people," Burn said. His ears sank in disappointment.

"We can't enter with so many soldiers on watch," Caprion agreed.

Crash remained silent, studying the temple.

"Perhaps if we climbed the hill, we would get a better view of the temple grounds," Sora suggested. "We might find a way to skirt around the soldiers." She waited for everyone's agreement, but no one spoke. Instead, they turned to the rolling hills.

They started walking up the long stretch of grass. The foothills were surprisingly steep, almost vertical; the lowest was almost a hundred feet high. Sparse patches of woodland grew in the trenches between the hills, fed by trickling streams of water from further up the mountain. No peasants camped this high up, where the wind easily blew away tents and fires.

It was an arduous climb. Sora kept her eyes fastened on the hill's crest, where a series of white windmills of varying sizes stood. Once they reached the peak, Sora left Burn's side and walked among the unusual structures. Some of the windmills were tall, practically the size of lighthouses, with swollen gray wood and chipped white paint. Their wooden arms were so long, they almost touched the ground. The smaller windmills stood only half the size, and appeared newer and far less weathered.

Sora surmised that the larger windmills had been used for grinding wheat, though they must have fallen into disuse a long time ago. The newer ones were more decorative, with blades fashioned from brightly painted wood.

"It's quite ingenious, really," Burn called to her. He trailed not far behind. "The windmills are tapped into underground wells. Using the force of the wind and a pulley system, they propel fresh water down to the city. I suppose that makes them more *water*-mills than windmills. "

Sora nodded, impressed. She noted the continuous wind along the hills. "So it all works naturally, like a snow runoff."

Burn grinned. "King Royce drew out the plans in his youth, and had the whole system established by the time he was thirty. A right genius, that one."

Sora looked at the windmills with a bit more interest. They weren't just decorative monuments—they controlled the water supply of The City of Crowns, and continued along the foothills as far as the eye could see.

Her gaze traveled to the northern end of the city, where she could see the white towers and bright flags of the King's palace. Even in the dim, overcast light it looked breathtaking. A river of snowmelt flowed down from the hills to the castle, and continued through the city in a wide channel until it reached the Crown's Rush. She remembered crossing the river earlier on their way to the Wind Temple. It ran parallel to the Royal Road, the main street connecting the King's palace to the West Gate.

She turned to ask Burn another question, but the Wolfy was lying in the grass a few feet away. Confusion knitted her brow. He looked asleep.

Suddenly she noticed someone standing at her shoulder. She gasped, turned, and met a pair of acidic green eyes. At first she thought of Crash, but this man was shorter, and a ragged cowl covered his face. He wore dark, frayed clothing, and strange metal gauntlets on his hands. He seemed to have materialized from nowhere.

"Who-?" she started.

The stranger grabbed her arm. His fingers found the pressure point above her elbow and dug in brutally. Then he swept her legs out from under her with a deft kick. She found herself on her knees, debilitated by the agonizing pressure on her elbow.

The man cocked his head to one side and stared at her with curious intensity. *One of the Sixth Race,* Sora thought, reeling. He must belong to the Shade.

"Pretty enough," the man finally spoke, his voice muffled by his cowl, "but unremarkable in the end, don't you think, Viper? I thought you preferred more experienced types."

Sora became aware of Crash standing a few yards away. He held his dagger tightly, a venomous look on his face.

Caprion stood over Burn's prostrate body, his wings shining.

"Release her," he called, his voice resonating with magic.

"No!" the stranger barked. His shadow darted across the ground and spread around the Harpy's feet, counteracting his power. Then he shook Sora by the arm, his grip like iron. She choked in pain.

"Fair trade, Viper. The Dark God's weapons for the girl."

"Stick to the plan, Cobra," said a new voice.

A second assassin joined his side. She was lithe and lean, her eyes narrow and menacing. A similar half-mask obscured her lower face. A long braid of black hair trailed to her waist, and a coiled bullwhip hung from her belt.

"Give me the girl," she said. "We don't have time for games."

Sora noticed several other assassins lurking in the shadow of the windmills. They were outnumbered.

Cobra didn't take his eyes off Crash.

"You may come with her if you like, Viper," he sneered. "Accompany your lover back to Cerastes. Or would you rather she go alone?"

Sora's eyes widened. She wouldn't be used as bait. The Shade couldn't gain the upper hand so quickly. She wouldn't allow it.

If she struggled, she would dislocate her shoulder, but she could bear the pain—she had done so before.

With a surge of willpower, Sora rolled away from him. Her shoulder popped as the bone slid out of place, but she used the pain to fuel her strength. She scrambled to her feet and took off through the windmills, then down the backside of the hill, skidding through the mud, away from the wind temple and the City of Crowns.

"After her!" the female assassin yelled.

Sora knew they would gain on her soon. Halfway down the hill, she plunged into a grove of pine trees. She ducked through branches and tore through wild thickets until she found a toppled tree trunk, then she crouched behind it. She drew her dagger from her belt. Her left arm might be useless, but she could still defend herself. She would not be taken by the Shade.

Crash didn't hesitate. The moment Sora rolled out of the way, he tackled Cobra and twisted him to the ground. The enemy assassin slipped through his grasp, but Crash kept him distracted long enough for Sora to escape into the forest.

Cobra released a wheezing laugh, then signaled to the female assassin. The woman darted into the underbrush, quick and nimble as a shadow. Two savants peeled away from the windmills and followed.

Crash pointed after them.

"Go!" he yelled to Caprion. "Help Sora!"

The Harpy leapt off the ground and flew down the back of the hill, faster than human legs could run. Crash could only hope he reached Sora in time—before the Shade.

Crash returned to his opponent. With a simple thought, he released the second gate and allowed his demon's strength to flex through his body. His vision flickered, adopting the demon's eyes. Now he could see Cobra's thick black aura trailing off his skin. He could taste it on his tongue.

*Mad as a wasp*, his demon murmured.

"I underestimated her tolerance for pain," Cobra said conversationally. "Did you teach her that little trick yourself? Are you *training* her? Is that your dear student, Viper?"

"What do you want with her?" Crash hissed.

"Just following orders." Cobra's voice lowered insidiously. "Nothing personal."

"She's useless to you."

"My master disagrees. He's very disappointed in your little tryst. Are you sure you won't meet with him, Viper?"

Crash's hand tightened on the dagger's hilt.

"Alright," he relented. "A new deal, then."

Cobra's eyes widened.

"I'll speak to him after I cut out your tongue."

Then Crash lunged. He aimed for the ribs. When Cobra blocked, Crash turned and jammed his elbow into his face.

Cobra stumbled, recovered, and swung his iron gauntlets. His hands moved lightning fast despite their heavy weight. Crash blocked with his forearm, but the jagged edge of Cobra's gauntlet cut into his flesh, drawing blood.

Crash grappled with the enemy assassin, locked together in a furious contest of strength. He didn't care who won the fight, so long as Sora escaped. Cobra finally broke away and tried to run into the woods, but Crash tripped him to the ground. He dragged his opponent beneath him, ready to plunge a knife through Cobra's neck.

Then, with a puff of black smoke, Cobra disappeared.

Crash's dagger sank into the frosty ground.

The fifth gate? Hairs prickled on the back of his neck. He sensed Cobra above him, ready to smash his iron fist into the back of Crash's skull.

He braced himself, unable to dodge.

Suddenly, a loud bellow shook the air. Burn charged across the grass, swinging his massive longsword.

Cobra raised his gauntlet just in time and caught the full might of Burn's blow on his forearm. His gauntlet shattered like porcelain under the Wolfy's heavy blade. Jagged chunks of metal flew off into the grass. Cobra fell down, holding his wrist tightly.

Crash regained his feet and faced the enemy assassin with Burn at his side.

Cobra stared at them, seething, his body curled around his injured limb.

"You're outnumbered," Crash said. "Give up."

Cobra's eyes traveled from the giant mercenary to Crash's solemn face.

"We'll meet again soon, Viper," he hissed. "Then we'll sort this out one-on-one...as it *should* be done."

The air wavered behind him, the shadows growing darker and thicker. Crash realized how Cobra intended to escape.

Burn, however, was a step ahead. He threw himself on Cobra's body, trying to pin the assassin to the ground, just as the black portal opened beneath them.

"No!" Crash yelled.

Burn and Cobra passed through the portal.

Instantly, it snapped shut.

Crash leapt after them, but he was too late. He landed amidst the green grass and spinning windmills. The wind gusted furiously across the hill. With a roar of frustration, he rammed his fist into the ground.

"Burn!" he yelled. "Burn! Answer me, dammit!"

But the Wolfy was gone.

Sora crouched behind the fallen tree with her dagger in hand, listening for sounds of approach.

Although she didn't hear the first assassin, she spotted his shadow flitting through the trees as he passed by. Lashing out with her knife, she caught the assassin in his upper thigh. The man grunted in surprise and went down. Sora yanked her dagger free and plunged it into the man's throat before he could twist away.

Then she sat next to the bush again, shaking with adrenaline, wondering what to do with his body.

Then the female assassin came charging down the slope, whip in hand. She unleashed a lightning- fast strike. Sora raised her good arm out of pure reflex, catching the end of the whip. It coiled around her forearm like a snake, and she was forced to drop her dagger.

With a firm yank, the assassin dragged Sora out of her hiding place. Her foot caught on a root and she fell to the ground, the female assassin continued to drag her through the mud until she sprawled at the woman's feet.

"Your first mistake was running," the woman sneered.

Then, suddenly, a bright light flared in her vision. Caprion hurtled through the trees, flying full tilt. Fierce vibrations filled the forest, pouring from his body in endless waves.

The female assassin turned, whip in hand.

Caprion barreled into her and tackled the woman to the ground. They rolled down the forested slope, over tree roots and thorny vines, to the bottom of the hill. Sora struggled to her feet and followed.

At the base of the hill, they spilled from the trees into a grassy glade. There, a fierce struggle ensued. Sora expected a cacophony of sound to fill the forest, but the Harpy and the assassin battled in complete silence. The woman abandoned her whip and drew a knife. She managed to land a wild blow on Caprion's arm, but then he grabbed her by the wrists and shoved her beneath him. The assassin moved like oil, twisting from his grasp. She broke away, scrambled to her feet and tried to run across the grassy clearing.

Caprion pulled a small, round object from his pocket, and it flared up brightly. A sunstone!

Sora's eyes widened—she hadn't known he carried one.

The Harpy lifted off and tackled the woman back to the ground. He pinned her firmly beneath him, pressing the stone to her throat. The sunstone blazed with power, and a burst of light from Caprion's wings filled the forest.

The assassin screamed.

Sora averted her gaze from the stone's brilliant light. The scream continued, the most excruciating sound she had ever heard. She covered her ears, willing it to stop.

For a minute, the forest seemed filled by summery daylight, at odds with the heavy, storm-laden sky. Then the light dimmed. The assassin's voice hitched and weakened.

Caprion ripped the mask from the woman's face. Sora couldn't see much at this distance. She stepped cautiously through the ferns and tall grass to the fallen assassin's side. Then she stared in surprise. The woman was...*young*, only a few years older than herself. Her face was badly mutilated. Long scars crossed vertically through each of her closed eyes, trailing down her cheeks like teardrops. A disgusting patch of shiny, wrinkled skin warped the side of her jaw.

Sora placed a hand over her mouth and turned away. Shaken, she tried to blink away the sight of the gruesome scars. When she looked back at the assassin, the woman's face had changed. It appeared flawless and smooth. The scars seemed to have vanished.

Sora opened her mouth, unsure of what she had seen.

Caprion knelt by the woman's side, inspecting the work of the sunstone, which was lodged at the base of the woman's throat. Sora caught a glimpse of blistered, angry flesh. She grimaced and looked away again.

She saw a familiar figure at the edge of the clearing. Crash came to a full stop when he saw the female assassin lying on the ground. Sora watched his face, looking for any sign of pity or empathy toward his own race—but his eyes remained cold.

She started toward him. He met her halfway across the small glen. His eyes searched her thoroughly. Without a word, he gently gripped her arm and guided it up until the bone slid back into place. Sora gritted her teeth the whole time, the fingers of her good hand digging into his shirt against the pain. She felt a pop as her shoulder slid into position. The pain flared, then lessened to a dull throb.

Crash ripped a piece of cloth from his cloak and helped her bind the arm in a makeshift sling. Then Sora turned back to the female assassin on the ground. Caprion still knelt next to her, taking her weapons. A small arsenal of weapons already lay in the grass: daggers, whips, and needles.

"Why would they come after me?" Sora asked Crash softly.

Crash's face remained grim. "We're about to find out." Then he approached the female assassin at the center of the clearing.

Caprion finished disarming the woman and stood over her prone body. Sora watched the Harpy closely. She couldn't figure out his expression, but it wasn't hostile. It was....

"Do you know her?" she asked, as they came to stand next to him.

He looked at her with a glimmer of surprise.

"No," he said briefly. After an awkward moment, he asked, "What shall we do with her?"

"Take her back to the ship," Crash said without hesitation. "Interrogate her."

Sora agreed. "We should move her before more come looking for her."

"They won't come."

Sora gave Crash a questioning look.

"She's expendable," he said flatly. "She's not important enough for the Shade to risk losing more men. But we can certainly use her in the meantime."

Sora hesitated. They didn't have much choice but to interrogate the woman—through her prisoner, they could finally find out more about the Shade. But how to get her back to the ship unnoticed? Sora chewed her lip in thought. Caprion would have to fly their new captive back to the ship directly. With luck, the Shade wouldn't be watching the skies. She and Crash could make it back on foot.

"Where's Burn?" Sora thought to ask, looking around the forest. She suddenly remembered him lying prone on the hillside. "Is he all right?"

Crash hesitated. "He's gone."

"What?"

"They took him."

Sora felt all her breath leave at once.

"He fell through a shadow portal," he explained. "I don't know where they went." His eyes focused again on the female assassin, "but I think we'll know very soon."

Suddenly Sora understood his coldness—his anger. She stared at Crash speechlessly, allowing the full impact of his words to settle. Burn, taken by the Shade? He was in mortal danger. *Or dead already,* she thought, with a sickening cramp in her stomach.

She abruptly grabbed a fistful of Crash's cloak. "Can't you follow them?" she demanded. "Work some spell and open another portal? We can't waste another second!"

Crash let her hang onto his cloak for a moment, then he firmly shoved her off.

"It was out of my control!" he snapped. "I can't follow them. I'm not skilled enough. I'm not...."

"We have to do something," she said. "Isn't there some way?"

Crash indicated the female assassin. "She'll have to tell us where he is."

"And she will," Caprion added. He stood up, lifting the woman in his arms. "We're not far from the docks. I will take her to the Dawn Seeker. Shall I come back and get you?"

Crash shook his head. "Too obvious. The Shade know we travel with a Harpy. They might be watching the skies to see where we take her." Then, after a pause, he announced, "We'll walk."

Sora wanted to groan in frustration. What a horrible waste of time!

"At least allow me to transport you over the city wall," Caprion said.

"That might be best," Sora agreed.

Crash relented, tucking the various whips and knives under his cloak. He hooked the long bullwhip to his belt. Then, with a few motions of his hand, Caprion's white light surrounded them. Sora felt a familiar sensation of vertigo as she was lifted into the sky.

Caprion kept low to the shelter of the treetops until he reached the wide hills, then glided smoothly to the east wall like a kite. He deposited them on the outer wall of the city and made his farewells, then carried their unconscious prisoner away over the rooftops.

Crash and Sora found a staircase leading down the other side of the wall to a narrow, winding alley. This district of Crowns belonged to the lower class. The streets were dirty and uneven. Cracked windows and chipped paint marred the low stone buildings. She caught a vague glimpse of the Temple of the North Wind, though it was half-obscured by drizzling rain and mist. The clouds seemed heavier and lower than before.

They walked for a good while in silence, Crash slightly ahead of her, his eyes endlessly scanning the decrepit buildings. He pulled his hood up as a light drizzle of rain began to fall. People averted their eyes when he passed. Sora knew why; he looked dangerous, his stride full of purpose.

Details of their fight with the Shade ran through her head. Cobra spoke to Crash as though they knew each other. *I thought you preferred the older, more experienced types.* Her nagging thoughts left her troubled.

Sora reached Crash's side and asked him, "Did you know those assassins?"

Crash's eyes shifted to her briefly. His expression became guarded.

*Of course,* she thought. "Tell me."

"They know *of* me," he answered, emphasizing his words. "But I don't know them."

Sora's frown deepened. "Did you have dealings with the Shade?"

"Of course not," he snapped, then fell silent as they passed a series of street vendors. The crowd thickened, then dispersed. "I didn't know about the Shade until you did. Have a little faith in me. You're beginning to sound like Caprion."

"Well, for good reason, I think you're hiding something. I can tell when you're lying."

He raised an eyebrow. "Can you?"

Something about his tone made Sora feel terribly self-conscious. She looked away, but she trusted her gut. She felt certain he was keeping something from her, so she tried again.

"Cobra said you prefer...more experienced types?" she asked. "Was that sarcasm...?"

"Perhaps," Crash responded dryly. "He was trying to get under your skin. Don't let him."

Sora's cheeks flushed. "It doesn't bother me!" she insisted. "But he acted so familiar toward you...."

Crash caught her hand. He paused his steps and looked at her sternly.

"I'm not part of the Shade, Sora. And I don't prefer more experienced types."

Sora didn't think she could blush any harder.

"I didn't think so."

"Then what's this about?"

"Just a terrible feeling that you know more than you're letting on."

Crash released a long sigh. Unexpectedly, he removed his cloak and settled it over her shoulders. It shielded her from the pouring rain. They continued walking.

"You can trust me, Sora," he said. "I need that trust, now that Caprion and half the Dracian crew look at me askance. The Shade will try to turn us against each other. Thanks to Caprion, that's already happening."

"And because you threw Tristan off the boat."

"You heard about that?"

"It's a large boat, but not that large," Sora said, quoting Burn from the beginning of their journey. Then she grimaced. "We have to find Burn. Perhaps Caprion can get that woman to talk...."

"I'm sure he'd rather watch me instead."

Sora's mouth twisted stubbornly. "Caprion isn't against you. He helped us escape the Matriarch—"

Crash cut her off. "Caprion has his own motives for being here. I wouldn't be surprised if the Matriarch encouraged him to travel with us. He suspects I'll lead him to the Shade."

"Well, haven't you?"

Crash didn't answer.

"And if Caprion were hunting down the Shade, that puts us on the same side."

Crash's eyes darkened. "If he distinguishes between the Shade and the rest of my kind, perhaps. But I doubt that. He's a seraph, after all. His highest calling is to destroy the Sixth Race. We shall see what side that puts him on in the end."

Sora considered his words. Seraphim were born with especially powerful magic for killing demons. Still, Caprion hadn't mentioned any plan to annihilate Crash's race. He had been friendly, if quiet, since leaving the Lost Isles. He helped around the ship where needed and kept to his own business. *Perhaps he's a little too quiet,* she thought.

She considered the sunstone Caprion used on the woman in the woods. He knew how to waylay an assassin.

Slowly, she said, "He seems dangerous, Crash."

"He is."

They turned down Tourmaline Street, an old and winding avenue that continued toward the docks. The drizzle thickened to a steady rain, and they tried to keep to the overhang of buildings. Finally, Crash flagged down a public coach.

"To the south docks," he said as he passed a few coppers into the man's hand.

Sora was relieved to be out of the rain, even if the carriage smelled like musty cigar smoke and mothballs. The coach was uncomfortably cramped. They sat face-to-face, their knees touching. She spent a minute adjusting for more room, then gave up.

"How do we rescue Burn?" she whispered. "The assassins are your kind. Don't you have any idea where they might be hiding?"

"If I did, I'd already be looking there."

"What if we can't reach him in time?"

"He's a warrior, Sora. We have to trust him to survive, just as he trusts us to find him."

His words struck her, and she felt guilty for doubting him. He wouldn't abandon Burn now, no more than he had back in Fennbog swamp or the Lost Isles. She sat back, wishing she could shake off her horrible sense of foreboding. What if they found him too late?

Silence filled the carriage as it rolled down the cobbled streets.

# CHAPTER 11

Lori's first sight of the seminary brought a familiar lump to her throat. About ten years had passed since she completed her training and achieved the elevated rank of Healer. She remembered the light smell of the river, its brisk, moist chill and the promise of snow on the wind.

She pulled her cloak tighter and waited for Ferran to finish securing his boat to the seminary's humble docks. Skiffs and fishing rigs filled the length of the boardwalk; more vessels than Lori had expected to see.

Ferran finished and joined her side.

"Ready?" he asked.

She nodded. They continued down the forested path to the seminary. She rounded a turn and caught sight of a gray tower jutting above the pines. It stretched upward until it blended with the overcast sky. She remembered the walk too well. With thick ferns and foliage on either side, it felt more like they followed a long tunnel through the wilderness.

Then the smell of smoke reached her nose—something new. She and Ferran came across a busy campground. Tents and lean-to's were spread across the road into the trees. She heard subdued coughing from every side and dim, broken sobbing.

Her steps hesitated. The seminary was a sanctuary and a center of education—a place of hope. Now the pallor of death seemed to hang over the woods. The school's stone walls looked grim and foreboding.

Lori forced herself to keep walking. *This is a dreary place,* she thought. *Not at all like I remember.*

As they neared the seminary gates, more people crossed her path. Many wore white Healer's robes, or the gray robes of novices. She even saw acolytes of the Goddess, their robes blue or purple, walking from tent to tent. The number of serfs and peasants outnumbered them ten to one.

Lori put her sleeve to her nose. Unlike Ferran, she was not immune to the plague. All of the Healers and priestesses wore gloves on their hands and handkerchiefs around their faces. She had no such protection.

"Seen enough?" Ferran asked.

Lori shook her head. "I need to speak to the headmaster. I need to warn the school. The best way to disperse the Shade's power is to expose them."

"Seems reasonable," Ferran muttered around his pick. "If you think they'll believe it."

"They'll have to." Lori surveyed the camp. How else could anyone explain this rapid spread of disease?

The seminary's wrought iron gates stood wide open before them, and they passed into the pavilion beyond. Sick patients lay on cots, stretchers and even haystacks, all moaning and coughing. She and Ferran continued to the seminary's front doors. No one stopped them. No one even looked up from their work.

Once inside, Lori looked around the flagstone landing. A twisting staircase proceeded upward to the seminary's central tower. The sick bay stood to her left, and to her right, a hallway to different classrooms. But where would she find the headmaster?

Lori led Ferran up the spiral staircase.

Three flights of stairs later, Lori found herself before a solid oak door: the headmaster's study. A series of dents and scratches marred its base, where students had vented their frustrations over the years. She remembered kicking it a time or two herself. She had stood in this very place when she first came to the seminary, homeless and looking for any sort of work: cleaning, mending or cooking....

But Headmaster Duncan had noticed her skill in the garden and how thoroughly she performed most mundane tasks. He had seen her way with people, and her potential. She owed him too much—her life, really.

She raised her hand to knock, but the sound of voices reached her first.

"It's repulsive," a clipped male voice asserted, "to have all these filthy peasants polluting our city with their disease. We must do something about it!"

"King Royce has the final say," a weary, familiar voice replied. "The nobility aren't the only ones who call this city home. Most of the lower class are visiting their families for the winter solstice. They'll leave again within a few weeks...."

"And leave the city reeking of their contagious residue? You're not so naive, Duncan. Think of the citizens who still have their health! We must shut the city gates. King Royce won't sign the decree, but perhaps, honorable Headmaster, if you spoke with him...?"

Silence. Lori waited. That clipped voice spoke again.

"You must see it's to the city's benefit. My only concern is for the strength of the Kingdom. Should King Royce himself fall ill...."

A longer silence ensued.

"I will have to think about it," the headmaster replied gravely. "Is there anything else, Lord Cedric? I have more than enough work to keep me occupied...."

A chill ran down Lori's spine. She stepped back from the door. Here, of all places—and now, of all times!

The oak door opened abruptly and she stood face to face with Lord Cedric Daniellian.

For a fleeting moment, she thought he might not recognize her.

But then his eyes narrowed.

They stared at one another. She didn't greet him, and he didn't speak. What could she say to the man who once tried to kill her?

She stepped out of the way. Lord Daniellian walked stiffly past her. His gray cloak swirled around his heels. She watched him stride down the hall. Somehow, the First Tier always appeared more vibrant than the average commoner: well dressed, polished and poised. They had the wealth to afford such things. The Daniellians were a fine-looking family, with ash-blond hair and sky blue eyes. But their pale hair matched their hearts, which ran white-cold with ice.

"Well, Cedric looks as jovial as I remember," Ferran said by her side. "Does he know you?"

Lori shrugged. "Wait here for me," she replied without explanation. Then she entered the headmaster's office.

Headmaster Duncan stood behind his desk, gathering a stack of parchment in his arms. He wore heavy white robes hemmed with purple brocade, and a gold medallion at his neck bearing the King's royal seal, which meant he now served on the royal counsel. Lori stood quietly for a moment, taking in the sight. He had aged surprisingly well over the decade since she'd last seen him. His hair, once gleaming blond, was now completely white. But it remained full and wavy, and his skin still held a healthy glow. Only his eyes were different, which looked dull and bruised from lack of sleep.

When he saw her, his face widened in recognition. Then his lips pulled into a bemused smile.

"Surprised?" Lori broke the silence.

"Of course—and not at all," he said. "Lorianne Blithe. I expected you to walk through my door at some point. I didn't think it would take this long."

"Wandered a bit far, I'm afraid."

Headmaster Duncan nodded absently. His eyes focused past her, caught by some distant memory.

Then his expression darkened. "Did Cedric see you on his way out?"

"He did."

"Well, that's an inconvenience."

Lori quelled her discomfort. Her scandal with Cedric had been long ago, but the memories seemed readily available in the room. She had been forced to flee the seminary, leaving the headmaster to sort out her mess. She wondered how much her scandal had cost him. The Daniellians were the seminary's biggest patrons. They might as well own the building, the grounds, and everyone within them.

Duncan sat back in his chair. He spoke plainly, as he always had.

"I'm glad you are well, but you've returned at the absolute worst time. You probably shouldn't have come back at all. I don't think any of the staff will remember you. Perhaps the older ones, but most are out in the field. It's a hectic time to visit."

"I'm not here to visit," she said.

"Oh?"

"I have information about this new disease."

He glanced at the small, ornate clock on his desk.

"I can spare about five minutes."

Lori considered herself lucky, and began speaking in a low tone, so as not to be heard by anyone outside the door. She began with the plague infecting the livestock near her village.

She held his attention for a full two minutes before she realized her mistake. The headmaster was human, and humans didn't believe in magic anymore. She got as far as the Shade's involvement, but at the look on his face, she didn't try to explain the Sixth Race or the Cat's-Eye stones. All too late, Lori imagined what she must look like—a Healer who, after many years of obscurity, returned with news of a rising Dark God only mentioned in storybooks. She probably sounded like a madwoman. Duncan didn't know her that well anymore. Perhaps he never had.

Lori allowed her story to dwindle to a hesitant conclusion. Hopefully Sora was having better luck at the Temple of the North Wind.

"Lorianne..." the headmaster began, "as you well know, all Healers serve the Goddess, but we must be careful of superstition. You have a sharp mind. I'm sure you're right about the disease spreading from the lower plains. But this business with gods and cults?" He shook his head. "Prayers can heal the mind, and perhaps even the body, if one is blessed, but to call this disease a curse and to say it was caused by magic...." He sighed, and the wrinkles on his face deepened.

Lori worried her lip, wondering if she should tell him about Ferran's Cat's-Eye necklace. At least that much she could prove. But the consequences could be extreme. Ferran couldn't possibly cure everyone in the seminary, and they might not let him leave. News would spread, and if the Shade caught wind....

"Headmaster, I wouldn't have traveled all this way if I wasn't certain of what I've seen."

"Even if it were all true, Lorianne, and a cult somehow caused this plague, that's not a stance the seminary can take. We are a learning institution meant to treat physical ailments. The matter of gods and curses belongs to the Wind Temple. Go there, if you are so certain."

Lorianne knew he had said his final words on the matter. She looked out the window at the courtyard below.

"How bad is it?" she asked.

Duncan removed his spectacles and cleaned them on the sleeve of his white robe.

"The worst I've ever seen. I suppose you heard Cedric harping about the city gates? He wants to close them. We might have to, if this illness endangers the King."

"Is it very bad in the city?"

"Not yet, but worsening. Especially now, with the winter solstice festival and so many visitors. We are trying to contain the infected areas. Most are on the west bank." He said *west bank* with a familiar sort of distaste. "Some of our patients come from farmlands farther south. They say the illness spread from their livestock, which is worrisome."

"Rare, that a disease travels from animals to humans," Lori agreed.

"Aye," he muttered. "It makes me wonder if the livestock aren't the culprit at all. Perhaps it came from the plants, which means it came from the soil. It could be in our food supply."

Lori sat back. She hadn't considered that. "Harvest season just passed...."

"Yes, and all of our food might be contaminated. If the Kingdom's soil is tainted with this disease, well, who knows how far it has spread, and from what region. Seeds fly faster on the wind than an ox on foot. We might very well be looking at the end of the human race."

The weight of his words seemed to darken the room.

"There is still hope," Lori said.

"Goddess willing," Duncan sighed. He looked very tired. "Was there anything more you needed, Lorianne? I have much to do."

"Ah...."

"I can't offer you housing, I'm afraid. The Daniellians are still our most generous patrons. We've moved past your little incident, but I won't defend your name. In a time like this, to lose their funding...."

Lori held up her hands. "I wasn't asking to stay."

Duncan seemed relieved. "Well, the Goddess has Her eye on you, I'm sure. You'll find housing in the city. But I'd stay away from The Regency and far from Cedric Daniellian while you're here. He is not a forgiving man."

Lori rose from her chair.

"Headmaster," she said, and bowed formally.

"Healer," he said, "good day."

She let herself out of the study.

Lori rejoined Ferran in the hallway. She shook her head at his curious expression. "I'll tell you outside."

She started down the staircase in a dismal mood. Their trip to the seminary felt like a complete waste of time. The Healers weren't going to help them, and she had her doubts about the Wind Temple. They ministered to so many superstitious types, they might not take her seriously, either.

Even worse, Cedric Daniellian had seen her face-to-face. As she went down the spiraling staircase, her mind jumped ahead to the gated pavilion. Was he out there, waiting for her? Could he hold a grudge for so long? From what she had witnessed among the nobility, and by Headmaster Duncan's own warning, she believed the answer to be yes.

When she reached the bottom of the stairwell, Ferran touched her shoulder unexpectedly. She jumped.

"Steady now. You're gnawing a hole through your lip," he said.

Lori looked around the flagstone foyer. Her eyes landed on an oak door that led to the seminary's rear gardens.

"Do you think Cedric is still on the grounds?" she asked.

"Most likely," Ferran said. "His family crest is stamped all over the building, and I think I saw his pleasure craft anchored at the docks."

"You don't think he's waiting outside, do you?"

Perhaps it was her tone of voice, or the way she glanced at the door, but Ferran took her chin in hand and forced her to meet his eyes.

"What's wrong?"

"I knew Cedric once, long ago. We have a history." She had worked at the Daniellian household for a year before running for her life. She hated even the memory of it. Surely Lord Cedric would have forgotten by now? Surely, she was being paranoid?

"Best to avoid him, I think," she said, pulling away.

Ferran studied her for a moment longer. "I'll do whatever makes you comfortable."

They left through the oaken door, down a short hallway, and out into the gardens. This part of the seminary was beautifully cultivated and landscaped with herb gardens, pumpkin patches, apple trees and blueberry bushes, not to mention countless rows of flowers, all turned a muted brown by winter frost. Unlike the rest of the grounds, it was blessedly empty.

Lori followed a familiar path through the garden. She remembered the cracked flagstones and the dormant apple orchard. The pumpkin patch was new, and the blueberries, and the garden shed.

She had been studying at the seminary when she first met old Lord Daniellian, Cedric's father. Most First Tier families employed Healers, but the positions were difficult to land. After her graduation, Headmaster Duncan recommended her to a place in their house.

The job had been a blessing at first, before she caught Cedric's eye. For months, he had tried to force her into his bed. Lori had refused him, even when he offered her gold, even when he offered her a house. She knew what happened to servants who slept with noble sons. If they were ever found out, she would be sent away, penniless and ruined.

She had evaded Cedric as best she could. But eventually, he grew spiteful. And eventually, he took his revenge.

She and Ferran reached the rear wall of the seminary and passed through a garden gate into the pine forest. Lori felt calmer under the trees. She wondered if she was overreacting. She had left the city years ago, time enough for old grudges to die, and the past to be laid to rest. Surely, Cedric wouldn't go to this much trouble to find her. Surely, he had better things to do.

# CHAPTER 12

Lori sucked in a quick breath when she caught sight of the docks. Lord Cedric Daniellian stood at the seminary's small marina, accompanied by his footman. The two men scanned the road, obviously waiting for someone's approach. *Her* approach.

"Bells," she muttered, watching them through the trees.

Ferran shoved his hands in the pockets of his greatcoat. "Waiting for you, I assume?"

Lori resisted the urge to cringe. She was a strong woman now, not that scared girl who fled the seminary. She would have to confront Cedric if they were to leave these docks.

"Let's get this over with," she said with resignation.

Coming out of the forest, Cedric saw them immediately. His light blue eyes targeted her like a hawk sighting prey. Then a charming smile split his face.

"Lorianne Blithe," he said endearingly. "Healer Lorianne. Lori. I wasn't sure I recognized you."

*Liar,* she thought.

"Then again, I'm not quite sure how I should address you, seeing as you've revoked your vows. What does that make you now? A peasant? A handmaid? A servant girl?"

Lori bit her lip. So that's how Duncan had settled this business—by making her disappearance seem more like a banishment. He had lied to protect her, of course. She had never revoked her vows as a Healer.

"What brings you back to the city?" Cedric said. He hadn't glanced once at Ferran.

"Winter solstice," she said briefly. "I didn't expect to see you here."

Cedric spread his arms. "Here? At the seminary? Why, this place is practically my home. I guess the same could have been said for both of us, once." His smile tightened.

The words hung between them, intentionally blunt.

Lori raised her chin a notch. "I assumed you and Headmaster Duncan worked everything out. Why dredge up the past? I've paid my dues."

"To whom?" Cedric murmured. "Certainly not to my family. You abandoned your post while my grandmother lay dying."

Lori couldn't believe her ears. A wave of heat crept up her neck.

"You forced me to leave," she began, outraged, "with all your hounding and harassment!"

"You brought it on yourself. You liked it, as I recall."

Lori's hands curled into fists.

"Easy," Ferran murmured.

"A Healer would never abandon a patient unless forced to! You tried to have me killed!"

"I wouldn't know anything about that."

Lori saw red. She took a threatening step forward, only to find Ferran blocking her path.

"Enough, Cedric," he said, standing between them. "Leave the woman alone. We're leaving the seminary now. Get out of our way."

Cedric's pale blue eyes turned upon Ferran for the first time. His lip curled in disgust.

"Riffraff. How dare you address me without my title! I'll have you thrown in the stocks for such disrespect!" He turned back to Lori. "And this wench can be sold to a whorehouse for the debt she owes me. She'd make a far better Healer on her knees."

Ferran lunged without warning. In two steps, his heavy knuckles connected squarely with Cedric's jaw.

Lori gasped.

Cedric collapsed. Ferran fell on top of him and began pummeling his face. Cedric's footman got hold of Ferran's arms, but Ferran threw him off with a heave of his wide shoulders.

The servant recovered quickly. Lori saw him reach for his belt. A knife glinted.

"Ferran! Watch out!" she exclaimed. She grabbed the footman's wrist and tried to twist the knife from his hand. They tripped over Ferran and Cedric in the process and fell together to the ground. Then the fight dissolved into chaos. Lori tried to find the hand holding the knife, but there were so many twisting limbs and bodies....

Suddenly a massive force struck her in the back. The impact stole her breath. She rolled away from the fight, then lay on the docks, stunned.

The fighting and tussling went on for a moment longer. Then Ferran disentangled himself from Cedric and stood up.

Lord Daniellian lay on the ground. Bruises covered his face and his nose was bleeding. He looked halfway dazed. His manservant knelt by his side and began dabbing the blood with a handkerchief.

"The city guard will hear about this," his servant spat.

"You can count on it!" Lori wheezed. "You stabbed me!"

"As I recall, Lord Cedric was attacked by a highwayman and a whore. I was defending my lord's life!"

"Oh, shut it," Ferran said. Then he crossed to Lori's side. She tried to sit up, but the muscles along her back were too stiff. Soon, she would feel the pain.

"Come," he said, after inspecting her wound. He gently slid his arms underneath her and lifted her from the ground. She ground her teeth. As her body shifted, she felt a deep, burning sensation where the knife had penetrated her back. Luckily, it had missed her lungs.

"Rub salt in his wounds. They'll heal faster!" she called over Ferran's shoulder as he carried her away.

Then a nauseating wave of pain tore through her. Her hands flew to Ferran's neck and she held on tightly. His steps quickened along the boardwalk back to his boat.

She realized he was speaking to her.

"Stubborn woman, no common sense. Can't believe you attacked Lord Cedric in plain daylight. That stab wound should be mine, and you should be the one carrying me back to the boat."

"You threw the first punch."

Ferran gave her a severe look. But he couldn't sustain it.

"As I recall, I was defending your honor against a cad."

Ferran boarded his houseboat without another word about Cedric Daniellian. He placed her on his cot, forcing her to sit up, then covered her lap in a blanket.

"Stay warm. Don't lie down. Wait here as I move the boat."

Then he left her side.

Lori faded in and out of awareness, her back throbbing. Her head spun with different remedies to ease her pain and treat her wound. She tried to bundle it all in order, but it was hard to focus.

*Stop the pain first... no, staunch the blood, then stitches... no, draw the knife out... disinfect... boil water...we have to sterilize a needle....*

Ferran returned to her side after an undesignated amount of time.

"Where are we?" she mumbled.

"Safely away from the seminary," he said. He grabbed a bottle of whiskey from beneath the cot and took a swig of it before passing it to her. "Drink."

Lori fumbled with the bottle for a moment. "I hate this stuff," she said. "It smells disgusting."

"Don't whine." He forced the bottle to her lips, making her drink.

She choked as the fiery liquid hit the back of her throat, and her muscles tensed. Then, as warmth arrived in her empty stomach, her body relaxed. The pain eased. She took another swig and pushed the bottle away with a groan. The bitter taste was still in her mouth.

Ferran corked the bottle and placed it next to the cot. Then he stripped off his white shirt, which was stained by her blood, to reveal his defined torso. Lori stared. His upper body was a flat board of solid muscle. He stood straight and narrow, tight as a longbow. A red phoenix tattoo stretched its wings across his chest.

Lori drank in the sight, unabashed. It was more potent than the whiskey.

Ferran noticed her blatant stare and a wry grin came to his lips. He flexed his shoulders. Lori's mouth opened in distraction.

Then he outright laughed. "One stab to the back and your walls crumble, hm? If I'd known, I would have done this sooner."

"It's the shock and the whiskey," she said, but continued to stare.

"Look as long as you want. It's not the first time I've caught you." He winked, then took her shoulders in his big hands and pushed her gently over, onto her stomach.

She gasped, the pain shattering the moment. Tears filled her eyes. Ferran wrapped his shirt around the knife's blade and pressed hard against the wound.

"You're too rough!" she snapped.

"And you're whiny."

"This is your fault, you know!"

"And you should have stayed out of the way!"

They fumed at each other for a moment, then Ferran reclaimed his patience.

"Do you need a stick to bite down on?" he asked, his own teeth gritted. He didn't let her answer, but handed her a long, twisted cinnamon stick from a box he kept near the stove.

Lori put it between her teeth, focusing on the harsh, spicy flavor. It cleared her mind—just enough to realize what he intended to do. *No!* she thought suddenly. *Wait!*

He set his hand firmly on the knife, then carefully drew it out. It made a soft, sucking sound as it left her flesh. He was rougher than she would have liked—clearly, he didn't have the delicate touch of a medic. But he worked confidently and quietly, keeping pressure on the wound.

When he finished, he placed the blade beside her so she could see it: about six inches long, short and elegant, suited to a footman. Judging from the line of dark blood, it sunk halfway into her flesh before jamming against a wall of rib and muscle.

Ferran threw his blood-soaked shirt aside, then grabbed one more from under the cot and pressed it down on the wound.

"My last tunic," he said, noticing her glance. "You owe me."

She would have grinned, but she could barely draw her next breath. Her body's natural defenses took over, and she felt her head slowly drift out of her body.

Ferran tore open her shirt, baring her back. He took a swig of whiskey, then splashed a large amount of whiskey onto the wound. Lori chomped down on the cinnamon stick. He held her firmly pinned to the cot, his strong arm across her shoulders. She groaned and forced herself to relax, submitting to the torment, and pressed her face against the rough material of the cot.

Then he lifted her hand and pressed the bundled shirt into her fist.

"Can you hold this against the wound?" he said. "I need to light the stove."

Lori summoned her willpower and, with massive effort, she did so. Her arm shook; her limbs felt heavy and useless.

Ferran lit the pot-bellied stove inside the cabin. As the coals heated, he drew a knife from his belt, rinsed it off in a bucket of water and held the blade inside the stove's iron furnace.

As Lori watched, she frowned, then dropped the cinnamon stick from her mouth.

"You're not....You're not going to...that's barbaric, I refuse! Take me back to the seminary!"

"And back to Cedric? He'll have a whole squadron of guards looking for you by now. We need to stop the bleeding, and I have no skill with a needle."

Ferran's face was drawn and tense, but when he met her eyes, his gaze softened.

"Consider yourself branded."

Lori snorted, then winced. "You're going to brand me? Like a cow of the Ebonaire estate?"

Ferran laughed, a short, ironic sound. "I'm disowned," he reminded her. "You'll be a poor cow belonging to a red-blooded scoundrel. But I'll treat you well. We'll roam the greenest pastures and wander wherever we like."

"Sounds lovely."

"It will be." He turned back to the stove. "Just keep thinking about that green, green grass."

She barely caught his words, and couldn't think of a response anyway. Her strength drained through the cot into the floorboards of the houseboat. She closed her eyes and focused on keeping pressure on the wound.

A minute or so later, she sensed him return to her side. He put the cinnamon stick back in her mouth. Her arm fell limply over the edge of the bunk. She couldn't prepare herself—she was too exhausted. She tried to focus on the taste of cinnamon.

Ferran sat across her legs, holding her body down to the best of his ability.

"Usually this is a two-man job," he explained. "Try not to move."

She bit down on the stick and braced herself.

Burning hot metal pressed into her flesh.

She screamed. The sound tore from her throat. Her ears rang, and her vision blurred. If Ferran hadn't been holding her down, she would have shot straight off the cot.

He pressed the searing hot blade against the wound for a few seconds, then withdrew it. He waited, inspecting his work, then repeated the procedure.

To Lori, each touch of the hot blade seemed to last for hours. Her muscles bunched and twisted. Ferran waited as each fit passed, cautious not to reopen the wound.

Finally Lori's senses dimmed, and she stopped feeling anything at all.

# CHAPTER 13

S ora stood in the cargo hold of the Dawn Seeker. As her eyes searched the wide space, she wondered if it would be secure enough to hold their new captive. Dense shadows obscured half the room beyond the light of Caprion's wings. Above her head, she could hear footsteps treading back and forth as various Dracians strode to and from their cabins to the mess hall. If the assassin got loose, there were no bars to hold her, no locks and no doors.

Caprion deposited the woman's body on the wooden floor planks, then stepped back. Sora noticed the way his eyes lingered on their prisoner. She wondered, again, if he knew her.

After a moment of silence, she asked, "Now what?"

"Now we get answers," Crash said. His words sounded brutal.

She hesitated. They hadn't broached the subject of the woman's interrogation during the coach ride.

"You don't intend to torture her?" she asked.

"What else would you suggest?" he said coldly.

Thoughts of Burn filled Sora's mind, causing her cheeks to flush with anger. She wanted to know if he was still alive, and where the Shade had taken him. She didn't know if this assassin could tell them, but so far she was their only source of information.

Still, Sora didn't know if she could stand to watch the prisoner being tortured.

"Look," Caprion said, drawing their attention. He knelt over the woman, and his hand hovered over the sunstone. "Do you see the way the light fades? She doesn't have a demon. So we don't need the stone."

"How is that possible?" Sora asked, surprised.

"She must have run into Harpies before," Caprion mused. "Given enough time, a sunstone can remove a demon from an assassin's body. It works similarly to a Cat's Eye in that sense. The demon will become trapped within the rock."

Sora frowned. In the Crystal Caves, she had learned that Cat's-Eye stones were formed from sunstones. Over countless centuries of resisting the magical friction of the ocean, shards of sunstone formed into Cat's Eye, absorbing the ocean's powerful energy so it wouldn't split apart the earth. That friction was the source of magic.

"It's not a pleasant thing to witness," Caprion added. "Ensnaring a demon, I mean."

Sora thought of the woman's scars, now invisible.

"The sunstone keeps her immobile," Crash pointed out.

"Yes, but so would a firm rope, and the rope would be less painful," Caprion said.

"Do you really have no pity for her?" Sora asked Crash. "A month ago, you were imprisoned with such a stone at your throat. Your voice still hasn't healed. Don't you care if she's in pain?"

"They have Burn, Sora."

She opened her mouth, then stopped. He had a point. The Shade wouldn't show Burn any mercy; they were the enemy. Still, she hated the sight of the woman's blistered flesh.

"How can you be so indifferent toward your own people?" she asked softly.

"The Shade are not my people." Crash's eyes fell scornfully to the woman. "For all the pain she's inflicted on others, I'm sure she can stomach this."

Sora shifted her weight uncomfortably.

"I'm going to remove the stone," Caprion interrupted. Not waiting for Crash's objection, he reached down and gripped the stone firmly with his fingers. He pried the stone from the woman's flesh. She groaned.

"Tie her hands," Caprion said.

Crash took a length of rope and quickly bound the woman's hands behind her back. Sora watched. The woman didn't look capable of fighting back, but perhaps it was an act. The Sixth Race were skilled at deception.

Once he secured their prisoner, Crash returned to Sora's side. They watched Caprion pull the woman up into a sitting position. He gripped her firmly by the shoulders. Her head lolled, but Sora saw her eyelids flicker. She was conscious.

Light shimmered around Caprion's body. Sora saw the ghosts of wings protrude from his back. His magic vibrated through the room, causing her skin to prickle. She noticed Crash draw in a slow breath as his hands tightened into fists. She knew this couldn't be comfortable for him.

When Caprion spoke, his voice reverberated with power.

"Your name," he commanded.

Sora felt her own throat tighten in reply. She touched her necklace. With a slight jingle of bells, she felt the Cat's Eye respond. Green light encased her skin, shielding her from the Harpy's magic.

"Tell me your name."

The woman stiffened in his arms. When she opened her eyes, Sora saw primal terror on her face, more fear than she could fully comprehend.

"I have no name," she whispered.

Crash folded his arms.

"What do they call you?" Caprion rephrased the question.

"Krait," she said hoarsely.

"Are you a member of the Shade?"

"Yes."

"Where does the Shade keep their prisoners?"

The woman's jaw clamped shut in resistance. Caprion moved his right hand to clasp her throat. Sora cringed. Considering the woman's burns, his grip must be painful.

"Tell me," Caprion intoned.

"My master—my Grandmaster," the woman choked. A trickle of blood fell from her lips. "He saved me."

Sora felt mildly impressed. The assassin's loyalty was so strong, she would not give up any information, even under Caprion's thrall. She glanced at Crash, but he stared at the woman without pity.

"Does your master have *The Book of the Named?*" Caprion asked.

Krait shuddered. "Yes."

"Why is he in The City of Crowns? Why does he want the sacred weapons?"

Krait didn't respond. Caprion's grip tightened slightly.

"I don't know," she murmured.

"Tell me."

"I don't know!" Suddenly the assassin's composure broke. Her expression changed. Vicious hatred twisted her features. "I'll kill you!" she shouted, writhing violently, trying to slip free of her bonds. "I'll cut off your wings, you bastard Harpy! I'll gouge out your eyes! I'll rip out your throat—agh!"

Caprion restrained her arms. His wings brightened until even Sora was forced to look away.

"Stop," Crash said.

Caprion's light dimmed marginally.

"I want to know—is she of the Hive?"

Caprion repeated the question.

The woman growled. "Harpies took me from the Hive."

Crash's expression turned thoughtful. "After you won your Name?"

Krait's head whipped back and forth. "My master gave me my Name."

Crash took a step closer, staring down at her.

"You're an impostor," he said. "You never earned your Name."

"No!" she moaned. "No, you lie!"

Crash smirked. Sora didn't expect such an expression from him. She grew cold watching him. This was not Crash; this was Viper. She could see it in his eyes.

"Why does your master want Sora?" Crash asked.

Caprion repeated the question. Krait shuddered and convulsed, then spat, "I don't know!" Her body stiffened, her face contorting with pain.

"The more you resist, the more you will hurt yourself," Caprion said softly.

"I don't care! I'll die before telling you—agh!" The woman convulsed again. Then she spat out, "He has the third wraith. He wants the last sacred weapon."

Tension ran throughout the room. Crash and Sora shared an alarmed look.

"What's a wraith?" Caprion asked, and glanced at Crash.

"We'll explain later," Sora said. "Ask her where her master hides."

Caprion did so. Krait twisted on the ground, but the Harpy's compulsion was too strong.

"In the city. I don't know where—agh!"

"Answer me," Caprion asserted.

The growl that came from her throat contained two words: "The Regency!"

Sora's eyes widened. "The Regency," she echoed. The private district of the city where the upper tiers lived. Her stepfather had stayed there before his death. But why would the leader of the Shade live there among the highest tiers? Was Burn there now?

"Ask her about Burn. He went through a shadow portal after Cobra. Where did he go?"

Caprion began to ask, but the woman cut him off.

"I don't know. Anywhere. He's probably dead," she croaked.

"No!" Sora rushed forward, but Crash caught her arm and held her back. "No! Where is he, you liar!"

A grotesque, choking laugh issued from the assassin's throat. "Cobra killed him. Your friend is dead. His neck was slit, his eyes plucked out, his teeth pulled from his head—"

"Don't listen," Crash said, and dragged Sora back. "She's lying. She can't know that. She's trying to provoke you."

Krait turned to Caprion. "Kill me now, Harpy. I'll happily die in service to my master."

Caprion looked repulsed. "What's become of you?" he asked.

Bound by the Harpy's voice, the woman answered, "By my master's will, my eyes were returned to me. I am a hand of the Dark God and will serve my master without fail!"

Caprion released the woman and turned to them. "It's pointless to continue this," he said.

Sora crossed her arms. "We don't have any answers yet."

"We know enough. The wraith. The Regency." Caprion gave Crash a solemn stare. "We will discuss everything tonight with Silas and his crew."

Crash nodded. He took Sora firmly by her arm and escorted her up the narrow stairs to the deck. Sora tried to pull away.

"If she wants to die so badly, you should let her!" she snarled over her shoulder. The thought of Burn's likely death filled her with helpless fury. "She deserves it!"

"Where's your moral high ground, Sora?" Crash asked dryly. "Perhaps you should recover it."

"Those bastards are going to kill Burn! How can you be so calm?"

Crash opened the latch to the upper deck and lifted her through it.

"I'm not calm," he said.

"Yes, you are!" she fumed.

Crash released her and they faced each other in the galley. Afternoon light filtered through a small porthole window at her back. Rain spattered against the deck above, thrumming hard and steady.

Sora planted her feet firmly on the galley floor. "We need to go back and question that woman until her throat is too bloody to speak!"

"Punishing her won't save Burn," Crash snapped. "Let Caprion work on her. Listen to reason. She wants us to kill her. Then she won't betray the Shade. Don't you see?"

Sora glared at him. She felt trapped. They needed to save Burn, but she had no idea where to start.

She spun on her heel and headed out the galley, through the mess hall and onto the outer deck. Rain fell hard against the wooden planks. A scant handful of sailors loafed about on the rigging, cloaked and hooded against the storm.

Sora dashed through the rain back to her cabin. Shadows engulfed her as she went below deck. Thoughts of Burn's injured body kept rising in her mind. She had seen so much violence since leaving her manor, she could easily imagine what the Shade might do to him. And all she could do was sit around and ask questions? It wasn't enough.

Caprion knelt above the female assassin. She glared up at him, blood leaking from the corners of her mouth. He knew that mouth, just as he knew her jawline, nose and ears. But her eyes were different, filled with malice, not as he remembered.

"You know me," he said.

She spat at him. "I know you're a sick winged bastard!"

"Do you remember the city of Asterion? The Lost Isles?"

She writhed against her bonds. "Cut me loose and I'll show you what I remember!"

Caprion gazed at her impassively.

"Tell me," he repeated. In his younger days, he would have abhorred the use of voice-magic to manipulate a prisoner's mind. But he was not so idealistic anymore, and she was nothing like the fragile girl he remembered.

Krait's body convulsed, resisting him, but he placed his hand over her chest. "*Tell me what you remember*," he pressed.

Her jaw worked. Her eyes fluttered. "They took me," she rasped. "They stole me from the Hive. The light!" A soft wail issued from her throat, a scream from long ago. "They held me in their prisons...they took my demon...agh!" She cried out again and thrashed her head from side to side. "Stop the voices!"

Caprion placed his hand on her forehead to calm her. Krait's eyes fluttered back and forth, trapped by some invisible memory.

"What else?" he asked.

Her eyes focused on his face. He thought he saw some flicker of emotion other than fear...but it vanished.

"No!" she cried. "No—what they did to me—I can't remember!" She clamped her jaw shut, grinding her teeth together. Her eyes rolled up toward the ceiling.

Caprion sat back, filled with doubt. He had known a young girl once, one of the Sixth Race, trapped on the Lost Isles. But she was long dead. Perhaps he was seeing a ghost.

This woman's memory was badly damaged, no doubt stripped from her the same day they stole her demon. He found it surprising that she had survived the experience. Most of the Sixth Race did not.

He felt an old, familiar sickness when he thought of what his race had done. The farther he traveled from the Lost Isles, the more pronounced that sickness became. The Harpies were no better in their cruelty to the Unnamed than the humans were to livestock. In fact, the sheer brutality of the human city astounded him. The incivility of it all, how men preyed upon men. But his race had no higher sense of morality, no greater claim to mete out justice.

He placed both hands on either side of her head. She twisted away, but he pinned her down with his knee on her stomach. He tried to be gentle, but her resistance made it difficult.

He had to know.

"Think back," he said, his voice swelling with the force of his magic. "I want you to remember all of it."

She coughed, her body shuddering. "The light..." she moaned. "Please...no more...."

"*Remember me*," he intoned.

She gasped brokenly. "I don't," she whispered. "Please, I don't know you."

She weakened. He felt the strength drain from her body. She fell back on the floor, unconscious.

Caprion released her and sat by her side. He rested his hand on her stomach, feeling her chest rise and fall with each shallow breath. Most of her memories had been stripped away by someone stronger than he. Whoever had blocked her memories, their command still lived inside Krait's body, even after so many years. Could it have been the Shade? How else had they tampered with her mind? She didn't seem at all like the girl he had once known, even if he recognized her face.

*This is folly,* he thought. Perhaps *he* was the one who didn't remember. Perhaps he was so desperate to see her again that he imagined this woman looked like her....

*Now what?* he thought. She was his prisoner, and for the time being, he would have to keep her in the cold, dank underbelly of the ship. How else could he restrain her? He would do his best to provide small comforts. Meals. Blankets. But he couldn't release her back to the Shade.

*Moss,* he thought. He remembered her well: the young girl he had met in the dungeons of the Lost Isles. He remembered her face in the dark when they chose her name. He remembered defending her against his race.

And he remembered the Matriarch's words when Moss died. *This is your fault. You should have kept away.*

Had the Matriarch deceived him? It wouldn't be the first time. Perhaps he was a blind fool, seeing a connection that didn't exist. Krait didn't bear Moss's scars. Her face was clean and clear, her eyes full of vision. Perhaps he was simply trapped by his past, clinging to the dream of a now-impossible future. *She's a demon*, the Matriarch's words rang in his mind. *You overstepped your bounds.*

He stood up. He turned from Krait's prone body and walked from the room. Whoever she was—Moss or Krait, or someone yet unnamed—he would not abandon her again.

# CHAPTER 14

L ori roused slowly from a deep, exhausted sleep, awakened by her own discomfort. She didn't know how much time had passed, only that it was night
outside and torrents of rain were lashing the window. The ship's stove burned
low and a single, small lantern lit the cabin.

She lay on her stomach on the cot, listening to the raindrops tap against the
wooden shingles above her. Her wound throbbed. She shifted and winced. Her
body felt unimaginably heavy.

"Ferran," she muttered, her throat hoarse. "*Ferran.*"

A body stirred on the floor next to her. Ferran sat up and ran a hand through
his mussed hair, dimly illuminated by the light from the stove.

"Ferran," Lori repeated.

"What?"

"Water."

The treasure hunter climbed to his feet, stretching as much as he could in the
cramped space. He stepped outside and brought back a heavy wooden jug. It
sloshed visibly, splashing a little on the floor. Fresh rain water. Lori licked her dry
lips at the sight.

"Here," Ferran said, and put a hand under her, helping her to sit up. Lori
moved in small, painful increments. She held the quilt tightly against her bare torso, clamping it under her arms like a towel, to retain some decency. She couldn't
stand to lean back and allow her wound to touch the wall. The burn was covered

by a light, airy bandage. She could feel a sticky salve on her skin. *Not bad,* she thought. Ferran had obviously tended several stab wounds over the course of his life.

He sat next to her and held the heavy jug of water up to her lips, allowing her to drink. The shift of position pulled against her back. She winced. First thing in the morning, she would send him to the Dawn Seeker for poppy extract to dull the pain.

She finished, and he lowered the water jug to the floor. Then he lifted a bottle of whiskey from under the cot. He took a swig from it. The smell assaulted Lori's nose, reminding her of the ordeal.

"Well? How do you feel?" he asked.

"Exhausted."

"And the wound?"

"Painful, what do you think?"

He gave her a rather charming look, then held up the whiskey bottle. "Best cure I know," he said. "Relaxes muscles, too."

Lori considered it. She didn't like to drink. But the muscles of her back felt tight enough to snap. She doubted she could fall asleep again like this. Finally she reached for the bottle and gave him an exasperated look, then plugged her nose and took several deep swallows. The liquid burned at the base of her throat, then settled into her belly, spreading a warm glow throughout the core of her body. On an empty stomach, the drink immediately went to her head, and she felt her shoulders slump, her back ease immediately. After the first two sips, the taste became less overpowering, and she kept drinking until Ferran pulled the bottle away.

"Slow down, Healer," he said dryly, then took his turn.

Lori felt lightheaded. She allowed herself to relax into his shoulder, a much better alternative than pressing her back against the wall. Ferran corked the bottle after a moment and set it back on the floor, then turned, allowing her to lie more fully against him.

"That's better," he said, running his hand over her hair. He had large palms, dry and warm, with long fingers and thick, heavy knuckles.

She glanced up to find him watching her. The dim light turned his eyes the color of wet stone, as gray and muted as the storm outside. His brown hair hung loosely across his brow. He looked roguishly handsome.

"Did you break your nose once?" she asked, noting the slight crook in it.

He raised an eyebrow. "Do you ever stop diagnosing people?"

"I never noticed before."

He shrugged uncomfortably. "I was fifteen. Got in a fistfight with Richard LeCroy. 'Little Dicky,' we used to call him. He broke my nose—and I broke his arm." Ferran wrinkled his nose slightly, as though testing it. "Our family Healer set it. Made sure it grew straight."

Lori nodded. Most First Tier families kept an in-house Healer. Some had several, depending on the number of sick relatives. She had once hoped to land such a position after graduating from the seminary...but it hadn't turned out that way.

The crook in Ferran's nose was barely noticeable—just enough to add to his rapscallion appearance. The Healer had done a good job.

"How about you?" he asked. "Where did you get those scars on your torso?"

Lori flinched. She hadn't thought about them in a long time. "Someone tried to kill me a long time ago. They failed."

"Obviously."

"I mean, I got them first."

His frown deepened.

"I don't think I killed them," Lori continued, the words slipping out uneasily. "Maybe I did. I ran before I could check."

"I imagine you didn't run far, judging by the scars."

"No, I didn't." She had never bled so much in her life. A slow, sick feeling began to rise within her at the memory. "I don't want to talk about it."

"Hm," Ferran murmured. He turned to face her fully, settling his back against the wall of the cabin. He placed his hands on her shoulders and pulled her closer. It took her a moment to realize what he was doing.

"Ferran..." she started, but didn't stop him. He drew her forward, draping her across his chest over the soaring phoenix tattoo. The smell of him tickled her nose: cinnamon, whiskey and old leather; the peppery tinge of sweat. In this position, his body stretched around her like a kingdom all its own, a terrain of strong limbs, wide shoulders, and sweeping collarbones. She slowly relaxed, her stomach pressed against his. She rested her head on his chest and listened to his heartbeat.

"You planned this all along," she said, too warm and comfortable to really care.

"Can you blame me?" His deep voice reverberated beneath her ear.

"It's hard," she murmured, "living alone as a woman. You can't trust people the same way. There aren't many good men out there."

Ferran snorted. "Aye," he agreed. "And there aren't many good women, either."

"Says a man who sleeps with whores."

He glanced down at her reproachfully, and she felt ashamed at her words. He almost looked hurt.

"What happened to you, Lori?" he asked. Usually he said it as a joke, but this time he meant it.

She bit her lip, thinking back to the day of her stabbing in the City of Crowns. She curled her hands on his chest and remained silent, unable to find the words.

"Whatever happened between us, Ferran?" she asked instead, changing the subject. "Why did we part ways?" *So many things could have been different.*

His hand traveled from her hair to the back of her neck, massaging her absently. "I set you up with Lord Fallcrest, just like you wanted. And then I left."

She tilted her head to better meet his eyes.

"Why did you do that?" she asked. "I mean, if you were an Ebonaire all along, why not just...."

"Shower you in bags of gold? Or marry you and ride off into the sunset?"

Lori winced. "No, I didn't mean...I know that's absurd, you were disowned, and we weren't...."

"Can't say I didn't think about it," he admitted, his eyes roving up to the ceiling in thought. "I should have for Dane. He asked me to look out for you. The honest truth, Lori, is that I was a selfish young bastard. I didn't know how to take care of a woman and a baby. And I knew you wouldn't have me either way."

Lori blinked, surprised by his honesty.

"Oh," she muttered. She had had no idea Ferran felt this way. After Dane's death, she had never considered marrying him as an alternative. Why run into the arms of a penniless, wandering rake? *We weren't so different back then,* she realized. Each had been reckless and impulsive in their own way.

"Do you remember...." Ferran started slowly. "That winter solstice festival? Just before you got with child?"

Lori thought for a moment. It was all so dim and long ago—twenty years in the past. Slowly, she dredged up the memory: a small town alight with lanterns and music. Villagers dancing in wooden masks, celebrating the end of the year. Endless bottles of flowing wine and spiced ale. She, Ferran and Dane had arrived the night before, en route to the excavation site, where Dane eventually lost his life.

"We spent the night dancing," she recalled. "And Dane...Dane was....?"

"With that buxom farmer's daughter. You two had a fight a few weeks prior and weren't speaking to one another. Remember?"

"Well, you certainly do." *Mindless drama,* she thought. She remembered the falling-out now, but not the reasons. She had tried to end things with Dane, before she knew she was pregnant. He had spent the entire festival trying to make her jealous by dancing with a sheep-farmer's daughter. Yes, she remembered now. And she had dumped an entire bottle of wine over his head in rage. Good peach wine, thick as syrup, the likes of which she hadn't tasted since.

She glanced up at Ferran. He watched her again, waiting for something. She wondered what he expected; then her eyes slowly widened.

"After all that dancing, and all that wine," she said softly, "we went to the shed behind the mill."

"Yes." His lips twitched.

"You kissed me?"

His smile drifted into an amused frown. "You don't remember?"

"I was awfully drunk, Ferran...." Bits and pieces of that night returned to her, seeming to drift across centuries. She hadn't once thought of it until now. Morning sickness began soon afterward and she became consumed with worries—about her child and her future with Dane.

He watched her through hooded eyes. "You really don't remember," he said, and repeated, "What happened to you, Lori?"

Her mouth went dry. She couldn't answer.

Ferran wrapped a lock of her hair around his hand and drew her closer. He angled her face toward his, a scarce inch between their lips, and murmured, "As I recall, I kissed you until you couldn't stand up. Then I lifted you against the wall. You grabbed me so hard, your nails ripped my back. I still have the scar."

Lori shuddered against him.

"Ferran," she said breathlessly. "Stop...my wound...."

"I know." He leaned down to brush his mouth against hers. He kissed her in a lazy, off-centered fashion, casually grazing her lower lip and trailing down her chin to her throat.

Lori gasped. She didn't want to tell him the truth—that she had lived a celibate life for longer than she ever intended. Getting close to men put her on-guard; she didn't trust easily. She had never recovered her nerve after the stabbing. Even now, Ferran's passionate touch caused a tremor of fear in her heart, something instinctive and primal that she couldn't rationalize or explain. Suddenly, she wanted to pull away.

He sensed her stiffen. He stopped, though he kept his soft grip on her hair.

"Did I hurt you?" he asked.

"No."

"You don't want me?"

She sensed the vulnerability behind that question; surprising, from a man like him. Lori pressed her cheek over his heart.

"No, it's not that. I just...."

"You were raped."

"I—" She struggled with that word for a moment. It sounded so terribly harsh. Not able to answer him, she looked away.

"I can tell by the scars on your stomach, and how you shy away from me. I've walked the low road, Lori. I've seen what street scum do to a woman. You were targeted. Someone had it out for you. I think I know who."

Lori swallowed hard. "I was attacked on the streets in the Smokeshack District. I don't know who found me, but I was close to death. The Healers spent hours piecing me back together...."

He wrapped his arms around her, cradling her to his chest.

"Was it Cedric Daniellian?" he asked. She sensed he already knew the answer.

"Thugs," she said. "I suspect he hired them. He wanted to bed me, but I had a job to protect, so I refused him. Humiliated him. He was furious." Her voice fell. "He became fixated on me. His rage was unrelenting."

Ferran let out a long, slow breath.

"Headmaster Duncan hid me and helped me leave the city. I guess he told Cedric I revoked my vows. All those years spent training, building a life for myself...I lost everything...." The tears streamed uncontrollably from her eyes. She couldn't finish.

Ferran adjusted the quilt to cover her more fully, then rested his chin on top of her head. Her tears ran down her cheeks onto his chest, blending with the lines of his phoenix tattoo. She could sense his anger, barely contained within the solid vise of his arms.

"I'll kill him," he said, deep in his throat.

Lori almost laughed, but was crying too hard. "Don't be ridiculous. He's a Daniellian, and you're not an Ebonaire anymore."

"Then I guess I have nothing left to lose."

"Really," she repeated, "it was seven years ago. There's no use retaliating. Believe me, I've spent a lot of time thinking about it." She paused. "I'm sorry, I'm not myself right now, the wound...and the whiskey....I'm fine. Really. It was long ago."

Ferran looked at her in a piercing way she didn't expect. She could see his disbelief. He didn't think she'd made peace with her past—and perhaps he was right. Cedric Daniellian had taken everything from her—her job, the seminary, her reputation as a Healer....And perhaps, most terribly, her ability to trust a man.

She told Ferran it took her weeks to walk on her own after the attack. During that time, she stayed in the seminary, paralyzed in fear, terrified Cedric would send someone to finish the job.

"He will never face any consequences...it's not right," Ferran said, his voice thick with anger.

"He's the First Tier. They sidestep the law all the time."

Ferran's jaw tightened.

She forced herself to smile, despite the tears down streaking her face. "I have Sora," she said. "That's enough."

"Right," he murmured. "You have your daughter."

Something about his expression gave her pause. She frowned, a forbidden thought stealing into her mind. "Ferran, on that winter solstice night, when you took me behind the mill...did we....?"

His gray eyes met hers.

She pushed on. "Did we...make love?"

All pretense vanished between them. She saw his expression soften, a look that terrified her even more than his anger at Cedric.

"If I told you we did," he said, "would that change anything?"

Lori sucked in a sharp breath. "Impossible. I would remember."

"Granted, it wasn't my best performance."

Lori pushed back on impulse, then cried out as the muscles in her back spasmed. He pressed her to his chest, holding her as she groaned. All the while, her thoughts spun in panic. *Would that change anything? Only the last eighteen years!* What if...what if Sora...what if Dane....

No, Sora looked like Dane, she had his wide lips....

Wide lips like Lady Ebonaire, who had visited the seminary once on a formal occasion. But Sora had Dane's long fingers...fingers like Ferran's, only smaller and sleeker....

Faces and features blurred before her. Lori had no picture of Dane to remember him by. She couldn't piece it all together anymore. What Ferran suggested seemed implausible...and yet....

"Tell me we didn't make love," she demanded.

"We did, Lori."

"But I don't remember! How could I not remember?"

"It was short and sloppy. We were both drunk. I didn't last long....And I think you called me Dane...." He paused awkwardly. "You've been through a lot since then. Hell, I only half-believed it in the morning. You and Dane made up. He was my closest friend, I wasn't about to say anything. I knew you didn't really want me. The only reason I remember," his voice lowered, "is because I didn't want to be a father. That's why I ran, Lori. And I've always wondered about it, and maybe regretted...."

"No!" she burst out. She wanted to pound her fists against his chest in frustration, but his arms held her immobile. "No, it's impossible. We were only together once. Think of the odds!"

"I know," he agreed. "But think of the *timing*."

"Why are you doing this to me?"

"Because you asked," he said in exasperation. "I'm not lying. I have the scars where your nails raked me. Has a kiss ever made you sink your fingers into a man's back?"

She couldn't listen to another word. She felt like she might throw up. "I can't think anymore," she groaned.

"I'm sorry. I shouldn't have said anything."

"Get off the cot," she said hoarsely.

"What?"

"I need to sleep." And just like that, she did the only sensible thing she could do—she pushed away. She sealed it all deep within herself, to be cracked open and inspected at a better time.

Ferran let out a long, frustrated sigh and worked his way out from under her, careful not to brush against her wound.

"I'm a damn idiot for bringing this up," he said as he sat down on the floor, dragging his thick coat around him. "Lori, none of this matters. What's done is done. But I'm glad you know the truth of it now."

"Go to sleep, Ferran." Her head began to pound. The alcohol made her feel sick. She pressed her forehead against her arm on the cot; her skin felt hot to the touch. She didn't need to dredge up the past. She really could have liked Ferran without all of these complications. Now...now, she didn't know what to think.

Her mind seemed to spin endlessly, but eventually the whiskey dragged her down into a heavy, troubled sleep.

Ferran sat for some time watching Lori sleep. Tumultuous thoughts raged within him. Eighteen years since he last knew her. Eighteen years. She was so different, so much less buoyant than he remembered. Now he knew why.

The thought of Cedric Daniellian awakened an old, iron hatred. Ferran originally stole his Cat's Eye from the Daniellian house, and it was Cedric's father—Maverick Daniellian—who ultimately turned the Prince against him. Maverick saw it as a chance to weaken the Ebonaire family, and caused Ferran's exile.

Ferran knew men like Cedric were common in the world; he had been one, once. He assumed Cedric was still the same spoiled, selfish brat of his youth. Perhaps even more now, as an adult.

He supposed he was lucky. Life on the road had taught him much. He had found a way to navigate through all the conflicting whims of his heart. Yet he remained a creature of habit in too many ways. The whiskey told him that much.

He had spent eight years traveling with Silas on the Glass Coast, wandering the great sand dunes on the border of Ester, an abandoned country where war-spells from the time of the Races still ravaged the land. Many lost artifacts had been discovered there, and many of them had been stolen or sold since. Where did the time go? Where did the *coin* go? He glanced at the whiskey bottle suspiciously. *Did you steal it from me?*

On the Glass Coast, he had spent many drunken nights staring at the desert stars, pondering the mistakes of his past, wondering if Lori's daughter was his, if she lived happily with Lord Fallcrest as a noblewoman of the Second Tier, raising her daughter in comfortable wealth. He had wished that for her, making silent toasts to the stars, comforted by the thought that even if he hadn't done the right thing, he had done the best he could.

After his falling-out with Silas, he had contacted Lori by letter, too much of a coward to show up on her doorstep. Not his grandest idea, but he didn't regret it. That's when he learned her address in the lowlands. It made him wonder. Teased him with the chance that he might have a home somewhere, waiting for him.

A home. In that moment, he had never wanted anything so badly.

The carefree girl of his imaginings differed greatly from the Lori before him. Perhaps she had never been that wild spirit. Perhaps over the years, he had distorted her face into some perfect image. Now, in his cabin, he saw a strong-willed woman, elegantly beautiful, intelligent, skilled. She combined the strength of the Goddess with a Healer's touch. He wasn't worthy of that. In his opinion, no man really was.

After returning from the Glass Coast, he had found himself on a plateau with nowhere left to climb. He feared the dark, swirling undercurrents of his habits. He had traveled that road too many times, and he was ready for something different, something stable that he could build. Meeting her in the dirty tavern of Pismo had turned him in a much-needed new direction.

Looking at all Lori had endured, and the life she had built from the ashes, he was too ashamed to explain his reasons. Too ashamed to share the tawdry, selfish details of his life. She saw him for who he was, and he didn't like that. *I can show her something better,* he thought.

He looked at the bottle of whiskey in his hand. *Small steps,* he thought.

He took the last swig, then flung the bottle out over the railing of the ship, into the Bath. It landed in the water with a solid, reassuring *plunk*.

Then a vague light illuminated the aft of his boat. Squinting, Ferran recognized Caprion hovering in the air. He stood, keeping one hand on the wooden frame of his cabin, swaying slightly.

"Hail, Harpy," he called, half-raising one hand.

Caprion floated above his boat like a lost star.

"We've called an urgent meeting," he said. "I will help guide your boat to the Dawn Seeker...if you can stand up straight."

"I'll manage," Ferran replied. "Lori is wounded. Don't know if I can leave her."

Caprion frowned. "Is she alright?"

Ferran shrugged again. "She's sleeping. The wound has been tended...."

"She will be safe once we reach the Dawn Seeker. I will move her to the ship's infirmary."

Ferran nodded. He took a deep breath and straightened his shoulders. "Let's get this over with, then."

Caprion made a brief signal with his hands; white light surrounded Ferran's body and his boat. Then Ferran's vessel began to move through the water by its own volition. Ferran sat at the tiller to steer, and together, they guided his houseboat through the dark, rainy night, across The Bath, back to the Dawn Seeker.

# CHAPTER 15

Sora stood in the captain's cabin aboard the Dawn Seeker. Captain Silas sat in bed, a blue coat thrown over his shoulders to cover his black silken nightshirt and matching pants. *He even sleeps fashionably,* Sora thought. She hadn't seen silk nightclothes since leaving her manor two years ago.

Caprion had summoned her only a few minutes ago. Crash and Ferran were already waiting when she arrived, though her mother was not there. The small space seemed doubly cramped by so many towering men.

Sora wondered why her mother didn't join them. Her eyes found Ferran. He was leaning against Silas' desk, twirling a cinnamon stick agitatedly between his fingers. He didn't look like his usual self, shifting from one foot to another constantly, his eyes framed by dark circles. He pushed a big hand through his brown, unruly hair. Sora caught a strong whiff of his breath—whiskey?

"Well?" Silas prompted. "What's this about?"

"We captured an assassin," Caprion said, and explained their encounter with the Shade and their new prisoner to Silas. The Dracian's expression became slack-jawed when he heard about Burn's capture.

Ferran remained pensively quiet.

"How do we recover him? There must be a way!" Silas demanded after Caprion finished. He turned to Ferran. "Can't you trace the portal, like you did on the *Aurora*? Discover where they've gone?"

Ferran looked solemn. "Not so easily done. Too much time has passed by now; the magic's grown cold. We'll have to find him another way." He looked Caprion. "Did you interrogate the prisoner?"

"Yes, and it appears the leader of the Shade resides in The Regency," the Harpy replied.

Ferran's voice dropped a notch. "The Regency?"

"Yes…"

"It's where the nobility live, separate from the rest of the city," Sora interrupted. "But why would the Shade hide there? It doesn't make any sense…."

"No, it doesn't," Ferran agreed. "Unless they have ties with the upper tiers."

"Forget the why of it." Crash's voice cut through the room. "We need to find their leader. Then all of this stops."

"We need a plan," Ferran disagreed. "We don't know who the leader of the Shade is yet. First thing's first—we need to find Burn."

Crash remained silent. He gazed down at his folded arms.

Sora watched him, troubled.

"We know they're in The Regency, so we should begin our search there," Ferran continued. "It's a gated community, so the city guards won't let us enter, especially dressed like…well…." He glanced down at his shirt, indicating the stains and patched holes.

"I can solve that." Silas raised his hand in a flourish. "I have quite an impressive wardrobe stashed aboard this ship. With a day's worth of tailoring, we can prepare all of you for your noble charade."

Ferran raised a skeptical brow. "Lovely. Wandering The Regency penniless in stolen clothes, and dressed by a pirate, no less."

Silas flashed him a gold-toothed smile. "I would have made a better lord than a pirate."

"And I, a better pirate than a lord."

Sora bit her lip. Were they truly going to infiltrate The Regency? The thought left her clammy with doubt. She could already imagine the grand houses, the marble statues and manicured lawns. She knew what the manors would look like, how the storefronts would be decorated, and the kind of people she would encounter. She had been raised a noble, and she didn't want to go back to that life, even temporarily.

"Do we just...wander about, then?" she asked. "The soldiers might catch on if we keep coming and going through the gates. We will have to find a place to stay in the Regency if we are going to spend any amount of time there."

"Yes, a fair point," Ferran agreed.

Silas chimed in again. "Of course, we do have one option, if our Lord Ferran will take the risk."

Sora looked at the two men in confusion. "Lord Ferran?"

"Aye," Silas winked.

Her eyes traveled to the treasure hunter. Did he have connections in The Regency?

Ferran leaned farther back against Silas' desk, his brow furrowed. Finally, he released a sigh.

"I suppose I could speak to my brother," he said reluctantly.

"Pardon?" Sora asked, still confused.

"My brother, Lord Martin Ebonaire."

The name didn't fully sink in at first. Sora stared at him, momentarily lost for words.

"Your brother is an Ebonaire?" she asked.

Ferran nodded.

"Then...you're an Ebonaire, too?"

He nodded again.

That name—Ebonaire—and all its implications finally sunk in. Sora felt decidedly lightheaded. The Ebonaire name was as well known as the royal family's, and often mentioned in the same breath.

Sora remembered word of a scandal long ago that still circled around the countryside. It had happened before her time...something about an exiled heir....

"You're the one," she said, her voice dropping. "You're the Ebonaire son who left the family?"

He nodded.

She still couldn't believe it, though he seemed to be telling the truth. He had no reason to lie.

Silas guffawed.

"There it is, old boy! Good on you! Admitting to your roots, this time sober—" he eyed the treasure hunter "—or not so much. It's decided, then. A week in the

Ebonaire House! They say there are blocks of gold hidden in the walls! Count this pirate's lucky stars!"

"You won't be joining us," Ferran glared. Then his gaze returned to Sora. "It's been a long time since I last spoke to my family. My homecoming might not be taken very well."

Sora frowned. "Are you sure we should take the chance? We could land ourselves in a lot of trouble, impersonating the First Tier...."

"But it won't be an impersonation, will it? Not entirely."

Sora considered that.

Ferran continued, "We need to find the Shade and rescue Burn, and retrieve *The Book of the Named*. The Ebonaires are the wealthiest family in the realm. If members of the Shade are hiding in The Regency, they'll pass through the Ebonaire house eventually. Everyone does." As an afterthought, he added, "I suppose I owe my family a visit, disowned or not. We'll have access to all parts of the city and a legitimate reason to be there, should anyone ask. It might be the best way to hide our presence here. The Shade would never suspect."

Sora nodded slowly. It was a bold plan, but their options were limited. If the Shade's hideout was in The Regency, they would need a way to search them out undetected.

On the other hand, they should be out searching for Burn, not sidling up to the Ebonaires. Ferran's family reunion could become a total distraction.

"Is it really worth the risk?" she finally asked. "We can't afford to get distracted. Burn's life hangs in the balance. Perhaps we should ask my mother's opinion as well...? Where is she, anyway?"

"We had an incident at the seminary," Ferran said. "She'll need a few days to recover."

"A few days? What happened?"

"We had a misunderstanding with some thugs on the docks. She was attacked."

"Lots of thugs around the seminary these days," Silas drawled, and Ferran shot him a look of annoyance.

"She's fine," Ferran enunciated.

Sora searched his face. She couldn't tell if he was hiding something or just drunk.

"How bad of an attack? A knife wound?" she prompted.

"Nonfatal," he assured her.

Still, the news was worrisome. Sora felt the need to go to her mother's side.

"If a knife wound isn't cleaned properly, it can lead to a dire infection...."

"I've tended her, and she will recover soon," Ferran repeated, and gave Silas another irritated look. "I expect the crew to check on her in my absence. She'll be up and about in a few days. Then she can join us at the Ebonaire estate, should we decide to follow through with this plan."

So Lori wouldn't be accompanying them. Sora felt a bit better knowing that. For whatever reason, she didn't want her mother watching her act the part of a noble. She imagined it would make them both uncomfortable and preferred to keep those two worlds separate.

"Must we really enter The Regency? Isn't there some other way to track down the Shade?" she asked, glancing around their circle. Ferran seemed solemn, if resolved. Silas's eyes were gleaming, envisioning gold coins. And Crash....

"If the Shade's hideout is in The Regency, it's our only option," he said. "You and Ferran have noble upbringings. You can play the part well."

"And you?" Silas asked dryly.

"A wealthy family will have a servant. I can fill that role. The First Tier have very specific standards." He looked sideways at Silas. "Different from pirate standards."

Silas flushed angrily. "I could walk into The Regency dressed in these nightclothes alone! No one would ask any questions. None of you have a lick of fashion sense."

"Still," Ferran said, "the assassin has a point. The nobility follow strict etiquette: proper greetings and titles, morning routines, late breakfasts and afternoon tea ...." He nodded to Caprion and Silas. "We'll meet with my family and send for the rest of you if we are able to stay."

Silas frowned, though he finally sat back on the bed.

"Then perhaps it's best if I stay on the ship," Caprion agreed. "I will watch over our new prisoner. See if I can't find out anything more."

"Bring us word immediately if you learn anything," Sora said, and Caprion nodded.

"Then it's settled," Ferran finished.

*Yes,* Sora thought, *it's settled,* though she wasn't excited at the prospect. With the right clothes, they might make it into The Regency. Perhaps the Ebonaires would even meet with them for a few minutes. But she couldn't imagine staying with such a family while under disguise. Her group would stand out like sore thumbs. Clothes couldn't hide sunburned skin, facial scars or unkempt hair.

And even if this all somehow worked, how would they find Burn? By somehow uncovering the Shade's trail?

*What other choice do we have?* her inner voice murmured. Weighing her options, she couldn't think of anything else.

Silas began to ask questions about wardrobe measurements and carriage costs. He went to his desk as Ferran outlined the gritty details of their plan.

Sora clenched her fist, trying to ignore her doubt. With every passing minute, Burn's survival seemed less and less likely. Infiltrating The Regency seemed like a huge distraction. They should be scouring the city right now, searching every street corner and dark alley for signs of the Shade.

But if the Shade were in The Regency, they wouldn't be in the city proper.

She cast a final look at Crash, then turned and left the room.

Crash followed Sora out of Silas' cabin into the wet night. That final glance concerned him. It contained a wildness, a desperation, that he recognized. He didn't know if she would confront their captive again, or leave the ship outright, but he had to make sure Sora stayed close. The Shade didn't want Burn, after all. They wanted her.

A distracting glimmer over his shoulder halted his steps.

"I have words for you," Caprion said as he exited the cabin.

Crash hesitated, watching Sora in a moment of indecision. She headed for her cabin, away from the galley and the cargo hold. At least she wasn't being rash.

Resigned, he turned to face the Harpy. The soft percussion of rain struck the deck. Behind them, the wide expanse of The Bath stretched off into a windy, throbbing darkness.

Caprion spoke directly. "It's time we put our differences aside, Viper. We can no longer waste time fighting each other." He gave Crash a searching look. "If you know anything about the Shade, you should tell me now."

Crash raised an eyebrow. "Tell me first why the Matriarch sent you."

Caprion paused for too long. Crash had expected as much; they both had their secrets.

"I am not in league with the Matriarch," Caprion finally said. "But you're right. I have not been completely honest about my purpose here."

"Surprise, surprise."

"I didn't think it was something you, Sora, or the rest of your group would understand."

Crash folded his arms skeptically. "Well? Let's hear it."

Caprion clasped his hands behind his back in a pose reminiscent of a soldier. "To be clear, I did not defy the Matriarch to come here. That would be impossible, because I outrank her. In the eyes of my people, she might be their queen, but I am their savior. She can control me up to a point, but when it comes to fulfilling my sacred purpose, she has no influence over me. I have not been sent by the Matriarch. I was sent by the One Star, the God of Light, to eradicate this darkness."

A beat of silence passed between them.

"You're beginning to sound disturbingly like our enemies," Crash said.

Caprion frowned deeply. "The last seraphim were born before the War of the Races. We are the heralds of things to come. My emergence was a sign that the Elements were out of balance. That once again, Darkness was outgrowing its bounds. It is my purpose, given by the One Star and the God of Light, to correct that balance."

"You seem very sure of yourself."

"I've been waiting for news of the Dark God for years. When I saw the sacred weapons Sora carried, I knew the time had come." He fixed Crash with a solemn stare. "I am here to eradicate the Shade and put an end to this threat. The Dark God cannot be allowed to escape His prison. That is my purpose."

Crash bowed his head to the rain. Then an ironic laugh broke from his throat. He shot the Harpy an empty grin.

"And now I should trust you? Knowing you were sent to kill off the Shade, and doubtless many more of my kind?" He took a slow step forward. "That's your mistake, Harpy—confiding in me. Assuming I care. We're not brothers in some fellowship."

Caprion's face twisted in anger. Crash watched the man's patience slip, savoring the experience.

"I am trying to help you, but you are withholding information. I saw you speak to that assassin in the woods outside the village. I know they've contacted you. They want Sora's Cat's Eye, and she needs to be protected."

Crash became guarded. "What happened in the woods was a pointless confrontation, no more than what you saw at the windmills. You don't know us well, Harpy. We've been fighting this battle for almost a year now. Sora doesn't need your protection."

"She does, from you."

Crash's hand drifted close to his dagger. He felt that inner darkness stir. This seraph knew nothing of what Sora had been through—what she'd survived, and what they'd shared.

"Your demon darkens your aura," Caprion said quietly. His eyes flickered around Crash's form as though watching flies dart through the air. "Your demon lives close to the surface of your skin. You're not as in control as you think, Viper. I don't know what kind of thrall you have over this girl, but let her go."

Crash hated the Harpy's words—their truth and their arrogance. "She chose me willingly to protect her. That's why I joined her side. But a man like you doesn't understand loyalty." He gave the Harpy a direct look. "You lied to Sora, to me, to this crew, even to the Matriarch—why are you here, Harpy? Be honest with yourself."

Caprion stared at him.

"Coward," Crash spat. Then he turned and walked away, back toward the row of cabins. He felt the Harpy's magic wash over him in a wave of frustration, but he ignored it. Caprion was just like the rest of his kind. Righteous to the world—deceitful to himself.

"If you won't tell me the full truth about the Shade, then at least tell Sora," Caprion called after him.

Crash looked back.

The Harpy's silhouette glowed vaguely through the rain. "Her life is at risk," he said. "You owe her."

Crash considered those words. Then he continued along the side of the ship. The Dawn Seeker smelled of wet timber and rain. He glanced up at the heavy mass of clouds overhead. No stars. No moon.

He thought of Sora, and of that name—*Cerastes*.

Yes, she was owed an explanation. They both were.

# CHAPTER 16

Golden light filled Sora's cabin. She sat on her small cot, her head in her hands. She couldn't stop thinking of Burn. She felt like they were already too late to save his life.

Finally she reached under her cot and pulled out a locked wooden box. Just touching the wood made her hands cold, and she felt the Cat's Eye stir at her neck uneasily. The box contained the Dark God's sacred weapons. They had already recovered two of them from Volcrian's wraiths: a sword hilt and a spearhead. The Shade was searching for them. Even more disturbing, it seemed that the third wraith had been captured. She wanted to question the female assassin again. How could the Shade imprison such a powerful creature?

And what did the Shade plan to do with the three sacred weapons?

*We need The Book of the Named,* she thought. But which was more important? Finding the book, or finding Burn? *It should be obvious,* she thought, but she had no answer.

Her skin prickled. The doorknob clicked. Sora stood up from her cot as the cabin door swung open, revealing the dark hallway beyond.

Crash stepped silently into the room. Candlelight flickered over his tall form, outlining his broad shoulders, powerful chest and narrow waist. Dark hair fell wet across his forehead. He looked brutal and wolfish.

Sora's lips parted in surprise.

He shut the door quietly behind him. The sound brought her back to herself.

"You shouldn't be here," she said. *And why should it matter?*

Crash stood facing her. His presence filled the small room. His shadow shifted along the wall, moving away from the light of the candle, seeming to have a mind of its own. The sight unnerved her.

"Our conversation from before was unfinished."

She blinked. "Really?"

He took the box from her hands and placed it on the bed. "I told you I didn't know the assassins who attacked us."

"Yes."

"But I didn't tell you all."

Sora's heart sank. Her instincts were right. *He lied again,* she thought.

In as few words as possible, Crash described the man who had once been his Grandmaster. She realized this was a rare moment of truth for him. He spoke briefly of his life in the Hive and his enigmatic teacher, Cerastes. She did her best to understand, not knowing much about the ways of assassins.

"So this Grandmaster is in league with the Shade?" she asked once he had finished.

"He is their leader," Crash admitted softly.

Sora didn't know how to feel. She couldn't meet his eyes. It was his way to keep secrets, but she struggled with the fact that he had kept such a vital piece of information from her—and from the rest of the crew. She thought of Caprion's suspicions, and the whispered rumors among the Dracians. Could she ever trust the assassin fully?

"Do you know why they want the sacred weapons?" she asked. "Do you know how they plan to raise the Dark God?"

Crash shook his head, but now she wasn't sure if she believed him.

"The Shade are separate from the Hive. What they believe, and the magic they practice, is not what our kind sees as normal." He paused. "But I think if Cerastes is in The Regency, then he has made some very powerful friends. I'm not sure why, but we will soon find out."

Sora nodded in silent agreement. *Cerastes.* In her thoughts, the name sounded like some insidious reptile. *Serraasteees.*

"I'm worried about Burn," she said.

"I'll find him."

"Alive or dead?" she asked bluntly. "We should be out looking for him right now. Why don't you go straight to your so-called Grandmaster and demand his release?"

Crash hesitated just long enough for her to worry.

"No," he said. "If the Shade wants you, then I won't let you out of my sight."

"My safety isn't important right now. If we must enter The Regency, then I'd rather you track down Burn. You know more about the Shade than any of us. You have the greatest chance at saving his life." Her eyes narrowed in anger. "Maybe, if you weren't so concerned with hiding the truth from us, you'd have saved him by now."

Her words sounded much bolder than she actually felt. Crash studied her. Sometimes he seemed to understand her silence better than her words.

"I'm staying by your side," he repeated.

"While Burn is tortured? He might already be dead! You can't take this decision out of my hands. I've grown, Crash. I'm stronger now. I don't need you hovering over me. Why can't you see that?" She thrust a finger at his chest. "I hate that you keep your past from me. I hate that you lie!"

Crash's face darkened. "You think I enjoy lying to you? In my race, deception means survival."

"Then I hate what you are, and what the Hive has done to you."

Crash stared at her. He seemed shocked by her words. His voice became low and tense. "You can't hate me for what I am. What I am is what shields you. *What I am* stands between you and a horde of demons! Why are you so infuriatingly blind? Everything I do—every word I say—is with you in mind."

Sora searched his face, trying to understand.

He glared for a moment, then his expression went stoically blank, like a mask sliding into place.

"I'll find Burn. That, I can promise you," he said directly. "But tomorrow I will accompany you and Ferran. I will make sure you're safe and settled in The Regency. You have no choice in that."

"*No choice*," Sora mocked. "What have you been training me for, if I can't defend myself against the Shade?"

"They're stronger than I thought," he started, but she held up her hand to cut him off. He grabbed it. "Listen to me. Cerastes is someone to fear, Sora. I *want* you to fear him because it just might keep you alive. If they took you and not

Burn...." He paused. "Stay as far away from the Shade as you can. Don't seek them out."

His words caused a chill to run down her arms. She had never heard Crash speak in such a way. She felt her anger deflate.

"You don't need to worry about me. In The Regency, I'll be among the nobility, surrounded by servants and the city guard."

He pointed at the wall as though they stood at The Regency gates.

"That's the Shade's territory," he said. "They will take you in a heartbeat, given the chance. Drop your guard on the street, in a doorway, in a shop, and they will take you. Cerastes will use you for his own dark purposes."

Sora glared at him, but his grip tightened.

"I know that defiant look," he said. "You think you can withstand him now, but Sora, you can't imagine what they're capable of." He grabbed her by the waist suddenly, his left hand cupping her rib cage over the white scar. "Do you remember this?" he asked.

Sora's pulse tripled. She could feel his warm palm through her shirt. She couldn't breathe. He pressed his entire hand against her.

Nervously, she ran her tongue over her dry lips. "You wrote me a note. *For the first time I felt fear*," she quoted softly.

Those words hung between them, rich with meaning. Her scar seemed to burn against his hand. For the first time he felt fear—because she had almost died. She struggled to retain her composure, hardly able to keep eye contact.

"Your life is far more important to me," he whispered. "I won't let them take you."

His words stole her breath. "We can't abandon Burn...."

"I know," he hushed, "but I will find him. I made you a promise. Let me handle this while you go with Ferran. Be safe. This is your quest, Sora. If you fall, we all go with you. Don't you see that?"

She frowned. Somehow, she had always thought of this as *his* story, his adventure, and she was just a bystander swept up in his wake.

He pulled her forward, his hands still firm on her waist. Sora gasped at the iron strength of his arms. He looked at her throat where her pulse pounded erratically, then at the Cat's Eye, gleaming around her neck, then up to her face, her lips....

Anticipation coiled in her stomach. She forced herself to breathe.

"Are you going to kiss me again?" she asked, her voice huskier than intended. "Because that didn't go so well last time."

A smile flickered across his face. Crash leaned down and set his forehead against hers.

"Does it truly matter what I do now? I tried to keep my distance. I wanted to protect you from the Shade, but they discovered you anyway."

"True."

"I wanted to avoid rumors on this ship, but I suppose that didn't work, either."

"No, not very well," she admitted.

Sora wordlessly pressed herself into his chest and closed her eyes. She felt wrapped in his presence, engulfed by his warm scent. She wished she could stay that way for hours, that he would tilt her head up and kiss her again, like he did on the Lost Isles.

Footsteps could be heard down the hall going past her door, reminding her of the crowded ship, and the stressful day looming tomorrow.

"With Burn's life hanging in the balance and the Shade so close," she murmured, "should we really talk about this now....?"

"We don't need to talk about anything."

She expected him to withdraw, but his arms stayed around her. They stood like that, for longer than she knew. The silence between them was comfortable and familiar, like dust on a warm hearth. The tension left her shoulders. She remembered a time when they had touched like this regularly, innocently, without a thought for the future.

*His self-control is admirable,* she thought. He must feel the heat building between them....

"Perhaps we *should* talk about this?" she broached.

"No," he said. "Let's not."

"When?" Something about his reply made her pursue it. "When shall we settle this?"

He searched her eyes with a bit of humor. "Is it really a matter to be settled? Like some business arrangement?"

She sighed, impatient. "Either we admit what's between us, or we don't. We keep returning to this, Crash, but I can't stand here with one foot in the water."

"Then perhaps you're the wiser one," he replied. The resignation in his voice caught her attention. She pressed her cheek against his chest and wrapped her arms tightly around his waist, keeping him as close as possible.

"You're pulling away," she said.

He curled around her like a living shield. Then he slowly detached himself.

"You said it yourself. All or nothing," he reminded her.

*I assume by that he means "nothing,"* she thought. She blinked hard, wishing her eyes didn't sting.

"We'll rescue Burn," he assured her.

She nodded quietly.

"I'll save his life," he repeated.

She nodded again.

He smiled faintly. Then, without another word, he turned and walked out of her cabin. His shadow trailed reluctantly along the wall.

Sora sat back again on her cot, a hollow feeling at the base of her throat. She thought of the familiarity of his embrace, his possessive arms and the touch of his forehead against hers. *Don't dwell on it,* she told herself. *He's made his choice.* Whatever was between them remained deep and uncharted, like an fathomless ocean. She couldn't call it love, but it went beyond fancy, beyond passion, and it was far from innocent.

*He's made his choice,* she reminded herself. But for this moment, between candlelight and darkness, she allowed herself to imagine what could be.

Burn's head spun. He felt sick to his stomach.

His Wolfy ears twitched. Somewhere in the distance, he heard the sound of churning gears, like a heavy jaw endlessly grinding. It made his head throb even worse, and he winced.

When he finally focused his eyes, he appeared to be in an empty, half-constructed room. Piles of rubble littered the floor and exposed wooden beams supported a heavy stone ceiling. By the thick walls and musty dry air, he guessed he was somewhere underground. He tested the chains on his wrists: solid iron. For the moment, unbreakable.

"Ah, he's awake," a voice murmured. A dim figure stood across from him at an open doorway. He could smell the man—Cobra, the one he had tackled through the portal. His head throbbed, but the memories were clear and sharp.

Beyond Cobra, another figure seemed to hover in the darkness. Burn squinted; his vision blurred again. When he moved, he felt sticky blood matting his hair.

*Why am I still alive?* he wondered.

"Keep him for a while," a low voice reached his ears. "Don't bother me again until you have the girl."

"Of course, master."

"And where is Krait?"

"Taken."

"Ah." The soft, sinister voice paused. "I'm sure she'll find her way back home."

The conversation stopped. Burn squinted again, but he couldn't tell if anyone was still in the room. He couldn't focus any more through the pounding in his skull. He closed his eyes and drew a deep breath.

"Better you kill me now," he murmured to the darkness. "You might not get another chance."

A soft laugh reached his ears.

"Spoken like a true mercenary," he heard. "But when my master says wait, we wait."

*Wait.* Assassins did not show mercy. The Shade wouldn't keep him alive unless they had a plan. A flurry of thoughts ran through Burn's head. They might use him as bait to lure his friends into a trap, or to bargain for the Dark God's weapons. He briefly strained against his bonds, instinctively trying to fight....

Then another streak of pain split his skull, and he found himself spinning into darkness.

# Chapter 17

Sora stood in front of the mirror in Silas' cabin—the only full-length mirror on the entire ship. She studied her yellow dress with a scrutinizing eye. In her younger days, she never would have worn anything so simple, but Silas had bought it last-minute from a vendor on the docks, and with winter solstice looming, pickings were slim. Everyone wanted a fancy dress for the festival.

The yellow, form-fitting bodice covered a long cotton shift with billowing white sleeves. Her flowing skirts of deep yellow opened at the front, displaying a wide section of white petticoats. Such a cut would have been highly scrutinized in the country, where petticoats were thought of as undergarments, but Silas assured her the style was quite in vogue. A fawn-colored jacket fit over the bodice. Her mother spent hours tailoring it, from her recovery cot on Ferran's boat, claiming she needed to keep her hands busy. When Sora asked Lori what she thought of their plan, her mother had only grimaced, her eyes focused hard on hemming.

Sora was surprised by how well the jacket fit, given their limited resources. Beneath her dress she wore a new pair of leather boots, appropriate for the cold weather.

Her friend Joan had braided her hair that morning and wrapped it decoratively around her head. A sprig of winter jasmine finished off the look, tucked just behind her ear. All in all, Sora thought she could pass for a rich merchant's daughter, or perhaps a country noble from a very meager estate. Not bad, considering how little time they had to prepare.

Last of all, she pulled on a pair of white gloves. She ran a hand over the rough crater at the center of her left palm, thinking of her battle on the Lost Isles. The scar on her hand, along with her calloused fingers, immediately betrayed her low status. Luckily, gloves were regularly worn both indoors and outdoors during the winter.

So much had changed since she last walked as a noblewoman. She wondered if she could still play the part.

There was a knock at the door.

"Yes?" she called. "I'm decent!"

Ferran entered. He wore a majestic red greatcoat with gold-trimmed cuffs. It fell elegantly over a starched white linen shirt and black vest. His tall leather boots reached up to his knees. Sora was amazed Silas had found proper shoes to fit Ferran's large feet.

She stared at him, suddenly awkward. Ferran Ebonaire. To most people in the Kingdom, the name Ebonaire was synonymous with wealth: First Tier elite, second only to the royal family. Two queens hailed from their lineage. He was a cousin to the prince, though somewhat removed. She remembered that their current queen was a Seabourne by blood.

And now he was a vagabond lord. Sora could still detect the wear of travel around his eyes. Still, in his new greatcoat and slicked hair, he looked every inch a noble. She wondered if her mother had seen him yet.

Ferran scratched the back of his neck. He looked uncomfortable in so many layers.

"Silas secured us a coach," he told her. "We're waiting for you."

Sora glanced back at the mirror uncertainly.

"Do you really think this will work?" she asked.

"We have to try," he said. "Feels strange, doesn't it? The whole..." he indicated both of them, "act."

"It does."

Silas had contrived their "family relationship" over breakfast: Sora would pose as Ferran's daughter, and Lori, his wife. Sora wasn't sure what possessed the pirate to devise the plan, but it made sense and would be an easy story to stick to. She didn't entirely mind, though she wasn't sure how her mother felt.

She took a steadying breath. Lying to the Ebonaire family? Claiming to be blood? *I must have lost my mind,* she thought.

She turned and offered her arm to Ferran, just as a lady would.

"Sir," she said, with a slight bow. She felt a little awkward, but he responded in kind, taking her arm and escorting her from the room.

Ferran walked with her across the deck. Outside, sullen rain clouds hung heavy in the sky and moisture lay thick in the air. A cold wind blew from the north and rippled across the waters of The Bath.

Ferran led her to the plank. She spotted Silas standing near a carriage some ways down the boardwalk toward the South Gate, but no one else looked familiar. She searched for Crash below on the docks, but didn't see him. She traversed down the plank to the boardwalk and started toward Silas and the coach. Ferran released her arm at that point and passed by her with his long strides. Admittedly, she took her time and enjoyed seeing the bustling wharf at dawn, the long row of fishing boats and the stacks of crayfish traps that lined the pier.

Someone fell into step next to her. She glanced sideways, then stared.

Gone were Crash's worn clothes and leather belts. His hair was slicked back against his head with Silas's expensive oils, emphasizing his angular face. His jaw looked clean and sharp. He wore a suit of black livery over a gray vest; a dark gray neckerchief tucked into the high collar of his white shirt hid his scars. A few stray bangs fell across his sea-green eyes.

He returned her look.

"Milady," he said solemnly.

Sora almost tripped over her skirts. Her predominant image of Crash was of a mud-stained, bristling warrior in various forms of ripped clothing, certainly a far cry from sophistication. But in his suit of livery, with his scars well-hidden and his back so straight, she could no longer deny he was a fine-looking man, his features sharp as steel.

He glanced over her fitted jacket and billowing skirts, allowing his eyes to linger. Sora felt her cheeks flush.

"You look sweet," he said.

"Sweet?" she rebuked. "What does that mean?"

"Trustworthy. As you should."

"Thank you, I guess."

"Of course, Milady." His words held a secret laugh.

"As a footman, you'll be at my beck and call," she grinned. "I think I might enjoy this."

"I'm Ferran's footman," he corrected.

"You'll soon see that means nothing to a Lord's daughter."

She stepped past him to the carriage and his eyes trailed after her.

Silas waited for her at the coach, and gave her a rather smarmy bow before handing her up. Her skirts caught on the door frame and she had to tug them loose.

"That can't happen when you get out of the carriage," Ferran murmured as he unhooked her petticoat from the door's latch.

"I know," she hissed, embarrassed. Her stepfather had always called her clumsy. In fact, she had even tripped and fallen at her own Blooming!

*But I'm not clumsy,* she thought, considering her training with Crash. *Just nervous. Be calm.*

Ferran entered behind her, while Crash took his seat outside, on the back of the carriage, as a servant should. Ferran settled across from her, giving her room for her skirts. Sora remembered quite vividly how much she had hated riding in carriages. She barely had room to breathe.

"I'll keep an eye on Lori for the time being," Silas said from the doorway. "Send word when you're ready for us."

"Us?" Ferran asked.

"Aye," Silas grinned. "What good is befriending an Ebonaire if you don't get to visit his house? I look forward to a glass of aged brandy when I arrive." He gave them a little wave and shut the door.

With a few quick words, Silas paid the driver and Sora heard a whip crack. She flinched on instinct, remembering her fight with the female assassin, Krait.

The coach rolled forward. Sora watched the city pass by out the window.

"Silas certainly seems confident," she mentioned.

"Perhaps we should try to do the same," Ferran agreed.

Tourmaline Street was one of the longest boulevards in the City of Crowns. It connected the South gate to the West gate, traveling parallel to the Crown's Rush. At mid-morning, the streets were heavy with traffic.

Sora watched out the carriage window at countless peasants, merchants, housewives and other city dwellers going about their daily business. She lost track of how many intersections they crossed. The carriage would pause briefly as children, dogs or other coaches meandered past, then continue on its way.

They trundled over many bridges, some arced like little rainbows, others broad, flat and utilitarian. Canals crisscrossed the city. The smaller canals in the poorer districts moved sluggishly, and the stench of compost hung heavy in the air. Not even the brisk wind outside could dispel it. The larger canals were more pleasant, with faster-moving water. Despite the gloomy weather, Sora saw pleasure crafts carrying well-dressed ladies down the wider canals, and merchant barges transporting goods.

At one point, they passed a ship that had become jammed in a narrow canal. Its forestay was broken and, from what she could see, its mainmast was snapped and buried part way under a low bridge. A crowd of excited onlookers watched as several guards spoke to the owner of the ship. Before the scene disappeared from view, she saw the city guards surround the captain and march him away. Apparently he disagreed with their fines.

The city transitioned through every level of poverty, from wooden lean-tos built against the eastern wall to low thatched houses separated by narrow alleys. Tourmaline Street became narrow and dirty. Then they crossed into another district. Sora watched the city transform into rows of polished storefronts and well maintained apartments.

A granite wall covered in ivy marked the border of The Regency, and their carriage stopped at a pair of tall, bronze gates. The emblems of different noble houses were carved along the wall at even intervals, and upon the gates, Sora recognized the crest of the royal family: a boar's head with mighty tusks. She had never been to The Regency before, but had heard plenty about it during her youth. A city within a city, the nobility had their own private parks, shopping districts and theater. Select merchants and tradesmen were allowed to run high-end boutiques, but most peasants never set foot inside the walls.

Sora tried not to feel nervous. Several soldiers guarded the entrance, their eyes stern under their helmets. One approached their coach through the misty rain, and Ferran climbed out. The moment his foot hit the cobblestones, his entire demeanor changed. He stood upright and raised his head, his chin thrust forward. His shoulders were pulled back.

Sora was surprised again by just how tall he stood, several inches above six feet. His narrow build only added to the effect. She watched through the open door of the coach. Ferran spoke to the guard calmly at first, then emphatically, making a few quick gestures with his hand.

Eventually, one of the guards let out a genuine laugh and clapped Ferran on the shoulder, then nodded to his fellows. A whistle blew somewhere out of sight, a wheel churned, and the heavy iron gates swung open on metal gears.

Ferran returned to the coach and signaled the driver to continue. He shut the door behind him.

As the coach rolled forward, Sora looked at him curiously.

"What was that about?" she asked.

"We weren't on the entry list," he said, "so I told them the truth: we were visiting the Ebonaires, and we had arrived a few days early."

"Wouldn't they ask for a letter of invitation?"

"I suppose this suit was enough." He flicked a bit of lint from his coat. "Should thank Silas later. Or maybe not. We'll see."

Sora sat back in relief.

They traveled down several streets of whitewashed townhouses. These would belong to the Second Tier, the less wealthy nobility. A frozen stream, crossed over by small footbridges, separated the row of townhouses from the cobblestone street.

Then they entered a district of sprawling front lawns and large manors. Here, the streets were wide and lined with impressive elm trees and footpaths where people could walk or ride horseback in the shade. She saw few people out on the street as the sky darkened with rain, and the storm grew stronger.

The carriage reached a wide cul-de-sac at the end of a long street. A copse of ancient oak trees stood like sentinels at the front of the long drive, blocking any view of the estate beyond. The carriage followed a single road through the thicket of trees. The tangle of ancient branches arced overhead, sheltering their carriage from the rain.

They left the oaks behind and entered a large field of trimmed green grass. The Ebonaire estate came into view. Their house looked like a castle in its own right, built of heavy gray stone, with spiraling turrets and endless rows of windows. Sora saw gargoyles hunched around the entryway, and two flags flapped in the wind. One carried the symbol of the phoenix, the insignia of the Ebonaire house, and another of a boar's head, the royal family. The Ebonaire bloodline went back to the founding of the Kingdom, and even before that, to the war-tribes of days long past. Their name was known by even the poorest urchin—as unquestionable as the King's own title.

Finally the coach came to a stop before the house. Sora was surprised to see no servants on the grounds. It looked deserted, perhaps because of the weather. At her manor in the country, stable boys always stood on call, ready to assist with horses or luggage. *But our arrival is unannounced,* she thought.

She glanced nervously at Ferran and noticed a slight sheen of sweat on his brow. He drummed his fingers against his knee. When the coachman opened the door, he sprung out of the carriage like a leapfrog and strode tensely up the front steps, forgetting to assist her from the coach.

Crash appeared in his stead, and helped hand her down. Her skirts seemed determined to catch on the doorway's latch, and he patiently assisted her with the dress. She gave him a grateful smile as she untangled herself. Finally she placed both feet on the cobblestones and they followed Ferran up the front steps, to the door.

He had already rapped upon the door. As they waited, he murmured, "Let me speak and don't interrupt."

"By all means," Sora replied under her breath.

They waited a long moment, and then she heard the doorknob click and the heavy door swung open. A man, most obviously a butler, faced them. He looked in his mid-fifties and stood with a dignified air. He reminded Sora a bit of a pigeon, with a long hooked nose and dark eyes placed close together. His hair was swooped back in a thin comb-over. His black and red livery were perfectly clean and pressed. His clothes were so nicely fitted, she almost didn't notice his large gut.

He glanced over them, taking in their appearance. Within seconds, Sora knew he had already decided their wealth and status. His eyes lingered on her dress, by far the most obviously out of place. Women's clothing of the First Tier was far more intricate than what she wore.

"May I help you?" he asked stiffly. Or perhaps he was being polite? Sora didn't know.

"Please inform Lord Martin Ebonaire that his brother has come to visit," Ferran said directly.

Sora glanced at him. To her ears, his words sounded rushed and a little tense, but perhaps the butler didn't notice.

The butler gave them a formidable frown. "Hmph," he said hotly. "A brother? And am I to presume you are Lord Simeon Ebonaire? He is on holiday with his new wife. You must take me for a fool, to think I wouldn't recognize Lord Martin's own brother!"

Ferran hesitated. "Not that brother," he corrected. "The elder brother. *Ferran Ebonaire.*"

The butler's scowl deepened. "I've heard of no such person."

"Then perhaps you should ask Lord Martin before you turn us away," Ferran said bluntly, a hard edge to his voice. "I assure you, he'll be most displeased if you do not announce us at once."

Sora had to suppress a smile. Yes, she recognized that tone—spoken like a true noble.

"Hmph!" the butler grunted again, stepping aside for them to enter. "Do wait in the foyer while I announce you." He followed them inside and headed up a wide staircase to the upper floors.

Ferran seemed less nervous inside the door. A familiar slouch entered his walk. He thrust his hands into his pockets. Despite his casual posture, he looked tall and impressive, in his deep red greatcoat and shining black boots. Despite twenty years of absence, he seemed immediately familiar with this place. He glanced around the foyer as though gazing at an old portrait on the wall.

Sora took in the sight as well: mahogany floors and wood-paneled walls, two sweeping staircases that led to the higher levels, and magnificent archways to her left and right. Through one, she caught a glimpse of a library, or perhaps a very grand study for entertaining guests. A grand piano stood in one corner, a recent invention she had seen once before. Through the other archway, she saw a richly decorated sitting room complete with stuffed leather couches, polished wooden shelves and a large liquor cabinet. She imagined many more rooms like this throughout the entire house. The Ebonaire manor could have engulfed her own country estate several times over.

Crash remained silently by her side. She found it hard to look at him. He was too clean. Too well-composed. Every time she looked over at him, she felt a rush of heat to her face and lost her train of thought.

"Where are the servants?" Sora finally asked, her voice soft and subdued.

Ferran shrugged. "They keep to the servant halls," he said. "It's bad etiquette for servants to walk openly about during the day."

Sora was surprised at that. Life in the country was much more lax. Servants, particularly the higher staff, were treated like family in her manor. Or at least, she had treated them as such. Her stepfather had not, but he had rarely been there.

Finally the butler returned for them. He gave Ferran a deep bow, then nodded to Sora. He ignored Crash, which was proper, as he was dressed as a footman and played the part well; he stood slightly behind them, a short distance away. She remembered him practicing a few basic protocols with Ferran yesterday, just enough to get by without arousing suspicion.

"Lord Ebonaire will see you now," the butler said, leading them up the staircase.

Ferran let out a slow breath, and followed.

The second level of the manor seemed covered by a maze of intersecting halls. Sora caught a few brief glimpses of the staff: maids in uniform airing out rooms or whisking laundry away down the hall. Several maids passed by them quickly, hardly stopping to bob a curtsy before continuing on with basins of water and stacks of towels. Sora frowned, recognizing a jar of herbs in one girl's hands: a mixture of yarrow, valerian root and mint leaves—common fever remedies. She wondered where she was off to.

"Is someone sick?" she asked.

Ferran shot her a *be quiet* look, but she ignored him.

The butler seemed uncomfortable. "Lady Danica is ill. Her condition has worsened over the past week...." He paused. "We are all praying for her swift recovery."

Lady Danica? Sora wondered if that was Lord Ebonaire's wife. Or daughter? Perhaps a visiting cousin? She wanted to ask, but Ferran's warning look stilled her tongue.

Finally they reached a waiting room in the manor's west wing. The butler led them through it and opened a pair of double-doors to a plush office. Ferran entered without pause, but Sora hesitated for a moment, unsure if she should join him. Were ladies often included in First Tier business, particularly between brothers? Was she overstepping her bounds? As a daughter, she had even less right to intrude....

Crash remained by her side, just as a footman would.

Finally, she entered through the huge oak doors.

# CHAPTER 18

Martin Ebonaire sat behind one of the largest desks in the Kingdom. It was almost the size of a dining table, and his chair could have replaced the royal throne. Behind him stood a tall, wide window overlooking the manor gardens, which lay thorny and dormant in the winter sun.

Ferran didn't expect this room to feel so familiar. Family portraits adorned the walls; he remembered each one. He noted a few new bookshelves full of ledgers, land deeds and reports. The entire left wall was taken up by a massive tapestry, spanning floor to ceiling. Upon it, all the names of the Ebonaire line were written in curling, stylized script. A tree connected them all together, with hundreds of thin branches spiraling out from a thick trunk. *A map of the family,* his father had called it. Ferran had been forced to memorize every name of each generation. *An Ebonaire must know his roots.* He had spent hours in this room with his father, Lord Rowland Ebonaire, who taught him to manage the estate.

The room seemed the same, yet the man before him barely resembled the younger brother of his memories. Martin Ebonaire faced him across the desk. He wore unusually macabre colors: a black waistcoat with silver embroidery and a ruffled gray tunic. Ornate white-gold cufflinks fastened his wide sleeves, and a pocketwatch fit snugly into his breast pocket. He wore his dark-brown hair slicked back, tied at the base of his neck in a short ponytail with a black ribbon. He looked a far cry from the adolescent boy Ferran remembered—a shy, sensitive lad who had followed on his heels through the royal court. Martin Ebonaire was now a sharply handsome man with steel-gray eyes and an inquisitive nose.

Ferran could only assume Martin had a wife and family by now, though he hadn't contacted his brother in many years. *A sister-in-law, nieces and nephews?* he thought, wondering how he would fit into the mix. Or *if* he would fit. He had written Martin once, shortly after their father died, but a wayfaring life made it hard to send and receive posts. He never received a letter back and didn't even know if his letter had been delivered.

His brother stared at him quietly over long, steepled fingers, his expression unreadable. The two regarded each other in static silence. It felt as though a storm of unspoken words filled the room.

Ferran fiddled with the cinnamon stick in his pocket. He had never expected to stand in this office again. He felt less than presentable—which was absurd, considering the expensive suit Silas had loaned him. But in this house, even the servants' livery was starched and creased to perfection.

*Forget about it,* he thought. He cast a look at Sora, who appeared pale, if composed. The young girl nodded to him, and he was surprised by the steadiness of her gaze.

Crash remained silent near the doorway, his arms by his sides, like a proper footman should.

"Lord Ebonaire," Sora said, unexpectedly leading the introductions. She gave an elegant bow to his brother—reminding Ferran, again, that she was raised as a noblewoman.

Lord Martin nodded back to Sora, taking note of her well-practiced bow. Then his scrutinizing gaze settled again on Ferran.

"Well, you look like my brother," he finally said. "Then again, you could also be a smuggler, thief, or some riffraff pulled out of the river. You'll have to wear more than a nice suit if you want to convince me of your name."

Ferran blinked. Not the response he expected.

"Prove your claim, or I will have Donwick throw you out," Martin said.

Ferran felt a bit of his usual fire return. "You think this is a charade?"

Martin raised a sleek eyebrow. "Last I heard, my brother drowned on a pirate ship off the Glass Coast, and not a word since."

"I sent a letter," Ferran said. "Though to my knowledge, you never returned one." He paused. Perhaps that wasn't the best tactic, given the situation. His letter might not have arrived. "If I'm not who I say I am, then why did I come here?"

"Why does anyone come to the Ebonaire estate? Our coin, perhaps? Do you have a debt to pay off? May I mortgage some land for you? Or is it an overseas venture? Come now, let's have it."

Ferran truly wasn't prepared for this. Why had he assumed his brother would recognize him?

"I want nothing, Martin, more than to give my condolences for our father's passing."

"Tactful," his brother said.

Ferran tried again. "I'll prove it, then." He pointed to his face. "I have a scar on my chin."

Martin regarded him for a moment longer. Then he stood and circled around his large desk, coming to stand immediately in front of Ferran. He gave his chin a measured look. Ferran stood just an inch taller than he. The two studied one another closely.

"There is a scar," Martin acknowledged.

"I don't suppose you remember how it came about?"

Martin nodded thoughtfully. "I remember. But do you?"

"I was taunting you with a rapier," he said. "You were ten at the time. You clocked me in the jaw, and I tripped down the staircase to the servant's quarters. Bled something horrible. Mother thought I'd slit my neck."

A faint smile grew on Martin's lips.

"I cussed like a sailor and the governess fainted," Ferran added.

Martin grinned then, just a flash. "There was another scar on your left hand."

Ferran raised his hand and displayed the back of it. A white line ran between his index and middle finger. "We were fishing on the lake behind our summer cottage." He remembered the place well—not a cottage at all, but a decadent villa residing to the south. Many of the First Tier owned land there because of the plentiful game and fishing. "You hooked me with your cast and tore out some flesh. I do believe you caught a steelhead."

Now Martin laughed—quick, ironic. "Biggest trout I ever saw," he admitted. "That fish was the size of a dog. Father mounted it in the cottage." He paused, remembering. "But which room?"

"The sitting room," Ferran said. "It replaced our family portrait."

Martin regarded him a bit longer. Then a spark of disbelief kindled his eyes.

"Well, a man can weave a good story, but you can't fake a scar." Then, "I must say this is quite unexpected. We haven't heard any news of you in eight years. We thought you'd drowned off the Glass Coast."

"I've drowned many times," Ferran dismissed him.

"Ha!" His brother clapped him on the shoulder, and it seemed as if a different man had taken his place. "This is truly a winter solstice blessing. It seems the Goddess has smiled upon me at last. To think, after so many years, here you are in the flesh!" Martin gazed at Ferran, his eyes clear and focused, as though truly seeing him for the first time. "My long-lost brother, returned home. You look like a hard-traveled man—but your coat leads me to believe you're doing well?" He flicked the shoulders of Ferran's red coat as though admiring it, which was all for show, considering his own wealth. "You look like a proper lordling."

Ferran grimaced. "Thank you, but I'm afraid my station has fallen a bit lower than that," he said.

"No doubt," Martin agreed readily.

Ferran felt slightly put off.

His brother turned and circled around his desk again. He drew a cigar box from a cabinet at the corner of the room.

"Smoke?" he asked.

Ferran's hand twitched. With a bemused smile, he pulled a cinnamon stick from his pocket.

"I'm sorry to say I no longer partake," he declined.

Martin shrugged and cut a cigar. For a moment, Ferran thought he looked exactly like their father. That unnerved him.

"For a while, we didn't stop hearing about you," Martin said as he sat down again in his chair. "All sorts of stories and adventures about your *procurement* service. Father denied any connection to the Ebonaire line, of course, but...." He paused, and his mood seemed to shift. He turned solemn, as though remembering a dark time. "Mother missed you terribly. She would ask the servants for news of *that dastardly treasure hunter.* Simeon and I always listened. We enjoyed the stories. Simeon collected some of them in a journal. Said he might write a novel someday."

Ferran fingered the cinnamon stick in his pocket. "A novel?" he asked.

"Yes. Of course, Simeon doesn't remember you as I do, he was so young. He could barely walk when you left." Martin grinned. "If he knew you a bit better, he might not feel so enamored by your adventures."

"Well, that was a long time ago," Ferran muttered.

Martin didn't seem to hear. "We didn't all agree with your exile, you know. Father was old-fashioned. Said the honor of our family had been questioned and we couldn't have a thief running the Ebonaire estate. But for what it's worth, no family like ours has a lick of honor. We've missed you very much."

Martin laughed at that while Ferran remained uncomfortably silent. He wasn't fooled by his brother's jovial manner. When his father threw him out, Martin certainly hadn't stood up in his defense. He had the entire estate to inherit. Ferran wondered if he was only being welcomed home because he wasn't a threat.

"Well, you've certainly filled my shoes as heir," he mentioned, watching for his brother's reaction.

"I suppose it's in the blood," Martin said easily, then changed the topic. "What brings you here, after so many years? You appear to have journeyed far. And who is your lovely companion?" His eyes lingered on Sora again, glancing over her with keen interest. He ignored Crash completely, typical of the First Tier.

Ferran felt a strange surge of protectiveness. Sora was a lovely girl in the prime of beauty. She had an innocent look about her—a heart-shaped face and full bottom lip with large, wide-set blue eyes. Her petite figure was toned with muscle and attractively proportionate. He didn't like the way his brother's gaze lingered on her.

"This is my daughter, Sora," he said, keeping to the roles they had rehearsed on the Dawn Seeker. But his satisfaction went deeper than that. He liked seeing the twitch on Martin's face. "My wife is a respected Healer who studied at the royal seminary here in Crowns."

Martin's eyes darted between them. "I have a niece?" he said, and a charming smile came over his face. He set the cigar down, stood up, and took Sora's hand. "My Lady, you certainly carry a noble grace."

"Thank you, Lord Ebonaire," Sora said, and curtsied while holding his hand. She released his grip with the perfect amount of propriety.

Martin turned back to Ferran. His tone became grave. "Your arrival must be serendipity. This season has been hard on us. There seems to be a particularly nasty illness spreading around this winter. My wife...." His voice faded. "The illness claimed her three months ago. And now my daughter, Danica, has fallen ill...."

A look of anguish passed over Martin's face, and Ferran felt his chest squeeze. He noted his brother's somber dress.

"You're in mourning," he said, making sense of the general malaise of the house. "My condolences. Martin, if I had known...."

His brother waved a hand. "My wife is sorely missed, but we are surviving our grief." He recovered his composure. "The Healer's seminary is overrun and our house Healer is unable to treat Danica's illness. We've brought in three other Healers, and they've tried everything, but Lady Danica only grows worse."

Ferran could hear the genuine concern in his brother's voice. He cleared his throat.

"It must be serendipity indeed," he said. "My wife, Lorianne, is quite skilled."

Martin's eyes flashed. "Perhaps, if your wife is so well-trained, she could see my daughter?" He glanced around the room as though Lori would appear any second. "Where is she?"

"She remains on our ship. She wasn't sure how we would be welcomed. But I can send for her...."

"I'll send a man to your ship at once," Martin said quickly. "Where are you docked? What's the name of the vessel?"

Ferran hesitated. He wondered if it was wise to let Martin's servants see their pirate ship. Or perhaps it didn't matter. What harm could a simple summons do?

"We're at the south pier, anchored at dock 54 near the bottom end. 'Tis a large schooner named the Dawn Seeker."

Martin jotted the location onto a piece of parchment. "This illness is unlike anything we've seen before," he said as he wrote. "You'd be wise to avoid some areas of the city. As many as a thousand have already died on the west bank. Can you believe that? A thousand! It's a wonder the King hasn't closed the gates. We're hoping Headmaster Duncan will persuade him. The King might listen to the head of the seminary." Martin sighed as though he had already abandoned that hope. "For now, King Royce is pacifying the lower tiers for the winter solstice. He has such a soft touch with his people. Too soft, some say."

"A travesty," Ferran muttered.

"I'd say so!" his brother agreed, missing the sarcasm. "The First Tier is pressuring the King to close the gates as soon as possible. It's for the good of the Kingdom. What if the royal family were to fall ill?"

Ferran shifted uncomfortably. "The lower tiers can't be left to face this affliction on their own."

"Then what do you suggest?" Martin asked. "There is no cure. This plague will pass eventually. The lower tiers will survive—the peasants are countless in number—but should the upper tier fall, who will replace us?"

Ferran searched his brother's face, not quite trusting the man's expression. Martin had never worked with his hands. He didn't see the peasants as his countrymen; he didn't understand their lives or day-to-day struggles. His brother was a true Ebonaire—arrogant and aristocratic, all smoothed over by deceptive warmth and charm.

"Please," Martin continued after he finished his note. "Stay and tell me of your journey. I'll have Donwick bring up lunch. This is a day for celebration. I have a new sister-in-law and niece, and my long-lost brother has returned home. Let's not argue about the Kingdom's fate."

Ferran nodded, still uneasy. He hadn't expected to be welcomed home warmly after so many years. Had all the hatred come from his father alone? He couldn't know for sure.

"Sit down, sit down!" Martin insisted, indicating the large armchairs around his desk.

At that moment, Donwick strode into the room with a prestigious air. Ferran surmised he had been standing outside the entire time.

"Send a footman to the waterfront to arrange for Ferran's wife," Lord Martin said, and passed him the small folded parchment. "And bring lunch for my guests, and a bottle of our best wine! This will be a day of tall tales!" He gave Ferran an engaging smile. "I want to hear *every last detail*."

Sora lay back on the stuffed feather mattress and stared at the wide canopy overhead. The bed was soft, like lying on a dense, woolen cloud. Rain thrummed against the tall window next to her. As she watched, the rain lessened and large white snowflakes began to drift down from the sky, glowing in the light of a single lantern on her bedside table. They looked like flecks of crystal drifting down from a pitch-black oblivion, silent as ash. The first snow of winter.

Her eyes roved restlessly around the dark room: two ornate bedside tables, a large writing desk, a majestic wardrobe and vanity. The walls were covered in oil paintings of spring gardens and placid sunrises. A wide, elaborate strip of crown molding framed the high ceiling.

*Ebonaire.* Ferran was their eldest disowned son, and she would spend the next two weeks at the Ebonaire estate. She still couldn't quite believe it. She half-expected to fall asleep and wake up back on the Dawn Seeker, still sailing up the Little Rain.

All this time, she had treated Ferran like a scruffy ragtag pirate, only to discover he was next to royalty. The reality hadn't fully struck her until she saw him standing in Martin's office, face-to-face with his brother, and she felt that air about him—the unmistakable confidence of a lord.

She put one hand on her head, still unable to absorb it all. How long had her mother known? The entire time? Why hadn't Lori told her?

Sora wished she could ask, but her mother wouldn't arrive until tomorrow. Meanwhile, Lady Danica's fever worsened in the room across the hall. She could hear the low chatter of maids as they came and went. She wondered if Lady Danica's health was the only reason for their stay. Martin Ebonaire was obviously desperate for a skilled Healer. He might have welcomed them warmly, but he had asked after Lori all through the afternoon, and again at dinner. Sora wondered if he would toss them out as soon as his daughter recovered.

The two brothers seemed like night and day. Martin was every inch an aristocrat, while Ferran sprawled rather than sat at the dinner table. Martin didn't seem to question their story, as Ferran told it. The treasure hunter claimed to have made gobs of wealth with his practice. He described the rolling sand dunes of Ester and the black, polished surface of the Glass Coast, where lightning storms ignited the sand. He described his retirement, including his marriage to Lori and the birth of their daughter. That's about where the story stopped. Sora remained mostly silent.

"*And after so long, why visit now?*" Martin asked.

Ferran shifted, as though truly embarrassed by his question. *"Father died,"* he finally said. *"Five years ago, I know, but I never made my goodbyes. Family seems more important now than it once did."*

The conversation continued until she sensed the late hour and retired for the night. Ferran and Martin remained awake, to her knowledge, still speaking in the drawing room. She wondered what Ferran would tell his brother after a few more glasses of brandy. How far would his story go?

Sora bit her lip and watched the snow drift languidly down from the sky. She tried not to think of the day ahead. She couldn't remember the last time she had socialized with other nobles. Her Blooming, perhaps. Martin said he would arrange for Danica's handmaid to escort her around the Regency tomorrow for a new wardrobe, fit for a daughter of the Ebonaire estate. In short—dress shopping. She writhed uncomfortably at the thought. She would much rather start hunting for the Shade, and track down Burn as quickly as possible. She was only too aware of their wasted afternoon. Her thoughts had returned to Burn over and over again. If he was found dead, she would never forgive herself.

But Crash was absent; he vanished later in the evening. She could only wonder where he went—perhaps he had already found the Shade's trail, and was hunting down Burn. She couldn't allow herself to hope.

Sora closed her eyes tightly, willing herself to go to sleep. She rolled over, away from the large window and swirling gusts of snow.

# CHAPTER 19

C rash crouched on the ledge outside Sora's window. The steeply slanted tiles of the Ebonaire roof made balancing difficult. Fragile snowflakes dusted the roof in a fine white quilt. He watched Sora toss and turn inside her grand bedroom.

Then he turned to the sprawling grounds of the Ebonaire estate. A blanket of snow obscured the wide front drive and expansive gardens. No light penetrated the darkness. Still, to his nocturnal eyes, he was able to make out the trimmed hedges, marble statues, and even the lumbering oak trees that marked the beginning of the driveway.

He felt neither the snowflakes nor the cold wind. As a creature of Fire and Darkness, his thoughts burned and simmered like hot coals.

Ferran was wasting their time. Crash didn't see any evidence of the Shade in The Regency, and Burn's life still hung in the balance. He couldn't wait for Cobra or Cerastes to show themselves. He had made a promise to Sora, and he intended to keep it.

He watched her for another minute. He wondered how she felt, surrounded by such decadence after so much time on the road. She didn't seem as comfortable as he had expected. She never spoke fondly of her life as a noble—and had not wanted to return to it.

He finally turned around and leapt from the window ledge, sliding easily down the side of the tiered roof. He caught hold of an ivy-covered trellis and climbed down the rest of the way to the ground and started his solitary way to the city.

*Burn.* He didn't want to frighten Sora, but their companion would be dead soon if he didn't act. His kind were not merciful. If he told her of Burn's looming fate, she would want to accompany him, and he couldn't allow that. Cerastes wanted her Cat's-Eye necklace, and he had to keep her away from the Shade.

*You're a fool,* he thought. She would never forgive him for this. But sacrifices must be made.

Once in the city, he flagged a coach to take him to the docks. Along the way, his thoughts dwelled on Caprion's interrogation of the female assassin. The Shade wanted the weapons of the Dark God, and although Crash loathed the thought of helping their enemy, he couldn't justify leaving Burn to die.

*Sentiment.* Such thoughts went against his brutal training.

Logically, he knew Cerastes would use the sacred weapons for his own dark purposes. So by bringing him the weapons, Crash played directly into his hands.

Perhaps that was the only way to win.

The coach arrived at the silent docks. Slipping aboard the Dawn Seeker was easy at this late hour, as most of the crew were asleep or exploring various pubs along the riverfront. He tied a black scarf around the lower half of his face, and pulled his hood down low. He didn't want to be recognized if he were seen. Then he scaled the side of the ship and pulled himself onto the deck.

He walked stealthily to Sora's cabin without incident, and found the small wooden box beneath her cot. It sent a tingle of energy through his hands, and he felt a stirring deep in his gut, just beneath his lungs. With a slow intake of breath, he removed the sacred weapons and tucked them securely under his cloak. Their freezing energy seeped through his shirt, and made his skin prickle like static.

The demon moved closer to the surface of his skin. *What are you doing, little snake?*

Crash didn't reply. He waited for its presence to fade. Then he turned to leave.

*Caution,* the demon murmured, but he ignored it. He was halfway down the hallway when a white light suddenly flared behind him.

He paused. Painful vibrations crossed his skin. *Damn.*

"Halt!" Caprion's voice rang with authority. The word struck the assassin's back like a gust of wind. "Who goes there?"

Crash fought against his own legs. By force of will, he broke the Harpy's thrall and took off running across the wooden planks. He heard Caprion curse and give chase. Another searing vibration rolled across his skin, and Caprion called out in authoritative command, "Stop!"

His body shuddered, wanting to obey, but his demon's strength flared and he shrugged off the compulsion. He reached the deck, but Caprion was following closely.

Crash ran directly for the railing, intending to jump into the midnight waters of The Bath, but he knew no matter how far he ran, the Harpy could fly and follow him. *Now what?* he thought in frustration. He needed the weapons to save Burn's life. He wouldn't let another friend die at his expense. Caprion couldn't understand that; he already thought Crash was allied with the Shade.

White light surrounded the assassin's feet. With a crack of power, the Harpy brought him crashing to the deck. The light engulfed his body and made his legs and arms heavy, his breath labored. The bright sheen burned his eyes. He found himself pinned to the floor, but managed to get onto his knees, resisting the Harpy's power, although his attempts were nearly futile.

"Give back the weapons," Caprion repeated. His words echoed as though he stood in a domed chamber, not on the icy deck of the Dawn Seeker.

*You'll have to kill me,* Crash thought, but didn't speak aloud. His voice would betray his identity.

Then, unexpectedly, a dark shadow pooled beneath him. It seemed to counter-act the light, and for a moment, the two forces strained against each other. Then the darkness spread. Crash glanced down, unnerved by the sight. He supposed the Shade would be watching their boat, but he hadn't thought they would act.

A man climbed out of the wooden deck—out of the portal.

Cobra leered at the Harpy. "Surprise!" he laughed. Then, to Crash, "What are friends for?"

Then he wrapped his arms around Crash's torso and dragged him down through the portal. It felt similar to sinking in quicksand. Disorienting black mist enveloped him; he saw nothing, heard nothing. He no longer smelled the river, or felt the snow pelting his skin.

When Crash next opened his eyes, he lay underground, on a cold stone floor.

His head spun. He wasn't used to traveling through portals, and his stomach churned for a long minute. He took several deep breaths to steady himself, then got back on his feet.

As his eyes adjusted to the gloom, he became aware of Cobra standing before him. The assassin wore a splint on one arm where Burn's mighty sword had cracked his wrist. His face was covered by a ragged black cowl.

"Come," Cobra beckoned in his wheezing voice. "My master expects you." He turned and walked away through a long corridor of heavy gray stone.

Crash hesitated before following him, but he didn't have much choice. The only path lay forward.

They walked in silence. The air was musty and stale. Cobra led him through a series of dark tunnels and half-built chambers. He noted the exposed wooden beams along the ceiling of each room. It appeared that their location was still under construction. The sound of churning gears echoed faintly through the rock. He tilted his head, trying to identify the sound, but could not discern it.

Eventually, they arrived at a central room where many different tunnels converged. The ceiling expanded outward into a wide, cavernous dome. A distant trickle of water echoed through the chamber. He couldn't tell which tunnel it came from. He suspected they were somewhere in the sewer systems beneath the City of Crowns, but he wasn't sure. They could be in an ancient mountain tomb, or the basement of a long-forgotten temple.

Then a shadow moved at the center of the room. His eyes detected a misty, evanescent figure. Suddenly, he recognized the wraith.

Crash's body stiffened, and his skin prickled in alarm. The wraith floated back and forth, hovering in the air. A tattered cloak covered its vaporous body. The creature seemed to continually dissolve and re-form out of mist, as though it only half-existed on the physical plane.

The specter took notice of him, changed course, and hurtled across the room with a piercing shriek.

Crash stumbled back and drew his dagger, expecting the wraith to barrel into him. But it abruptly stopped mid-flight. A keen of frustration split his ears. The thing raised its arms, skeletal hands clenched, and pounded against some unseen barrier.

Crash slowly lowered his dagger and glanced down. On the floor, a circle of white powder kept the wraith contained. At first he thought it was salt, but it was too fine. Sand? Powdered bone? *What kind of sorcery is this?* What magic could imprison a creature from the underworld?

"Don't look so surprised," a low voice said. "This spell is but a single page in *The Book of the Named.*"

A tall figure uncoiled from the shadows across the room. Crash's throat tightened, but he forced himself to remain calm. He knew the man's stride before he saw his face.

Cerastes approached him with a deliberate step. He seemed to glide rather than walk, as darkly ethereal as the wraith. He paused a few yards away, and the two men stared at each other. Cerastes was a tall man, his muscular physique visible through his layers of robes. Long black hair trailed down to his navel. His cheeks were thin and gaunt, his eyes like hollow lanterns. Deep lines around his lips marked his age. His aura permeated the room like black smoke. The Grandmaster's demon had grown so strong, its presence bled into the air like a toxic cloud. Cerastes' skin looked paper-thin, merely a costume to be worn as the demon's guise.

"I take it you've come for the Wulven mercenary?".

Crash nodded. He didn't trust his voice yet.

"Then you've brought me the weapons." A thin smile twisted Cerastes' lips, utterly meaningless.

Crash felt numb, somehow paralyzed. He wondered if he had made a mistake...but it was too late to change his mind. If he showed any sort of weakness, any sort of hesitancy, he would be killed.

"Release the Wolfy," he said directly, "and you will have your weapons...if he's still alive."

Cerastes' lips quirked. His gaze traveled to Cobra. "Bring him out. Let our snake see for himself."

Cobra bowed. Shadows gathered at his feet, and a second later he disappeared. Crash gazed at where the assassin had stood. The fifth gate. He was sorely reminded of his own shortcomings. He might be renowned in the Hive for physical combat, but his other skills were limited.

Cerastes folded his arms and turned back to him. "Now, Viper," he said, "why are you really here?"

Crash shifted. He knew Cerastes had carefully planned this confrontation. His Grandmaster was cunning, above all else. He wanted something more than just the weapons.

Crash wondered if he could use that to his advantage, and if he could learn more about the Shade's plan. He would surely need to choose his words wisely.

"I wish to join the Shade and continue my training."

Cerastes considered him for a long moment. "I already know where your loyalties lie."

Crash expected this. His Grandmaster was not a fool. He tried again.

"I allowed myself to develop sentimental attachments, but now I see the error of my ways. I want to unlock the fifth gate. I wish to join your side, if you will have me."

Cerastes studied him. "No," he said. "I don't believe that's true."

Crash didn't know how to reply.

"You wish to kill me," Cerastes said.

The words surprised him, but Crash kept his face composed. *True,* he thought. Now what?

After a long moment, Cerastes' cold smile returned. "I can read your silence. You wish to kill me, and you think you might succeed. But what I've built, Viper, extends far beyond me. You have no idea what I've become."

"Then show me," Crash said. "If your power is so great, you have nothing to fear. I brought you the weapons. Have I not earned a modicum of trust?"

Cerastes' smile broke into a laugh, like a dry gust of wind. "Fear and trust?" he rasped. "I fear no one, and I trust no one. I will confide in you, little snake, if that is what you wish. But you might regret it." Cerastes fixed him with a piercing stare. "I know who you are, Viper, and I know what you truly want."

Those words resonated in Crash's bones. He shuddered, and his demon rippled through his mind like an eel through black water.

Cerastes turned and with a wave of his hand, summoned a portal. He beckoned Crash forward, and as one, they stepped into the darkness.

Crash felt a familiar sense of vertigo. Suffocating shadows enveloped him. Then a sudden red light pierced his eyes. He squinted against the unexpected glare and raised his dagger, prepared for an attack, but none came.

After a few seconds, his eyes adjusted. The light came from a burning, vibrant sunset. Hot, dry wind rippled his hair, carrying flecks of grit and sand.

He looked down, realizing he was standing on the edge of a steep cliff. Rusty red rock stretched hundreds of feet below him into a vast desert. He saw a large encampment with endless campfires and pitched tents spread out at his feet. At this distance, the occupants looked like tiny ants marching to and fro.

He immediately regretted stepping through the portal, with no assurance that Cerastes would return him from this place.

His Grandmaster stood behind him, his arms crossed, his hands tucked into his billowing sleeves.

"Where are we?" Crash asked.

"Here is where your brethren come to train," Cerastes replied. "See for yourself all those rejected by the Hive. Here, they have found a new home."

Crash looked back at the tiny ants below. "You brought them here."

"They came of their own will."

"Why?"

Cerastes raised an eyebrow. "Why? Can you really not imagine? To find a higher purpose. To stand in the Dark God's shadow, and enact His will upon the world. Is that not the true purpose of our kind?"

Crash frowned. "The Hive does not teach this...."

"The Hive is weak, and our race's knowledge has been diluted." Cerastes swept his arm out, as though to encompass the entire desert and all the lands beyond. "This world has been stolen from us. The humans have destroyed our history, our heritage. Why should we allow ourselves to quietly vanish? Why should we let the humans keep what is rightfully ours?"

Crash shifted. "The war ended centuries ago," he said. "They won."

"No," Cerastes said. "We gave up the fight."

Crash turned to face his Grandmaster. "You intend to start a war against the humans?" he asked incredulously. "We can't win. Even with all the races united, there are too many humans to kill on a battlefield."

An empty smile pulled once again at Cerastes' lips. "Not a war," he said. "Something more final. A complete and total ending, if you will."

Despite the harsh heat of the desert, Crash felt himself grow cold. He looked back at the rows of tents far below, hundreds of them, perhaps thousands. The Shade's numbers were far greater than he imagined. Cerastes was forming an army, that much he could tell.

His Grandmaster watched him. "Why do you think I am showing you this?" he asked quietly.

Crash thought he knew the answer. "Because you intend to kill me."

"No, Viper," Cerastes murmured. "Because I intend to save you. I intend to bring you home."

Crash flinched at those words, as if he had been struck in the face. *Home.* It should be a meaningless word, and yet he wondered what it would feel like to have a place to return to, a place to belong.

*Don't listen. These are not your people.*

"And the Dark God's weapons?" he finally asked.

Cerastes' eyes glinted. "They are the key to everything."

Then he turned toward the cliff face, waved his hand again, and another portal opened.

"Come," he said. "Let us return to the snow."

Crash followed him, and a few steps later, found himself once again in the wide stone chamber under the earth. The sudden change was unnerving. Moist air engulfed him, and the stale scent of old water, and he knew they must be somewhere near The City of Crowns, far away from the desert heat. The wraith hovered before him, still trapped by the circle of white powder.

The sound of heavy chains rustled in the darkness, drawing Crash's attention. He looked up. Cobra entered the chamber, with Burn limping slowly behind him.

The sight of the Wolfy brought Crash back to himself. He remembered again why he had come here. The history between himself and Cerastes was difficult to ignore, but he had other bonds now: new people who needed him, who trusted him, and who had shown him a different way of life.

Blood matted Burn's hair from a head wound, and he staggered as he walked. Pain dulled his eyes. Crash could guess Burn's thoughts. He would rather die than put his friends in danger. But Crash's mind was already made up; he was not going to let Burn pay the price for his own mistakes.

"Release him," Crash said. "I'd gladly exchange my life for his."

"An intriguing offer, but no."

He faced Cerastes, now angry. "What more do you want? I've brought you the weapons you seek."

"I have need of a Cat's Eye."

"The Sixth Race cannot wield such a stone. None of the magical races can."

Cerastes was calm. "Then I shall need the bearer as well."

Crash remained silent.

The Grandmaster became amused. "You've gone to great lengths to keep her from me, but I know about your little tryst. Bring her to me and prove your loyalty."

Bile rose at the very thought, yet Crash knew he tread on dangerous ground. Despite his Grandmaster's promises, Cerastes would kill him if he refused to obey, and then no one would stand between Sora and the Shade.

"I know of another stone, another bearer," he began.

"The girl, Viper." Cerastes' voice was ice. "I want the girl."

Crash's fists clenched. He knew, then, that this was personal.

"I will do your bidding," he relented.

"Yes, you will," Cerastes said. "And until then, I will keep the Wolfy to ensure your obedience."

"That wasn't the deal."

"You're right; it wasn't."

Crash glared. "I brought you the weapons. Now release him."

"No," his Grandmaster said firmly. "Not until you prove your loyalty to me. And in exchange for your silence, I will keep the mercenary alive." His tone became low and lethal. "Don't forget what I have shown you."

Crash looked again at Burn. He should have expected this; all sense of control had been effortlessly pulled from his grasp. The Wolfy's golden eyes told him to turn back, but it was too late.

"You could have played this better, Viper," Cerastes said knowingly. "I taught you better, and I will teach you more, should you bring the girl to me." He spread his arms. "The fifth gate. Mastery of your demon. A place of prestige and power when the Dark God rises. What more could an assassin want? What more could *my student* want?"

Cerastes' words summoned a strange yearning within him, a yearning Crash tried to deny. After all these years. His Grandmaster's presence still held power over him. Those simple, targeted words seemed to burrow into his mind: *I taught you better.*

A crack formed in his armor, and doubt slipped in. How could he stand against his own Grandmaster? He was the Viper, a Named assassin, *he who hides in the grass.* He couldn't leave that life behind. Not when it stood in front of him, mocking him, beckoning him closer.

An eager stirring began in his chest. The demon wanted to overtake his sense of morality, shirk the burden of human guilt and release its chaotic will upon the world.

Crash knew the demon's desires well. He had fought to overcome them for years. Now, disturbingly, as he felt pulled toward Cerastes' promises, he suddenly understood the fanatic loyalty of the Shade. His Grandmaster offered his demon the purpose—and power—it desired.

He bowed his head, and in an instant, he knew he had promised too much.

# Chapter 20

The next morning, Sora was awakened by Lady Danica's handmaid and a serving girl from the kitchens. Her room's large bay windows overlooked the front of the manor. She could see a thin blanket of snow dusting everything except the driveway, which had been shoveled clear and salted. The clouds above remained sullen and ominous, threatening more snow to come.

The serving girl laid out her breakfast tray on the bed and quietly left the room. Sora pounced on the silver platter of food: cinnamon toast, honey, eggs and black tea. She was left with Lady Danica's handmaid—Olivia, as the woman introduced herself. She was slender, with short blond hair and wide brown eyes. Unsmiling, she curtsied and went to the wardrobe, where she selected several outfits.

As she ate breakfast, Sora watched her new handmaid curiously. It was common knowledge that a handmaid took on the mannerisms of her mistress. Olivia walked with her head held high and her prim nose raised slightly in the air, exactly how a servant of the First Tier should look. It made Sora wonder about Lady Danica's tastes. What kind of person would her new "cousin" turn out to be?

"This is the fashion?" Sora asked, inspecting the elaborate dresses Olivia laid out, one in deep magenta, another in forest green, and a third in royal blue.

"From last season," Olivia admitted. "You'll find it more than appropriate."

An inkling of doubt entered her mind. Fashion changed slowly in the country, but in the City of Crowns, the fashion center of the Kingdom, she wondered if wearing a dress from last season would mark her as an outsider or draw unwarranted attention. Did the Shade know anything about dresses, hats and boots? *Most likely not,* she thought, then felt a little silly.

"We'll make do," Sora said.

She meant the words as a peace offering, but Olivia looked offended and turned up her nose a little.

"Lady Danica is generous indeed to offer up her wardrobe, given her current condition," she sniffed. And then, with a change of emphasis, "Lord Martin entrusted your new wardrobe to me. We will have you fitted today in the Flower District."

Sora felt suitably chastised.

"The Flower District?" she asked.

"The women's district, where all the women's boutiques are," Olivia replied, distinctly unimpressed. Her expression said it all—what noble-born lady didn't know about the Flower District?

Sora decided to keep her mouth shut from then on. Lord Martin must have kept some information from his staff, and perhaps hadn't revealed Ferran's fallen state. Olivia seemed skeptical that Sora was really noble blood.

That could be worrisome. The staff was probably abuzz with speculation. If anyone could tell Sora didn't belong, it would be a lady's handmaid. How fast would news of Ferran's arrival spread through the servants' corridors to the neighboring estate's kitchens? How long before he was identified, and all the servants of the First Tier knew? Surely the older servants would remember him. Surely someone would recall his exile. And then what?

Sora indicated the royal blue dress, deciding she liked the color. Olivia put the other two back in the wardrobe. Sora studied the design: a tight bodice with a square-cut neckline, and a heavy velvet skirt that opened at the front to reveal a length of white petticoat underneath. In the country, long skirts were made to hide a woman's petticoats, which were considered undergarments. In her opinion, the dress looked quite risque, but she stopped herself from mentioning that.

Olivia brought out a set of panniers, wide hoops used to boost the many skirts she would be wearing. The panniers would considerably exaggerate her figure.

"Is that necessary?" Sora balked. What if she needed to defend herself? Where would she put her daggers? With the hoops, it would be next to impossible to land a kick, or even touch her toes.

Olivia didn't bat an eye. "It's the style. The dress is made for it."

Sora crossed her arms. "Well, I don't like it. "She no longer cared about impressing a house servant. "We're going to the market, not a royal ball. I'd like a simpler dress."

"A simpler dress?" Olivia asked. "My Lady, it's winter and the summer styles are packed away."

"You're wearing something practical," Sora said, indicating the maid's simple black skirts and bodice. No hoops or adornments, just long pleats and an apron.

Olivia looked startled. "You wish to dress as a peasant?" she asked slowly.

Sora hesitated, torn between her desire for comfort and her need to play her role. Which was better—disguising her identity from the Shade, or being able to defend herself? What would Martin Ebonaire think if she chose to wear peasant clothes?

Finally, she said, "I suppose it shall do, if there's nothing else. Let's see how it fits."

Sora walked cautiously down the long set of stairs to the ground floor of the Ebonaire manor, balancing carefully in her dark blue skirts, which spanned several feet from her waist. It all came back to her slowly—the weight of the panniers, the sway of heavy fabric, the thin heels on her shoes. Her posture was naturally straighter, so she could walk gracefully. The dress constricted her breathing; her hair was pinned tightly about her head in a braid. Yes, she remembered this.

Olivia escorted her to an informal breakfast room, then bowed briefly.

"I'll have a driver bring 'round a carriage," she said, and excused herself.

Several comfortable chairs of varying styles sprawled in a half-circle around a large fireplace. A tea tray had been placed on a low table. Martin Ebonaire sat across from her, facing the entryway, a porcelain cup half-raised to his lips. Ferran was seated next to him. When they saw her, their conversation stopped. Martin's brown eyes widened marginally as he set his cup down.

Sora blushed under his intense gaze. She had to admit, Martin Ebonaire was a strikingly handsome man, if a bit too old for her taste. She thought he resembled a younger, less-weathered version of Ferran. His skin was smooth and clean, his features sharp and intelligent, with high cheekbones, a proud chin and shiny dark hair tied loosely at the nape of his neck. He wore an elegant black riding jacket over a vest of gold brocade, with a silk neckerchief tucked around the high collar of his shirt. Sora imagined Silas drooling over the whole ensemble.

"My Lord," she murmured, and dropped into a stiff curtsy. As an afterthought, she bobbed her head to Ferran as well. "Father," she said. The word felt strange on her lips, but at least she was playing her part.

"You look lovely," Ferran said.

Sora focused on her role as a noblewoman. "Oh, this?" She plucked at her skirts. "Lady Danica generously loaned it. Lord Martin has offered me a new wardrobe."

Martin gave her an approving look. "I'm sure your beauty would outshine any dress, my dear niece. I am happy to help you prepare for the winter solstice. No niece of mine shall go wanting."

Ferran snorted, but said nothing.

Martin Ebonaire rose from his armchair. "Please, will you join us before your visit to the Flower District?" He offered her a seat.

Sora tried to think of a polite way to decline. She glanced awkwardly around the room, then paused. A man sat in a chair behind her. She hadn't seen him at first because her back was turned, but she recognized him. Her heart stopped.

She had last encountered Lord Gracen Seabourne—captain of the King's personal guard—two years ago in Mayville when she fled her father's manor. In fact, he arrested her and accused her of murder. His brown hair was considerably more gray now, though she knew him to be a young man, around thirty years old. There were dark circles under his eyes. Still, he harbored the aristocratic grace of the First Tier, and was well-dressed in a dark green, velvet morning jacket.

He studied her intently, and she felt self-conscious. Did he recognize her? She couldn't tell.

Dumbfounded by his presence, Sora took the offered seat and accepted a cup of tea from the maid. Ferran met her gaze curiously but she looked away. *Calm down*, she said to herself firmly. She needed to regain her composure. She played with the teacup, and wondered again if Lord Gracen recognized her.

The conversation continued. Sora listened to Martin chat idly about a joint business venture with the Daniellians. Ferran leaned forward with interest when he heard the name. She noticed he asked quite a few questions about the doings of

Cedric Daniellian, now head of the Daniellian estate and a patron of the Healing seminary.

As Ferran and Martin spoke, Lord Gracen turned to her with a wan smile.

"It's a pleasure to make your acquaintance, Lady Sora," he said. "*Sora*," he repeated. "That's a unique name."

"Oh?" she replied. Her mouth went dry.

"Yes," he continued, unconcerned. "In fact, it reminds me of an incident quite a few years ago. I was called out to the high plains to a small estate. Lord Frederick Fallcrest, a country noble, was murdered at his daughter's Blooming. The whole business was very strange. Sadly, his daughter ran off into Fennbog swamp and was killed by wild beasts."

Sora did her best to look shocked. She even gave a small gasp. "Eaten by wild beasts?" she murmured, hoping she sounded appropriately disgusted.

"We couldn't find her body, but the swamp is nigh impassable. The hunt was abandoned years ago."

"Ah," Sora muttered. "How very sad."

"I don't think you've told me that story," Martin interrupted.

Seabourne crossed his legs. "Well, they were Second Tier country nobility. No one important."

Sora felt ruffled at that. "If it was so unimportant, why were you called out to the countryside?" she asked. "Seems strange you would travel so far, just for the murder of a country lord...."

Gracen frowned. "Lord Fallcrest invited me to his daughter's Blooming and asked for a private audience. Sadly, we never had the chance to speak."

Martin held up his hand. "Wait. I think I remember this Fallcrest fellow. A bit round in the middle, with a wide drawl. Balding, I think. Didn't he stay in the city a few years ago?"

"Aye," Seabourne confirmed. "He tried to strike up a business arrangement with a few investors, something about importing goods from down the coast. I assume his plans fell through."

"We met briefly," Martin recalled. "I suppose my business sense served me well. Can't have a man dying in the middle of a new venture." But he seemed troubled. "Whatever happened to his estate?"

Sora focused hard on her teacup.

Gracen sat back thoughtfully. "It was absorbed by the King. Fallcrest's brother tried to claim it, but it was tied up in court. Letters were found in Frederick's desk implying he had committed treason...or was it tax evasion? Some such vagary. The matter was swiftly sorted and closed. No one likes to admit it, but the royal family can do what they like. They sold off the land in parcels, I believe."

Sora felt her heart plummet, but she hid her reaction behind a handkerchief. She pretended to dab at her lips. Sold off? A hundred questions filled her mind, and she struggled to keep them in check.

At that moment, Olivia appeared at the doorway. She bowed to Martin Ebonaire. "My Lord," she said. "I'm sorry to interrupt. The carriage is ready and we must be leaving."

"Excellent timing, as I do believe we have an afternoon ride planned," Lord Martin agreed. "And remind Donwick that Ferran's wife will be arriving this evening, will you? We must prepare a room for her." He stood up, as did the other men.

Sora set down her tea and got up. Lord Martin took her hand in farewell; his touch was surprisingly warm and gentle. "I've given a stipend to Olivia for your new wardrobe. Don't hurry, take your time and enjoy the city."

"I will take my leave then," Lord Gracen said in farewell. "I have business in the Gentleman's District, then off to the royal court for a hearing this afternoon."

"An eventful day, as always," Martin grinned. "And tomorrow? Will you be busy with the parade?"

"Same as every year," Lord Gracen said dryly. The weight of his many responsibilities dampened his voice. A maid entered with his cane and coat. He donned them both, turned and strode away, his cane tapping rhythmically on the polished wooden floor.

Sora gazed after him, filled with both relief and burning curiosity. Her stepfather, accused of treason? Her estate dissolved? It didn't sit right. She craved to know more.

And then, that long-ago question—who had hired Crash to kill her father? Was the culprit here in this very city? In The Regency, perhaps?

She sighed, wondering where Crash had gone. He hadn't shown himself all morning, and she had expected him to accompany her around The Regency. His absence bothered her more than she wanted to admit. What if they ran across the

Shade? Olivia wouldn't be much help in a fight. Weren't they supposed to look for Burn and the Shade's hideout?

She shared a look with Ferran; his eyes cautioned her to be careful. Then she curtsied elegantly and left the room, with Olivia in tow.

# CHAPTER 21

By noon, The Regency streets were crowded with foot traffic, and carriages traveled slowly down the cobblestone roads. In some places, the snow had melted and formed slick patches of black ice. Horses picked their dainty way to and fro. The air felt crisp and moist through the open window of the Ebonaire carriage; each breath tasted of fresh snow and pine.

The Flower District spanned four blocks on the far west side of The Regency. Sora thought it resembled something out of a storybook. Clean cobblestones and wide flagstones paved the road. Signs painted with fancy gold-leaf lettering hung above each boutique. Despite the layer of snow dusting the streets, winter blossoms grew in long planters by the side of the road. Flowers bloomed beneath window sills, above doorways, or in large pots next to the entrance of each store. She recognized bright pink camellias, dainty white snowdrops, sprawling winter jasmine and bushels of purple violets, all hardy plants with small, bright petals that could resist the frost. She imagined in Spring the District would be overflowing with color and rich perfume. *And bees,* she thought.

Many ladies walked slowly along the street with their maids or footmen. Older women traveled with their servants or a single companion, while the younger girls moved in large packs, giggling and laughing with each step. They wore skirts supported by wide panniers, just like Sora's, and fur-lined cloaks buttoned tight around their shoulders. Some wore decorative hats above lavish, curled hair.

Sora remembered Olivia trying to thrust such a hat upon her this morning. She had declined, and wore her hair braided. Her lack of glamour seemed to impress Olivia not a jot.

She didn't know which families the women on the street hailed from, but judging by their dress, she realized Olivia's extravagant gown wasn't over-the-top. Lady Danica obviously had expensive taste, but her gowns were elegant, almost understated. Some of the girls wore dresses with large, puffy sleeves and gaudy patterns, or feathers pinned every which way on their bodice. They looked like bright, bejeweled peacocks. Sora glanced down at her royal blue skirts again and thought, *Expensive, but tasteful.*

As their carriage pulled up alongside a group of stores, the driver opened the door and helped them step out.

"Here, Milady," Olivia said, directing her to the nearest boutique. "First, we shall secure several day-gowns, then a few dinner gowns, and a costume for the winter festival, which we can get at a store up the street. How many weeks will you be staying? Have you given thought to your mask for the festival? Black is very much in-style this season."

"Black?" Sora asked, surprised.

Olivia nodded. "Traditional, I know, but the queen wore a black swan costume last year, and now all the young ladies want one. Lady Danica had her costume specially made by the Queen's own designer. She likes to compete with the princess, you see. This season, she aims to win."

Sora stared at the maid, unable to think of a response. Olivia politely ignored her shocked expression. Lady Danica, competing with the royal princess?

Olivia linked arms with Sora and escorted her up the street. "You've come a bit late in the season to have your costume made," she continued, "but perhaps we can find a seamstress who's willing to make alterations to a previous design .... You *are* staying for winter solstice eve, are you not?"

Sora grimaced at that. "Yes," she said shortly. *But not for the dancing.*

Olivia led her to a nearby boutique. The building's facade resembled a quaint country cottage. A stone lintel arched over the door. Inside, the floor was made of gleaming mahogany wood and white plaster walls. Rolls of fabric and strips of embroidery lined a long, narrow aisle through the small store.

Upon setting foot inside, Sora noted a large desk to their left. A short, gray-haired clerk sat behind it, poring over a bundle of dark green fabric. He glanced up over his thick spectacles. His gaze drifted over Sora to focus on Olivia with immediate recognition.

"My darling!" he exclaimed. He immediately rounded the desk and grasped Olivia's hand. With a flourish, he kissed the back of her palm. "My dear girl, how are you? And who is this lovely lady you bring into my shop?"

"Oh, Edward, you are too much!" Olivia gushed, then stepped aside. "This is Lady Sora Ebonaire, a cousin of Lady Danica's who is visiting for the winter season."

A spark appeared in the clerk's eyes: *Ebonaire* meant wealth. He turned to Sora with a vibrant smile. "Lady Sora!" the clerk greeted her. He said her name in a way that sounded respectful and endearing all at once.

Sora became acutely aware of her deception. She forced herself not to curtsy in return. An Ebonaire would only bow to those of equal or greater rank—namely, the royal bloodline—so she remained aloof.

The clerk recovered from her silence. "Welcome to *Winsome Couture*, a boutique specializing in the most current fashion trends!" he said, even more eager to please. "Our seamstresses work extensively with the royal family and all the upper tier. We just finished a new ball gown for Lady Marcella LeCroy, a good friend of Danica's. Have you met?"

"No," Sora replied.

"Ah, well, you are in good hands, I assure you. Let's take your measurements."

Edward led them down the narrow aisle to the back of the store. Sora felt suffocated by so many reams of cloth. Every kind of fabric imaginable spilled from the walls: bundles of silk, piles of brocade, streams of chiffon, rolls of cotton and velvet. Finally, she found herself at the rear of the boutique, in a quaint circular room surrounded by mirrors. Potted ivy and large indoor ferns grew along the walls. Sora was mildly impressed. Despite the fact that the boutique resembled a messy closet, it was still decorated in style.

Olivia led her behind one of the mirrors to a small changing stall. There, Sora removed her dress and panniers until she wore only her undergarments. She hesitated when Olivia tried to escort her back to the measuring room, and the maid smiled sweetly.

"Don't worry, Milady. This is routine," she assured.

Sora nodded. Strange, that she could traipse around the Lost Isles in a ripped shirt and no shoes without a second thought, but removing her skirts in The Regency gave her pause.

Olivia escorted her back into the room and helped her onto a small footstool. Then Edward returned with a strip of measuring cloth. He bustled about with a professional air, and Sora stood patiently as he measured her arms, bust, waist and hips. He jotted down numbers, occasionally muttering to himself.

"Thank you, Milady," he said as he finished. "This has given me much to work with."

The short ritual finished, Olivia assisted her back into her dress and they returned to the front of the shop.

"Do you have a certain style in mind?" the clerk asked. "Let me show you our design book."

Sora opened her mouth to respond, but Olivia took over at that point, explaining to him that several dresses were to be made. She listed a series of possible fabrics and cuts. Sora stayed behind as Edward led Olivia to the design book at his desk as ideas rolled easily off his tongue. Her eyes glazed over. She wanted to go explore the city, not spend all day standing on a stool, wrapped in cloth and stuck full of needles.

She looked out the front window at the line of shops across the narrow street.

An hour or more had passed since they had arrived at the shop, and the clouds were thinning overhead as the afternoon sun grew warmer. At times, a ray of sunlight broke through the dense sky to melt the frozen cobblestones.

A carriage passed. Sora frowned. Was that the Seabourne crest painted on the door?

The carriage stopped across the street, and she watched two young women step out of the coach. She wondered if they were directly related to Lord Gracen. One looked like she could be his sister and the other was younger, perhaps a niece. They walked into a perfume shop across the way.

Sora's mind traveled back to her conversation with Lord Gracen that morning. She had the sudden desire to ask him more questions about her stepfather's demise. Had her father truly committed treason? Why had Lord Fallcrest invited him to her Blooming? Did Gracen know who ordered her father's murder?

She took two steps toward the door, then paused. Lord Gracen wasn't at the Ebonaire estate anymore. He left already, saying he had business in the Gentleman's District.

She wondered how to excuse herself from the tailor's shop. Her patience had shortened admirably in the last year.

*Enough of this nonsense,* she thought. *Time to do something useful.*

She walked up to Olivia and Edward, who were still huddled over the design book. She placed her hand on Olivia's arm and said crisply, "Well, are we having any luck?"

Olivia started. "I've found a few gowns that might work, should you approve."

"Then I'll leave this in your very capable hands," Sora said. "Edward," she added to the store clerk, "Don't let me down!" Then, with a swift turn on her heel, she started back across the room, striding with a purposeful gait, her pointed slippers clicking on the wooden floor.

"But, My Lady, we are not yet finished! Where are you going?" Olivia called after her.

"To get some fresh air. I'll be close by!" But of course, she had no intention of staying close to them. She felt a little guilty for lying, but she hadn't come to The Regency to shop for dresses. If she couldn't hunt down the Shade, she could at least investigate the demise of her estate.

She passed through the archway into the frozen street, then started toward the Ebonaire coach.

Ferran returned around mid-afternoon from an uneventful ride with his brother.

They had shared only a few words over many hours. Eventually, his brother had broken the silence by pointing to an old deer trail and recalling how he and Ferran used to hunt game during the summer months. Ferran had relaxed somewhat after that, but he still didn't know how to act around his brother. Did he keep up his pretense of nobility, or slide into his familiar habits and ways of speech, allowing his brother to see how the last two decades had changed him?

He didn't have an answer upon returning to the stables. He wished Lori would arrive. At least then Martin would have someone else to focus on. After dismounting, they chatted idly for a minute about his brother's thoroughbred horses. They were a quality breed for hunting, with a bloodline that could be traced back to the war-stallions of the founding tribes of the Kingdom. Then Ferran excused himself, saying he needed to bathe and dress before Lori's arrival. He couldn't walk fast enough back to his rooms, where supposedly he would take a long bath.

Actually, he was headed for the second floor, to Martin's private study. His brother's behavior that morning had piqued his curiosity. Martin seemed uncomfortable around Lord Gracen, who had joined them unexpectedly for tea. At times, their conversation had sounded more like an interrogation. Ferran wondered at their friendship. Had Gracen been close to his brother for some time, or was Martin under suspicion of the King's guard? It wasn't any easy question to ask aloud.

Ferran had spent many years in low places. He knew a guilty conscience when he saw one. He could practically smell his brother's anxiety around Lord Gracen. He wanted to know what Martin was up to, and why.

He had seen something strange in Martin's study the night before, and he couldn't get it out of his mind: an old map splayed out on his brother's desk. It didn't look like a blueprint for a new estate, or a piece of land his brother might purchase. No, it was sketched in faded ink, the edges worn and creased, and it looked...*complex*.

Ferran, as a treasure hunter, had an affinity for old maps and considered himself a specialist of sorts. He had seen hundreds, both real and fake. But why would Martin—who loved horses, numbers and good business—take an interest in a faded old map?

He walked up the staircase and past Danica's bedroom to the upper floors. He knew Martin would take another hour or so inspecting the dozens of steeds in his well-stocked stables. His brother had always been an avid equestrian.

He finally reached Martin's private study. The door was locked, but that wasn't an obstacle. He rummaged in his pocket for two thin, hooked needles—lock picks—and inserted them into the brass knob. After a bit of finagling, the door clicked open.

Martin's study was exactly as it had been the night before, except Ferran didn't see the map. With a frown, he began shuffling through papers on the desk. Land deeds. Contracts. A few half-penned letters to various lords around the city. He glanced over a few, but read nothing of interest.

The left bottom desk drawer was locked. With a few quick twists, he sprung it open. Small leather-bound books were inside. He saw a carefully folded piece of parchment tucked between the pages of the top notebook, and identified it immediately. The map was wrinkled and worn, stained with age.

He gently pulled it out and unfolded it, then laid it on the desk. The map was about sixteen inches long and ten inches wide. A network of intersecting lines crossed the page. After a long moment, he detected square symbols for buildings and dark circles for monuments. A small scale in the corner explained land elevations.

He sucked in a quick breath. It was a blueprint, a very old one, that showed the original layout of the sewer system beneath the city.

"But why?" he murmured, unconsciously pulling a cinnamon stick from his pocket. He sucked on it for a moment. The spicy, burnt flavor made his tongue sting. "Why would he have this?"

The map was very detailed, showing not only access points but larger drainage tunnels. The sewer system followed the same natural model as water running off a mountain. Tributaries ran down from the windmills to the King's palace and The Regency, bearing fresh water. Following the pull of gravity, those same lines eventually connected to larger and larger pipes and tunnels that eventually emptied into the Crown's Rush, where wastewater was naturally swept into The Bath and then over the waterfall.

*Truly, a brilliant design.*

Ferran ran his finger eagerly over the map, thoroughly absorbed. Six main drainage tunnels emptied into the city's canals, which then flowed into the Rush. He frowned and counted again, then traced the lines back with his fingers, trying to find the origin of each one. The city's sewage system seemed larger than was actually needed; all sorts of tunnels didn't connect to the main drainage run-offs. His finger found a rather large access tunnel that appeared to run beneath the royal palace.

"Strange," he murmured.

He pocketed the map and bent over the drawer in search of something more. He thumbed through a few notebooks, finding ledgers full of numbers: loans, gambling debts, unlabeled tallies, but nothing to explain the map.

Then his Cat's Eye glimmered at his wrist. Ferran glanced at it. A sharply sweet scent, like mint and lavender, filled his nose. A single word passed through his mind—*Caprion.*

Light from the Harpy's wings came through the window. Ferran looked over his shoulder. He couldn't quite believe his eyes. Was Caprion flying in broad daylight? Had the man lost his mind?

Ferran unlatched the window and the Harpy drifted down from the overcast sky. Caprion entered the room with a gust of cold wind. His wings brought a shower of snow from the roof that immediately soaked the rug on the floor. Ferran winced; Martin would definitely notice that later.

"What are you doing?" he asked, irritated.

Caprion fixed him with a firm stare. "The weapons are gone."

Ferran didn't quite understand. He frowned. "The weapons...you mean, the Dark God's weapons?"

"They were taken from the ship. I tried to retrieve them, but the Shade opened a portal and escaped. I've spent hours trying to track them down." He hesitated. "I suspect one of our own betrayed us."

Ferran drew a slow breath, trying to arrange his thoughts. The news shocked him.

"Silas?" he finally said. "Did Silas take them?" The Dracian pirate had a thirst for gold and a questionable conscience at best....

"No," Caprion said. "I suspect the assassin, Viper."

"Crash was here at the manor last night. Did you see him take the weapons?"

Caprion remained confident. "I didn't see the thief's face, but it was one of the Sixth, I am certain, and who else would know where the weapons were hidden?" The Harpy searched Ferran's eyes. "Was Viper with you the entire night?"

Ferran thought back. "He left with Sora when she retired...."

"Is he here now?"

"Actually, no." Ferran's frown deepened. "I haven't seen him since last night. I thought he went with Sora to the Flower District...." With growing alarm, Ferran realized he hadn't seen Crash anywhere in the manor since their initial meeting with Martin. "There must be an explanation. He wouldn't betray us."

"I must speak with Sora," Caprion said. "Where is she?"

"The Flower District, on the west side of The Regency." Ferran put a hand on the Harpy's arm. "Wait," he said. "Don't draw attention to yourself. The shopping district will be crowded at this hour. If anyone sees you...."

"Sora could be in danger." Caprion shrugged him off. "I must go immediately."

"You can't just fly through the city! You'll start a riot!"

"The clouds are low enough to hide me," Caprion said. "If Viper has sided with the Shade, they might already have her. I must go."

Caprion turned to the window again and leapt easily into the open air. Ferran watched in vague admiration. The Harpy's wings glimmered briefly against the muted daylight, and a strong breeze lifted him up and away. In seconds, he disappeared among the clouds.

Ferran rubbed the Cat's Eye on his wrist. If anything happened to Sora...*Lori's going to kill me,* he thought.

He shut the window again, sat down heavily in Martin's plush leather chair, and placed his head in his hands. The weapons were gone. He didn't know for sure if Crash would betray them, but Caprion's suspicions made too much sense. How else would the Shade know the location of the sacred weapons aboard the ship? And where had Viper disappeared to?

Ferran's first instinct was to leave the manor and find Sora, but Caprion would reach her much sooner. By the time he had readied a carriage and made his farewells, an hour would have passed. *Sora is a strong girl. She can defend herself,* he reasoned. She had a Cat's Eye, and the necklace would protect her at any cost.

The distant thrum of footsteps caught Ferran's attention. He looked up. A female voice drifted down the hall--a maid humming as she went about her housework. He stood up and briefly scanned the desk, then he pocketed Martin's map, closed the drawer and locked it.

He hesitated. Was it wise to leave Martin's papers so disorganized? His documents had obviously been rifled through. Would his brother notice?

Ferran shrugged. If Martin brought up the map, what of it? Perhaps he could ask his brother some honest questions. *I highly doubt my brother has taken a sudden interest in plumbing.*

And if Martin didn't mention the missing map, perhaps he was hiding something after all.

He waited for the maid to pass and left Martin's office, carefully locking the door behind him. Then he moved down the hallway, away from the maid's voice.

Ferran felt the folded parchment in his pocket. He couldn't wait to find a quiet, secluded room where he could study it again. A familiar tingle began at the base of his neck—anticipation. This map contained a hidden puzzle, a secret he couldn't wait to uncover, and he was itching to get started.

# CHAPTER 22

S ora climbed into the carriage and with a quick rap on the roof, told the driver her destination. She didn't know exactly where Lord Seabourne might be in the Gentleman's District, but she had to look.

Within minutes she had left the Flower District behind. Her carriage passed a large opera house, a beautifully landscaped park, and several streets of small, exquisitely decorated shops. Finally she entered the Gentleman's District, proclaimed by a decorative brass sign planted on a broad street corner. Here, the storefronts were made of sturdy brick and polished wood, with large thatched windows displaying various goods. Sora saw leather workers, tailors, barbers, tobacco shops, pubs and more. Only two highborn ladies walked the street. They looked like proud family matriarchs, with graying hair and lined faces. She guessed that young, unmarried women did not frequent this area.

Luckily, she spotted Lord Seabourne's carriage on the second avenue they turned down. She tapped smartly on the roof, and the driver pulled over to the side of the road. Sora didn't wait for him to hand her down, but exited by herself, stepping onto the windy street.

The driver looked down from his bench at the front of the carriage. "Milady," he said, "Are you certain of your destination? This is the Gentleman's District."

She nodded. "Yes. Just wait here for a moment."

He tipped his velvet hat. "Do be careful," he said.

Sora looked around, wondering which shop Lord Seabourne might have entered. Her eyes landed on a large sign outside the building in front of her: *Brookworth's Distinguished Club. Gentlemen Only.*

She gripped her skirts, uncertain. Filled with burning curiosity, her first instinct was to dash headlong into the club to see if the Captain was inside. But as a lady, she would not be welcomed, and her presence might cause quite a stir.

As her eyes scanned the road, she noticed an alley to one side of the building. It looked deserted. Perhaps she could circle around the club and catch a glimpse of Lord Seabourne through one of the many windows. If not, she might just have to wait until he returned to his carriage.

Sora lifted her heavy skirts and walked carefully along the slick cobblestones to the side of the building. The alley was wide and clean, the snow fresh and unbroken. A series of low, dark windows ran along the side of the building. She tried to see through them, but the glass was thick and distorted to protect the privacy of the patrons. She gnawed her lip as her feet carried her further and further from the main street. Should she look for a back door? Perhaps a cook or waiter might help her.

Crash sat on the rooftop on the overhang of the second story, watching Sora walk down the alley.

She looked different, far from the fierce and wounded girl on the Lost Isles, when dirt smudged her cheeks and saltwater matted her hair. Now she resembled the other ladies in The Regency—doll-like, fragile, proper and clean—just like the night they had met. He remembered that first sight of her clearly: a small speck on the ballroom floor, spinning before an audience of the Second Tier. Later, when she ran into him face-to-face, he recalled the fear and startling innocence of her blue eyes, and her green Cat's-Eye stone glinting at her neck.

That had been selfish of him, taking her for the necklace. He had ripped her away from her life, purely for his own devices. *You bastard,* he thought. He owed her a debt that could never be repaid.

His thoughts drifted uneasily as he continued to watch, with no intention of doing anything else.

Without warning, a shadow portal opened nearby. Cobra materialized on the roof next to him, and sank down at his side. He gave off a tense, eager energy.

"Well?" he hissed, and followed Crash's gaze to the girl below. "Our master grows impatient. Why are you stalling?"

Cobra knew very well why. Cerastes doubtlessly knew as well.

Crash lingered on his options. He could bring Sora to the Shade to save Burn's life, but then, could he save them both? He had now put Sora in more danger than he had ever intended.

"A pretty young blossom," Cobra hissed, gazing at the girl below. "Too pretty for you."

Crash felt a deep yearning to draw his knife and shove it through Cobra's throat. He knew this kind of assassin well—too impatient, too ruthless—the kind that savored inflicting pain.

"Act," Cobra pressed him.

Crash clenched his teeth. "Not yet."

"Are you betraying us so soon? If you don't grab her, then I will."

Crash didn't reply.

With an idle shrug, Cobra dropped silently into the alley.

A curse fell from Crash's lips. His gaze fastened on Sora, who walked from window to window, still trying to see into the pub. She hadn't noticed Cobra's descent.

Now what? If he followed, she would see the two assassins together and think Crash had joined the Shade. But, if Cobra attacked her?

*She has a Cat's Eye,* he thought. He suspected it would block Cobra from using the fifth gate. He would have to wait and act as needed.

Sora may have been distracted, but she wasn't deaf or blind. She saw a shadow flicker out of the corner of her eye, and heard a soft, muffled thud as a body landed in the snow. Not a bird, she thought. She glanced up briefly, but saw no one. Still, she felt certain she was no longer alone.

As she pretended to peer through the window before her, she wondered what to do. If she retreated from the alley, would she be followed? *Better to face the stranger,* she decided. Her unseen visitor might be from the Shade, and she didn't want to turn her back on an assassin.

Finally, she straightened up.

"Show yourself," she called.

Her eyes scanned the alley. A cold wind gusted by, carrying flakes of snow and dead leaves. She waited.

A familiar assassin stepped out from behind a pile of broken crates. He wore a splint on one arm, a new addition since their last encounter.

"Hello, dear," Cobra said.

Her stomach twisted in disgust.

"You..." she seethed. Surprisingly, she was not afraid, but filled with bitter anger. "Where is Burn?"

The assassin approached her at a gliding walk. "Your Wolfy friend is in capable hands," he sneered. "Never fear; he is alive. I will make you a deal. Come with me, and I'll release him."

Sora took several steps back, trying to keep her distance. She remembered Cobra's hands vividly—he could debilitate her with a single touch. She wouldn't let that happen again.

"If you kill him, I'll make you pay," she growled.

"How rude," he mocked. "And here I thought you were a lady."

She reached for the knife in her bodice and drew it.

Cobra's eyes followed her hand, then crinkled behind his cowl. "How endearing. You didn't tell me she was so feisty, Viper. This is truly a delight."

*Viper?* Sora glanced around the alley. Her eyes scanned the rooftops, but she did not see Crash anywhere. Still, Cobra's words left her cold with doubt. Was Crash here, or was Cobra toying with her?

She tightened her grip on her dagger. "Come any closer, and you'll regret it!" she warned, even as she grew nervous. The Shade rarely traveled alone. How many more assassins were hiding on the rooftops? Was Crash among them?

*Don't be silly,* she thought, even as she glanced over her shoulder at the mouth of the alley. She was too far away to make a run for it.

"I didn't come here to fight, but to make a deal," Cobra repeated in his oily tone. He halted a yard away. "Come with me, and we'll release the Wolfy."

Sora hesitated. For a moment, she actually considered his offer, but she wasn't fool enough to make a deal with the Shade. The sad truth was that Burn might already be dead.

"Why?" she called instead. "Why does Cerastes want me?"

Cobra sneered. "My master has use of you."

Sora gripped the Cat's Eye at her throat. After Krait's interrogation, she had a vague idea of Cerastes' plan.

"You'll have to kill me if you want the necklace, and then it will be useless to you. It only works with a bearer, and your kind can't touch it." She raised her head. "I won't go willingly."

Cobra scoffed. "You forget, my dear, we are in a city full of humans. You are easily replaced."

"Don't be so sure," Sora countered. "To control the necklace and kill a wraith, a bearer needs training."

Sora held his gaze in defiance.

Finally Cobra shrugged, "As you wish," and vanished.

Sora felt a gust of wind brush her left cheek. She ducked just as his heavy gauntlet swung past her face. She grabbed Cobra's arm, dragging him forward, off-balance, and over her hip. She threw him into the snow.

Cobra landed on his back. He lay stunned for a moment, but then she heard him laugh. The eerie sound echoed off the alley walls.

"Well-played, little girl," he wheezed. "But you won't be so lucky twice!" He leapt to his feet and lunged at her.

Sora braced herself, knowing she was outmatched. Cobra slammed into her, his crushing grip on her wrists. She gasped, anticipating the pain. He twisted her arms behind her; fire shot up down her spine. She collapsed to her knees with a choked sob.

Cobra laughed. "Just a weak little human after all, hm?"

She couldn't focus on his words through the pain. Her eyes fell to the cobble-stones, and she saw a dark shadow gathering beneath her on the ground. A portal.

*No, I won't be taken!* she thought. With a firm command, she activated her Cat's Eye. Green light encased her skin as the necklace counteracted Cobra's magic. With a loud crack, the portal snapped shut.

Cobra cursed and dragged her up from the ground. Sora screamed—she thought he would break her arm.

"You crafty little fox," he seethed. "Must we do this the hard way?"

Suddenly, a strong vibration passed over her skin. Bright light spilled into the alley, dazzling her eyes, and she felt strong arms wrap around her. Cobra lost his hold as she was dragged away from him.

*Caprion*, she thought. It had to be.

The bright light disoriented her but faded quickly. When her vision cleared, she saw Cobra at the opposite end of the alley. Skid marks in the snow revealed he had been pushed, or pulled, away from the fight. And then a shocking sight met her eyes. Her heart stopped. Crash stood next to him. She blinked twice. He seemed to look straight through her.

"If you want to fight, you can fight me," Caprion said from her side. How had he found her?

The two assassins glared menacingly at the Harpy. Sora tried to recover, although she couldn't stop staring at Crash. He still wore his suit of dark livery, but somehow he looked different. Not himself.

Cobra hissed, and the shadows darkened at his feet. Crash grabbed his arm. Within seconds, they vanished into a portal, and the alley was empty. A lonely gust of wind swept over the snow. Sora waited, wondering if they would reappear and continue the fight, but after a long moment, she relaxed in Caprion's hold. It seemed that Cobra had fled.

Caprion gently released her, and Sora stood shivering in the snow. She couldn't look away from where Crash had stood just seconds before.

She turned to the Harpy. The wind ruffled his pale hair. His eyes scanned the alley and surrounding rooftops, still prepared for an attack. He was dressed in a clean, white tunic, soft tan breeches and tall black boots.

He turned and touched her arm, the one she had dislocated two days earlier.

"Are you injured?" he asked with concern.

His hand was surprisingly gentle. She brushed it off awkwardly. "I'm fine, thank you," she said. "How did you find me?"

He pushed his pale hair away from his eyes and said in a weary voice, "Ferran told me you were in The Flower District. I didn't know if this was the place, but I spotted you from above."

Sora frowned. "Ferran sent you? Why?"

"No, not Ferran. I came by myself. I feared you were in danger. The Shade are much bolder than we anticipated." He paused solemnly. "The sacred weapons are missing from the ship."

Sora blinked twice. Then her face became pale. "What?" Her bodice suddenly felt too tight. "But how...? When?"

"A thief came in the night and took them." His expression darkened. "I suspect the Viper."

Caprion's words made her stomach cramp. "Crash," Sora corrected automatically. She wanted to forget her entire encounter with Cobra. "It can't be...he was with us last night."

"And this morning?"

She found herself reluctant to answer; Caprion seemed to know her reply already. She shook her head. "I didn't see him at the manor this morning, but that doesn't mean anything."

"No," Caprion agreed, "but we just saw him with Cobra."

Sora's thoughts were sluggish. Although she secretly hoped Crash's appearance was an illusion, or simply a trick played by her eyes, Caprion had seen him as well. How could she justify that? She knew in her gut that Crash wouldn't betray them. Not after everything they had been through together.

"It must be a trick," she muttered. "Magic of some kind, or an impostor. The Shade are cunning, they want us to turn on each other...."

Caprion remained silent. His unwavering gaze made her suddenly angry.

"Was no one guarding the ship?" she asked. "Did anyone see who took the weapons?"

"I did," Caprion said. "I couldn't see the man's face, but he was one of the Sixth. And he had Viper's height and build."

Sora found herself becoming defensive. "Obviously the Shade have been watching us," she said. "They must have seen where we hid the weapons. They sent someone to steal them. Crash wouldn't betray us...not with Burn's life in the balance." The sickening knot in her stomach grew tighter. *Burn. Crash promised to save his life.* Would he actually go to the Shade on his own, without telling her?

*No,* she thought. *No, he's not that foolish....*

Again, Caprion didn't respond to her outburst, but she thought she saw pity in his eyes. She hated that, and had the sudden urge to cover her ears and scream.

"I came here to check on your safety," he repeated, "and I'm glad I reached you in time. We should return to the manor and keep you indoors. Cobra still might bring more warriors." His eyes returned to the rooftops. Without further explanation, he grasped her gently by the arm and started back to the main road. "We should hurry."

His concern was obvious, but Sora resisted. She wanted to argue for Crash's honor, and convince Caprion that the assassin was not their enemy.

She dug her heels firmly into the snow. Caprion came to a stop.

"Why are you always against Crash?" she asked fiercely. "Assuming we really saw him—perhaps he has good reason to go with Cobra. Perhaps he is trying to rescue Burn, or gather information, or do *something* useful while I'm forced to squander a full day buying dresses!"

"If that's the case, then why didn't he tell us of his plan?" the Harpy asked logically. "He gave the sacred weapons directly to the Shade's leader. That sounds rather counterintuitive, doesn't it?"

Sora scowled. "Perhaps he went to barter for Burn's life."

"Then why has he not returned? We would know by now if he was successful."

"They must have tricked him somehow, coerced him into helping Cobra...."

Caprion chuckled dryly. "Now who sounds far-fetched?"

She twisted toward him. "You don't know him the way I do!"

"True," he said. "But consider—perhaps you are too close to him, and perhaps that makes you blind."

Sora bit her lip. Caprion's words caused a small crack in her heart. She knew deep down that her eyes hadn't deceived her. She knew who was standing next to Cobra; she would recognize him anywhere. But why would he go to the Shade? Why had he not helped her fight? Why hadn't he protected her life?

More than anger, she felt confusion. Hadn't he sworn to protect her in The Regency? Why would he leave without telling her?

She continued to walk numbly through the snow toward the street. Caprion followed.

"What are you doing out here alone, anyway?" he asked.

Sora sighed—she had almost forgotten her quest to find Lord Seabourne. She didn't feel like explaining their sordid history to Caprion.

"I'm looking for someone, but I didn't find him," she said briefly.

"Someone connected to the Shade?"

"No," she snapped, annoyed. She picked up her skirts and walked faster, trying to leave the Harpy behind. She didn't want to think of Crash, where he was now, or what she had just witnessed. *This has to be a mistake. He's back at the manor with Ferran. Cobra is trying to trick us.*

Suddenly, she heard a shout from the street. Horses whinnied and a carriage rolled past. She spotted the Seabourne crest on the door.

"Damn!" she cursed, and took off running. She sensed Caprion behind her. She had to see where the carriage was going. Perhaps she could follow it in the Ebonaire coach.

Sora sprinted through the rest of the alley and around the corner of the Gentleman's Club—and skidded headlong into an unexpected pedestrian. *Wham!*

She yelped as her nose smacked against a forehead; her foot slipped on the ice and she started to fall. Thin arms grabbed her, but the short stranger couldn't support her weight. They both stumbled awkwardly to the cobblestones, falling together.

"Bells!" Sora cursed, trying to untangle her limbs from the stranger's. She felt her skirt rip, and wanted to tear off the rest of it in frustration. Lord Seabourne was long gone by now; she stood no chance of catching him.

"By the North Wind, forgive me, Lady, I'm so sorry!" a voice twittered in her ear. The girl disengaged herself and got back on her feet, then tried to help Sora up.

Sora regained her feet and put a hand on her stinging nose. The stranger immediately began adjusting Sora's dress, mindlessly apologizing all the while.

"Oh, no, your pretty dress is torn! Forgive my clumsiness, milady. Please, you must allow me to fix it, I am quite skilled at needlework."

Sora finally refocused. Standing before her was a young woman dressed in pale skirts covered by a simple apron; a handkerchief tied back her dark brown hair. Long bangs hung low across her forehead in a stylish cut.

"I can't apologize enough!" the girl babbled. "I admit I wasn't paying attention. We're out of flour, you see, and the cook sent me across the street. I didn't see you..." then she paused. "By the Goddess," she whispered. "Sora?"

Sora's mouth opened in surprise. "Lily?"

They stared at each other.

Sora tried to think of something reasonable to say. Lily had served as her handmaid for twelve years. They had grown up together on the Fallcrest estate. Lily was the closest Sora had ever had to a best friend. In fact, Lily would remember the night of her kidnapping and her father's murder. She would know all the tawdry details of her disastrous Blooming, the warrant for her arrest and her mysterious disappearance into Fennbog swamp....

And perhaps she had more information about Lord Seabourne and the fate of the Fallcrest estate.

"Um, hello," Sora managed.

Lily's face darkened. "Hello? *Hello?* I haven't seen you in years! You were declared dead!"

"I can't explain right now," Sora stammered, remembering Lord Seabourne's vanished carriage. "I mean, I *can* explain, just not here. Please. We have to leave right now!"

Lily gave her a suspicious look, then glanced around. "Why?" she asked. "Are you hiding from someone? Are you in trouble? Well, you're in a world of trouble, I suppose—your obituary was published a year ago. By the four winds, Sora, you have to tell me what's going on!"

"What is an obituary?" Caprion interrupted.

Lily looked over Sora's shoulder. At the sight of her attractive male companion, Lily's eyes widened and her jaw went slack.

"Oh," she said. "Is he with you?"

Sora grabbed Lily by the arm and began to walk her up the street. Lily tried to resist but Sora was much stronger. She practically lifted the poor girl off her feet toward the Ebonaire coach.

"It's a long story, and should be told in private," she said. "By the way, what are *you* doing in The Regency?"

Lily glowered. "Well, I had to find work somewhere after you ran away! That dratted uncle of yours fired me last year, sold off his townhouse and left the city. But that's neither here nor there. You're alive!" Lily stared at Sora as though she couldn't believe her eyes. "I knew it! Everyone thought you met a terrible fate in Fennbog swamp, but I knew you weren't so foolish! You'd never set foot in that place!"

"Right," Sora agreed.

"Goddess," Lily continued, "the entire Fallcrest staff owes me a fortune in bets right now...."

Sora's eyes combed the street, hoping for another glimpse of Lord Seabourne's coach, but it was long gone. She cursed loudly.

"But how?" she muttered. "How did he sneak back to his carriage without me noticing?"

"Perhaps he was in a hurry," Caprion offered.

"Who was in a hurry?" Lily asked.

"Lord Seabourne," Sora said.

Lily's eyes grew large. "Ooh! Wait, why would you want to speak to Lord Seabourne? He's the last person you want to see! He organized a manhunt after you—"

"I know," Sora snapped.

Lily fixed her with a searching gaze. "I don't follow. If you're alive now, then you never died, which means Lord Seabourne might...."

"What? Arrest me? Confiscate my fortune? Renounce my title and nobility?"

Lily blinked. "Ah. I see. Well, if you're so set on meeting him, I know where to find him."

Sora raised an eyebrow.

"He's in charge of security for the winter solstice parade," she said. "I know the tavern where he briefs his men. I can take you there tomorrow before the parade begins."

Sora clasped her friend's hand eagerly. "You're certain?" she asked.

"Of course!" Lily said. "But I'll have to go with you as an escort." She eyed Caprion again. "And I'd like a proper introduction to your friend."

"Don't you have a job to get back to?" she asked, indicating Lily's uniform.

Lily untied her apron. "Nonsense," she said. "And risk never seeing you again? There are more important things than money, you know. And if I'm not mistaken, aren't we standing outside an Ebonaire coach? Is this your transportation?"

Sora blinked and realized they had been standing there for some time; the driver was impatiently checking his pocketwatch. "We'll be just a minute," she said to him, then turned back to Lily. "Yes, I'm staying at the Ebonaire manor...and I see you're still quite the opportunist."

Her former handmaid winked.

"I suppose I could use a handmaid," Sora mused, though she wondered how that would go over with Ferran and the rest of their group. Still, Lily's presence was comfortably familiar. She needed people she could trust, and she needed to meet Lord Seabourne.

"We're not staying in the city for long," she said. "I don't think you should leave your job for me."

Lily rolled her eyes. "There's no shortage of jobs in this city," she said. "Don't worry about me."

Sora found herself sharing another smile with her old friend. She introduced Lily to Caprion and all three climbed into the carriage. The driver cracked his whip, and the coach jolted forward down the icy road, back to the Ebonaire manor.

# CHAPTER 23

Lori arrived at the Ebonaire estate that afternoon. The sky was dark and overcast, making the hour seem much later in the day. The size of the manor was overwhelming at first, but she had lived and worked in such places before. She gazed out at the wide lawn, with its maze-like hedges, as the coach traveled up the front drive.

She adjusted her long white Healer's robes and held her summons tightly. Her eyes scanned over the curling script for the tenth time.

> *To Mrs. Lorianne Ebonaire,*
>
> *Dear sister, although we have not met, I extend my warmest welcome to you. It is my desire that you come to stay at the Ebonaire residence for the remainder of winter solstice, and indefinitely, as you wish. Please arrive post haste as Lady Danica Ebonaire has fallen ill, and your skills as a Healer are sorely needed.*
>
> *Fondly, your brother,*
> *Lord Martin Ebonaire III*

Her eyes roved over the first line: *Mrs. Lorianne Ebonaire.* Ferran's wife, and with a proper surname, at that. Ferran must have been successful in reconnecting with his brother.

She swallowed hard, and cursed Silas a hundred times for concocting such a ludicrous story. The Dracian captain couldn't possibly know about her shared past with Ferran; her guise as his wife was cruelly ironic. She didn't know if she could pull it off. Perhaps if Ferran had never told her of their time together, she could simply act her role and be done with it. Instead, his possible link to Sora remained constant in her thoughts. They crossed a line on his houseboat when he cared for her after she was wounded; their friendship had changed. She wasn't sure what Ferran truly wanted, or how she felt.

The coach rolled to a stop and she walked stiffly to the front door. Her stab wound twinged uncomfortably with each step, but the pain was tolerable.

A portly butler opened the door and, after reading her summons, welcomed her inside. A maid whisked away her cloak. The manor seemed subdued and quiet, more like a mausoleum than a house, and she noticed that all the servants were wearing black. That sight left her unsettled; there must have been a death recently. She wondered who had passed.

A half-minute later, Ferran bounded easily down the wide staircase, taking three steps at a time. Lori sucked in a short breath when she saw him. He looked tall and dashing in his noble attire: a vest of gray and silver brocade fastened over a white tunic with billowing white sleeves. His brown hair fell across his brow in a slight wave. He looked younger, somehow, his face clear, his features less worn by living on the road.

Reaching her side with a wide grin, he looked unusually relieved to see her, took her hand and quickly kissed it. "My dear," he said. "Welcome to the Ebonaire estate."

The kiss took her aback. Lori wasn't sure what to say.

"Why, she is the spitting image of Sora!" another voice interrupted. "Or rather, Sora is the spitting image of her mother. Hello, Lorianne."

A dark-haired man entered the hall, dressed in a long black coat and green vest. He walked with an ramrod-straight, regal air. Lori thought the two brothers looked alike. Ferran's younger brother Martin had a clean-cut, aristocratic look about him, where Ferran was decidedly more roguish. Still, their mouths and eyes both tilted when they smiled, and they both seemed to habitually thrust their hands into their pockets.

Ferran introduced them properly, and Lori curtsied before asking about Lady Danica. She would rather skip the First Tier formalities. "Thank you for the warm invitation," she said, her tone polite and professional. "Is your daughter very sick? I should see her immediately."

"Come this way," Martin said. "She has been sick for almost a week. Her mother came down with the same illness several months ago...."

Lori looked at Martin gravely. "Did she survive?"

"No," he replied shortly. Then, in a softer tone, "It has been difficult for us."

That explained the somber attire of the staff, and the general sense of malaise in the house. Lori allowed Martin to lead her upstairs to Lady Danica's grand bedroom on the second floor. She looked about the magnificent room with a bit of awe. It was large enough to encompass her entire house; the ceiling was so high, she couldn't imagine how the maids dusted the corners.

She had never understood the nobility's need for immense indoor space, which she had always found quite wasteful. Yet as a work of art, the room was immaculate, decorated in hand-woven tapestries, oil paintings, deep burgundy curtains and a polished dark wood floor. Plump sofas and large armchairs surrounded an ornate fireplace. The furniture and mantel were gilded in gold leaf; or perhaps it was truly made of gold, she couldn't tell. Danica's bed stood on the opposite side of the room near a row of tall windows. The bed was large enough for four people to lie there side-by-side.

Lady Danica rested silently and completely still, surrounded by a mountain of pillows. Two maids attended to her with a bowl of warm water. One swept a damp cloth across the girl's brow.

Lori immediately went to Lady Danica's side and dismissed the two maids. First, she checked the young girl's vitals—the patient looked to be around fifteen years old. Her pulse was weak and fluttery. She forgot Ferran's and Martin's presence in the room as she went to work.

Her first assessment of the patient was unexpectedly positive. Fever blisters, yes, and a heavy cough. But no blackened nails.

"She had chills," one of the maids said, "so we heated the room as best we could...."

"You should move her to a smaller room," Lori said absently as she listened to Danica's breathing. "Less drafty, with a fireplace closer to the bed."

The maid nodded.

"Is it the plague?" Ferran asked softly. She hadn't noticed him by her side.

"No," she said as she straightened. Her eyes traveled to Lord Martin, who hovered at the foot of the bed. "A very bad case of pneumonia."

Ferran barely hid his surprise.

Martin stared at her. His hand clutched the bed frame. He seemed staggered by the news.

"Pneumonia?" he echoed. "The other Healers said it was incurable...."

Lori snorted. "They probably mistook it for the plague," she said, "but I've seen both. She will recover with proper care." Then her tone changed, becoming gentler. "Tell me, has your daughter always suffered from poor health? Fainting spells? Is she easily bruised?" She glanced at Danica's sleeping form. The girl looked as white as the bedsheets.

"Yes," Martin said, showing his surprise.

"She has a blood condition. Something she was born with. It makes her frag-ile," Lori said. "I've seen this before. Red meat will help. And beets. And fresh honey each season for her allergies."

Martin looked at Ferran with raised eyebrows.

"She's very good," he said, referring to Lori.

"I've seen a lot of illness," Lori replied.

Martin gave her a short bow, which Lori found quite unexpected. He caught her eye when he raised his head again. "Thank you, sister. You are as intelligent as you are beautiful." Then he turned to Ferran. "You've done well for yourself."

Lori noticed Ferran's flush of pride, then his silent bristle of annoyance. She wondered at his response. Was he jealous? Or perhaps simply embarrassed, as they weren't truly married?

Martin looked satisfied. "I'll leave you to your work, then," he said. "I have business to attend to upstairs. Letters to write and ledgers to balance. Shall I see you at dinner?"

Lori remembered to curtsy again. "Yes. Until this evening, Lord Ebonaire."

He winced. "Please, just Martin. We're family now." He turned and left the room. The maids were behind him, carrying a basket of soiled towels.

Ferran waited until the door was shut. "That went well," he said softly, shoving his hands into his pockets. "Martin has been very welcoming so far. I suppose we're lucky." His eyes lingered a bit too long on her. "How are you?" he asked.

Lori hesitated, wondering if he meant her dagger wound, or her overall reaction to being in the Ebonaire manor. "Fine," she replied briefly. "And you?"

"As well as one can expect," he said quietly.

Lori sensed he wanted to tell her something. He shifted his weight, but didn't speak.

She cleared her throat. "Have you found any evidence of...?" She glanced cautiously at Danica's sleeping figure.

"We're looking," he said.

"You should have asked me before deciding to come here," Lori chided. "There must be an easier way to track them down; too much is at stake. And where is Sora?"

"She should be back soon. She went shopping for dresses," Ferran explained.

Lori raised an eyebrow. "Shopping?" she asked. "That sounds *very* productive, Ferran."

He shrugged. "She's searching The Regency as well, looking for signs of the Shade. We just arrived here, Lori. We've barely had time to explore the house, let alone hunt down a cult—"

"Hush," she murmured. Danica stirred. Lori waited until the girl's breathing became deep and even and then continued, "We shouldn't be here. It's a distraction."

"Caprion said the leader of the Shade is staying in The Regency. Now that they have the weapons—"

"Oh, you heard about that already?"

"Caprion arrived an hour ago, then went to find Sora."

Lori sighed. She had been shocked and dismayed that morning when she heard the news. She had spoken to Caprion at length about the weapons theft. He suspected Crash, but she didn't know if she agreed. She was more concerned about her daughter.

"It seems we've delivered the weapons straight into the Shade's hands," she said grimly. "I think they planned this, Ferran. I have a sense they are biding their time, waiting for the ideal moment to strike. They know our faces, but we are still blind. We fell into a trap by coming to this city."

Ferran looked uncomfortable. "Perhaps," he said, "but what other choice did we have?"

"The Regency is a dangerous place for us," she repeated. "I'm not welcome among the nobility. I have a past here. Did our encounter with Cedric at the seminary mean nothing to you?" She absently touched her bandages. "If he were to stumble across us again...."

Ferran frowned. "You have nothing to fear from Cedric Daniellian. That spoiled bastard will get what's coming to him."

Lori fixed him with a discerning stare. "Is that why you were so ready to come here? To get another shot at Cedric? I won't have it. We need to stay focused on our original quest. Cedric Daniellian is of no consequence."

"To you, mayhap," Ferran muttered.

"I won't discuss it," Lori said brusquely, and wiped her hands on a clean towel. "Seven years have passed. I've made my peace. I just want to avoid him, especially while I stay in this house. Can we manage that?"

Ferran nodded and passed her a jar of salve for the fever blisters on Danica's lips.

Lori applied the salve with a light touch, then pressed a damp cloth to Danica's head. The girl's fever seemed to be calming now that she wasn't under so many blankets.

An uneasy silence fell between them. Ferran cracked the knuckles on his left hand. His Cat's Eye gleamed at his wrist. She wondered what he was thinking.

"The Shade will show themselves eventually," he finally said. "I wouldn't have returned to this house if I didn't think our plan would work. I didn't come here for Daniellian. I know what's important, Lori. I'm not an ignorant pirate. I'm not some drunken fool."

"You were when I met you."

"For a stage of my life, yes. But that's not who I am."

Lori remained silent. She didn't want to delve into this conversation. Their current predicament was stressful enough. They were staying at the Ebonaire house and she would have to put up with it. She wondered how her daughter was holding up, and hoped Sora would stay out of trouble.

"When you're finished here, I want to show you something," Ferran said abruptly.

Lori glanced up.

"Meet me in my room," he said. "It won't take long. I found something of note." Then he strode out the door.

Lori watched him go. She wondered what he was referring to. Perhaps old family memorabilia...or gold? Rumor had it the Ebonaires hid bags of gold in the walls of their estate. Silas had made several comments about that.

She wondered how Ferran felt, being in this house after so many years away. His brother Martin was not what she expected—better, in fact, than she had imagined. He seemed a good man, although still a businessman; he played his role well.

Unspoken tension was obvious between the two brothers. She wondered if Martin would invite Ferran to the upcoming First Winter's Ball. Would Ferran be allowed to make a public appearance? It would be quite the coming-out. Despite twenty years having passed, many of the nobility would remember his exile, and his double-life as the notorious Redhanded Ferran.

For now, Ferran seemed surprisingly well-adjusted. But she still noticed his anxious passage through each room, and the way his eyes lingered on family portraits, particularly along the first-story hallway. He didn't appear in any of them. In some ways, he stood out like a misplaced vase. He belonged in this house...but where, exactly? How did he fit?

Danica coughed. Lori lay a soothing hand on the girl's chest. Only fifteen, she already looked like a woman, with long, dark curls and porcelain skin. She could tell Danica's height by her length on the bed. Tall, like the Ebonaires. Long-boned. Elegant. Their bloodline was strong, and Danica looked far more like Martin or Ferran than Sora did.

Perhaps Ferran had made a mistake. Perhaps Sora *wasn't* his daughter. Perhaps he and Lori's encounter meant nothing, and she could move past it.

*Yes,* Lori thought to herself. *Nothing's changed.* Lori had her daughter, and of their own relationship, she could be certain.

She patted Danica's hand gently. "Your mother worries about you very much," she said, thinking of the portrait downstairs. Lady Ebonaire had kind brown eyes and a sweet, dimpled smile. Lori felt certain her spirit sat in this very room, watching over her sick daughter. She could almost feel the woman's imprint on the bed. This house seemed full of ghosts.

The maids returned and set a simmering pot of water over the fire, then left again. Lori waited until the water boiled and released a cloud of minty steam into the room. It would clear the girl's lungs and draw out the infection. Lori expected significant results by morning.

She stood up. Her back ached, and her wound pulled with each breath. She took a moment to gather herself. Thirty-six could not be called old, and yet her age was beginning to catch up with her.

She shut Danica's bedroom door softly behind her, and headed for Ferran's room.

*Goddess!* she thought, her footsteps faltering. Lord Ebonaire thought they were married, and had given them the same suite.

Sora said goodbye to Caprion outside the stables.

"I'm glad you're safe," he told her. "I regret that I cannot stay. I must return to the ship and make sure our prisoner has not escaped. The Dracians mean well, but they are easily distracted."

Sora clasped his arm briefly. "Until next time we meet," she said.

Caprion hesitated. "I don't like the thought of you here without protection. The Shade found you in The Regency, and they might know where you are staying."

"I'm not afraid. Ferran and Lori are here, should I need help...."

Caprion ignored her. "I intend to return, if only for your peace of mind. If you see Viper again," he cautioned, "don't let your guard down."

"If you insist."

His warning left her uneasy. She still hoped to find Crash inside the manor, and discover that this whole ordeal was a misunderstanding.

Their hands remained clasped for a moment. Then Caprion released her and walked swiftly toward a copse of trees, from which he would undoubtedly take to the skies.

Sora turned back to the stables and the sound of Lily's voice, which rose and fell in apparent outrage. It sounded like an argument.

She entered the wide doorway to the stables and paused when her eyes landed on Olivia, who looked slightly haggard and very irritated, standing with her hands on her hips.

"Lord Martin asked me to escort her! I am acting as her handmaid for the time being!" the maid exclaimed. "Now back to the docks with you! We are not hiring, and we have no love for thieves or riffraff!"

Sora cleared her throat.

Olivia looked up at her.

"Where have you been? And who is this?" she demanded, and thrust a finger at Lily.

Sora considered Lily's dress. She looked like a serving girl or a cook's assistant, far from a handmaid or even a kitchen girl in a lord's house.

"This is my maid," she said curtly, and raised her chin. She felt a push of confidence—her noble upbringing came to the surface. "Lily was delayed on our ship, but she found me in the Flower District."

Olivia said wrinkled her nose slightly. "She smells like seaweed. Hopefully she brought a change of clothes."

"Watch your tone," Sora said coldly.

Olivia came back to herself, and curtsied abruptly. "My apologies, Milady. Your mother just arrived. She will be joining you in an hour for dinner. Perhaps you'd like a warm bath?" Then she turned on her heel without batting an eye and went back into the manor.

Sora wondered if Olivia meant her question to sound like an insult.

"Olivia," Sora called, a sharp edge to her voice. The maid halted mid-step. "From here on, Lily will assist me as my handmaid. I relieve you of your duties."

Olivia's lips parted in shock.

"Please show Lily to her rooms. She will be staying with us in the manor." Then Sora turned to catch Lily's eyes. "I will need a dinner dress."

"Yes, Milady." Lily gave her a perfectly elegant curtsy. As she rose, a small smile played about her mouth. Then she followed Olivia to the house.

Sora trailed further behind, taking her time as she walked through the snow. Her eyes scanned the stables and the outside courtyard in search of Crash. She prayed for a sign of him--anything to prove he was safe in the Ebonaire manor, and not among the Shade--but she saw no one, save the cold marble statues in the garden.

# CHAPTER 24

S ora met with Lori and Ferran briefly before going to the dining room. She clasped her mother in a tight embrace, relieved to see her recovered and walking around after her knife wound.

"We only have a few minutes before dinner," Lori said quickly as Sora released her from their hug. "Tell me about your day."

Sora briefly described her trip to The Flower District, Cobra's attack and Caprion's unexpected arrival. It seemed Ferran and Lori already knew about the missing sacred weapons. They seemed more relieved than surprised that Caprion had tracked her down.

Sora left out a few details. She didn't bother explaining her search for Lord Seabourne, nor her discovery of Lily, which she figured could wait for breakfast. She skirted around any mention of Crash and the Shade, but Ferran brought it up.

"Did Crash accompany you to the Flower District?" he asked.

Sora felt sick to her stomach. "I thought he stayed here with you?"

A troubled look passed over Lori's face, and the two shared a worried glance. Sora didn't need them to explain; Caprion had obviously shared his suspicions. Now, in the halls of the Ebonaire manor, Crash's absence and possible betrayal seemed far too likely. Sora still held onto the hope that this was all a misunderstanding, and the assassin might appear from around a corner or closed door. She kept watching the hall, anticipating his appearance at any second.

Olivia arrived to escort them to the dining hall. The main banquet hall could seat hundreds of guests, but Olivia led them to a quaint room near the front of the house, meant for smaller parties. They joined Lord Martin at the table and partook in a savory five-course meal. Sora found the conversation slightly forced.

"Tomorrow I will be participating in the Winter Solstice Parade," Lord Martin told them as the second course was brought out—roasted chicken and carrots and gravy. "You are all welcome to attend and watch."

Lori responded first. Her words seemed practiced. "A generous invitation, but I have to decline. I wish to keep watch on Lady Danica in case her condition worsens."

Sora saw relief and gratitude in Martin's eyes at the mention of his daughter. She felt momentarily guilty, as she hadn't thought of Lady Danica's condition all day.

"Thank you for watching over her," he said sincerely.

Sora fidgeted, thinking of her plans with Lily to find Lord Seabourne. The parade would be a fine excuse to leave the manor.

"I wish to see the parade," she said.

Lord Martin smiled. "You will be amazed, my dear. You should attend with a proper escort; the crowds can become quite rough. Where is your footman, by the way?" He glanced around the room, then turned to Ferran. "You arrived with a footman, did you not? If you'd like, I have other trained servants you can use."

Ferran seemed taken aback. "He returned to the ship," he finally grumbled. "Yes, another footman would do well." The lie seemed paper-thin, and when Ferran looked into Sora's eyes, she knew Crash had vanished without a word.

After that, Sora fell into deeper and deeper silence until she could barely look at her plate. As Ferran and Martin exchanged stories of their youth, she found herself acknowledging the truth—Crash was gone. Even Lord Martin noticed. She couldn't doubt herself any longer; she had seen him with Cobra. But why would he go to the Shade without telling her?

Sora excused herself early, blaming her exhaustion. She kissed her mother on the cheek and retired quickly to her room, where Lily assisted her out of her dress and into a nightgown. The fabric pooled on the floor around her feet, obviously hemmed for a much taller lady, possibly Danica.

Sora sent Lily away as soon as her hair was braided. Then she stood in front of the mirror in her room, studying the angles of her heart-shaped face, her thick blond hair and the nightgown that trailed on the floor behind her. She looked older in the firelight than she expected. Her skin was too tan for the First Tier. She flexed her arms curiously and noted the lines of her biceps; too much muscle for a noblewoman. The upper tiers prized soft curves, bordering on plump, and pale skin. She looked like a farmer's daughter. Considering Lori's ranch, that wasn't far from the truth.

She stripped off her gloves and looked at the scar on her left hand. It was an undeniable testament to the journey she had shared with Crash. She couldn't staunch the overwhelming feeling of betrayal.

Sora crossed to the window of her grand apartments and looked out upon the Ebonaire front drive. Several lanterns glimmered like fireflies in the black distance. Her gaze traveled from the distant lanterns to the tiled rooftop of the stables, to the front steps and the circular courtyard below. She knew her search was futile. Crash was not on the grounds, and even if he gazed back at her through the darkness, he wouldn't show himself to her now.

Her eyes stung, and she clenched her jaw firmly. She couldn't imagine why Crash would give the sacred weapons willingly to Cerastes. It was far too great a risk. Did he intend to barter for Burn's life?

Sora grasped her Cat's Eye in her scarred hand, then crossed the cold wooden floor and slipped into bed. With a sigh, she forced herself to relax back against the pillows. She couldn't allow herself to feel so weakened by Crash's absence. Her worry would interfere with her necklace's bond. She could already sense the Cat's Eye becoming distant and stifled. She needed to meditate, especially on nights like this when her mind spun in useless circles and sleep seemed impossible.

She closed her eyes and slowed her breathing, allowing her thoughts to drift to and fro, entering her mind and leaving like birds flying across the sky. Eventually, all she knew was darkness. She looked down to find the glowing green rope once again in her hands. Then she stood outside the horse corral behind her country manor, except now the grass had turned brown with frost. Icicles formed on the iron bars of the corral. She hesitated to put her bare hand against the frozen metal. The fence seemed much higher than before.

She remembered she had brought gloves, and withdrew them from her pocket. She pulled a glove over each hand, hiding the scar on her left palm. Then she climbed the gate of the corral, carrying the green rope slung over her shoulder.

No sooner had she entered the corral when the shadow of the *garrolithe* fell across her. It was not sleeping, but hunched over with its back turned, digging furiously into the icy ground. Clots of dirt, ice, dead grass and moldy leaves flew through the air. Sora held up her arm to protect her face. A shudder of fear moved through her. The *garrolithe* was intimidating, to be sure...but was it bigger than before? She didn't remember its limbs so long and lean, or its teeth so yellow and curved.

The beast sniffed the air abruptly and turned its lion-snout upon her. Long horns spiraled up from its head, thrusting out from a bristling mane of sharp quills. Electric eyes blazed with blue fire. The beast released a low, coughing roar that ended in a howling screech. All the hair on her neck stood up.

Sora dropped her rope to the ground and scrambled to climb the bars of the corral. Her foot slipped on the metal rungs and she almost fell. She heard the earth crunching beneath the garrolithe's weight as the beast approached. She could feel its panting, fiery breath upon her back, and imagined its jaws opened wide, ready to bite through her neck....

It was just a dream. She woke up with a gasp and struggled against her heavy quilt.

A white light glimmered at the foot of her bed. Her heart lurched.

"Don't be alarmed," Caprion intoned.

Sora sat up and pulled her blankets up to her chin, a natural defense. "What are you doing here?" she asked, though she already knew the answer. Truly, she hadn't expected him to return. She glanced at the wide bay windows, and took note of a wet puddle on the floor. He must have unlatched the windows and let himself in.

"I came to check on you," he said. "What were you dreaming? You cried out in your sleep."

"I wasn't sleeping, I was meditating...and it wasn't going well," she grumbled.

He smiled at her. The kindness on his face took her off-guard. His skin glowed vaguely in the dark. His eyes were a strange, luminescent violet, his hair the color of moonbeams. He truly was a beautiful man, his features evenly measured, both masculine and cultured. He looked like a prince bathed in starlight.

Sora shook her head. She had no business thinking of Caprion in that way. All Harpies carried such ethereal beauty; she was simply unaccustomed to it.

He walked around the bed to her side, and much to her surprise, he sat down next to her.

"I know you can defend yourself," he began. "You defeated the bloodmage Volcrian, which is no small feat...so please forgive me if I'm wrong," he paused, "but I think you're used to traveling with many companions. Burn is not here, and the assassin is gone. Lori and Ferran reside up the hall. You are without the protection of numbers." His eyes turned to the row of unlocked windows. "Perhaps you will allow me to stay."

Sora raised an eyebrow. "I assume if I refuse, you'll sit outside on the roof all night?"

"Yes."

She sighed. She wanted him to get off the bed and leave her to her gloomy thoughts. But she also felt horribly isolated in the large room. She hated admitting her fear. She didn't want to wake up in the darkness to that sick bastard Cobra sneaking through her window—or worse, materializing from a shadow portal. The thought of his cruel hands made her cringe.

The Shade wanted her. They might have followed her back to the manor; they might be watching her right now.

Wordlessly, she made room for Caprion on the bed. He kicked off his boots and stretched out next to her, keeping a respectful distance away, not touching her. Slowly she began to relax.

Still, every time she closed her eyes, she found herself facing the *garrolithe* again. It waited for her on the fringes of sleep, watching, and pounced whenever she entered a dream. She kept waking up with a start. The beast's presence throbbed at her temples. After a half-hour of tossing and turning, she finally placed her hands on her head.

"I have a horrible headache," she muttered.

She knew Caprion wasn't asleep. He lay nearby, facing the windows. She could clearly see the lines of his strong back against his tunic. His shoulders were wide enough to block her view of the room.

Eventually, he cleared his throat. "My people often use music for healing. I know a song that will calm your mind, if you wish."

Sora hesitated and touched her Cat's Eye in thought. "All right," she agreed, and deactivated the necklace.

A soft hum began in Caprion's throat, and eventually flowed from his mouth. His strange language swirled around her, full of long vowels and soft, soothing murmurs. His words moved like a dance. She felt her headache slowly recede, and images of the garrolithe dispersed with it. Soon, she drifted to sleep.

Lori finished unpinning her hair. It had grown an inch or so, just long enough for her to braid it with a few flowers. She allowed a section of bangs to fall across her forehead. She wore a simple off-white gown with a green bodice, the colors of a Healer, nothing too fancy. Martin Ebonaire knew she was not of noble blood, but luckily, he held her in high enough regard to invite her to dinner.

The meal had been grand—the conversation, not so much. She felt anxious every time Martin referred to Sora as his niece, because it contained a seed of truth. *Curse Silas!* she thought for the hundredth time. The Dracian couldn't have picked a more troublesome charade.

Ferran sat behind her at a large mahogany writing desk. A tall window loomed behind him, revealing thick white snow pelting down from a black sky. A burgundy rug covered the polished oak floor, and a wide fireplace graced the wall across from a grand canopy bed. Even Lord Martin's guest rooms were decadent and richly furnished. A peasant could sell every item in this bedroom and live happily for years.

She allowed herself a half-smile, wondering if she was in the wrong profession. A thief would make out rather well in The Regency.

"You're laughing at me," Ferran said.

"Always a possibility." Then her smile slowly faded. She felt at once awkward and comfortable sharing a room with him. If only she could forget the night on his houseboat, she might actually enjoy herself. But his claim to fatherhood lingered on her mind. She couldn't truly see Ferran anymore, just a giant question with no answer.

She had hoped coming to the Ebonaire house would make Sora's heritage clearer. No, her daughter did not look like she had Ebonaire blood. She was short and stocky, where Lady Danica was tall and long-boned. But the girls had a certain similarity about their lips and chins, the curve of their fingernails and the shape of their thumbs....

Sora's eyes were a vibrant blue. Ferran had gray eyes. Dane had brown eyes.

So wouldn't Dane's child also have brown eyes?

Lori turned away from the mirror, pushing her confusion aside. She looked at Ferran, who now had the map turned sideways and held up to the light. He was obsessed, though she couldn't blame him. Ferran had a certain fondness for old maps. Her treasure-hunting days had ended with Sora's birth, but not his.

"We need to stay focused on our original plan," she cautioned, partially chiding. "You're getting distracted. It's just a map of the sewers. What does any of this have to do with...."

Ferran gave her a wary look. Servant corridors traveled from room to room behind the walls, and conversations were easily overheard. "It all connects," he said. "I can feel it."

Lori shrugged. "Show me, and I'll believe you."

"You barely glanced at the map before. Try looking again."

Lori raised an eyebrow.

"Come look," he beckoned.

Ferran couldn't ignore the fresh scent of roses as Lori leaned over his shoulder. Was she wearing perfume, he wondered humorously, or had she actually stuffed rose petals down her bodice? She brushed against his shoulder and he itched to raise his arm and swing her easily into his lap. But he sensed her stiffness, her discomfort. He wanted to ask what burdened her mind, but he knew her too well. She would tell him when she was ready.

"I don't see it," she finally said as she glanced over the endless lines of canals and channels. "Perhaps the King is renovating the sewer system and the Ebonaires are footing the bill?"

"Perhaps," Ferran mused, "though you'd think Martin would have mentioned it. Surely it would have come up last night after a glass of strong brandy."

"True," Lori allowed. She bent over the map again, brushing Ferran's shoulder.

He picked up Martin's notebook from the desk. "This is half-full of history," he said, thumbing through the pages. "Not my brother's favorite subject. He always preferred numbers. He writes about the wind temples and the City of Crowns."

As Lori took the book and thumbed through its pages, Ferran released a silent breath of tension. He couldn't think straight when she stood so close.

"I think the two are connected," he said.

"Do his notes mention water canals or sewers?"

"Not exactly...." Ferran replied. But the base of his neck tingled, and he trusted his intuition to a fault. "Perhaps Martin is searching for something in the original layout of the city...but what?"

Lori put the book down and turned back to the map. After a long moment, her finger landed on a glint of blue ink among the interwoven black lines.

"Look," she said. "If you hold it up to the light, you can see its color. Isn't blue ink a recent invention?"

Ferran's eyes widened, and he held the map close to the lantern. "Indeed it is blue," he murmured. In the dramatic shadows of the room, he hadn't noticed.

Lori straightened and pushed a strand of blond hair from her face. "Well, blue ink or not, unless we find something concrete tying Martin to our shadowy friends, I say we abandon this business and go back to our hunt for the Shade."

"I *am* hunting," Ferran argued. "Caprion's prisoner said the Shade's leader lives in The Regency. The only reason I can think of is, they need rich friends—and who is the richest friend you can have in the Kingdom?" Then he put his finger on the map. "This blue line you discovered—it's an access tunnel that leads through The Regency, and if you follow it...look here...it travels under the royal palace."

"And then branches into half of the city," Lori pointed out. "Half these tunnels were probably built as escape routes in case of a siege. King Royce isn't a fool. You're grasping at straws. We need to find *The Book of the Named*; only then will we understand the Shade's plan. All we've done so far is sit around this manor!"

Lori paused after her outburst and placed a hand against her back. Her stab wound had begun to throb.

Ferran watched her with a frown. He wanted to help, but he knew she would refuse.

"Anyway," she continued, "if Crash has indeed turned against us and joined the Shade, our cause might be lost completely. They have the three sacred weapons, and we have no more leverage. I'm trying not to lose hope, Ferran, but our chance of stopping the Shade looks bleak, at best."

"Are you planning to attend the parade?" Ferran asked. "We could hunt for the Shade's hideout then."

Lori shook her head. "No," she said. "I should stay with Lady Danica and make sure she doesn't relapse."

"The staff is more than capable, I think...?" Ferran asked searchingly. "I don't want you—*my wife*—acting as a servant."

Lori gave him a pointed look. "I am acting like a Healer, not a servant, and Lord Martin has been more than welcoming, considering your history. Besides, I'm not in the best condition to go romping around the city. Let's continue this in the morning, shall we? I am exhausted."

She turned and walked toward the double-doors that led to the rest of their suite. A maid was waiting on the other side to help her into her night garments.

"And where will I be sleeping?" Ferran called after her.

"The chaise," she replied stiffly.

He sat back with a long sigh and rested his hands behind his head. Why were dresses so provocative? The mysterious sway of skirts, the alluring cut of the bodice, the scent of roses....*Focus,* he thought. *Don't be distracted.* Oh, if only it were so easy....

He folded the map and slipped it in his pocket, then stood up. Perhaps Lori was right. Perhaps the map and the notebook meant nothing. But Ferran had a nose for buried treasure, and he could feel the hunt in his bones.

# Chapter 25

The desert wind was cold at night, though not as cold as the freezing snows of the City of Crowns. Large bonfires lit the Shade's encampment; orange flames danced across the sand and sent shadows leaping.

Crash walked behind Cerastes, following up and down the rows of soldiers. They didn't wear uniforms, just ragged clothing dyed black and gray. The Shade moved around him as the firelight flickered. He knew their practiced formations, their chains of attack. Every kick, every forceful punch reminded him of his own training.

*He's building an army,* Viper thought, studying the ongoing rows of soldiers. He wondered again why Cerastes would show him this. The Grandmaster had brought him here and left Cobra behind, which made him uneasy. Cobra couldn't be trusted, and was stronger than Crash had first thought.

Cobra had transported him back to Cerastes after their brief encounter with Sora. He had reported the entire debacle, and seemed frustrated when Cerastes didn't punish Viper for his hesitation. Instead, Cerastes sent Cobra away and brought Crash here again, further into the desert, deeper into the world of the Shade.

*Is he trying to impress me?* Crash thought as he trailed in Cerastes' wake. No, his Grandmaster was not so vain. But why bring him here? Why further expose the Shade's secrets?

His Grandmaster walked along the ranks, occasionally singling out a savant and correcting his or her form. The students practiced with wary attention. Viper saw countless mistakes as his experienced eyes swept over the younger assassins. He felt no desire to correct them. He was no longer part of this world.

After almost an hour of listless walking, Cerastes reached the front of the ranks and traveled along the first row. Viper's eyes immediately landed on a young soldier whose feet were trailing heavily in the sand. He saw Cerastes stiffen marginally as he picked his target.

"Wake up," Cerastes snapped. His hand flashed out and grabbed the young savant by the arm, just above the elbow. He didn't have to squeeze hard to bring the man to his knees.

Cerastes dragged the savant out of line and threw him before the ranks of soldiers. At his brief signal, the leaders of each row stopped their practice. The ranks came to a graceless halt. Viper stood back several paces, wondering what the Grandmaster intended.

Cerastes turned to his army. When he spoke, his voice was louder than before; it seemed to rise from the earth and shake the air. The hair prickled on Viper's neck. This was not a man speaking. Cerastes' demon was powerful indeed to hold such influence over the physical realm.

"This soldier can hardly keep his eyes open. He is failing before his brethren. He is too weak to stand in the Dark God's shadow. Laziness will not be tolerated among the Shade." Cerastes clasped his hands behind his back. "What are our four tenets?"

The soldiers shouted back: "*To stand as His feet, to lift as His hands, to serve in His shadow, to obey His will: We are children of the Dark God.*"

"A lazy servant cannot carry out our God's will," Cerastes intoned. Then he indicated Crash. "The Dark God has honored you all by returning his child to us: this is Viper, Named at the age of fourteen. My protegé—and some day, a new leader among your ranks. Viper," Cerastes turned to him, "if you were commander of my army, how would you punish this man?"

The Grandmaster's words caught him entirely off-guard. Viper found himself returning the silent gaze of a thousand or more nameless soldiers. The attention upon him was palpable. His heart quickened as the firelight leapt, but he remained composed. This was another test. His Grandmaster was trying to corner him. He thought he knew Cerastes' intention. He wanted Viper to remember himself, to confront the past he had buried.

He turned to the soldier on the ground. Slow, smoldering anger entered his thoughts. Cerastes was trying to manipulate him into joining the Shade. *Too soon,* he thought. *You've misplayed your hand.* He would not be put to the reins like a beaten horse. Cerastes thought he knew the inner workings of his student. He thought Viper was still the same man who left the Hive, exiled and assumed dead, cursed to endlessly wander the land. He thought Viper was like the rows of savants before him, broken down by years of solitude, battling the savage desires of his demon.

But he wasn't like them. He had something else to live for.

The soldier before him knelt on the sand, waiting for his punishment. Viper felt his lips twist. An assassin didn't wait like a servant to be struck.

He reached down and dragged the man to his feet.

"Stand," he said.

The savant obeyed.

He stared briefly into the man's eyes, unnerved by their glassy appearance.

"Strike me," he said.

The man's eyes focused on Viper's face. "What?"

"Show me your skill." Viper spread his arms in silent invitation.

The savant drew a crooked knife from his belt, and with a heavy, stumbling gait tried to plunge it into Viper's chest. He was clumsy and off-balance. Viper easily dodged and disarmed the man by twisting his arm behind his back. Then abruptly he released the savant, who fell forward into the sand, with his back fully exposed. And there he stayed.

"Why not defend yourself?" Viper demanded.

"You did not order me to, Named one," the savant said with a lowered head.

Viper felt disgusted. What kind of fools had Cerastes created? These were rejects of the Hive, and for a cold moment, he understood why. This man was not worthy of any title, let alone that of an assassin.

His demon stretched through his thoughts like an uncoiling snake. *Look at this weak little worm,* it whispered. *Kill him.*

Viper's hand tightened on his dagger. He stared down at the man's exposed back. Adrenaline flooded his muscles and he tried to control his demon's strength.

*There is no reason to kill him,* he thought. The soldier was young, and exhausted to the point of delirium. He was not worthy of death.

Crash tried to suppress his demon's ruthless desires, but the creature seemed stronger than before, its presence amplified by Cerastes' dark aura.

*One sick man weakens the horde,* the demon whispered. Its voice sounded identical to Cerastes. *One lame man burdens his fellows, and makes the fight twice as hard. The weak have their place. Do what you must to survive.*

*This is not a battlefield,* Viper thought.

*Nature has its order,* the demon pressed stronger. Viper felt his muscles cramp. *Release him to our god.*

"We are waiting, Viper," Cerastes murmured behind him. "Your army is watching."

Cerastes' words held a mysterious power. Viper felt his control slip. This was a public demonstration. What would the soldiers say, what would they think, if they saw his weakness? They knew his Name now. If he betrayed their Grand-master, the entire army would fall on his head.

And for what? To save a nameless stranger, who had doubtlessly committed evils in his own life, who had lived as an outcast of the Hive, killing for money in the back alleys and underground taverns of human cities....

What of Sora? What would she think?

*We belong here,* the demon hissed. *A home.* The word resounded through him with strange clarity. He hadn't belonged anywhere for a long time. He hadn't thought he needed a place in the world. But suddenly, standing before all these eyes at his master's right hand, he wondered if Cerastes was trying to entice him with something more. Not just a home, but a place of honor, a sense of prestige he would never gain elsewhere.

Viper felt the hive-mind stir. A damp heat filled his thoughts. He tried to suppress it, but demons ran in packs, and the influence of the horde around him was too strong. Cerastes' indomitable presence hovered over them like a curtain of black smoke, influencing them by proximity alone, bringing their primal instincts to life.

He knelt and grabbed the man's head. In a swift motion, he ran his knife along the base of the man's throat, cutting his jugular. Then he released the body to the sand.

Krait's head lolled to one side. The wet, musty scent of the river awakened her, and the gentle roll of the ship. She winced. Her neck felt raw. Each swallow burned like a dagger slipping down her throat. Her senses quickly sharpened.

She tested the bonds on her wrists. Firm.

A loud clatter from the deck above caught her attention. She heard rattling plates and not-quite-distinguishable conversation. She guessed she was under a mess hall. Chairs thumped against the floor. Breakfast hour?

Her eyes adjusted easily to the shadows of the ship's hold. She saw boxes, crates and barrels held down by heavy nets, fastened to brass rings on the floor. She was tied to a similar brass ring. The smell of seaweed and pickled vegetables assaulted her nose. By the gentle sway of the ship, she guessed they were still docked on the banks of the river. *Good,* she thought. She was still in The City of Crowns. She could still escape and return to her master.

Her eyes scanned the darkness for a sharp object that would cut through her bonds, but she saw nothing of use among the wood and ropes. She repeatedly tightened her hands into fists. How long would they hold her? A few days? A week? Indefinitely? She sneered to herself. The Harpy wouldn't let her go. She suspected he would kill her soon.

As though summoned by her thoughts, she felt a subtle prickling on the back of her neck. Krait looked up just as the hatch opened on the other end of the cargo hold. Dim light, too white to be a lantern, teased her eyes.

Her chest tightened when she recognized the Harpy's glow. Instinctive panic surged. She would never admit it aloud, but she feared the race of Wind and Light—*feared,* which was not a word in her native tongue.

The light brightened at the Harpy's approach. She shuddered. She couldn't see his wings, but that didn't mean he was harmless. A piercing glow emanated from his skin, burning her sensitive eyes.

He knelt before her. She squinted and bowed her head to avoid his light, and suddenly, it dimmed. The vibration rolling off his skin changed in texture and intensity. Surprisingly, his magic didn't hurt her as it had during her interrogation. Rather, his aura washed over her in cool, calming waves. The tension in her shoulders loosened.

He set a bowl of oatmeal and a tankard of water next to her foot.

Krait almost laughed. "Come to feed me, like a chained-up dog?"

The Harpy—Caprion, they called him—gazed at her with violet eyes.

She kicked the wooden bowl away. "Take your gruel elsewhere," she hissed. She couldn't look directly at him. The glow of his skin bothered her, but his expression was worse: she saw no loathing, no disgust. His lips were set in a patient line. He obviously didn't fear her in the least.

The race of Wind and Light were known for their physical perfection: symmetrical faces, alluring voices and ageless, glowing skin. Caprion's face held a vulpine edge, both masculine and intelligent. He looked like a highborn prince, meant to study magnificent books and rule with a gloved fist. He did not appear like a brutish warrior, but a man of higher birth.

She felt repulsed by him.

He hovered for a moment, made buoyant by the power of his wings; his feet did not quite touch the wooden planks. Then he sat cross-legged before her, eye to eye. She could no longer look away and met his luminescent gaze. His eyes were so strange, so unusually colored. His platinum hair fell in ruffled waves around his face. His nose and jaw seemed chiseled from stone.

"Why don't you kill me?" she asked.

"I considered it," he said, "but I decided it would be too much of a reward."

She sneered at him. "I would gladly die for my Master's plan."

"My thoughts exactly."

"I am not afraid of torture. I won't betray the Shade."

"You won't have a choice," he said dryly.

Rage made her neck ache. She fixed him with a withering glare.

"My master will come for me, and when he does, he will rip your wings from your back and your wiggling tongue from your head."

He studied her, unperturbed.

"What if I told you," Caprion said slowly, "that I knew a girl once, and you remind me of her?"

"Did you lock her up too? Did you torture her? Did you kill her?"

His gaze hardened and he didn't answer.

Krait's sneer widened. A long moment of tense silence passed. Finally she snapped, "So what happened to this girl?"

"I tried to save her life, but I don't know if I did in the end." He watched her.

Krait rolled her eyes. "Is this a new tactic?" she taunted. "Tell me your secrets, and I'll spill mine? Are we friends now? You *tried* to save her life. You *intended* the best. Am I supposed to feel pity?" She didn't care about his memory of some dead, nameless girl.

He watched her warily. He sat so close, she could see the small imperfections on his glowing skin, a slight scar on his left brow, the small lines around his eyes.

"You're ugly," she snapped without warning.

He blinked, and she liked his surprise.

"Oh, has no one told you that before?" she grinned.

"Yes, actually. An old friend, once."

She leaned forward. "You're uglier than a rat carcass."

A smile cracked his lips. "Really?" He leaned a little closer. "Is it my nose? Or my hair?"

Krait felt a bead of sweat drip down her brow. She suddenly couldn't think of what to say. Her eyes darted to the door, then quickly up to the ceiling.

He sat back again. "I suppose you have some sort of daring, resourceful escape planned?" he asked, following her gaze.

She glared at the slanted boards of the cargo hold, but didn't reply.

Unexpectedly, he took her face in his hand. His touch was as cool as she imagined. He managed to be firm without causing pain.

"Where is *The Book of the Named*?" he asked softly.

"I told you already. My Master has it. I know not where," she replied.

"Surely you must know something of the Shade's plot. Tell me what you left out. Any small detail." He laced his voice with magic. She tried to resist, but his words had a way of weaving into her mind, forcing her to speak....

"Winter solstice," she choked, trying to swallow back the words. "He needs the three weapons by winter solstice."

"Why?" Caprion demanded.

She shook her head. "I don't know. He doesn't tell us."

"Who is he?"

Pain split her skull, but she bit her lip, withholding the Name with all her might. "My Master," she gasped. "He saved me." She tasted blood in her mouth.

A ripple of anger crossed the Harpy's face, marring his perfect composure. He stood up, distancing himself from her.

"Saved you," he mocked. "And you would sacrifice yourself for him now."

"Gladly."

"I won't let you."

"What?"

"I won't let you sacrifice your life for a demon. I won't let you fulfill your vows to the Shade." His shadow fell across her. She didn't think Harpies could cast a shadow, but his was large, all-engulfing.

"You can't take the Shade from me," Krait burst out. She didn't know why, but his words made her heart pound. The Dark God's code was all she had, all she knew. "My Master will come for me. He will *end* you!"

"What makes you think he can take you from me?" Caprion's gaze darkened. "I'm a seraph. I'm not afraid of a Grandmaster, or the Shade, or any other entity that lurks in the dark." His eyes swept over her. "I am, however, just a little afraid of you."

"Why?"

"Because some day, I might just let you kill me."

She stared at him, uncertain if she had heard correctly.

He continued speaking. "Your kind is used to pain. You've endured it all your life. It's how you understand the world. And from that pain, you turn cold." His voice lowered. "But I know what hurts you the most."

Then, unexpectedly, he drew his hand down the side of her cheek. She felt gentleness in that touch. Reverence. It pierced her.

"Don't mistake my patience for weakness. I am your keeper now."

She shuddered, wholly unnerved. The timbers creaked. She heard a spatter of hail against the deck above. And for a moment, fear overwhelmed her again. She knew the pain of a Harpy's wings; she knew the burn of a sunstone at her neck. But the endurance of his eyes? His unwavering voice? He promised a kind of torment far deeper than that of the flesh.

Caprion stood up and turned away; her eyes lingered on his retreating figure. He climbed out of the cargo hold and shut the trapdoor, and she was once again left in the dark.

# CHAPTER 26

S ora and Lily rode in the second carriage from the Ebonaire manor to the Royal Road, which cut through The City of Crowns and connected the West Gate to the King's palace. Lord Ebonaire rode before them. Large plumes of red feathers and trailing black streamers marked his carriage. People lined the side of the road to cheer for the Ebonaire coach. Sora saw other carriages marked with various house colors ahead of them. The entire city turned out to watch as the procession passed by. Some flew bouquets of winter flowers at their feet.

"Is this the parade?" Sora asked.

"Oh no. This is just the beginning," Lily assured her.

Sora felt a flutter of excitement. That morning, Lord Ebonaire had dressed in extravagant armor displaying his house colors. He had donned a chest plate of dazzling silver over a black tunic. A dashing sword hung from his belt with rubies and diamonds embedded along the pummel. A crimson cloak, with the symbol of a phoenix sewn on the back, had finished the ensemble. Before leaving, the servants had delivered a black porcelain mask into his hands.

He would wear the mask when he boarded his parade float. The parade, after all, was a story in and of itself: through props and costumes, the history of the Kingdom and its founding tribes was retold. Each of the First Tier families wore their inheritance with pride.

The *floats*, as they were called, were floating barges decorated for the parade. Some represented the First Tier families, while others represented the wind temples or the Healer's seminary. The floats traveled down the main canal from the King's castle to the Crown's Rush, then onward down to The Bath, where they were docked and dismantled. Then, at night, all was set alight in a grand pyre. The entire city flooded the streets, dancing and reveling.

The Ebonaire carriage before them, drawn by four magnificent black horses, headed inland toward the King's palace. People cheered as it sped past, throwing flowers or dyed feathers into the street. The arrival of the First Tier families stirred almost as much excitement as the parade itself.

Sora's carriage continued toward Tourmaline Street. She wished she could join the merrymakers outside and watch the entire parade, but she had to find Lord Seabourne. Lily assured her he could be found at The Knob, a well-known tavern off the canal where the parade would pass.

Outside the carriage window, gray clouds covered the sky. Icy wind swept the streets, with the promise of snow to come. Light rain misted the air. The weather only seemed to excite the city, rich and poor alike. The farther they traveled down Tourmaline Street, the bigger the crowds became. Some people flew kites shaped like autumn leaves, snowflakes or stars. Shopkeepers decorated their storefronts with black and silver ribbons. They hung ornate wooden masks, painted pine cones and shiny glass ornaments on their doors.

Lily's short black hair bobbed gently with the sway of the coach. Her large, doleful eyes gazed dreamily out the window.

"Look, performers!" Lily exclaimed, pointing out at the snowy streets. A large group of brightly dressed troubadours marched down the cobblestone road, their masks painted yellow, blue and red. They pounded on drums and trilled on flutes, readying the crowd for the parade. People scurried to and fro, calling to their friends and interrupting traffic.

Sora tried to memorize each and every sight. Hundreds of people walked toward the wide canal to watch the parade. Twenty minutes passed before Lily directed their driver to the side of the road.

"The Knob is just ahead." She pointed down the street as she climbed out of the carriage.

Sora followed determinedly. Her skirts were much easier to walk in today. That morning, she had discovered her new clothes wrapped in brown paper packages by her bedroom door. She was surprised by the expediency of the shops; in the country, several weeks might pass before a new dress arrived by mail. She suspected the tailor had modified a few older designs. Still, she felt much more graceful moving about in a properly fitted corset, which clasped her correctly under the arms and pressed up her cleavage to a daring height. A lacy white bow decorated the front of her dark green bodice, and more lace trailed from the ends of her sleeves. Her skirts were made of a green velvet, and a white fur-trimmed cloak covered the ensemble.

Colorful? Yes. Seasonal? Apparently so. And every other woman on the street was equally dressed up.

Lily led her down Tourmaline Street a brief way. They passed a dozen street vendors and countless peasants before reaching the end of the block, where a square building sat on the corner. Several chimneys sprouted from its roof, releasing wisps of gray smoke into the air. Her eyes combed the white plaster walls and exposed wooden beams of the inn. Icicles dripped along the edge of a wooden shingle roof. Despite the hubbub of the streets, the noise issuing from the building was even louder.

Lily ushered Sora through the door of The Knob. "The parade will start soon. Hopefully, Lord Seabourne is still here."

Every sort of person crowded the interior of The Knob: sailors and merchants, off-duty soldiers and just as many women, all dressed up for the parade. As Lily led her through the room, Sora tried to guess their occupations. Thick forearms indicated field hands, bricklayers or bakers, while housemaids and store clerks dressed with a lean sort of elegance. Others appeared to be merchant daughters or farm girls from the surrounding countryside. Sora remembered the days when such a crowded room would have intimidated her. Now, she felt more at ease in the busy tavern than she had in The Regency.

Several women took note of Sora's expensive dress when she passed. A few turned away as though jilted. One woman near the door glared at her outright.

"Looky here!" she said drunkenly, and grabbed the man next to her, almost spilling his drink. "Her Ladyship lost her way! You're a bit far from the henhouse, aren't you, chicken?"

Sora ignored the jeer, but Lily faced the woman full-on.

"Shut your crooked mouth 'afore your teeth fall out from drinking that sewage water!" she spat.

The woman sneered, displaying a wide grin with two missing teeth, and raised her tankard. "Only the finest sewage in Crowns. Take your rich friend elsewhere. Let us working girls have a place of our own."

Lily made an obscene gesture with her hand, then stomped further into the room.

"Ignore her," she seethed. "She's just sore because you're taking all her attention."

That's when Sora noticed the men glancing in her direction. Their eyes lingered on her tight bodice and the outline of her cleavage. A few leaned over to murmur to their companions. She didn't know what they noticed more—her expensive dress, or her lack of a male escort.

She followed Lily through the massive room. The ceiling was tall and vaulted with exposed wooden beams. Black, silver and white ribbons decorated the rafters. She noticed less seasonal decorations: deer heads, furs, fishing nets and other outdoor memorabilia. A large rowboat hung across the ceiling. It was old but well-kept, made of beautiful rich oak, polished to a shine. The craftsmanship was impeccable. Her eyes traveled to a massive catfish almost 12 feet long hung across the back wall of the tavern. It looked more like a sea-monster than a fish, its mouth twice as wide as her head, weighing at least 300 pounds. Sora stared in awe, wondering if it was real. Beneath the fish hung a large plaque that read *The True King of the River*.

Finally, they reached a private table at the very back where Sora saw soldiers with the King's insignia on their pauldrons and helms. More than two dozen soldiers sat around a wide map spread over the table. She recognized Gracen Seabourne's long, dark-blue cloak. He was the only one who didn't wear armor. He pointed to various locations along the parade route as he spoke.

As Sora recalled, the captain of the King's personal guard was a position reserved only for nobility, and usually handed off to younger sons of a family close to the crown. Contenders for the station had to prove their unquestionable loyalty to the throne. In this case, Gracen Seabourne was the queen's youngest brother. He went through the same training as most soldiers, though perhaps more intensive, considering his private tutelage as a noble. He was charged with protecting the royal family's safety, particularly in times of war.

Sora took a moment to quickly compose herself. *Today, I'm an Ebonaire, the most powerful family in the realm. I'm in charge. Ignore the soldiers!* Then she stepped confidently up to Lord Seabourne.

Lily hung back, as a servant would.

"Lord Gracen," she said pointedly. "A pleasure to see you again."

Gracen looked up. If he was surprised, he didn't show it. His face appeared drawn and tense, weighed down by heavy thoughts. He looked so serious, she forgot his relative youth.

"Lady Sora. How strange to meet you here."

Sora tried to think of an excuse, but decided to cut to the chase.

"I tracked you down, actually."

"Really."

"I have something of great importance to discuss with you."

Lord Seabourne considered her for a moment, then glanced at Lily. Recognition kindled his eyes. He looked back and forth between them, and Sora knew, with a bit of anxiety, that her charade was up.

Gracen's brow lowered. He didn't appear angry, but intrigued. He turned back to his men.

"West Gate patrol, to your posts," he said. "The rest of you, wait for me."

The soldiers saluted as Lord Gracen left the table and joined Sora's side. He offered his arm, following First Tier etiquette.

"Milady," he beckoned.

Sora found herself looping arms with him. She couldn't very well refuse in front of his men; that would start their conversation off entirely wrong.

He escorted her outside, onto a deck built over the wide water canal at the back of the tavern. Lily remained inside with the soldiers; Sora watched her maid put on her most charming smile as she approached their table. The door to the tavern swung shut. They were alone.

A light layer of snow dusted the wooden planks of the wide deck, and a thin blanket of frost speckled the channel. Soon, the water canals would freeze over completely. Sora shivered against a cold wind that blew across the water.

Lord Gracen noticed her discomfort and unexpectedly pulled her closer to his side. They stood shoulder-to-shoulder at the railing. He regarded her with a thoughtful expression.

"You know who I am," she said. A year ago she might have been afraid, but after so many months of travel and peril, Lord Gracen seemed as threatening as a small dog. Or, perhaps, a large dog. Still, she saw no issue in smacking him across the nose, should she need to.

"I'll admit, you had me guessing." He searched her face again. "I thought I'd lost my mind after our first meeting. Sora Fallcrest, alive after all this time, and somehow staying at the Ebonaire house? Congratulations for escaping the King's law." His eyes glinted with a sudden, smoky sense of humor. "I can't imagine why you've come to the city."

Sora had to ask, "Are you going to arrest me?"

"Difficult to arrest a dead woman. Your obituary is long past, my dear, and your estate dissolved. Enjoy your freedom. Think of what it's cost you." He looked ready to go back inside.

Sora tightened her grip on his arm. Lord Gracen paused, not expecting her to be so strong.

"Actually," she said, "I have a few questions."

"Oh?"

"Why did you attend my Blooming? Did you get a chance to speak with Lord Fallcrest before he died? Do you know who killed him? Why did you travel to the country?"

"That's quite an interrogation," Lord Gracen said. He studied her with even more interest than before. "All right. We don't have much time before the parade, so I'll explain quickly. Since the beginning of the king's new project, the Gillian Square Clock Tower, there have been a wave of mysterious deaths. Now, most of the victims were peasants who worked on the construction crews, but some were wealthier merchants and investors."

Sora frowned but stayed quiet. She didn't see how this related to her Blooming.

"The deaths all seemed accidental," Gracen continued, "but eventually I realized that each victim was connected to the Ebonaire family: either working for them, or locked into contracts...except your father. He met with the Ebonaires, but no agreement was struck. He left the city after that, perhaps the very same day. Then he wrote to me. We weren't companionably close, so I found that strange.

He said he had important information, but needed to share it with me in person, and he couldn't meet me in the city."

Sora's brow knit with thought. "And my Blooming?"

Lord Seabourne shrugged. "A timely excuse to visit." He looked out over the frozen river. "He was killed before we could speak in private."

Sora shuddered. She remembered her stepfather collapsing to the ballroom floor amidst the shattered skylight and screaming guests. She had panicked and fled the manor, without realizing he was dead. Several days had passed before she had learned of the assassination...and that she traveled with his killer.

It all seemed so horribly tangled. Hadn't Crash done the dirty deed and offed her stepfather for payment? In that light, he was surely a villain. She thought of his likely involvement with the Shade and felt sick to her stomach. What if she truly didn't know Crash at all?

Lord Gracen cleared his throat. "My condolences for your loss," he said.

Sora blinked. No one had ever told her that. "Thank you," she stuttered, fumbling for something to say. "I remember you from my Blooming. You caught one of my scarves."

Gracen cast her a vague smile. He looked much younger when he was at ease, almost handsome.

"So I did." As an afterthought, he added, "You were quite charming."

"And you thought I killed my own father?"

"Easier than pinning it on Martin Ebonaire or the Prince," he replied. "They're second cousins, you know. They look out for each other. In truth," he added, "I wanted Lord Fallcrest's death to be simply explained. I wanted my suspicions about the clocktower deaths to be wrong. I let that desire blind me. Instead, after some time had passed and I was able t o reflect upon the situation, your father's assassination convinced me that something very rotten was afoot. Frederick Fallcrest knew something. He discovered something, likely by accident, and it got him killed."

Sora didn't know how to feel.

"Yet you made me out to be a murderer," she said through gritted teeth. "You made it impossible for me to return home. Then you pronounced me dead, and the Fallcrest estate is no more."

His face grew older again, and she saw the regret in his eyes.

"It was a mistake, Lady Sora. I am only human. Just by looking at you, I see the error in my ways. You are not a killer."

She shifted on her feet, uncomfortable at his words. She might not be a killer, but she had killed before. She wondered how much her new dress weighed into his assessment.

"Did you ever find out who caused the clocktower deaths?" she asked.

"No." Lord Gracen's eyes traveled over the cold water. "I thought Fallcrest might be a lead, but the moment he offered to talk, he was killed." He folded his arms. "Again, I'm sorry I couldn't save his life. Something is horribly amiss in this city, and it's circling in the higher tiers. Assassins aren't cheap, and nobility aren't easy to kill, no matter their rank."

"Assassins aren't cheap," Sora echoed. Morbidly, she wondered what her stepfather's life had been worth in coins. Crash had never told her; he never spoke of it at all.

She wondered if Crash had lied to her all this time, and if he knew who had paid for Lord Fallcrest's death. She had forgotten about how much he used to frighten her, how much she had distrusted him in the beginning. Maybe he was just a killer, and her heart was simply too open.

Lord Seabourne stared out over the gray waters. His energy was as strong and consistent as the river's flow. She felt safe next to him, despite standing in the open.

Slowly, she realized he wasn't a threat. He was only interested in protecting the royal family. Martin Ebonaire might be a much darker person than she had first realized. If he had hired Crash to kill Lord Fallcrest, what if he did the same to Ferran? *We've landed in a snake pit.*

Lord Gracen must have noticed the concern on her face, because he said, "I'm sure you're fine, staying in that house. Just know when to leave. Martin is a gracious host, but he can grow weary, especially if you make trouble." He paused, considering his next words. "Martin is a sly one. We all are, even our good King Royce. Only wolves survive in the First Tier. Either become a wolf yourself, or run."

Sora thought of the garrolithe and the scar on her hand. She wasn't going to run.

"Now, I have to ask: why are you staying at the Ebonaire house under such a disguise?"

She hesitated before speaking. How much should she tell him? Humans thought the ancient races were extinct. They didn't believe in magic. Lord Gracen didn't seem interested in superstition, but in facts.

"It's a long story, to be sure." She searched for a convincing lie, knowing how the nobility talked. Gracen Seabourne seemed like a good man, but he was not her friend. Not yet. "You might know the name of Redhanded Ferran. Well, I ran into him on the road, and I joined him. He and his wife adopted me, in a sense." She laughed, but it sounded forced, and Lord Gracen gave her a pointed look. He could sense her hidden story.

Her tone became serious. "To be quite honest, I'm trying to recover what I've lost. I'm in the city to find a match and Ferran Ebonaire agreed to help me."

"That's rather bold."

"One has to be bold to survive in this world." Sora held his gaze evenly, and she wondered what Gracen saw there, because eventually, he glanced away.

"I will keep my eyes and ears open around the Ebonaires, if you like," she offered. "We would make good allies."

"A deal," Lord Seabourne said, though he didn't sound very enthusiastic. "Just don't give me cause to arrest you. Because I will."

She nodded, a little wide-eyed.

"Come find me if you uncover anything suspicious. In exchange, I'll keep your little secret."

"Thank you." She forced herself to smile.

Lord Gracen appraised her with his dark eyes. He was an intense man, she decided, but he carried the weight of his responsibilities well.

"I found you quite pleasant at your Blooming," he finally said. "A pity the ball ended as it did. I would have asked you to dance."

"You and I, dance at my Blooming?" Sora laughed unexpectedly. "What a disaster! I appreciate the sentiment, though I know that you, a Seabourne, wouldn't dance with someone of the Second Tier."

His eyes sparked. "You were shy and uncertain, perhaps, but lovely all the same. Who knows, eh? I might have made a suit."

Sora flushed. A suit? After tripping at her own Blooming? He was flattering her.

"I know how to dance, truly," she stuttered.

"Perhaps I'll find out at First Winter's Ball."

"What?"

"You're going, aren't you?" he asked. "If not, I'll see to it. Please accompany me as my guest."

Sora was absolutely flustered. His guest? What did that mean?

"Is that...is there some way—"

"I'll put your invitation in the mail in the morning." He smiled. "And if we can't dance, then perhaps we can talk."

Ah, yes. She was an informant. She could look at it that way.

Lord Seabourne took her hand. "Until next time we meet, Lady Fallcrest," he said. Then he put her hand on his arm and escorted her back into the tavern.

Sora left Seabourne with his men and went to find Lily, who stood at the bar sipping a tankard of ale.

"Well?" she asked. "Did you find what you came for?"

Sora glanced skyward. "He invited me to First Winter's Ball as his guest."

Lily's eyes widened. "His guest? Are you sure that's all?"

"Please don't make a big fuss about it. He wants to talk to me, no doubt to find out more about Lord Ebonaire."

"Maybe, if that makes you feel better." Lily gave Sora a rueful wink. "But I wish I had a dress like that to wear around the city."

Sora smacked Lily's shoulder, and her maid laughed. Lily downed the rest of her tankard in one gulp, then slid it back across the counter.

"Well?" she asked. "Shall we watch the parade?"

Sora knew she should head back to the manor, back to Ferran and her mother, to organize a hunt for The Shade. But she wanted to see the parade for herself. When would she get the chance again?

"Let's watch for a few minutes," Sora agreed.

They backtracked through the tavern, then exited the building. Lily took Sora's arm and pulled her toward the parade route. As they walked, fine snow began to fall. Sora watched the delicate snowflakes land on her skin and melt.

She couldn't help but imagine the life she could have lived. What if she had never found the Cat's Eye? What if her father hadn't been murdered, and she had stayed at her manor? She might have received a marriage suit after all. She might have joined the First Tier and come to live in the City of Crowns, becoming Lady Sora Seabourne, wife to the Captain of the King's Guard.

She wondered what that life would have been like. Did she feel regret? She tried to quell her uncomfortable thoughts. She had made her choice, and it was useless to imagine what might have been.

The sound of music reached her ears and Lily dragged her closer to the canal. "The parade!" she gasped. "Look there! Isn't it wondrous?"

Countless people rushed to the side of the water to watch the floats drift by. Sora and Lily followed them. Sora found an open space on the banks and gazed out over the broad channel. She had never seen anything like it before. Small barges drifted past, displaying miniature scenes of country-and-city life. Sora heard a child's voice cry out, "That one! That's my favorite! No, wait, the next one is better!"

Then each of the First Tier floats drifted past: the Ebonaires, Daniellians, LeCroys, Seabournes, and others she didn't recognize. Flags and banners, displaying different house colors, decorated each float. Then came the royal entourage: The King, Queen, Prince and Princess sat upon bejeweled thrones atop a large float painted gold.

Then the seminary's barge passed, then a float for each of the four winds: North, South, East and West. The largest was the North Wind, the messenger of the Goddess. A man on stilts stood at its center, wearing a costume of red, gold and purple. A porcelain mask covered his face, he carried a scepter in one hand. Several silent figures wearing silver uniforms and white-painted masks, symbolizing the wandering spirits of the dead, danced around him.

Next, another exaggerated figure dressed in sheer purple scarves played the West Wind. She sat languidly upon a velvet cushion, and held a set of scales in one hand. Her porcelain mask was carved into the shape of a single, all-seeing eye—the fortune of the Goddess. The countless bells that decorated her float symbolized Barcella, home of the West Wind, which Sora remembered visiting.

The East Wind appeared as a bearded, grandfatherly man that reminded Sora of Headmaster Duncan. His float looked like an apothecary, full of dried flowers and glass vials. His hat resembled a giant stone mortar and pestle full of flowers, roots, and vines. He symbolized the Wind of Life, the light of the Goddess.

Finally, Sora saw the float of the South Wind. Four fierce warriors stood upon it, dressed in colorful suits of armor—the King's Wanderers. Their armor looked like stained glass glinting in the light. At this distance, she couldn't tell if they were men or women. The masked figure of the South Wind stood at its center, carrying a massive warhorn. The mask was twisted into an angry red scowl, and a tall, swooping helm bedecked her head: the South Wind, the Wanderer's Wind, the might of the Goddess.

Sora's eyes drifted to the four actors who twirled their weapons on the barge. Each twirled a staff in hand, and entertained the crowd with acrobatic leaps and flips. They served as reminders of Kaelyn the Wanderer, the first chosen warrior of the Goddess.

She drank in the sight, knowing she might never see anything so grand again. Before she realized it, a full hour had passed.

Finally Lily tugged on her arm. "We should leave to go back to the manor," she said.

Sora nodded. She disliked leaving behind such rare and glorious sights, but Ferran and her mother had asked that she return by midday, and the sun was already high in the sky.

As she turned away from the parade, a shout went up from down the street. The energy of the crowd changed. She heard voices rising and falling, and people pushed forward, trying to see.

The crowd gasped as several dots of light arced into the sky. She craned her neck. At first she thought they were part of the parade, but the crowd's response told her differently. Flaming arrows, she realized. Fire! An attack?

A squadron of the King's soldiers rushed past her on the street, shoving aside the revelers. Several people fell to the ground. Panic swept through the crowd and Sora found herself caught up in a tide of movement. Peasants began running and jostling each other back and forth. Some fell into the icy canal, while others screamed as they were trampled underfoot. Within a minute, the happy crowd turned into a panicked mob.

Sora tried to fight her way through. She grabbed Lily's arms and dragged her along. At one point, she heard her dress tear and her panniers crack. She held back a cry of pain as the wooden hoops dug into her hips. With her small stature and heavy clothes, Sora realized she was in danger of being dragged underfoot and began shoving people out of the way, landing deft punches where necessary to protect her life. Lily followed close behind her.

Finally they waded to the side of the road and took shelter in an alley between two tall buildings. Lily unhooked Sora's panniers and stripped off her heavy outer skirts, which were now torn and stained beyond recognition. Sora was left in her bodice and petticoats.

"Take my cloak, Milady," Lily said. "Tie it around your skirts...."

"No time for decency," Sora cut her off. She grabbed her maid's hands and looked her in the eyes. "Go back to the Ebonaire manor. Tell them what's happened."

Lily looked shocked. "Alone? Without you?"

"I need to help."

"Have you lost your mind?" Lily demanded. "What could you possibly do?"

"I don't know yet, but I must do something. Just find Ferran and tell him what's happened!"

Sora shoved Lily out into the street. Like a river's current, the crowd picked her up and swept her off around the corner. Sora then turned in the opposite direction and darted through the alley to its other side, where she entered a less crowded street. Then she doubled back toward the water canal and the parade.

The fires aboard the King's float burned a fierce crimson red. She didn't know exactly what to do, but she knew she couldn't let the royal family be killed.

Then, suddenly, a hand grabbed her from behind.

# CHAPTER 27

S ora tried to resist the cruel grip of the man behind her, but she succumbed to
his strength with little choice. By his touch, she knew him: Cobra. He shoved
her ahead of him, and she stumbled. Her soft leather boots offered no grip on the
ice. The crowds were so panicked, no one seemed to notice her being forced up
the street.

"Seems you know better than to struggle," Cobra hissed.

Sora wondered where he was taking her. She knew she had to escape, but
couldn't see an easy solution. If she put any sort of pressure on her arm, it would
snap.

"It must be difficult to know your lover has abandoned you," Cobra said. "He
belongs to Cerastes now. Don't worry, my master will take good care of him, just
like he will take good care of you."

Sora realized he was talking about Crash.

"He would never join you. He hates everything you stand for. He is nothing
like you!" Her conviction sounded much fiercer than she felt. In truth, she was
agonized by Crash's possible betrayal.

"A liar, am I? No matter. You'll have the chance to ask him yourself soon."

Cobra dragged her around a corner. They entered a network of alleys between
a cluster of tall brick buildings. After another turn, he dragged her into a small
courtyard. An iron grate in the ground marked an entrance to the sewers. Cobra
dragged her toward it.

"Where are you taking me?" she demanded, trying to break his grip. He didn't answer. She knew, if he got her underground, she would be lost for good.

Then someone dropped down from the rooftops.

Cobra stopped, and Sora stumbled. She raised her head and stared.

Crash stood before them. He looked hardened, his expression sharp as a dagger. She sensed a low, simmering energy about him. She couldn't quite place what had changed, but he looked different, his cheeks gaunt, his lips tight.

"Cobra," he said curtly. "This is my task. Give her to me." He drew his knife.

Cobra sneered. "I knew you would show yourself if I stole your little doll. Cerastes gave you direct orders, but he seems content to watch you flounder and fail. Well, I'm tired of waiting for this all to shake down."

"No," Sora uttered. "No, it can't be true...."

"Give her to me," Crash repeated.

"You took too long," Cobra hissed. As he twisted Sora's elbow, her entire body turned. If she resisted, he would break her arm. "You're not worthy of our Master's favor."

"Favor?" Sora asked. She searched Crash's chill gaze. "You've sided with Cerastes?"

He looked straight through her to Cobra. "Let her go, or I will tear off your arms."

Crash saw doubt and betrayal in Sora's eyes. She stared at him as though he were a stranger. He wanted to reassure her in some way, but instead, he focused on his enemy.

"Too late, Viper," Cobra said. "Now she's mine."

Crash felt a horrible pressure building inside his body. His temples throbbed—his patience vanished. He acted.

He lunged and slid forward on the ice, to his advantage, and tackled his enemy. He broke Cobra's grip on Sora's arm and hurled him into a wall.

Sora stumbled away, and Crash let her go—at least she would avoid being involved in the fight. He turned fully on Cobra and kicked the enemy assassin to the ground, then threw himself on Cobra's body, ready to slit his throat.

His opponent vanished in a billow of black smoke as Crash's blade struck the cold cobblestone.

Cobra materialized a few feet away, and the two assassins faced off. Crash studied his opponent through white clouds of breath. When he lunged forward, Cobra didn't try to evade him. Crash grabbed him by the throat through the folds of his cowl. His neck was not straight and strong, but mangled, like rotted wood.

Crash dragged the assassin sideways by his crooked neck and slammed him into the side of a building. Too easy. Why didn't he fight back?

"So angry, Viper," he hissed with a wheezing laugh. "Where is your control?"

Crash's demon awakened, as though summoned by Cobra's words. Anger couldn't describe the darkness that stirred beneath his skin. That maddening sense of pressure continued to build, causing his flesh to tingle and burn. *I'll show you control*, the beast grinned. *Take his head!*

"Run back to your master, little worm," Crash said, in a lethal voice.

"And miss your complete undoing?" Cobra breathed. "Our Master's precious Viper, protégé of the Hive, now loyal to a human?" A hoarse laugh escaped Cobra's throat. "Dare I say, bound by love? Humans are too frail for the likes of us. Just look at your lover now, demon—I believe she's fallen ill."

Crash glanced over his shoulder, and his stomach tightened. Sora was leaning heavily against the wall in the alley, with one hand pressed to her chest as though unable to draw air. She hadn't run, as he had expected. Blood ran down the side of her neck.

Cobra's grin widened. "A small cut just behind the ear. She hardly flinched. The poison works slowly—slow enough for my purpose. I want her to see the monster you are." He pulled out a knife from his sleeve and plunged it into Crash's torso.

All the air left him. Crash sank to his knees, his blood staining the snow.

"*Fight me*, Viper. Fight me as you truly are."

A gust of wind blew past them, moaning down one alleyway into the next. Crash focused on breathing as searing pain twisted through his torso. He wondered if the blade was poisoned.

"Why?" Viper asked, holding the knife hilt. "Why are you doing this?"

Cobra's eyes narrowed. "You don't remember the Sandsorrows?" he murmured. "You don't remember what you did?"

The name momentarily jarred him. Crash stared at Cobra for a long, hard moment.

"Impossible," he said through clenched teeth.

"Unlikely, perhaps, but once I heard your Name, I knew I couldn't let this opportunity pass. You might not remember me, but my memories of you have remained pristine over the years. How could they not, when you left me so beautifully disfigured?" His voice grew sharp. "First I will kill you, and then I will kill the girl, and then I will burn you both in the vengeful fire of our God—as I was burned."

Crash shuddered. Images of that night leapt briefly before his eyes, but he couldn't lose himself to memory now. He gripped the handle of the blade lodged in his torso—how could he fight with a dagger stuck four inches in his gut? He hesitated, on the verge of wrenching it free. So what if he bled out all over the street? He had to kill Cobra. He had to fight....

Then, in the dark recesses of his mind: *You need me.*

*No,* Crash struggled against the demon's strength. It could feel his desperation. Its presence remained firm.

His heart began to pound.

*You can't do this alone,* the beast murmured.

*You'll destroy her, and anything else you touch.*

The demon grinned. *I'll destroy the one who touches her.*

Crash didn't trust that voice. Was the demon not loyal to Cerastes? Did it not crave the power of the Dark God?

And yet, in that moment, he could feel the beast's strength pulsing through his arms, his legs, his throat. His demon was a simple creature ruled by baser needs. It desired whatever lay immediately before it—something to fight for, something to protect, something *to own.*

He didn't have a choice. Sora was debilitated by poison and couldn't escape. Even now, he could see her strength wane as she slid further down the wall.

He couldn't waste any more time; he had to make a decision.

The demon made the choice for him. The pressure in his body reached an unbearable pitch. Then the beast overcame his mind in a rush—Crash felt his bones crunch and his sinews tear as his body changed. His limbs elongated as his skin blackened and hardened. Long spikes jutted out from his shoulders and arms. Wings twisted up from his spine, bursting through his skin like spears. Where his hairline would be, a myriad of short black spikes covered his skull. A thick cloud of mist trailed around his body, half-obscuring his seven-foot frame. The heat of his power melted the snow on the ground.

Cobra's gaze filled with rapture.

"Let's not drag this out any longer," Viper replied, his words distorted by his long teeth. Through his demon's eyes, he could see a toxic cloud hovering around Cobra's body. He could hear the labored rush of Sora's breath across the alley and smell the poison in her blood. The frosty winter air cut through his nose like glass.

He met Cobra's eyes with a deadened stare.

"Aren't you worried?" Cobra asked the man inside the beast. He tapped his own head emphatically. "Will you let the beast kill her as well? One more life for your demon's altar?"

Viper growled, a noise similar to a roaring flame. *Rip out his teeth,* the demon thought. *Strip his spine.*

From deep behind the demon's eyes, Crash watched.

*Shall we kill him,* the demon murmured, *or shall we play first?* A surge of excitement accompanied the thought. *Shall we? Shall we?*

Crash was considering. For once, he and his demon wanted the same thing. He liked this new sense of common will.

He ran at Cobra, who activated the fifth gate and vanished beneath his claws, but Viper expected this. Cobra reappeared behind him, and Viper spun around. His fist connected powerfully with his enemy's jaw.

Cobra's body flew clear across the alley and smashed through a brick wall.

Viper prowled after his prey. He spotted Cobra lying on the other side of the wall. Shards of broken stone and mortar surrounded his body. His cowl lay ripped around his neck, revealing an unexpectedly gruesome sight: half the man's lower jaw was missing. His skin hung loosely like stretched cloth. His neck was mangled and distorted by scar tissue and burn marks.

Crash tried to remember that night, but couldn't. He only saw the vague impression of flames and the shadows of a burning village, feeling the demon's bloodlust heavy in his mind, like a wet, humid cloud. Had he truly created this man?

A ripple of darkness along the ground caught his eye: Cobra's shadow. The darkness coiled around his feet, and suddenly Viper found himself immobile. With a roar of frustration, he lunged forward, trying to break the shadow's grip, but dark magic held him bound.

Cobra sat up as smoke rose from his body. The snow around the brick wall began to melt. Viper could see the man's demon form boiling beneath his skin, a visible force yearning for release.

Cobra's maimed face pulled into a scowl.

"I would have been a Grandmaster if it weren't for you." He climbed to his feet and stood, hunched and faltering, as his body contorted. Speaking through a cracking jaw, he said, "Forget the Shade and its schemes. You're dead, Viper."

"So very devout of you."

Cobra's body pitched forward. A second set of arms exploded from his torso. His limbs became long and sinewy, and his skin turned mottled brown, not unlike a praying mantis. Wicked green claws, dripping venom, sprouted from his fingers and toes. Wide yellow eyes bulged from his skull, and a gaping mouth full of pointed fangs finished the transformation. His teeth were so long, his mouth couldn't shut properly, and his jaw fell open awkwardly to one side. Yellow saliva fell to the snow and sizzled when it struck the ground.

The two demons were like night and day. Viper, of the Mistmire Hive, encased in hardened black skin and long protruding spikes, like bristling armor from the underworld. And Cobra, damp and oozing with toxins, like the Sandsorrow Swamp from which he hailed.

Viper took Cobra by his first set of arms. He used his grip to lever himself over the demon's body in a fantastic leap. As he fell, he dragged his blades down the slimy mottled skin on Cobra's back, landing the first blow.

Yellow pus spilled from Cobra's wound and sizzled when it hit the ground. It smelled rancid.

"Careful, demon," Cobra hissed as the two faced each other. "My blood is toxic to humans. Hit me too hard, and the girl might catch some on her skin."

Viper placed himself between Cobra and Sora's small body. She lay in a tight ball beneath her cloak at the side of the alley. He could hear her ragged breath, but he didn't know if she was still conscious.

His enemy lunged at him, swinging his venomous claws, but Viper grabbed Cobra's arms. With a mighty heave, he threw Cobra over his shoulder, breaking his long, spindly insect arms in the process.

Cobra released an inhuman scream. As he fell through the air, he activated the fifth gate and vanished. The row of spines on the back of Viper's neck prickled. He turned, prepared for Cobra's strike.

Cobra reappeared behind him, and Viper plunged his claws into his soft underbelly.

A look of shock passed over Cobra's face. He opened his mouth and spat yellow pus. It struck Viper's skin, burning, blistering, but Viper didn't let go. His claws remained firmly lodged in Cobra's vitals until his skin rippled, his face shrunk, and his insect arms receded into his torso.

Viper waited until Cobra took his human form. Then he ripped his claws free. A strand of entrails accompanied his hand.

Cobra lay kneeling in the snow, a pool of red blood growing around him. He stared at the unraveled rope of his intestines.

"Kill him." He met Viper's gaze. *"Kill him."*

"Who?"

"Kill Cerastes. Our kind are not meant to rule. Better to worship no man, no god, than become a slave...." Cobra looked like he intended to keep speaking, but his eyes became cloudy and unfocused, and he slumped forward. Life drained from his body.

Crash considered him through his demon's eyes. He thought of Burn, of the Dark God's weapons, and the hopeless task he faced. Cobra was right. The Shade's new order went against their nature. Better to live alone—separate from the Hive and the Shade—than become a mindless slave to a demon's will.

Then his thoughts turned to Sora.

A surge of protectiveness rushed through him. His first instinct was to charge across the alley to her side. Crash considered asserting himself over the demon's mind and reclaiming control, returning to his human form, but the stab wound in his side still hadn't closed, and he was further injured from his fight with Cobra. If he transformed now, he would bleed out swiftly into the snow, and wouldn't have the strength to carry Sora to safety.

Still in his demon form, Viper returned to her unconscious body. He leaned his face close. Cobra had pricked her with a poisoned needle behind the ear. He could smell the taint of nightshade, red sage and foxglove. She would be sick for some time. Nightshade and foxglove, especially, would cause mental confusion, even hallucinations. She would be hard-pressed to keep down food. He couldn't leave her alone.

Viper sat back on his long heels and considered his options. He could return her to the Ebonaire estate and seek out Lori, but that would be risky. Caprion had recognized him in The Regency with Cobra. Ferran and Lori wouldn't trust him, and for good reason. If he showed up with Sora in his arms, he would be blamed for her condition, and maybe even attacked. His demon form was more than threatening, and he didn't know if he would be able to control it.

The demon's will was strong in his thoughts. He felt a fierce animal need to protect her and find shelter. His demon demanded a cave, somewhere warm and dry and easy to defend. He tried to think rationally. He used to live in this city. He knew many places to hide. One, in particular, stood out in his mind.

He picked Sora off the ground and spread his wings to fly.

# CHAPTER 28

Burn opened his eyes. The pain in his head was more manageable now. He couldn't see much in the absolute darkness of his prison, but if he used his ears, he could hear through the earth, down long tunnels into the distance, where gears churned endlessly through the rock.

*Empty*, he thought. The sewers were empty. He did not hear The Shade's footsteps or the rustle of their weapons. Where had they gone?

He climbed heavily to his feet and fumbled to the door of his cell. It was locked, but the iron was poorly made. Using his brute strength, he smashed the chains on his wrists against the cell's lock until the gate bent outward and the hinges snapped. Then he shoved the door to the ground.

His head throbbed and the world spun, but adrenaline kept him on his feet. The Shade had disappeared from the sewers. He didn't know why, and he didn't care. He had to escape while he could.

Burn limped quickly through the underground corridors. No torches or lanterns illuminated his path, but with his heightened senses, he was able to smell the most used passages. He knew he traveled blind. He could be lost for hours. But he needed to find an exit, and this following The Shade's trail seemed the most likely. Hopefully he would find a way to the surface before they returned. If they returned.

Ferran rode in the Ebonaire carriage alone. He had left Lori in an argument with Olivia, Danica's handmaid, back at the manor. Olivia outright claimed that Lori's treatments were "out-of-vogue country cures" not used in the city. Lori had looked ready to skin the maid alive.

He shook his head quietly to himself. The First Tier even had trends for medicine. Olivia had accused the Healer of brewing up bunk concoctions that might ruin young Danica's mind. He had half-expected Lori to smack her in the mouth. That's when he had made his exit.

The coach carried him deeper into The Regency. Ferran unfolded the map from his pocket and tried to direct the driver. He used landmarks and street intersections to follow a particular access tunnel on the map that Martin had traced in blue ink. It was all very troublesome, as some streets had been repaved and renamed, or alleys had been built in-between. Twice, he lost all sense of direction. The sky was solidly overcast and there was no sign of hills or the river. His driver had to backtrack several times.

Finally, Ferran found himself in front of a house on Timberlin Lane. The townhouse appeared dark and quiet, with no servants or horses in sight. Perhaps it was a vacant guest house for a much wealthier family?

He stopped the coach and got out. A wrought-iron fence surrounded the property. The gate was locked. A navy-blue door stood atop a series of flagstone steps. He frowned for a while, looking over his map. A special symbol in blue ink marked this house, and the sewer tunnel appeared to run directly beneath it. He didn't know what that meant, but he had to investigate.

He placed his hand on the iron gate to open it, and immediately felt a tingle of energy run through his fingers. Magic? Some sort of ward or concealment spell protected this house. He wondered how many people noticed the building on a day-to-day basis—probably not many.

With a command to his Cat's Eye, he deactivated the spell and entered the yard, though now he was on high alert.

"Looks like a storm a'brewin,' Milord," the driver called from his seat on the carriage. "Will this be a long visit?"

Ferran glanced at the sky. The clouds appeared coarse as wool. Yes, snow would fall soon, and heavily.

"Not very long. Wait for me."

"Aye, Milord."

He walked to the front door and tried the knob without bothering to knock. It was locked, and he sensed a second ward. Now thoroughly suspicious, he disabled it with his Cat's Eye and used his lock picks to spring open the door. Then he hesitated. Their prisoner, Krait, had said the Shade's leader lived in The Regency. Could this possibly be their base of operations? It seemed improbable in such a quaint neighborhood, but what if he ran headlong into a nest of assassins?

He listened, but heard no sounds from inside. *Nothing else for it,* he thought. He entered the front door.

A short hallway led into a wide-open sitting room. Through an archway, he glimpsed a second hallway leading to the kitchens, no doubt. The furniture in the room appeared untouched.

He walked carefully from room to room. The dining hall was immaculate, as was the drawing room and the servant quarters. A staircase led to the upper levels, but he didn't hear any noise from the floor above. He began to wonder if he was in the right house. He took a quick glance at the kitchen—the oven was clean and unused, the pantry empty. He saw nothing unusual. He scanned his map again, puzzled.

On his way out, he passed an unassuming door in the hallway. He opened it, just to be thorough, and found a reading room with a large bay window overlooking the front of the house. It caught his attention, because the hearth contained a pile of smoldering ash. He touched the stone of the hearth, and found it was still warm. That unnerved him. The house must not be abandoned after all—perhaps the occupants were out and about. If he had a lick of sense, he would leave before he was discovered.

But Ferran was not a man of good sense. As his eyes scanned the room, he found himself staring at a bookshelf. His Cat's-Eye gleamed at his wrist, and he touched it in thought. *Something's here.*

He crossed the floor and stood in front of the bookshelf. His Cat's Eye glowed brighter. The books looked worn and well-used. He pulled a few out to examine them: *Origins of the City of Crowns, The First King,* and *Legends of the Six Gods.*

Ferran thumbed through the books and paused when he reached the back page—each one carried the seal of the royal library. These books belonged in the King's palace. Why were they in this house?

His hand hesitated over another volume: *A History of the Wind Temples.* A strange tingle of energy shot up his fingers. He pulled it from the shelf. The moment he touched the leather, the book's cover shimmered before his eyes. A concealment spell.

The letters on the binding dissolved, and he recognized the dilapidated cover of *The Book of the Named.*

Ferran could hardly believe it. He turned the book over in his hands. The Shade must be confident indeed, to hide such a priceless artifact in plain sight. Then again, they hadn't dealt with an experienced treasure hunter or a Cat's-Eye stone.

But why was it in this house? And why was this house marked on Martin's map?

He opened the book and flipped through a few pages, then a slow, uncertain frown grew on his face. All the pages were all blank. Another concealment spell? He rested his hand on the book's heavy parchment and activated his Cat's Eye, but he sensed no magic.

His frown deepened. This book was no doubt enchanted. Silas would know more about it; he used to own it. Ferran slipped it into his pocket and glanced around the room again. *Someone very important must live here,* he thought. Someone he didn't want to meet quite yet.

He left the room, ready to flee, but a distant thud sounded from deep in the house. *Just go,* he thought, *before The Shade arrive...*but the pounding didn't stop, and it didn't sound like footsteps. He hesitated, his shoulders rigid with indecision, but his curiosity won out.

With a muttered curse, Ferran followed the sound past the sitting room to a door under the staircase. The pounding intensified. He opened the door cautiously and discovered a second staircase leading down to the basement.

His eyes widened. A sewer access tunnel might be under the house after all. He could at least take a quick look. The staircase led him to a cramped room--undecorated, musty--with a metal grate in the floor. Someone appeared to be trapped on the other side of the grate. There, the clanging continued. Ferran wondered if he should leave before inviting more trouble.

Then a deep, muffled voice cried out, "Can anyone hear me? Help! Let me out!"

Ferran recognized the voice immediately. He rushed to the grate and slid it to one side. A massive set of shoulders came into view.

"Burn!"

The Wolfy gazed up at him with obvious exhaustion. Blood matted his hair and smeared his face.

"You're not who I expected," he said.

Ferran grabbed the man's thick forearm and hauled him out of the tunnel. Burn collapsed wearily onto the floor.

"You're alive, you lucky bastard!" Ferran exclaimed. "Are you being followed?"

"No," he grumbled. "I think not."

"Come with me." Ferran helped him to his feet. "A carriage awaits us outside. This has been a strange day, indeed."

Burn stood a bit straighter and tried to walk toward the staircase. Pain glazed his eyes. Ferran slung the Wolfy's arm over his shoulders and supported him up the stairs. He listened for any sign of The Shade while he escorted Burn through the silent house. All the while, he gnawed his lip. Why had this place been marked on Martin's map? Did his brother have dealings with the Shade?

"Where are we?" Burn asked as Ferran led him back to the Ebonaire coach, thankfully without incident.

"The Regency in The City of Crowns. Don't worry, old boy. We're headed to safety."

"And a hot meal, I hope."

"Of course, after we patch you up...."

"A roast, two blocks of cheese and a loaf of bread," Burn said very seriously. "I'll eat first."

# CHAPTER 29

Krait's head spun. She felt delirious from dehydration, but wouldn't touch the food or water laid out before her. She wouldn't accept the Harpy's kindness at any cost.

She hadn't seen him in several hours and she didn't think he was aboard the ship any longer. The crew was unusually quiet as well. Now would be a good time to attempt an escape, but she couldn't break the chains that bound her.

She let her head roll down to her chest. *Dark Redeemer, come for me,* she thought. *Return me to Your shadow. Engulf me in Your flames.* She imagined a wave of black fire consuming her body until, with a billow of ash and smoke, she was released into the realms of the underworld.

When she next opened her eyes, she found the ship's hold darker than before. She quickly scanned the room; a pool of shadows condensed at the opposite end of the hold. A familiar shiver moved down her back. *My Master comes.*

The shadows formed a pool of ink on the floor. The timbers creaked as a long body materialized from the wooden hull. Krait bowed her head in reverence.

Cerastes stepped from the portal. His presence chilled the air, and frost formed on Krait's breath. Their eyes met. He crossed to her side, his robes rippling in a silent wind. With a touch of his hand, the metal chains rotted from her wrists and fell to the floor in a pile of dust.

"Master," she rasped. "I knew you would come. I never lost faith...."

"Where are they?"

She gazed at him, confused by his question. Did he mean the Dracian crew, or the Harpy who had captured her?

"I haven't seen anyone in several hours."

"A pity."

Her Grandmaster stood and walked away from her, to a ladder at the far side of the room.

Krait fell into step behind him. She tried to walk in a straight line and not show her weakness.

"Master, may I ask, why have you come for me now?"

"It was time."

Krait understood. They must follow the Dark God's plan and His perfect timing.

"You should have eaten their food," Cerastes admonished her. "Then you would be able to carry out the Dark God's work."

Krait bowed her head. She felt guilty. "I'm sorry."

"Our god values silence, not words."

She clamped shut her mouth. Did her Grandmaster not see her devotion?

She followed him through the silent mess hall. They exited to the aft of the ship. Four Dracians stood at the railing, casting lures into The Bath. They wore heavy cloaks and hats against the blustery weather.

The sailors turned when Cerastes appeared on deck. Their eyes widened. One dropped his pole in surprise.

"Aye! Stop there! Who are you?"

"Idiot Dracians," Cerastes said softly. Then, in a louder voice, he called, "What is the name of this fine vessel?"

"The Dawn Seeker," one said, and shared a bewildered glance with his fellow.

"Then we shall light it up like the dawn...."

Cerastes raised his hands and a long stream of words began under his breath. The back of Krait's neck tingled. She glanced at the deck and saw the ice begin to melt around Cerastes feet. Her lips parted in awe. Black fire rippled across the deck. It sprung from the railing, trapping the Dracians on board.

*He's going to burn down the ship,* she thought.

Then a powerful sound-vibration rolled through the air with enough force to push Krait from her feet. She fell to the deck. Even Cerastes staggered against the sudden wind. The Dracians all shouted and pointed at the sky.

Light burned her eyes. Krait lifted her arm to shield her gaze. The seraph had arrived.

Caprion hovered just beyond the aft of the ship, his wings blazing strongly against the overcast evening sky.

Two members of the Sixth Race stood below him on deck. Krait, he recognized, but the insidious stranger next to her looked like a powerful enemy. A black aura surrounded his body, stronger than any presence Caprion had felt before.

*A Grandmaster,* he thought. And, he suspected, the leader of the Shade. He met the man's piercing gaze without fear. He had killed demons before.

"Release your servant," he called, and pointed to Krait, who cringed away from the light of his wings. "She is mine now."

The Grandmaster smiled, a horrifying look. "Take her, then. Kill her if you wish. She is of no further use to me." He spread his hands. "A pity your fellows are not here. I hoped to burn you all while you slept. I suppose I will throw you instead to the Dark God's fire."

With a stroke of his wings, Caprion released another crushing vibration. It tore through the railing of the ship, creating a hole in the black fire where the Dracians could escape. The four pirates lost no time flinging themselves into the Bath.

Caprion hovered closer, now that the Dracians were safe. He drew his sword from his belt. The blade glowed with crystalline light. Shards of sunstone infused the blade. They gleamed inside the metal like quartz.

"Your cult is a twisted lie, and you are the king of liars," he called. "Leave or die, demon."

"You may be a seraph, but you are a child, untried and unskilled. I am not afraid of you."

Caprion allowed his second set of wings to glimmer into existence.

The Grandmaster sneered. "You challenge me? So be it."

Black fire spread from Cerastes' feet to engulf the deck. Soon it created a shield between the Grandmaster and the Harpy. Krait disappeared, as well, into the flames. The black fire spread down the side of the ship and across the surface of the water, melting patches of ice. Soon The Bath began to steam.

Caprion swept the flames back with massive wing strokes as he tried to approach the two figures on deck. He cared less about the Grandmaster, who might escape through a shadow portal, and more about Krait. He didn't think she could withstand this fire. She had no demon and no magical ability.

Finally, the flames parted and Caprion saw his opening. He dived through the flames and dropped to Krait's side. Before he could rescue her, however, the Grandmaster materialized through the fire. A wave of black energy shot from his hand, but Caprion's giant wings deflected the darkness. He gritted his teeth. The fire was closing in around him, threatening to set light to his clothes. If he didn't hurry, he would burn alive.

He whirled upon the Grandmaster, spinning his blade through the air, slashing left and right. He forced the man away from him.

They stood facing each other as the flames spread. The Grandmaster regarded him with narrow eyes, no doubt considering his wings and his sword, and how long a battle of this magnitude might take. Caprion already knew he would flee, and had decided he wouldn't give chase. He would much rather get Krait to safety.

The demon's gaze flickered to the girl on the deck.

Caprion pointed his sword at the Grandmaster. "Leave her."

After a long minute, the Grandmaster's aura receded. The black fire on the ship slowly changed to a more natural orange.

"Another day," the demon said briefly. Then, with a flurry of shadows and smoke, he disappeared, leaving Krait behind on the burning deck.

Caprion lifted the woman into his arms. She had passed out from the smoke. Even though she was unconscious, he felt her stiffen when his arms encircled her.

He lifted off the deck, using his white magic to fly across the lake. Singed feathers fell from his wings as he passed over the water. He could fly, but not far. His wings were burnt and damaged by the Grandmaster's fire. It worried him. The demon's magic shouldn't be able to affect him like this.

He glided over the waters of The Bath and landed a brief distance away from the southern docks. He turned back to the burning pyre of the Dawn Seeker and saw a growing crowd of humans gathering to watch the inferno. Nearby boats were catching fire as well. He watched a group of sailors on the docks attempting to rescue other vessels. The orange flames from the Dawn Seeker leapt and spread ravenously, with a supernatural appetite.

Then snow began to fall.

Caprion's wings flickered and disappeared. He pulled his cloak about his shoulders and his hood low over his head. Carrying Krait in his arms, he slipped behind the amassing crowd and started toward the southern gates of the city. Between the weather and the fire, no one paid him any mind. He didn't see any Dracians in the mix; perhaps they had already left to find Silas. He wondered how the poor captain would react when he heard about his ship.

Once inside the city walls, Caprion tried to flag down a coach, but was refused service as he didn't have any coins. People rushed by him in the streets, jostling him to and fro. With no other option, he began to walk back to The Regency with Krait clasped close to his chest.

# CHAPTER 30

Viper flew to the Smokeshaft district. It had a proper name, Enderlane View, but no one used that other than the king's tax collectors. Here, the apartments had poor structural foundations, so they leaned and sagged in all manner of ways. Some resembled broken accordions laid on their sides; others looked like old men leaning against each other.

Residents of the Smokeshafts burned peat, not wood. A dense forest of chimneys spewed gray-and-black smoke into the sky, thick as fog. What snow didn't melt turned soot-gray and sticky, and stuck to windows like wet clay.

Viper swooped through the gritty air, with Sora held tightly against his chest, until he found the rooftop he sought. A flame-ravaged hole in the roof provided easy access into the building. Crash dropped down and landed in one of the upper apartments, where the fire had destroyed most of the top floor many years ago. He left the first room and entered a long hallway. This level had once housed six small apartments, all of which had been eaten by fire, except one at the end of the hall. He walked to it carefully and nudged the door open with his shoulder. It creaked on its hinges, ready to collapse. He entered the room cautiously.

A musty cot stood in one corner beneath a grimy window, and a cast-iron stove with decent venting sat to one side. He searched for signs of inhabitants, but saw no traces of food or belongings. Everything in the room looked forgotten. Perfect.

He laid Sora down on the cot. Her skin was moist and clammy. Cold sweat beaded her brow, and her breath came in short gasps. He inhaled, taking in her scent. In his demon form, he could smell the toxins in her body. Strangely, it made him salivate. A row of black spines flexed along the back of his neck.

He forced himself to back away from the cot. The smell of her stayed with him, an irresistible perfume.

Crash looked down at his claws, his hardened black skin, and the dagger-like blades protruding from his arms. He ran a hand over his head, feeling the short thumbnail spikes. He shifted his bulky wings.

*How do you think we appear to her? She's afraid of you,* he thought to his demon. *She can't love us like this.*

The demon didn't seem to listen. It stayed focused on her sleeping form.

*Is this what you desire?* Crash asked the beast. *Where is your love of the Shade? Of the Master you sought to follow?*

The demon still didn't reply.

*Why do you fight for her?*

The demon looked curiously at the prone body.

*Heat,* it thought simply.

Together they gazed at Sora, two wills through one set of eyes. Crash, who fiercely desired to defend her, and the demon, who smelled the residue of poison in her blood and thought it to be a very fine perfume.

*Share her warmth,* the demon murmured.

Crash knew that need well, and he shared the beast's longing.

He stroked the bristling spikes on his head again. No. Sora could not wake to see him like this.

He reclaimed the throne of his mind. The demon withdrew. For once, their wills seemed one and the same. With a long groan, Crash took over his limbs. His wings shrank into his back; his body returned to its normal size. Finally he collapsed to the ground, shirtless in the frosty winter air and overcome by exhaustion.

For a long moment he could only lie on the floor, wheezing in pain. The dagger wound in his side felt twice as sore, though thanks to his demon's strength, it had stopped bleeding. He dragged himself up next to Sora on the cot, and wrapped her firmly in her cloak. Then he turned to the door. He needed to gather wood and light a fire in the stove. There wasn't much he could do about the poison, but he could at least protect her from the blizzard outside.

That, and he needed time to compose his thoughts before they spoke face-to-face.

Sora woke to the scent of musty blankets. Her head pounded, and the world tipped every time she moved. She tried to take stock of her surroundings. She recognized the slight curve of a dresser on the opposite wall. Through a musty window, she saw thick flurries of snow swirling down from a heavy, overcast sky. Cold air seeped through the rotten window pane, making her shiver.

She was alone.

She sat up and looked around the room. She remembered...*someone.* She thought harder. She remembered, quite suddenly, the appearance of Cobra at the parade. She remembered being dragged through the alleys. But what then?

Floorboards creaked beyond the closed door. A jolt of adrenaline sharpened her senses. Her only instinct was to defend herself.

Dizzy and disoriented, she managed to slip from the bed and crouch low at the foot of the cot. She found a piece of splintered wood on the ground and held it like a knife. Perhaps it was a knife. Her vision kept wavering; she squinted, waiting for the unknown intruder.

The door swung back, groaning in resistance. A dark figure filled the doorway: Cobra. Fear gripped her, and her vision swam again. She felt the need to rub her eyes.

The assassin looked around the room. She could sense his lethal intentions. He wanted to kill her.

He stepped inside, walking with a slight limp as though wounded. Perhaps she had wounded him before; perhaps she could escape.

Sora waited until he was closer, kneeling before a potbellied stove, then she lunged. She intended to sever the tendon at the back of his leg and debilitate him. Then her sense of balance abandoned her completely. She stumbled and missed her strike.

Cobra rose to his feet and kicked the knife--the shard of wood--from her grasp. He grabbed her and lifted her clear off her feet. She tried to struggle, but the room kept spinning and she couldn't seem to organize her limbs.

"Sora!" Cobra hissed. His voice didn't wheeze as it usually did. "Sora, be calm! Look at me!"

She almost slipped his grasp, but he locked his arms around her waist. He force-carried her to the cot. Sweat dripped down her forehead and gathered at the back of her neck. Suddenly, she couldn't seem to get enough air.

He placed her on the cot and she stared up at him, weak and panting. She waited for the room to stop spinning. When it finally slowed, she saw not Cobra standing above her, but Crash.

*Crash.*

Another jolt of near-panic sent her scooting across the bed. She curled defensively into the farthest corner of the cot. Yes, she remembered now. Crash was helping the Shade. He must have helped Cobra abduct her from the parade.

Her thoughts felt slippery. She didn't know what she remembered or what she had dreamed, or if she was dreaming now....

"Where am I?" she finally asked, her voice low.

"The Smokeshaft District," he answered. "I'll return you to the Ebonaire manor in the morning. You're safe here."

She blinked, doubting him. "Where have you been...?"

He didn't meet her eyes. "I made a promise to you. I tried to save Burn's life by going to the Shade. I should have never taken that risk."

Her head spun, and for a moment she saw Cobra sitting before her again, his eyes crinkled in a leering grin. Then his face rippled like water, and she saw someone else. The shadows suggested an older man, past his prime, with long hair and sunken cheeks. She didn't recognize him at all, and she recoiled in fear.

"Who are you?" she asked hoarsely.

His face shifted again, and then Crash stared back at her. He looked solemn. Her question didn't seem to surprise him. "You're sick," he said firmly. "Cobra poisoned you."

She stared at him. She understood his words, and yet the delirium overcame her. Now he looked more like a ghost, his skin pale as snow, his eyes large as moons.

*A fever,* she thought rationally, though it didn't clear her vision.

"I never meant to put you in danger," he said heavily.

"It's true, then? You've gone to the Shade?"

"It's not so simple," he murmured.

Tears stung her eyes. "You took the Dark God's weapons to Cerastes, and now he's done something to you. You're not the same. I can sense it."

He didn't deny her words, but watched her closely.

"He won't let you go now. That's what you won't tell me."

Her words took him off-guard. She could see it on his face.

"I'm afraid I've caused much more harm than good," he admitted.

Sora felt suddenly frail. She couldn't imagine the days to come. What if Crash never left his Grandmaster's side? What if the Shade dug their way into his mind? She didn't fully understand what had happened, but she felt the change in him, like a distance that she couldn't measure.

A sense of helplessness descended. She couldn't save him from his past. She couldn't help him.

"Are you loyal to him, now?" she half-choked. "Take me to Cerastes if you must—I can't fight against you."

"No." He reached, grasped her around the waist and pulled her across the cot. She stiffened, but she couldn't resist. His arms enfolded her. "No, Sora. Not that. *Never* that. I don't know where I've been the last few days. Cerastes is powerful, and he has a strong influence over the Shade, but when I saw you again, I knew everything he stood for was a lie." He looked into her eyes fiercely. "You brought me back."

As she gazed up at Crash, his words frightened her. Could he forget who he was? Could Cerastes assert such a powerful hold over him? As silence filled the space between them, and she began to think back on their journey together, on everything she knew about Crash and why he would choose to stay with his Grandmaster. She almost understood. He had never laid to rest his past. He was still running from it.

In some ways, they were more alike than he must realize. When she had first entered The Regency, she had felt drawn back into her old life. Old thoughts had resurfaced: her preoccupation with her appearance, her desire to be accepted—or perhaps, to be found acceptable. Old wounds had reopened. She had wondered about the life she had left behind.

Yet now, with Crash, she remembered who she was: a girl who didn't doubt herself, who didn't seek after the approval of others. A girl who had confronted Lord Seabourne face-to-face. Wealth and prestige no longer intimidated her. She knew her own worth now.

"We all have demons, Crash," she said quietly. "But we don't have to let them control our lives."

Surprise registered on his face.

"If you need to return to Cerastes, do so. I understand. Just remember what's in the past, and what's in the present. Remember who you are, right now."

He lowered his eyes. She suddenly sensed how lost he was, how lost he had always been. He might show the world an uncaring facade, but he wasn't dead inside, just raw. His wounds still bled.

She felt the need to continue.

"We all make wrong choices, Crash. We fall into old habits. But every day, we get a little better and a little wiser. We learn. You're not the same man who left the Hive. You're not going to lose yourself to Cerastes...and you're not going to lose me, either."

"Big words for a naive little girl," he murmured.

"I know," she grinned. "See? I've changed, too. You helped with that."

He grunted.

"I relied on you in the past, perhaps too much. Maybe I need to stand on my own for a while."

He studied her closely. "You're already strong, Sora, in ways I don't know how to be." He brushed the hair back from her face. Without speaking more, he pressed her into his shoulder and cradled her head against his wide chest.

Then she felt his lips brush against her forehead.

She raised her face blindly, seeking him out. She kept her eyes closed until she found his lips, which became an anchor in her spinning world. Soon she found herself sprawled across his body. He grabbed her wrists like two shackles and she couldn't break away, not even to breathe, not even when she thrashed against his chest. Her heart raced. Heat surged through her, and she forgot about the poison, about the darkened room, or the snow falling outside the window.

She knew it was Crash, yet sometimes, when the poison brought on its wave of hallucinations, she opened her eyes to a complete stranger.

"Do you trust me?" he asked against her temple, after another feverish wave had passed.

She lay passively in his arms. "I do."

"Don't give up on me, Sora. Don't be afraid."

She opened her eyes and saw him clearly.

"Will you return to me?" she asked.

He didn't answer with words, but with the touch of his lips against her burning skin.

# CHAPTER 31

Ferran looked up when Martin entered his study. His brother wore a blue velvet dinner jacket over a simple white shirt. He looked warm and comfortable, if a bit sore after his fall into the river.

Ferran had returned to the manor an hour earlier. First, he had deposited Burn in the horse stables, trusting him to hide in the hayloft until Lori could tend to him. He had meant to bring him food and water, but the manor had been in an uproar. From the kitchen staff, Ferran had learned about the attack on the winter solstice parade, and his brother's incident with a flaming arrow. Luckily, Martin had leapt into the river before his costume could catch fire.

Ferran had managed to grab Lori's elbow and direct her out to the stables before Donwick the butler found him. Now he sat in an armchair next to Martin's desk. A large fireplace warmed the room with the scent of burning pine. His brother didn't acknowledge him immediately, but went to his cabinet and took out a thick cigar, then lit it. After a few puffs, he offered the cigar to Ferran.

Ferran felt his hands itch, but declined.

"I've noticed some of my papers are missing and I think I know where they went," Martin said casually.

Ferran watched him fill a cup of malt wine to the brim; apparently, Lord Ebonaire planned to make a night of it.

Ferran chose a direct response. He had spent the last twenty minutes considering how to confront his brother about the map, and he wasn't in the mood for word-sparring.

"I took it. You're right. Now what are you hiding, Martin?"

"Nothing at all," his brother replied. "The King is building a new clock tower; you might have heard about it. We're funding the construction. But a few drainpipes were in the way, so we needed to look over the original plan. Nothing strange about that." He opened his hands, as though to show he had no cards up his sleeve.

Ferran placed his palms solidly on the desk. Martin was still his younger brother, and he could hear the lies on his tongue.

"I know trouble when I see it, Martin," he said. "This map is unusual, to say the least. Was it drawn by the King's own hand? Why seek out an original? And why write on it?"

"Ah. So you followed the map to the house, I take it? One of the royal advisors lives there, a friend of Prince Peric's to be precise. I brought blueprints to him several months ago. See? Nothing to worry about."

Ferran searched his brother's face. *The Book of the Named* rested heavy in his pocket. Was the leader of the Shade an advisor to the King? The thought was alarming.

"Martin," he began slowly, "Have you run into some bad business? I can help you."

"Help me?" Martin demanded. His jaw tightened. "Why would you help me? Our father exiled you. You just want a share of the profits."

Silence filled the room.

"That's truly what you think of me?" Ferran asked, his hand still pressed to the desk. "That I would drag myself here, after so many years, just to worm my way back into the family fortune?" Martin be damned. He stood up and turned to leave the room.

"No, Ferran, wait," Martin said, walking around his large desk to stand between Ferran and the door. "I spoke wrongly. It was unfair of me to accuse you. I've been grappling quite a bit with our family's past since your arrival...."

Ferran raised an eyebrow. "Have you now? By that, I assume you mean *my* past."

"Father exiled you, and I did nothing!" Martin burst out. He ran his hand through his dark hair; a few strands fell around his face. "The family could have revoked your exile twenty years ago, but instead, we let you slip off on your own. I let father kick you out on the streets. I wanted the title, Ferran. I wanted your birthright."

Ferran allowed his brother's words to settle between them. Finally, he replied, "I know."

Martin blanched. "You do? Ah. I suppose you would. Quite the realist, I presume?"

"Well, I'm not naive."

"Then you know I'm a selfish man at heart."

"What Ebonaire isn't?" Ferran thrust his hands in his pockets. "That was twenty years ago, Martin. If I still held a grudge, you would know it. I didn't come here for gold, or any claim to my title. Honestly, life has treated me well..." *as well as to be expected.* "I simply thought it was time to make an appearance. I never had a chance to see Father before he died. You are my true family. I only wish I'd come sooner so I could have met your wife."

Martin stiffened at that, then seemed to relax. He clasped his hands behind his back and turned to the window in thought. Ferran watched the flurries of snow outside.

"It really should have been you," his brother finally said.

Ferran almost snorted. *No,* he thought. "How so?"

Martin's words sounded bitter as he sipped his port. "Father prepped you so thoroughly, for all your life, until you left. I wasn't ready to take over the business, and father was never pleased with my performance. Said I had no imagination, and wasn't willing to take risks. And then," waving his glass, "when I decided to take a risk, it turned into a horrible mess. Perhaps he was right."

"Seems our father was a hard man to please," Ferran said dryly. He wondered what risk Martin referred to. He couldn't quite feel sorry for his brother. *Such a hard life, running this golden palace,* he thought.

"I've had many dark thoughts of late, Ferran. Our family has enemies, you know. I worry, now that my wife is gone and I haven't remarried, what might happen to Danica. She is so young. I fear one day those enemies might come for our family, or for me, and she won't be ready."

Ferran thought of Sora, so strong and independent, and only a few years older than Danica. But that was after several years on the road. He didn't know the girl she had been before, at the Fallcrest estate.

"Danica will survive," he said. "She's an Ebonaire. She will see her enemies coming down her front drive well in advance."

Martin didn't laugh, and Ferran realized his brother was being gravely serious.

"I worry about the Ebonaire line, should anything happen to me. Simeon is young. He wouldn't know how to handle our accounts." Martin abruptly reached into a drawer and withdrew a stack of leatherbound papers almost six inches thick. "This alone is not even one-quarter of the trade contracts and disputes we deal with every year. I used to hire bookkeepers and stewards to manage the accounts, but it's hard to know whom to trust. I caught too many hands in the cigar box, so to speak...." Martin gave him a pointed look. "Some I still employ because I have to, but I must always check the numbers and make sure it all adds up. Beyond all that...Simeon is a spendthrift. He burns through his allowance like feeding reeds to a fire. If the Ebonaire fortune were to fall into his hands, well, one can't keep a fortune by spending a fortune, hm?"

Ferran recalled his father saying much the same thing.

Martin raised his glass in a mock salute. "I wish to make an announcement at First Winter's Ball," he said, "and I would like you to be there."

Ferran felt awkward. "Martin, you don't need to reintroduce me to society. I didn't come here to lay claim to anything."

"I know," his brother said. "And that's why it *must* be you. Father thought you were an irresponsible, thieving rake when he exiled you. But that's not the man I see before me." He examined his port thoughtfully. "Taking the map shows keen observation and intelligence, and a certain boldness I have to admire. You always were the bold one, Ferran. Fearless, I imagine."

*Far from it,* Ferran disagreed, touching the map in his pocket.

"I think you've learned the right lessons over the years." Martin offered him a small toast. "It would be an honor to have you rejoin our family. This punishment has lasted long enough."

"You're joshing," Ferran choked.

"No. Let's drink to it. You will be by my side at the ball for the announcement. No talking me out of it, now."

"I don't think I could," Ferran said, then paused. *Thank you* seemed small and inadequate, and he wasn't sure this was an occasion to be thankful for. Should anything happen to Martin, he would have to take on a vast world of responsibility. Perhaps his brother would sober up and change his mind; he couldn't possibly want to reinstate Ferran as heir to the estate.

Ferran took the goblet Martin handed him and quickly drank a toast. The port burned his throat.

Martin refilled his glass. "You've certainly changed, Ferran," he said. "I sense the future holds many grand possibilities. This is a night to celebrate. Come, drink with me."

Ferran sat down resignedly. But one thought still nagged at him.

"What of Danica?" he asked. "She is the current heiress, isn't she?" Property usually went to children before wives or brothers.

"She's only fifteen," Martin said. "She can't take over the accounts. And who would leave an estate this large in the hands of a child? She'll need guidance."

"Surely you can't expect anything dire to happen that soon?"

Martin shifted his gaze to the wide, dark windows. "Hard to say, brother...but let's not dwell on that."

"I can help you," Ferran repeated softly.

"You already have."

Ferran sat back in his chair. Martin had his secrets, and perhaps after a few more glasses of wine, he would tell a few. But his brother seemed afraid to speak. Perhaps, in his own way, he was trying to shelter Ferran and Danica from his own failures—from the true extent of their family's danger.

Ferran's eyes wandered to a tapestry that hung on the north wall of the room. Their family tree stretched up and up, becoming lost in the shadowy corners of the ceiling. *A map,* his father had called it. A chart of the Ebonaire line. His name had been removed from it years ago, but now it would be returned. He would belong to those branches again.

Ferran raised his glass to his brother, and then to the tree, and drank deeply.

# KRAIT'S REDEMPTION
## Read a special preview of Book 5!

S ora stood on an open expanse of meadowland behind her stepfather's
manor. Instead of green grass cushioning her feet, a layer of snow and
ice caked her boots. Winter had overtaken the Fallcrest estate. The trees were
licorice-limbed and sugar-coated, and the sky was a white, woolen quilt.

She glanced behind her. A rose bush grew against a low stone wall, its limbs
naked, its thorns menacing, its branches arced like claws against the sky.

A chill wind blew her blond hair over her shoulder. She shuddered, wrapping
her arms around herself. She didn't wear a cloak. Her skin felt as cold and stiff as
marble.

She remembered this place. She had traveled here before in guided meditations.
But the snow was new. The season had changed.

She trudged up the icy hill. Before long, a gated corral came into view, ringed
by thick metal poles. Her stomach tightened, and she unconsciously reached for
the Cat's-Eye stone at her neck, which sent only a little warmth to her hand.

A monster waited beyond the corral's closed gate, a monster whose strength she
needed to harness. But every time she neared the *garrolithe*, it attacked her with
terrifying rage. It stood on four legs, a great beast taller and broader than a bull. Its
mane of bristling quills could pierce her skin. Its gaping jaws could swallow her
in two wolfing bites. How could she tame a beast of such ferocity? The creature
wasn't flesh and blood, but formed of magical energy centuries before her time.
How could she control it?

Here, in the dreamscape of her mind, she must try.

She walked across the snowy meadow to the corral. As she neared, her sense of
unease grew. The corral's gates dangled off their hinges like broken iron wings,
the metal twisted and warped beyond use. Inside was empty.

A sudden, low growl erupted behind her.

Sora turned, numb with fear. She stared into the blue-fire eyes of the monster. Its teeth stretched as long as her forearm. A mane of bristling quills stiffened along its neck. It stood on four legs with shoulders as powerful as a bear.

Sora tried to find her courage, but she could only summon thoughts of Crash. *He's gone*, she thought, her fists curling at her sides. *He's left my side. How am I supposed to be strong?*

Her sense of hopelessness grew. The struggle seemed pointless. She couldn't win against the *garrolithe*—she couldn't win against herself. She knew, this time, she would be devoured.

The rumbling growl, deep in the *garrolithe's* throat, continued.

Sora took a shaky breath. A small cloud of mist formed between herself and the monster. The beast breathed with her as one. Within its fiery eyes, she saw her own reflection. She saw someone small, her face too pale and thin, her brows too low and gaze too focused.

Then the *garrolithe* widened its lionlike jaws. She closed her eyes and succumbed to its strength, to its dominion. She knew this moment was inevitable. A sense of relief filled her. *This is the only way.*

She felt like a deer in its final moments, after a long and harrowing run from the wolves.

The dank cave of the *garrolithe's* mouth enveloped her, its hot breath on her hair, her face. Her fists tightened as she braced herself. The first prick of the beast's fangs pierced her neck.

Ferran slammed his hand down on the desk.

"She's lying," he asserted.

"She's not lying," Caprion said.

The red stone at Ferran's wrist glowed in response to the Harpy's voice. *Magic.*

"A spell to sooth my temper? You arrogant bastard."

"Force of habit," Caprion didn't sound sorry.

"Bells!" Ferran swore. "Winter solstice is only three nights away. At this rate, we'll all be celebrating the end of the Kingdom, if not the human race. We need answers—we need this book."

"I realize that."

"Krait is lying, she has to be," Ferran repeated. "Of course she can read *The Book of the Named*. She's a Named assassin!"

"I showed her the pages, and she said they were blank."

"And you believe her?"

"She can't lie under my voice's influence," Caprion reminded him. "Only one explanation makes sense: she isn't truly Named at all. She's an imposter. Viper suspected as much during our initial interrogation."

"So it's possible?" Ferran asked.

"Of course," Caprion said. "Other races lie about their names; they just don't hold as much significance."

"Then we need Crash."

Caprion folded his arms. "He has joined the Shade."

Ferran kicked a footstool across the room, where it smashed into the wall next to a wide stone hearth. He glared at the stool. He had meant it to sail into the roaring flames.

He and Caprion stood in a small library on the second floor of the Ebonaire manor. Mahogany bookshelves lined the walls. A row of windows to Ferran's back revealed a night sky thick with falling snow.

Ferran shook his head, even more frustrated. Only a few days ago, he had managed to steal *The Book of the Named* from the Shade, but the pages were blank, and remained blank no matter who tried to read them. His Cat's Eye detected an enchantment on the book—an ancient spell soaked into the binding like old liquor—but his stone couldn't remove it. The magic seemed impossible to pry from the book's unassuming pages.

Only a Named assassin could read *The Book of the Named*. Semantically, it made sense. Crash could have read it, but he had vanished almost a week ago, when they had first arrived at the City of Crowns.

"She said her Name was Krait," Ferran repeated, his voice tight and controlled. "Under the influence of your voice, she swore it."

"Her mind is broken. Cerastes has manipulated her for years. He must have tricked her into thinking she was Named. Perhaps she isn't the only one of the Shade to carry a false title."

"If Crash were here..."

"Would you really trust his word, after what happened to Sora?"

"We don't know if he was involved."

Caprion looked like he wanted to argue, but he shut his mouth. He turned away and paced the room, his feet an inch above the floorboards. Silence fell as heavily as the snow outside the window.

"Has she improved at all?" Caprion finally asked.

"No."

Ferran stared blindly at the falling snow. No one knew what had happened to Sora, exactly. A hired coach had arrived at the Ebonaire manor the morning after the winter solstice parade, with little explanation from the driver, except that a cloaked figure had placed the girl in his carriage and given him this address.

For the last two days, she had laid unconscious in her bedroom, pale as a ghost, as her mother slowly cleansed the poison from her system. The wound at her neck was minimal, hardly a needle's prick, and yet the poison in her veins was powerful indeed. The herbs Lori needed were difficult to find this time of year, and the tonic took a master's hand to brew. They didn't know when Sora's fever might break, or when she would return to consciousness. Lori had left yesterday to the Healer's seminary, to purchase more herbs to treat Sora's condition. Doubtlessly the storm had detained her.

Ferran blamed himself. He should have searched for Sora when she didn't return from the winter solstice parade, but a fierce blizzard had made the city streets impassible.

"Only an experienced assassin could have brewed that poison," Caprion pointed out.

"That doesn't implicate Crash. There's an entire cult of assassins in this city."

"It doesn't prove his innocence, either."

Ferran glared at the Harpy. "Right then. We know the enemy poisoned her, but how did she escape on her own? She had help. The driver said a 'cloaked man' put her in that carriage. Perhaps Crash saved her life."

"A mystery left unsolved," Caprion said flatly.

Ferran pulled out *The Book of the Named* from his pocket and turned it over in his hands. It looked like a leather-bound journal, though obviously ancient. He flipped through a few of the blank pages. The parchment carried no stains, no rips, no creases. Unlike the book's binding, it looked hardly a day old.

The creak of floorboards distracted him. Ferran glanced at the closed door, listening. Who else would be awake at such an early hour? A strange scent filled his nose: sharp and brisk, like clear mountain air. His Cat's Eye glimmered at his wrist, indicating magic. Ferran tried to place the smell. The Sixth Race's magic carried the scent of mildew, like a pool of stagnant water, while the First Race was sharper and more metallic. Dracian magic always carried a burnt flavor, like campfire ashes or heavy incense.

The midnight hour had long since passed. No one in the manor should be awake....

"What is it?" Caprion asked, watching him warily.

Ferran crossed to the door, cracked it open and peered out into the hall. He checked left and right, but saw only darkness, no candles, no lanterns. At night, the Ebonaire manor became a maze of shadows and solemn doors. Walking about without a light came at the risk of breaking one's neck.

He sniffed the air, but the scent was gone. He touched the Cat's-Eye stone on his wrist cuff, but it remained dormant. He finally closed the library door and turned back to Caprion with a troubled frown.

"Nothing," he said. His red Cat's Eye had turned dark and quiet. He rubbed a hand over his jaw. He needed a shave.

"The hour grows late," Caprion said, perhaps in response to the weary look on Ferran's face. "I will return to our prisoner."

"Ask her again about the book, would you?"

Caprion's lips tightened. The Harpy always had an arrogant look about him, but his expression intensified it.

"Cerastes is winning," Ferran pressed. "I don't know what else we can do."

"Sleep, perhaps."

Ferran knew he was right. They had been burning the midnight oil since the parade, and nothing had come of it except more frustration. He was too tired to do anything now, even think clearly. Perhaps new ideas would come in the morning.

"I pray sleep finds me." He bid Caprion goodnight. The Harpy glided from the room like a ghost, his feet hovering just above the carpet.

Ferran rummaged in his pocket and withdrew a cinnamon stick, which he rolled back and forth between his fingers, thinking. His eyes turned to the falling snow outside the window. Then he moved across the room to an armchair and sat down heavily, allowing his head to loll back against the cushions. Perhaps tomorrow, they would find some other way to interpret *The Book of the Named* and discover Cerastes's plan. Until then, they were at an impasse.

# CAPRION'S WINGS

*How did Caprion become a seraph? Learn about Caprion's story in this exclusive novella, available now on Amazon! Here's a special preview.*

I n the dream, he always stood in the same place——Fury Rock at the far end of the Isles, gazing into the darkened sky, counting the brilliant stars. They seemed impossibly close, bright white orbs as tangible as lanterns, hanging inches above his head, moments away from his hands. One by one, the stars detached themselves from that net of sky and danced around him softly, silently. Then they would slide apart, opening like a great curtain.

And there——billowing across an ocean of darkness like white sails——would be his wings.

He would reach for the gentle slope of white feathers, their great lengths like bars of light. He could never quite grasp them. They hovered just out of reach, beckoning him to step from the rock, to take hold of his wings. Yet he couldn't. He remained paralyzed, immobile, wary of the darkness beneath his feet. Fury Rock stood at the very edge of the Isles; the top of the cliff dropped hundreds of feet into the ocean. He couldn't fly yet. How could he leap——how could he claim his wings——if he couldn't fly?

But on this night, the dream unraveled differently. His wings sailed closer than ever before, pure light solidified into bone and flesh. He reached for them, hands grasping a half-inch away.

The ground suddenly rocked beneath him, pushing him forward. He gasped, wavering, struggling for balance. But the earth kept quaking, shuddering and lurching, and a great shadow rose from the ground, seeping through the rock, gathering at his back. He stumbled, tripping into black space. His arms swung out, thrown before him, but there was nothing to stop his fall.

He plummeted off the rock into darkness, away from the stars and his wings, icy wind rushing past him, freezing his skin, gripping his heart. A voice rose from the abyss; a lethal, insidious voice, oily-slick. *Your people are dying....*

Caprion awakened in a cold sweat, his pale hair damp against his face. He sat up in his cot and turned his frantic, violet eyes toward the window, taking comfort in the light of the sun: the One Star that shone upon the world, giving life to all things. He closed his eyes momentarily, breathing out a prayer, dispelling the darkness that lingered in his mind.

For months now, he had experienced the same dream, but this time it was different. Darker. Somehow malevolent. *We do not dwell on these things,* he heard the Madrigal's voice say. *We do not acknowledge them with our thoughts, nor our words.* A Harpy's voice, after all, was a tool for magic. It must remain pure. He shook his head, trying to clear it.

"Caprion!" he heard from the window. Something struck the wall—a rock, perhaps. "Caprion, wake up!"

"I'm awake," he muttered, passing a hand over his face. He felt drained, exhausted despite a full night's rest.

"You're going to be late! It's past the greeting hour! They've called your name twice now!"

A jolt of panic shot through him. *Flight!* He slept late! He leapt to his feet and pulled a white silken robe around his lean, tall form. It hung a few inches above his ankles, slightly too short. The novice robes were made of smooth silk, soft against his skin, weightless. Gold thread embroidered the neckline and wide cuffs. Caprion slipped on his leather sandals, fastening the buckles at his ankles, then he ran outside.

He lived in the novice district, a part of the city reserved for young Harpies who had yet to gain their wings. The buildings were small, circular and domed, made of chalky white limestone. The surface of the stone was easily carved. Generations upon generations had decorated each of the houses, etching patterns and symbols or scrawled blessings and poems across their facades. Some of the dwellings had been built before the War of the Races, when the great island of Aerobourne had flown through the sky, hovering over the mainland, the pinnacle of Harpy civilization.

Now the great floating island lay in a series of isles, scattered across the ocean, a cracked shard of its former self. The city of Asterion, once the capital of Harpy society, had grown old. Flagstone paths had fallen to disrepair, cracked and split by weeds, sprawling tree roots and wildflowers. Untamed foliage crawled down alleyways, up windowsills and across the road.

Caprion followed the main footpath over a slight hill and through a small patch of forest that separated the novice district from the main city. A second figure joined him——Esta, his laughing younger sister. She matched his pace easily, her feet barely touching the ground. She was only thirteen, but she had gained her wings three months ago in the early Spring. They gleamed at her back, two small figments of light, each barely three feet in length and a foot wide. Small wings, those of a seamstress, horticulturist or tutor. She currently worked with the younger Harpies in the academy, teaching them to sing.

"Sleepy head!" she teased. "It's like you don't even want to fly!"

"Quiet, little bird," he grumbled back.

She stuck her tongue out at him, still laughing. Her long pale hair shone in the wind like a gleaming pearl. It fell almost to her waist, decorated with bluebells in honor of his Singing——she was the only one who bothered to attend.

"If I hadn't come to find you, you would have missed the entire Singing!" she said heartily, as though this were some big joke.

"I was awake," Caprion said defensively.

"Liar," she grinned.

Like their older brother Sumas, Esta gained her wings at a young age. She found her star on her first attempt at the Singing——a small, yellow orb of variable light that flickered and flared in the pre-dawn sky. The light of its magic had entered her body, manifesting as wings, pure energy that sprouted from her back. She could now practice true magic, not just simple singing spells.

His brother Sumas, the pride of their family, had experienced even more success. At twenty-five, he was now a celebrated soldier, rising quickly through the army's ranks, his wings spanning fifteen feet, a sign of his star's strength and magical ability. The girls all gushed over tall, strapping Sumas, with his deep-set gray eyes and proud, square jaw. They followed him around and gossiped about his latest escapades. They said he was the most handsome in the city, the most unattainable, the most highly respected.

It grated on Caprion's nerves. His brother carried himself with a certain vain confidence that begged to be knocked down. The same confidence that Caprion had once carried, before his years of embarrassing failure. Without wings, he might as well be a cripple. The girls shied away from him in the streets, averted their eyes, cut short their conversations. He tried to ignore the sick, bitter jealousy that arose at the thought.

As a Le'Nasir, his family held a prestigious reputation. Several Matriarchs had risen from their bloodline. The entire city expected him to succeed as swiftly and easily as Sumas. But five years of failure had chipped away his sense of confidence. He had always expected great things, a unique destiny, some unnameable purpose. Now, at nineteen—his eleventh hour—he could feel his future slowly slipping away. He could already hear the Madrigal's voice: *The stars are ever moving, fledgling. The sky is different now than it was an hour ago. Your lateness may have cost you everything.* His last chance to succeed.

Depending on a Harpy's hour of birth, the Madrigal could predict where his star would be, what time of day he would find it, what season, what hemisphere of sky. But five times now, the Madrigal had predicted, and his star had not shone. It left a hollow feeling at the base of his throat. To remain a Harpy without a star, without the ability to fly, was a mortifying concept. Those without wings were excluded from many parts of the city, which could only be reached by flight. The wingless often worked at night when most of the population slept. They cleaned the streets, mended buildings or served the more prominent families. It was a life sentence, shameful and uncompromising.

And the worst part? He couldn't find any reason or logic behind it—no way to fix the situation. Perhaps his Song was not strong enough, his voice did not carry across the vast emptiness of the heavens. Or perhaps...perhaps the rumors around the city were right. Perhaps he simply did not have a star.

No, he couldn't think such disturbing thoughts, not before his Singing.

By this point, Caprion had traveled well into the city. Asterion had once been a grand spectacle of ornate architecture, and it still showed. All of the buildings were carved of gleaming quartz and white limestone, towering domed structures interconnected by bridges and balconies, arches and entryways, with hardly any doors. The windows were of shining crystal. Ancient mosaics decorated the walls and archways, symbols of stars and moons, patterns that mimicked the ocean and wind. The buildings stretched up and up; almost half the city was only accessible to those who could fly.

The wilderness had crept up over the years. Trees sprouted from between flagstones, small saplings yet to bear fruit. Vines crawled over balconies, cascading onto the street. Grass and weeds abounded, conquering flower pots and wide planters, framing tall columns and porch steps.

A few familiar faces called out to him. Caprion waved but kept running.

"You're lucky Sumas is busy this morning," Esta sang out, keeping pace nearby. "He'd be furious to know you slept late."

Caprion grimaced and ran faster.

"You know," Esta said, "I forgot how big the city is on foot. I can reach the Singing Chamber in a few minutes with my wings!"

"You're not helping," Caprion panted.

"I know," she said and smiled cheekily at him, just as a younger sister would.

Finally, Caprion turned off the main street onto the Road of Remnants. Statues of ancient warriors and diplomats lined the thoroughfare, some in fierce armor with swords in hand, others in great robes carrying stone parchment and books. He passed the statues quickly, having seen them countless times. The city fell behind him. The road led him up a great hill to where the Singing Chamber resided at its peak.

"Do you want me to accompany you?" Esta asked, falling slightly behind.

Caprion waved a distracted arm. "No," he replied, panting. "I'll meet up with you after. Wish me luck!"

"Luck, and the One Star's blessing!" she called, then fell back, returning to the Road of Remnants.

Caprion felt relieved. He didn't want an audience on this day. No audience meant no one to witness his failure. He tried to stay positive, but this late past his Singing hour, he hardly expected to succeed.

The Singing Chamber had existed long before the city of Asterion ever came to be. A great wealth of sunstone formed a giant bowl, carved deep out of the center of a hill, magnifying all sound and light. Once inside the Chamber, a Harpy's voice could be cast far above the world, through the sky, into the realms beyond. In this way, a Harpy could find his wings.

Panting from exertion, he finally reached the peak of the hill. The gates of the Chamber stood before him, tall iron structures twisted into intricate patterns. He slowed his frantic pace and paused at the gates, leaning over, trying to regain his breath.

When he looked back up, the blue robe of the Madrigal greeted him. Caprion bowed his head again, both to catch his breath and to show respect. His face flushed. He was almost two hours late; he wouldn't be surprised if the Madrigal told him to go home.

"Rise," the man said briefly.

Caprion straightened, wishing he had a minute more to rest. The Madrigal was very tall, very thin. His hair was long and billowing. Creases lined his face. His skin had a slight glow about it, a white sheen hardly visible to the eyes. As Harpies aged, they eventually dissolved into light; his glow was an indicator of his years. Madrigals lived longer than most. Some said that he was a thousand years or older. He had lived before the War of the Races——before their current Matriarch even came to power.

His wings, for that moment, remained hidden. The most powerful Harpies had the ability to hide or display their wings at will. Caprion had glimpsed the Madrigal's only once, years ago at the One Star's Dawning, the first day of Spring. Fully manifested, his wings were so large, so bright, Caprion had been forced to turn his eyes away or else go blind.

"I'm sorry-" Caprion started.

"No time to speak," the Madrigal said. "We shall discuss it when you are done. The hour has grown late. You must sing before the sky changes further. Have you prepared your Song?"

Caprion nodded. Last year, the Madrigal had suggested he practice a new Song, since his old one was not working. It had been a huge embarrassment. His mother hadn't spoken to him for weeks, muttering always to herself, *"I taught him to sing well. He knows how to use his voice. What is wrong with my boy?"* She had prayed to the One Star over and over again. Finally Caprion left the house, moving into the novice district, where the wingless fledglings resided. He couldn't stand to hear her pray anymore. He couldn't even look at her face.

He entered the outer halls of the Singing Chamber. Unlike the rest of the city, the hall around the chamber was built of thick granite. The rock had to be dense and heavy to keep extraneous noise from interfering with the Singing. Usually the halls were full of wingless fledglings practicing their Songs, learning about the sacred bond between Harpy and star. But this morning the halls were silent. Eerily so.

Caprion sighed. He had a feeling the Madrigal requested it. Probably to help him concentrate, but it only reminded him that he was different——close to an outcast. All of his friends had gained their wings and moved on to other pursuits, becoming soldiers, medics, song-casters and architects. Some were already expecting their firstborn children. A Harpy's life was long, but only if one found their wings. Otherwise, he'd be lucky to last a few decades. His days of childhood were almost over; once he finished developing into an adult, it would be too late.

The Madrigal led him without ceremony to the very end of the hall, where a tall statue of the God of Light stood. The statue was carved of white marble and stood more than fifteen feet high. The God of Light's face was beautifully masculine, tilted upward toward the sky. In one hand, he held a long scepter, the symbol of a sun perched at its top, the One Star, raised slightly above his head. In the other, he held a long stone sword. The One Star was a symbol of the God of Light, a sign of His strength. It was thought that the God of Light carried the sun across the sky on a mighty scepter.

A metal tuning fork had been placed on a dish before the statue. Caprion knelt on the ground before it, bowing his head in respect. The Madrigal picked up the fork and struck it firmly on the side of the dish. A loud, pure tone resonated from the metal, echoing around the empty halls. Then he turned and held it above Caprion's head.

Caprion could feel the vibrations resonate off his skin like a small shower of rain. *"May His light shine upon you, may His voice speak your name,"* the Madrigal prayed. *"May the shadows flee, may the mind know peace, may the heart speak clearly,"* he struck the tuning fork one last time. *"God of Light, we ask that you listen, that you accept this Song as an offering. Show your son, Le'Nasir Caprion, his star."* He struck the fork one last time, the sound resounding off of the vaulted ceiling.

Caprion felt the pure tone in his bones. His skin tingled. He whispered his own prayer to the One Star, hoping it would be enough, that he would be heard.

The sound faded. Caprion climbed to his feet somberly. Contrary to the Madrigal's prayer, anxiety clamped down on his stomach. After this Singing, he would no longer be a child. The magic would fade from his body and he would be too old to find his star.

The Madrigal led him behind the statue to a stone archway. A long, dark corridor sloped downward through the rock. This hall would lead him to the Singing Chamber.

"Remove your robes," the Madrigal ordered.

Caprion slipped the smooth silk from his pale body. He was young and strong from daily sword practice, his muscles taught and defined, though he had yet to reach the width and height of a fully grown Harpy. He bowed one last time to the Madrigal, then started down the long hallway.

*Continue the story in* Caprion's Wings, *available now in print from Amazon. com, and on all major ebook retailers . . .*

# Meet the Author

**T. L. Shreffler** is a noblewoman living in the misty forests of Snohomish County, Washington. She enjoys long hikes through the wilderness, drinking strong coffee or teas, exploring the unknown reaches of her homeland and unearthing rare artifacts in thrift stores. She holds a Bachelors in Eloquence (English) and writes Fantasy and poetry. She is the author of *The Cat's Eye Chronicles*, *Skydust Kingdoms* and *The Dragon Pearl* series.

# Follow
# *T. L. Shreffler*
## on Social Media!

### Email
therunawaypen@gmail.com

### Join the mailing list!
www.catseyechronicles.com

### Instagram
@catseyeauthor

### Tiktok
@catseyeauthor

### Pinterest
www.pinterest.com/catseyeauthor

### Facebook
www.facebook.com/tlshreffler

SIGNED COPIES!

Tarot decks!

VISIT
T. L. SHREFFLER'S
# AUTHOR STORE

BOOKISH STUFF!

Gifts & Things

**authortlshreffler.etsy.com**

www.ingramcontent.com/pod-product-compliance
Lightning Source LLC
Chambersburg PA
CBHW051956240626
47153CB00005B/1778